Nicola Barker

lives and w ... e winner of the David Higha ... joint winner of the Macmillan Silver ... our Enemies, her first collection of stories. H ... y collection, *Heading Inland,* received the John Lle ... Rhys/*Mail on Sunday* Prize. Her novel *Wide Open* won the IMPAC Prize in 2000. Her most recent novel is *Behindlings*. She has been selected as one of Granta's Best Young British Novelists of the decade.

SMALL HOLDINGS

is set in an attractive park in north London. Phil, a chronically shy gardener, feels at home only with his plants. In love with Nancy, he is tortured by the malevolent Saleem, and by Doug, his imposing, unpredictable and terrifying supervisor. Phil strives nobly to maintain his equilibrium despite being systematically mystified, brutalized, drugged, derided and seduced. But when he loses his eyebrows, he decides to fight back.

Praise for *Small Holdings*:

'This marvellous short novel explodes into action, with Barker letting off fireworks and flares in all directions, performing dazzling verbal gymnastics. She has a great talent for the creation of eccentric characters, and the assorted misfits in *Small Holdings* fizz with playfulness and the author's obvious delight at her own powers of invention. A hilarious and remarkably assured novel.' *TLS*

'Funny and intelligent. Barker's sense of plot and comic timing is faultless: she goes for big effects, which resound brilliantly within the small space her narrative describes, and holds the whole thing together with writing that is resolved down to the last detail. *Small Holdings* paints the big picture on a small canvas, capturing in it the universality that is the essence of good writing.' RACHEL CUSK, *The Times*

'Edgy and comic, it succeeds by virtue of Barker's flamboyant sense of the absurd.' *Elle*

A Granta Best British Novelist

NICOLA BARKER

REVERSED FORECAST

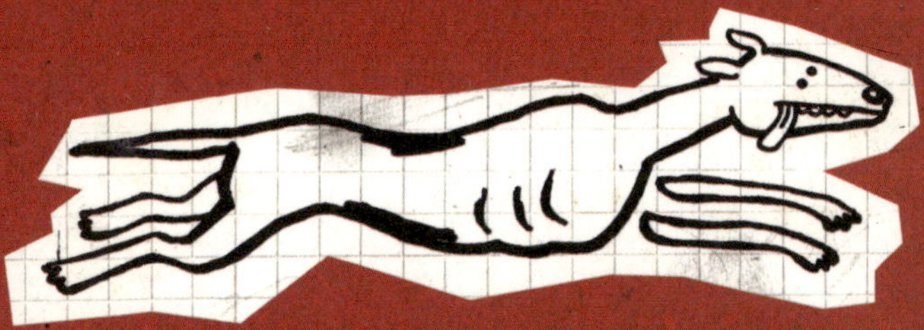

'A strange [redacted] and wonderful novel'

THE TIMES

Photograph of Nicola Barker

NICOLA BARKER

Small Holdings

Flamingo
An Imprint of HarperCollins*Publishers*

By the same author

Love Your Enemies
Reversed Forecast
Heading Inland
Wide Open
Five Miles from Outer Hope
Behindlings
The Three Button Trick

Flamingo
An imprint of HarperCollins*Publishers*
77–85 Fulham Palace Road,
Hammersmith, London W6 8JB

Flamingo is a registered trade mark of
HarperCollins*Publishers* Limited

www.**fire**and**water**.com

Published by Flamingo 2003
9 8 7 6 5 4 3 2 1

Previously published in paperback by Faber and Faber Ltd 1996
First published in Great Britain by Faber and Faber Ltd 1995

ISBN 0 00 716399 1

Set in Palatino

Printed and bound in Great Britain by Clays Ltd, St Ives plc

Empty-handed I go, and behold the spade is in my hands;
I walk on foot, and yet on the back of an ox I am riding;
When I pass over the bridge,
Lo, the water floweth not, but the bridge doth flow.

Shan-hui

THREE DAYS

Wednesday
Thursday
Friday

Wednesday

SOME PEOPLE OPEN up like flowers; slowly, painstakingly, each petal unfurling, reacting, affirming. Responding, simply, to warmth and to tending.

Other people can be peeled; like a fruit – like an orange or a pomelo – the skin comes off, and underneath is something full and ripe, perfectly segmented, waiting to be apportioned by deft and inquisitive fingers.

Doug was like an egg. A boiled egg. Hard-boiled. He was knocked once, twice, many times, and his shell cracked, and it crumbled, and underneath was something slippery and rubbery and not especially digestible.

If he hadn't been hard-boiled, he would have dropped from his shell, moist, sloppy, just a mess. In certain respects, in retrospect, that might have been preferable.

I'd been wrong about Doug all along. I'd thought he was an oyster: barnacle-hard outside, abrasive even, but with a vulnerable interior, maybe a pearl in there somewhere, hidden, precious, protected. I also considered at certain points that he might be a beetle. Beetles, it seems, like some other insects, have a skeleton on the outside and the flesh, the soft bits, inside. People are traditionally soft on the outside, and the bones, the frame, the supports are hidden away within layers of skin and fat and muscle. That's exactly how I am. Soft and yielding, like tripe to the touch.

Well Doug, Doug was a boiled egg, hard-boiled with a blueish pallor – white turned blue – a pale yellow yolk (his heart, not soft either), and he was extremely entrenched, obscenely contained and mystifyingly, ridiculously, maybe even *deceptively* proud of himself.

We'd all worked as gardeners in the park for several years before the whole enterprise was privatized and a group of us – me, Doug and not forgetting Ray (Big Ray) – formed a partnership and along with Nancy, our driver, made a successful bid for the contract.

Doug was always nominally in charge. I'm too shy to do anything but blush and blunder. Ray, well, he's moonish, and tender and completely unfocused. Doug is incredibly reasonable, too reasonable – monosyllabic, in general, admittedly – awesome, though, terrifying, as hard as a nut; a literal tough-nut. He is fair-minded but merciless. If he has a rule book (and he'll usually find one close at hand) then he'll play by it.

Working with Doug is like playing a game of snooker. The park is the green baize. We all look after the baize, we nurture it, we love it – but more of that later – and Doug is the white ball. He sets all the other balls in motion. He doesn't confer, he doesn't request, he doesn't even cooperate. Doug simply knocks into the other balls, slams into them, bangs into them. Balls of all colours. And I'm a red ball. Shy. Embarrassed. Always the first to be pocketed, to scamper and scarper.

Doug's technique is remarkably simple. Physical. He's the big ball, the biggest ball. That's all. He is also, and I guess this is ironic – or else this whole snooker business just isn't working – Doug is also the black ball. He is the first and the last. If he leaves the table then the game is over.

There's one question you should never ask Doug. Never ask Doug where he's from. I know where he's from because many is the time I've heard him talking French, a strange French, like a list of exotic ingredients from a fancy cookbook, to his wife, Mercy, who he walked out on a fortnight ago after thirty years of marriage.

Doug comes from a place full of bright birds and sun and tall trees. I can imagine this place so clearly, can even imagine Doug there, kicking up sand, shouting at people. It's an island. One island in the Lesser Antilles: Martinique. I looked it up in my big old atlas. I saw the arc of Doug's islands, islands humped in the Caribbean sea like the backbone of a long-forgotten animal. Barbuda, Antigua, Guadeloupe, Dominica, Martinique, St Lucia, St Vincent, Grenada, Doug's Islands.

Everything about him gives him away, external things, so he holds himself in, his real self, his inside-self, every-part.

Every muscle tenses, resists, contains. That's Doug all over. With his neat greying beard, his black hair, his hands like clams, his dark, bloodied eyes, his accent which is as strong and thick as rich molasses.

In fact, though, in truth, he comes from Palmers Green, North London. We all do: me and Ray and Doug and Saleem (one-legged Saleem, our squatter, my persecutor, our old curator) and Nancy. That Nancy.

Well, the park is my soul. I live off it, I work on it, I live for it. I love it. Doug loves it too, but lately he's taken to growing vegetables – out back, in the greenhouses which are no longer open to the public. Giant vegetables. He thinks the punters don't notice when they peek through the glass, expecting succulents, orchids, exotica. He thinks they aren't surprised, shocked, maybe even *piqued* when they see only row upon row of onions (Doug's an onion, yes, I like that. An onion) or marrows, cabbages, tomatoes. The occasional giant, merry sprig of a carrot top.

'Phil,' Doug said, last time I broached the subject of the vegetables – and the other things too, more recent peculiarities – 'Phil.' (He takes every opportunity to say my name, rolls it on his tongue, pronounces it 'feel', which never fails to activate something in me, something inside, something vulnerable and inadequate, something connected to feeling too much but expressing nothing, something soft and sad.) 'Phil, whosoever diggeth a pit shall fall in it.'

Doug has another saying, equally incomprehensible, which he'll interchange randomly with this one; 'Phil, Phil, what-ya gonna do when your well runs dry? Huh?' He won't wait for an answer. He's too preoccupied. He'll saunter off (that saunter, a true gardener's gait) and he'll be rubbing his hands, jangling the keys in his pocket and expectorating; drawing something deep from his throat which he'll expel neatly into the border as he wanders past the perennials.

By then I'll be blushing. Fool. I'm thinking about 'Feel'. *Feel.* Whosoever diggeth a pit.

Ray was digging a deep hole next to the perimeter fence on the east side of the park and preparing to sink a gate-post into it. He was glossy with sweat. He stopped digging as I approached.

'Whosoever diggeth a pit,' I said.

'Now that,' Ray answered mopping his wide forehead with his fat arm, 'That's Bobby Marley.'

'You're kidding me. I thought it was biblical.'

Ray shrugged. 'Could be originally, but I'm sure I heard it in a Bob Marley song.'

Ray must be well over twenty stone, has long, frizzy blonde hair, a straggly beard, green eyes, the face of a cherub. I told him Doug had requested a meeting at five, in the house, the kitchen.

'Fine.'

'You, me, him and Nancy.'

Ray rested on his spade. 'It seems like Doug's finally cracked,' he said, grinning gently. 'At long last. And that's what comes,' he added, 'that's what comes of being too solid for too long.'

I didn't like this kind of talk. 'He's only left his wife,' I said calmly. 'That's all.'

Ray remained undaunted. 'He's talking to himself.'

'I do that too, sometimes, when I'm not thinking clearly.'

'You're like royalty. You talk to your plants. Doug's just talking. All the time.'

'He's got a lot on his mind. There's the meeting with the council to re-assert our tender on Friday. That won't be much fun. It won't be easy. And Doug's the man to pull it off.'

Ray nodded his assent. 'Doug's the man, yes, but he hasn't done a stroke of work in weeks now.'

I shrugged. I said, 'He's keeping busy.'

Ray scowled. 'He's up to something,' he said. 'He's tipping the scales . . .'

Ray made a strange, scale-tipping gesture with his two arms. 'And I don't know,' he added, 'what that actually means for the rest of us, and for this place.'

He looked around him, at his spade, the mud, the grass, the fence.

I cleared my throat. I said, 'Things are chugging over, just like they've always done.'

Ray shrugged, yanked up his spade and returned to his digging. 'Someone,' he said, grunting out every syllable with each cut of the soil, 'Someone is going to have to do something.' And after he'd finished speaking, the slice of his spade added a further five syllables: *And it won't be me.*

I watched Ray digging for a moment. If only, I thought, Doug'd opened up gently, like a flower.

I had a thorough understanding of how flowers worked.

How big is it? Christ knows. An average size. Not a grand park. Not your Victoria, your Hyde, your Hampstead Heath. It seems small because of its unpretentiousness. Even so, it has pretensions. Used to have a Tudor museum – black, white, criss-crossed beams – stuck wham-bam in the middle of it, facing the water, reflected in the water; three little lakes and a round ornamental pond over to the right where kids paddle – contravening the park regulations – in the summer.

The museum was burned down, years ago now, but its black, burnt-out shell remains, and Saleem, its curator, well, more about her later. We used to have a proper athletics track: red, official, fenced off, very impressive, but we grew it over a while back. Athletes go down to Tottenham or up to Enfield now.

The tennis courts – six of them, slightly overgrown, but in working order – stand adjacent to the greenhouses. There's also a wild section, which is purposefully unkempt, circled by silver birch, where the squirrels dart. A bandstand, Doug's pride and joy, recently built at his instigation out of raw, dark-stained, splinter-pushing pine. An adventure playground that any park would be proud of.

To the north is the hill which is grass, mainly, where people come to picnic. We have public toilets – Ladies, Gents – and behind these are the private areas, staff-only places, which consist of a barn – a lovely barn – and the house where Saleem squats, where Doug is skulking, now he's left his wife. Now he's opened up and gone crackers.

It was three o'clock that same Wednesday afternoon and I was planting geraniums over by the bandstand. I had twenty plants in all and wasn't particularly optimistic about the contribution these would make to the display as a whole which was scruffy and sparse and relatively shambolic. This was Doug's patch, supposedly.

I was deciding whether to plant them in a half-moon, close to the border, or whether to distribute them more freely among the spider plants – this display's main constituent. The spider plants had been Ray's idea. His reasoning was that they grew quickly, reproduced easily, and that they were, most importantly, green. I doubted whether they'd last the winter out, but they'd cost us nothing which, as we're broke, was all that really mattered.

Nancy had promised to drive over a new, cheap assortment of annuals from Southend at some point. She'd arranged to get them on credit. She has the gift of the gab, and it's a useful gift. I wish I had it.

I dug a hole with my trowel near to the front of the bed. Behind me, as I worked, I could hear the gravel shift and scuffle, and another familiar noise, a plunging, a sucking-plucking. *One-legged Saleem*. I could see her from the corner of my eye, swinging over, staggering over. I pretended to be engrossed.

'Phil,' she said, 'what's up?' She drew very close. 'Planting pansies, eh?'

'Geraniums.' I popped one in and pressed the soil firm around its roots.

'Yeah? What's a geranium do?' She poked her stick out, automatically, and pushed it into the soft soil to the right of the new plant. 'How's that?'

'Thanks.'

I widened the hole with the trowel and placed the new plant.

'What's it do? I love knowing what they do. You're clever like that.'

'You could dry the root. It's astringent. A kind of tonic. You could take it internally for diarrhoea or use it as a gargle. It's a good gargle.'

'Who'd've thought it?' She bounced a step back and made a further hole. I moved over and planted the next one. 'Who'd've thought it, eh?'

I grimaced. She stared at me closely, 'Are you busy, Phil? Are you working too hard? Are you hot? Catching the sun, maybe? You've got bright little flames in both cheeks.'

I tried to distract her, to evade her questions, to drag her eyes away from my skin which always ripens at her approach, always reddens. 'You're getting mud on your stick.'

'Huh?' She inspected it, 'Nah, Soil's dry. Needs a water.'

'It's moist for August.'

'*It's moist for August*!'

She guffawed and threw herself down on to the grass verge. I glanced at her for a moment and then turned my back and carried on planting.

Saleem has long, black hair and a lean face. Skin the colour of caramel. Half dark Hindu, half Greek. A curious hybrid. She looks like a cobra in a wig. She speaks with a forked tongue. She hates me. I don't know why.

'Can we talk, Phil?'

'I'm working.'

'While you work, then.'

I smell her hate, always, and it's a hot-hate, has a hot smell which makes me shrivel, inside, outside. And she loves to stare, to invade, to gouge. She lives for it.

'While you work, then,' she repeated.

I said nothing.

'Am I irritating you or something?'

'No.'

She prodded the base of my back with the tip of her stick.

'Stop that.'

I swatted her stick with my arm but didn't turn.

'You're just too sensitive,' Saleem said, and by the sound of her voice she had a smile on her lips. 'And usually,' she added, 'I wouldn't care, but lately, well, things are coming to a head and I'm looking to you for some kind of decisive action.'

I didn't respond to this, didn't rise to her, and she, in turn, was silent for a minute, sitting up straight, viper-still, her amputated leg jutting out in front of her like the short butt of a cigar.

'You know, sometimes, Phil, your natural reserve comes across like a kind of hostility. Turn and look at me, Phil,' she added, almost whispering. 'Turn and look, go on. Go on, Phil. Turn and face me. Look at me. Go on.'

'I'm busy.'

My head was so low as I spoke that my chin touched my chest. She laughed at this. Her incisors are protrusive, are very clearly pointed. I could picture them in my mind, and the very idea of them scorched me, scalded me. She prodded me again, sharp in the back with her stick. 'Go on, Phil, go on. Go on.'

And I blocked out her taunting, was working, like I'd said, was busy, was working, was planting, was digging. Quickly, busily. Five plants, then four plants. Then three plants left, only three, and after I'd placed those I'd have to turn to face her and she'd see, with glee, that I was burned by her proximity, that I was red as beet, purple-red as beet. Two plants left. One plant.

I turned. But Saleem wasn't looking at me. She was a hooded reptile, yes, still a reptile, drawn up to spit, rocking, readying herself, but suddenly not focusing on me, but staring beyond me, over my shoulder, at the museum, its black shell. I thanked God for it, the museum. That was a skin she'd shed a long time ago, but she kept on inspecting it, sniffing at it, mulling it over.

I turned away again, shuffled the soil into smoothness with my palms, broke down lumps with my thumb and forefinger, patted it, softened it. And for a minute or so I was still blushing, red and ripe and bright as a poppy. Blood. My curse.

You see, I blushed before I could walk, before I could talk. People's eyes invade me and make me anxious. Maybe because I think too well of other people, or maybe because I don't think well enough of myself. My schooldays were tortured, my teenyears a wash-out, and when I grew older, my only recourse was to disguise. Girls wear green-tinted make-up. Yes, that helps to hide blushes, apparently. I grew my hair, a mass of curls that fall over my face, cover my ears, which always tingle first, sting and heat up. A neat and moderately well-spread beard – up my cheeks, down my neck – helps to shelter further exposed flesh. I am Monkey Man. I am Mountain Man. I am Scott of the Antarctic after a very long expedition.

Doug told me once, in a lighter moment, that my face was a vagina – all curls, all hair, with pink lips protruding and a small nose, labia-like, just above – a tender fold. After that I knew I didn't just feel strange, vulnerable, like a whelk when its shell has been jerked open, but that I seemed strange to others, that I looked strange to others.

It's all so complete, so perfect. A sun, a moon, a circle, a cycle. Maybe I think too much. Maybe I don't think enough. Saleem knows all this. She smells it. She sees it with her yellow eyes.

'What's that?' she asked suddenly, pointing with her stick. I followed its line. To the right of the museum I could see Doug in the distance, carrying what looked like a small tree.

'Doug.'

'What's he up to?'

'I don't know. He's working.'

'Come off it! Anyway. I don't mean Doug. I mean *that* . . .' She continued pointing and added, 'A plant. Inside the building, the museum.'

I squinted. It was too far to see anything, not clearly.

'It's a plant,' she insisted, 'crawling up where the chimney used to be.'

I looked again, still not seeing but vaguely remembering – the park, its constituent parts, every small thing etched in my very heart – I said, 'I think it's a passion flower, growing up in the charcoal and old cinder.'

'What kind of a plant?'

'A creeper. It has a beautiful flower. White and very ornate. In Jamaica they have a variation which they call a grenadilla. Doug might know more about it.'

'I bet it grew from my leg,' she said. 'My skin and foot. During the fire, that's where the burning beam fell, right there.'

I stared at her. She was warped. She was rubbing the stump of her knee, smiling. I shuddered.

'What does it do?'

'It works like a kind of morphine, affects the circulation and increases the rate of respiration. In homeopathic medicine they use its narcotic properties to treat dysentery. Sleeplessness. Some types are used for treating hysteria and skin inflammation.'

'Yeah? How?'

'I'm not sure. Dry the berry or boil the root. Something like that.'

Saleem started drawing a pattern in the grey gravel of the path with her stick.

'Let me tell you something, Phil,' she said. 'I was talking to Doug this morning, over breakfast. And guess what we talked about?'

I didn't turn but I shook my head.

'We talked about the Gaps.'

I carried on smoothing the soil, thinking of softness, soil-softness.

'Are you listening, Phil? The Gaps. Does that mean anything to you?'

I said quietly, 'It doesn't mean anything.'

'What was that?'

Saleem. My tormentor. I turned. 'I don't know.'

'OK,' she said, 'OK, so Doug has this theory, right, about why London doesn't work. It's to do with the postal districts. He has this theory about London not working . . . Did he tell you this yet?'

I shook my head.

'Oh, you'll love it. You'll love this. Here's how it goes: Doug says that everything in nature moves in a circle, OK? That's how nature works, a kind of winter–spring–summer–autumn–winter thing. A kind of sun-follows-moon-and-earth-revolving thing. Sort of oriental. He's into all this stuff lately. Anyhow, Doug has now decided that the city of London is a life form too, kind of like a complex bacteria, and as such, everything should fit together. But *unfortunately* . . .' She stressed this word until it stang with venom. 'Unfortunately, Phil, London can't work properly because of the Gaps. Sounding familiar yet?' I shook my head, although suddenly, strangely, it did begin to sound familiar. Doug. Circles. Doug. The Gaps. It did sound familiar.

In the gravel Saleem had drawn a circle. 'That's London,' she said, completing it. She drew a horizontal line through the centre of the circle, cutting it in half. 'And that's the Thames,' she added. 'So that's London and everything connects to everything else. And these are the postal districts, OK?' She drew them in. 'We've got plain North London, we've got plain West London, we've got plain East London . . .' As she spoke she pointed, and I could hear the gravel kissing and knocking.

'But here's a problem, right. There's South-West London postal districts and there's South-East postal districts, and they, sort of, meet in the middle, which means that there's no South. No plain South. And Doug's upset about this. And there's another problem too, right. There's North-West and South-West and South-East, but there's no North-East. Another Gap. No plain South and no North-East. And according to Doug, this is why London doesn't connect. This is why London doesn't work. Things aren't properly linked. See what I'm getting at, Phil?'

I nodded.

'You see, the city is *fucked*, Phil, because of this little problem with the postal districts. And Doug is worrying about it, Phil. He's thinking about it. These Gaps.'

I stopped feeling the soil. I turned.

'So what's the problem? Why are you telling me this?'

Saleem's eyes popped. 'Because Doug's going absolutely fucking crazy. He's got this meeting on Friday. Our whole fucking future depends on it, and he is going crazy. He's crazy.'

I turned away again.

'Say something!'

'He'll be fine.'

'No he won't be fine. And that's the worst part of it. You seem determined to ignore what's going on right under your nose. He's gone mad. I know all about it. I'm living in the same house as him. And no one asked me, incidentally, whether I minded or not. He just moved in and that was that. Anyhow, I can see my way around the whole thing but no one wants to know what I've seen.'

Saleem scratched out her Postal District London and prepared the gravel for another design: a large phallus. Medieval. A two-foot phallus pointing west to her north and east to my south. Pointing, I decided, towards Ray, far away, digging his pit.

'Doug's OK.'

'OK? Jesus! You don't know anything,' she said, slitting her eyes, angry now, 'You're so *in* on yourself. There's stuff going on here that you don't know anything about. Private stuff. Everything's a secret with Doug. You don't know about Mercy and the diarrhoea. You don't know about that mad man, that Chinaman, slinking about the place, poisoning everything. You don't see anything through all that fucking hair. You don't see *anything*.'

Saleem pushed herself up, used her stick to pull herself up by. She works well without her leg, admittedly, is lithe when she wants to be.

'And the thing is, she said, 'I know you love this place. It matters to you. You depend on it the same way I do. But you won't ever *act*, you won't ever *do* anything. You're *dormant*, just blind. Turning in on yourself.'

I was surprised to be connected, all of a sudden, in a rush, like this, with Saleem. It was a curious sensation, this connection.

'Forget it, then,' she said, sounding defeated and afterwards, almost instantly, sounding defiant. 'Looks like I'm going to have to be the one,' she muttered, turning her back, 'Me. Saleem. I am the one who'll have to save things. Ray's too stupid. You're just a yak, a blob. And Nancy . . .' She laughed. 'I am the one,' she said, darkly, stalking off, 'just watch me.'

SO THIS IS the problem, I told the exhaust on the back of Nancy's truck. The Park's got another four months to run and we're almost broke. On Friday Doug's going to meet Enfield Council's Park Management Committee to re-assert our tender.

Doug's been cryptic about his intentions. He's said he has plans, big plans, but he hasn't discussed them with me or Ray, he hasn't told us what he's up to. Saleem thinks that he doesn't care any more, that he's losing it, that he's liable to do just about anything. Now he's left his wife. Now he's left his home. I can't help thinking, though, somehow, that Doug's just like me, that he cares too much. But there's no telling, not with Doug. Doug won't tell. His lips are zipped. Like Saleem says, he's private. He's impenetrable.

And of course we're all frightened of him, apart from Saleem. Maybe even Saleem. He's getting bigger and bigger. Sometimes I glance at his eyes and see the whole world in there, streaming in – light and colour and nature and history. God only knows what he might do.

My one compensation is that at least I think I know what he's capable of. I know the perimeters. There are none.

And I love Doug for that very reason. I see my own smallness reflected in his hugeness, and because we are opposite we are almost the same.

I'm thirty-four years old and I can't even hold a conversation. I'm soggy and I'm limpid and I've never truly believed in anything but the things that I do. My work, this park. And I like plants. I can make them grow, and I like the sky, how it goes up and up with no lid, and I've never even kissed a girl. And I'm in love with Nancy.

At least I think I am, and for all the wrong reasons. I love Nancy because she never looks me in the eye. That's her way. She's too preoccupied. There's something in her gaze that doesn't focus, doesn't invade. I am only a voice in her head, so I'm safe, it's a safe love. You see, she isn't like other girls.

Nancy's our driver. She has two great passions in her life: to drive her truck and the truck itself. (A Leyland Daf Roadrunner, 'Truck of the Year,' she tells me proudly, 'when it first came out.' Seven tons of silver and metal and diesel.)

Also, Nancy likes to run. She has a body like a wasp; so clean so neat, so sharp. She can be very mean, potentially, but she often chooses not to be. She's a man-woman, an Amazon, an outlaw. She has a small, silver pistol in her truck, in the glove compartment, smokes slim cheroots, wears denim jeans ripped off above the knee, and her muscles, smooth like cream, leg muscles, arm muscles, a tan, darker down one side of her body and face, a driving tan.

In summer she'll wear a short leather halter-top. Her small breasts, like two beige damsons, jutting up, vibrating as she pulls the truck in, struggling in low gear, still when the engine's off. She's a reconstructed Suzi Quatro, a Joan Jett of jammed-up junctions. Sticky and tricky.

She is strong. She moves the load, effortlessly, at speed. She likes picking people up, can even pick Ray up, can do basic judo, play football, baseball, basketball. Has broken both arms, both legs, her collar bone in motorbike accidents. She told me so, she did.

She is covered, like a cactus, in tiny blonde hairs: her face, her arms, her legs. And the light shines off her, and the sweat, when she's hot (always hot), beads on her and transforms her body into a silken web, so ornate, wondrous, one of the wonders of the world, in the world, out of this very, very world.

Nancy.

Nancy switched off her engine.

'I'm fucked,' she said, staring past my ear and into the middle distance. 'My side-light's gone. I'm gonna have to tell Doug. He'll blow.'

'What happened?'

'I dunno. Some guy pulled out and I didn't see him. Halfway to Southend. I was too uptight, too stressed. Just stupid. It's been churning in my stomach all the way home. Third claim in two months. Here's the paper,' she slung me a copy of the *Guardian*, 'that's all they had left at the services.'

'Anything in it?'

'Nah.'

I rolled up the paper and stuck it in my back pocket, then said, 'We're having a meeting in a minute, in the kitchen. D'you need a hand unloading?'

'Nope. I'll be fine. Better start without me.'

'Why?'

'Doug'll blow when I tell him about the bump I had. I can't face it right now.'

'D'you want me to tell him?'

She climbed out of her cab. 'Would you? If the moment's right? If he's in a good mood. Don't mention it otherwise.'

'Fine.'

'Would you?'

'Sure.'

'Thanks. You're a gem.'

She rolled up her sleeves and went to let down the truck's tail.

Ray was in the kitchen devouring a packet of ginger-nuts. He offered me the packet.

'No thanks. Seen Doug?'

'He's on the phone.'

I started preparing a pot of tea. Saleem appeared in the doorway, 'That's fine, Ray, those are mine but just help yourself.'

'Sorry.' He put down the biscuits and furtively brushed some crumbs from his beard.

'Let me do that.' Saleem pushed past me and picked up the teapot, took off the lid and peered inside. 'Doug never rinses this properly.'

I took the paper from my pocket, opened it, held it high and started turning the pages. On the third page, in the Reuters column, two small items had been outlined in blue ink. I peered more closely at them. The first had the heading THUMB SALAD. It said:

> A nurse who found the tip of a thumb in a take-away salad was awarded £200 compensation. Rebecca Pothecary, who bought the food from Anthony's Take-Away on Tottenham Street, central London, 'felt something resist her bite', Clerkenwell magistrates were told. The sandwich bar was ordered to pay £600 in fines and costs for breaching health regulations.

Outside my paper-wall I could hear Ray reaching quietly again, gently, for the ginger-nuts; the crackle of the packet, his fingers prodding inside, his nail catching the rim of a biscuit and easing it out. Saleem had her back to him, engrossed in the task of filling the kettle, fitting on its lid. I heard the water slosh inside it.

The second item in the paper, underlined, directly below the first, had the headline, 100-DAY PROTEST. It said:

> Peter Hawes yesterday spent his 100th day welded inside his roadside café. Mr Hawes, 48, is fighting a government decision to close down the lay-by at Guyhirn in Cambridgeshire, where he has cooked for travellers for years.

Ray had the ginger-nut between his teeth now, bit down softly. I heard the sugar snap and then an unobtrusive crunching, a short silence, another snap, more crunching. Saleem pushed the kettle's plug into the wall and then turned on the power switch. I waited to hear the water in the kettle starting to gurgle, I waited for Saleem to notice Ray's chewing, I waited for Ray to gag and swallow, but all I heard, suddenly, was silence, like each sound had been extracted, sucked out, expunged. I tried to turn a page of my paper but it didn't move. My eyes focused in front of me, on the words *felt something resist her bite*, the words *felt something resist*, the words *felt . . . resist* the word *felt felt . . . felt*. Doug was standing in the doorway. Doug was standing next to me.

'Phil.'

Feel. All the sounds returned in a rush. At once. Doug was standing there and he was smaller than I'd remembered and he had his hands in his pockets and he was smiling.

'If this is our meeting,' Doug said, 'our business meeting, then what is she doing in here?'

Doug tipped his head towards Saleem. Saleem bridled, 'Aren't I even allowed in my own kitchen now?'

Doug continued to smile. 'This is not your kitchen, Saleem. It is our kitchen. This house belongs to the business. You used to work here, yes. You used to have some right to live in this place. When you were a curator. But now the museum is gone, you have no function. You stay here on sufferance, you have stayed here for years, on sufferance, because you have one leg and you lost the other one in a fire, and I feel sorry for you and Ray feels sorry for you and Phil, too, feels sorry for you. But this is not your kitchen. This is our kitchen and we let you borrow it. And you should remember that fact. Now would you get out, please.'

'Fuck you, Doug,' Saleem said, calmly. 'D'you know what a grenadilla is?' she asked, not sounding in the least bit ruffled.

'I know what a grenadilla is, yes.'

'I gave my own flesh for this place,' she whispered. 'What can you give?'

Doug said nothing. He watched her and then he said, 'Go away.'

Saleem laughed. I moved the paper up closer to my face as she swung past me. 'And what're you doing?' she asked, saucily. 'Eating that thing?' Close up she smelled like a bunch of watercress. A peppery smell. I folded the paper, my face tingling. 'If you don't mind,' she added, 'I'll borrow that.'

She snatched the paper and swung out.

Doug filled the kitchen. Ray's fatter – twice as fat – and I'm big enough and hairy enough, but Doug has personality. Doug has backbone, is a true vertebrate. Ray and I are rheumy, watery creatures that ride the waves but Doug's already clambered on shore.

'Where's Nancy?' Doug asked.

'I dunno. Phil?' Ray looked to me.

'Outside. Unloading.'

Doug leaned against the sink. 'Nancy's got to go,' he said, 'I just got a call from our insurance. She had another accident this morning. Almost killed two people. Her fault.'

Ray and I stared at each other.

'We can't afford the insurance premiums any more,' Doug said. 'They keep on going up and up. It's out of control. We've got to tidy this stuff away. Nothing will work until we tidy this stuff away. That's all I'm saying.'

'And just hear this,' he added, warming to his subject now. 'She only went and contacted the insurance people from the services on her way back and said she'd pay the difference herself and something extra if they didn't tell us. If they didn't tell me. That's what the man just told me on the phone.'

'I can't see why she shouldn't do that,' Ray said, boldly.

Doug ignored this, 'She wouldn't even have mentioned it, not a word, not a single word.'

I almost said something, but when I opened my mouth I was only coughing.

'That's deception,' Doug said. 'We can't trust her. She's a liability.'

'I like her,' Ray said cheerfully. 'She's OK.'

Doug focused on Ray. 'Ray,' he said, 'you have all the business sense of a Savoy cabbage.'

Ray smiled. 'True,' he said, 'I see your point, Doug.'

After a short pause, I said, 'I think we should wait a while before we make any decisions. Give it some thought. Take a vote, later on. And maybe we should think about the meeting on Friday before all this other business.'

'It's under control,' Doug said, haughty. 'I want Nancy out. I can't operate, I can't deal with that kind of deception. I'll tell her to her face when she crawls in here. No problem.'

'It's just . . .' I said, 'It's only . . .'

'First things first, Phil,' Doug said, calmly. 'We'll lance her like a boil. Tidy things up a bit.'

Ray's face began to move, to curdle, like he was having a

thought which was germinating in his big, fat cheeks, swelling, expanding, filling him up.

'Doug,' he said, his thought at last finding a voice, a small voice, 'Doug, we were all thinking that maybe you should take things a bit easy for a while . . .'

Doug stared calmly at Ray, his eyes taking in Ray's pink lips and his yellow beard, his several chins, the dimple in his cheek.

'You're going crazy, fat boy, you're crazy if you think I need to take things slow. I'm only just starting. I'm taking stock, fat boy. I'm seeing things big and I'm seeing them better than I've ever seen them. Better than ever.'

Ray looked at his hands. Ten fingers, all in good working order. 'Uh, fine,' he said. 'It's just that Phil . . .'

Doug turned, 'Phil?'

I scratched my neck, my brain fizzy and empty. The kitchen is only a small room and it hasn't been decorated in years. Above the oven, grease has stained the wallpaper a steamy yellow. The grey floor tiles are full of prints, footprints and mud-prints and cat-prints.

'Is there something you're wanting to say to me Phil? Anything? The meeting on Friday? Anything you think I can't handle? Want to tell me?'

It's not exactly that I *couldn't* say anything, more that I didn't really have anything *to* say. What was my evidence, after all? Doug was being strange, but thinking about it, he'd always been irascible, changeable, unpredictable. It wasn't so much anything in particular, any special fact or detail I was burdened with, more a feeling, a sensation.

Saleem had said that we were connected in some way, she and I, the two of us, connected together, against Doug, because Doug was thinking about Gaps, and thinking about making Gaps. And Nancy . . . and Nancy . . . And I was contemplating all these things when I suddenly heard a voice and the voice was saying, 'I love this place, Doug. I love this place.' It was my voice. Blood rushed into my cheeks. I felt a stabbing sensation in my chest.

Doug's face broke into a broad grin. His teeth were tombstones.

'Phil,' he said, laughing, 'I'm going to the greenhouse. Gonna have a little talk to my big vegetables.'

And off he went.

As soon as Doug had gone, Saleem bounced back in. She put her stick down on the table, pulled out a chair and sat down.

'Now what? Nancy's in some kind of trouble?'

Ray nodded. His expression was so mournful and forlorn that it looked like his cheeks were in danger of melting and dripping and dribbling down on to the table. 'Oh God,' he said, 'her timing's less than perfect.' I couldn't think of anything to add. Eventually I said, 'Let's not get this all out of proportion.'

'No?' Ray glanced up, hopeful, 'You think it'll work itself out?'

'More than likely.'

'Oh shut up, Phil,' Saleem snapped. 'What the fuck do you know?'

My skin felt tight. I looked at my watch, 'It's nearly time to knock off.'

'I need a drink,' Ray said, 'and a few packets of crisps. Want to come to The Fox for a while?'

Before I could answer the kitchen door opened slightly and Cog wandered in. Cog was the park's cat who behaved like a dog, was dogged and doggish, ran for sticks and didn't mind a cuff and a wrestle. Nancy was two paces behind him.

'Me and Cog are going for a run together,' she announced. Her voice was just a fraction too loud.

'Did you see Doug?' Ray asked nervously.

'Doug? I saw him.'

She walked to the sink and rinsed her hands. She seemed calm.

'Did Doug say anything?' Ray asked, even more nervously.

'Doug says a lot of things, Doug's a sandwich short of a picnic.'

'Doug's elevator,' Ray grinned, 'doesn't stop at all floors.'

'That's as maybe,' I said, 'but above all else, it's Doug who holds this place together.'

Saleem cocked her head at this. 'I don't think so,' she said. 'It's you that holds this place together, and Ray, and even Nancy. Doug holds the business together.'

'It's the same thing,' I said, confident of this fact.

'Not at all.'

Nancy dried her hands on a tea towel. 'I'm going for a run,' she said, 'Come on, Cog.' She slapped her thigh. Cog came to heel.

'Didn't Doug say anything?' Ray asked, for the second time. Nancy started jogging gently on the spot, warming up. 'Did Phil tell you,' she asked Ray, still very loud, 'that I had another knock in the truck?'

Saleem intervened on my behalf. She said, 'Doug already knew. The insurance people rang him.'

'I was unloading the privet from the van,' Nancy said, 'and Doug came over and asked me to load it up again.'

Saleem, I noticed, was watching Nancy closely, staring at her, and she had a smile on her lips but her eyes were full of something else, an intensity, a fixity, a cruelty.

'Privet?' I asked, unable to stop myself. 'You were unloading privet?'

Nancy nodded, distracted. 'Neat bushes with small, dark green leaves. A ton of them.'

'You don't need to tell Phil what privet is,' Ray said, smiling glumly. 'He's the Plant King.'

'Come off it.' My cheeks tightened a fraction more and I started to glow.

'Yeah, well,' Nancy tucked her T-shirt into her running shorts. 'I'm going for a run,' she said, and before anyone could respond, she'd slammed her way out and sprinted off.

Saleem turned to me. 'He's gone and sacked her,' she said. 'So what are you two going to do about it?'

Ray stared towards the door, after Nancy, his expression inscrutable.

'Let's just sit this one out,' I said. 'Doug won't actually get rid of Nancy. He's just letting off steam.'

'I don't know.' Ray looked uncertain. 'I mean, I like Nancy and I respect Doug. I like them both. But they've both done things and they've both said things . . . I dunno.' Ray picked up the packet of ginger-nuts and ate another one.

'What's Nancy said?' Saleem asked, suddenly sounding interested. I turned too, focused on Ray, slightly daunted by his apparent overview.

'Huh?' Ray stopped chewing.

'What kind of things?' Saleem persisted.

'Stuff.'

Saleem looked towards me and said tartly, 'Maybe you should go and catch up with her. Tell her you and Ray'll sort something out. The way I see it, if Doug can get rid of her that easily and you're both too spineless to do anything about it, then he can also dispense with your services too, if and when the fancy takes him.'

'She's running.'

'Catch up with her. See that she's OK.'

'Maybe Ray should go?'

'Not me,' Ray said, 'I'm not nimble enough.'

Saleem smiled at Ray. 'Anyhow, me and Ray,' she said, 'need to have a quiet little chat.'

Ray's eyes bulged nervously at this prospect. I smiled to myself and slunk out.

Ten minutes later, after a cursory stroll around the sections of the park in which I was least likely to find Nancy – Christ, she would have been half way up Alderman's Hill by the time I'd left the house, and anyway, what could I have said to her if I did catch up with her? What could I promise? And how could I be sure that the words would come? I couldn't be sure – I found myself travelling past the main lake, past the ducks and clambering on to the bandstand and settling myself in a shady corner where I fully intended to dawdle for ten minutes before returning to the house, back to Ray and Saleem.

It was cool and green here, and the water sloshed to my left, and in the distance I could hear a spaniel barking as it ran for a ball, and the thwuck and the swish as it caught the ball and returned it. To my right, I could see one of the tennis courts, and one of the greenhouses, and I could also see, if I stretched my neck, a small man in a white shirt who was limbering up, bending and stretching and bending and stretching.

And I found a fuzzy rhythm in this corner. A wooziness. And as the lids on my eyes descended, cutting my view in half, I felt a terrible certainty, in my gut, in my soul, that nothing could change the way things were, it wasn't possible, because nature didn't work in jerks and starts, but in a rhythm, a cycle, a circle, and Doug, of all people, was aware of that fact. And so was I.

Then out of the blue, out of the sky, a fistful of sand landed in my face. I blinked, shook myself, and then a clod of soil landed to my left followed by a small geranium plant, then a further clod of soil.

I stood up and saw for the first time that the innocuous little man in the white shirt was bending and stretching in the middle of my newly planted flower bed, plum in the middle of my freshly planted flower bed, and he was yanking up plants and tossing them. My new geraniums, the spider plants, other things. This way and that. An arc of soil flew over him.

I jumped off the bandstand and made my way over to him. As I drew closer I saw that he was Chinese and wearing kung-fu robes and he was older than I'd initially thought – sixty or so – but his hair was black and his face was hooded, and something in it was scary, was withered, was fundamentally unpleasant.

And yet his expression was in such direct contrast to his body, his movements, which even in his present task were as fluid and beautiful as a seal's. I appraised his body as I approached, calculating my chances in the likelihood of any kind of physical confrontation.

He was small but he was also solid and thorough and focused; clenched like a little nugget, a meteorite. Plain like a stone. I drew closer to him, but he ignored me. I drew closer still. I said, 'Excuse me. I think you'd better stop what you're doing.'

His head turned, a fraction. 'You fuck off.'

He wasn't nice. His voice was like a dry cork twisting in the neck of a bottle. A tight voice.

I said, again, 'I'd like you to stop what you're doing, immediately, please.'

He plucked a geranium, and weighed it in his hand, looked straight at me, took aim, and thwack! He hit me with it, in the centre of my chest. It had quite some clout, for a geranium. I stepped back slightly, and it was then that I thought I saw Doug, in the doorway of his greenhouse, and even from a distance it looked like Doug was smiling.

'You know him?'

Squeaking voice. I turned back. 'Pardon?'

He pointed towards Doug, 'You know him?'

'Who? Doug?'

'I have a message for him.'

'For Doug?'

'D'you know me?'

I glanced over towards Doug again, but Doug had disappeared, had gone. I guessed he'd withdrawn, back to his tomatoes.

'Do I know you? No. I don't know you.'

'I am Wu.' He offered me a small, slightly muddy hand. 'Shake.'

Gingerly, I offered him my hand. He took it and squeezed it and his grip was like steel.

'Wu! Wu!' he barked softly. 'Like a dog, huh?' And my hand was crumbling and grinding and liquidizing.

'Let go of my hand, please.'

Wu pulled me close to him, so close I could feel little sprays of his saliva on my neck as he spoke.

'Your friend,' he said, 'I don't like him and I don't want him near me. I don't want him watching me, see? All the time I feel his eyes on me. And you can tell him, from me, that a frog cannot turn into a green leaf.'

'I'll tell him. Let go of my hand.'

He lessened his grip a fraction, pulled me even closer, stood on his tip-toes and whispered directly into my ear, 'I hope I didn't break your knuckle.' Finally, after one more, gentle squeeze, he let go. He wiped his hands clean on his robes and walked off. Slowly, calmly, treading softly.

I looked down at my hand. I tried to wiggle my fingers. I could move my thumb but nothing else. My fingers were purple, the joints were white. The whole hand was burning. I ran over to the lake and dipped my fist in it. But the water didn't help to cool me. It was warm as saliva at its edges. I took my hand out, held it in front of me like a trophy, and went to find Doug.

Doug was watering some tomatoes in his greenhouse. The house was warm and had that rich smell of damp compost which always makes me feel like sneezing: a fine, ripe smell.

Doug watered his tomatoes with enormous tenderness. He didn't take his eyes off them as he spoke.

'So he got you, did he?'

I stood next to his marrows and his radishes, both of which seemed to be coming on well. The radishes were already the size of tennis balls. 'I think he broke my hand.'

'Wu. He's a devil.' Doug chuckled to himself before adding, 'I can't take my eyes of him. My fault he destroyed the bed. I can't stop myself from watching him and he's warned me. He gets irritable.' He chuckled again.

I said, 'I've never even seen him before.'

Doug moved on to the next bush.

'Phil, someone could squat down and shit on your foot and you'd hardly notice them.'

I let this pass. Pain had made me bold. My hand hurt so much that I could hardly contemplate any other kind of feeling. I said, 'I don't think you want to have too much to do with that man in the future, Doug.'

'Wu!' Doug said, delightedly. 'Did you see the way he moves around this place? Flowing, flowing. Like water. Like he owns the whole damn park. And the sky. That special kind of movement. Inside out. Round. That strange oriental kind of moving. Tip-toeing but very sure.'

'I think he broke my hand.'

Doug turned off the hose. 'I've been following him about since I moved into the house. Early in the morning he comes to the park, climbs over the fence before we even open, and he does all that strange, slow dancing. Tai Chi. I've been watching him, I even approached him for a talk but he didn't want disturbing. I think I broke his concentration,' Doug said, 'and so it's possible I've started getting on his nerves.'

'He said that. He told me to tell you that you were getting on his nerves. I don't think you should pester him any more.'

Doug gave this some thought and then for the first time he turned his eyes on me. 'That sudden violence,' he said cheerfully, 'I like it. I like the *idea* of it. It's clean.'

'He's destroyed the flower bed. I spent half the afternoon planting it.'

'He's cleaned it out,' Doug said, unperturbed. 'Good luck to him. I have plans for that section anyway,' he added, 'a couple of big ideas. Icing on the cake.'

'But for the time being . . .'

'And if I've learned one thing from that tough little man,' Doug said, 'it's that you've got to have your own vision and stick to it. Ignore the rest of life's radish.'

'Life's radish?' I echoed, bemused.

Doug nodded. 'No more rubbish. Only truth.'

He then moved a few feet across, fingered the bright shoot of a large onion and said, almost to himself, 'This one's going to be a giant. I can feel it. I can smell it.' He scratched his nose. 'Do you smell it, Phil?' He glanced over at me. 'Smell it, do you?'

'Smell what?'

Doug sucked his tongue, irritated. 'You don't see it, Phil, do you? You just don't see how there's a real logic to an onion. One layer inside another layer inside another layer. All circular. Like a maze. A puzzle. Nothing missing. No gaps. Just simple.'

My hand was swollen now. It had swelled up like a puffer fish. 'If he tries to assault me again,' I muttered, 'I'll call the police.'

Doug carried on talking to his onion, 'One layer inside another layer.'

'Doug. About Nancy . . .'

'Whosoever diggeth a pit, Phil, shall fall in it. Nancy dug her pit. She's fallen into it.'

'Even so . . .'

Doug began to scowl. 'I want big, Phil, and I want neat. Big, neat, clean, true. Not just the park itself, but everything. The whole lot. The business, the talking, the ideas. Big, *clean*, neat, true. None of that muddy stuff, none of that green fruit, nothing unripe, none of that murky water.'

I looked down at my hand.

'I'll fix the bed in the morning,' I said, 'before we open. I don't think I can replant right now with my fist all swollen.'

Doug waved me away with his hand, 'Go away, Phil. Go. I'm busy with this onion. There's work to do here.'

I hesitated.

'Phil,' Doug barked. 'Go away. Let's get tidy. And I don't just mean weeding and replanting. OK?'

I nodded. I retreated.

'Where's Ray?'

Saleem was in the kitchen alone. She had Cog on her lap and she was stroking him. Cog's purr almost lifted the tablecloth.

'He's gone,' she said, 'to the pub. You didn't find Nancy, I gather?'

'No.'

'Fuck. Your hand's all swollen. What did you do?'

'I crushed it in the mower.'

'You've been out mowing?'

'I was putting it away.'

'Is it broken?'

'No, the mower's fine.'

She knocked Cog off her lap. 'Let's see it.'

I backed off a fraction. 'It's in the barn. I locked it up for the night.'

She gazed at me, unsmiling. 'Do you seriously think I'm going to hurt you, Phil?'

'Hurt me? No.'

I inspected my shirt-front. Wu's geranium assault had left its mark.

'Sit down Phil. I want to talk to you.' Saleem pulled out a chair and pointed at it.

'Ray's expecting me. Maybe I'll go to casualty with this hand.'

'Sit. Screw Ray. Screw your hand.'

I sat down, but on the edge of the chair so she'd sense I wasn't staying.

'OK,' Saleem perched herself against the table. 'Picture the worst case scenario . . .'

I studied my hand. It was still smarting. I thought about the pain.

'If Doug gets any more erratic and irascible than he already is, then there's no way we can let him go to the meeting on Friday.'

'He has to go. No one else can.'

'You could.'

'Doug has to go. I can't go.'

'Why not?'

'I just can't. Doug needs our support. He needs to be kept on an even keel, that's all.'

'Ha!' Saleem rolled back on her hip, victorious. 'So even you've noticed that something's up. Even you, finally, have noticed.'

'I'm only saying . . .'

'Picture the worst case scenario.'

'It's hardly going to come to that.'

'If Doug can't go, you'll have no choice but to go yourself. Ray's a moron. You understand how the park works.'

'But I don't have anything to do with the business side of things. That's Doug's department.'

'You'd just have to acquaint yourself with a selection of the most salient facts, that's all. I could help you.' She pointed towards one of the kitchen drawers. 'It's all in there. The papers, the bills, receipts, accounts. Everything we need.'

'It won't come to that.'

'Look,' Saleem pushed herself up off the table, 'I've got something for you. It's kind of last-minute, but I think it might help.' She picked up her stick and disappeared from the kitchen.

Cog came and slithered around my ankles. My knuckles felt like they were growing. Expanding. I looked around and my eyes settled on a tea-cloth over by the sink. I stood up, grabbed hold of it, dampened it in some cold water and tried to apply it to my hand. Saleem returned.

'What're you doing?'

'I'm trying to tie this around my knuckles.'

Saleem was holding a book. She put it down on the table and came over. She snatched the tea-towel, wrung it out and tied it on firmly. I winced. Pain and her proximity left me squeamish.

'Sit.'

She pushed me down on to the chair again. She picked up the book. It had a red cover.

'See this?' She held the book up to me. It was called *I'm Not Angry, I'm Hurting* by Dr John Sledge. 'Guess what, Phil?'

'What?' I wished the book didn't have a red cover. Not red.

'You're not angry, Phil, you're hurting.'

I inspected my makeshift bandage. I said, 'I think I'm feeling a little of both, actually.'

Saleem ignored this.

'I went to a psychiatrist, after the accident,' she said, 'after the museum burned down and I lost my leg.' She paused for a moment and then grinned. 'Fuck all wrong with me, though. But for some reason, that quack gave me this book. Obviously, it's all bollocks. Most of it. But there's something in here, Phil, that I think might help us. Kind of like the inside of a nut.'

'A kernel.'

'Exactly.'

She paged through the book. She pushed the pages flat on Chapter four: 'How I Feel, How You Feel'. She handed me the book. 'Read.'

I closed the book. I said. 'I'll read it later. I think I should go and see Ray.'

'It's a quick fix,' Saleem said, undaunted, 'and if you're going to attend that meeting on Friday then we're going to need a quick fix, because you know and I know that you won't have the balls to stand up in front of five people and present a good case for our tender without some kind of divine intervention.'

'It won't come to that.'

'It might.'

She took the book back and opened it again. 'The main point Sledge makes is this, right. He says, it's not *what* happens in life that screws you up but how you *interpret* events. See? So sometimes, if you're very sensitive, then often it's not like bad things have actually happened, only that they feel bad to you. So it's all a question of getting things in proportion, yeah?'

I gave my sore knuckle a little squeeze so that the pain would distract me. A kind of anaesthetic.

'And right here's how you go about it. Chapter Four. Right here. Cognitive Behaviour Therapy. Something called the three Cs. Cool, calm, confident. Uh . . . rhythmic exercises and stuff. Breathing.'

I scratched my beard. 'Did Ray say he'd be in The Fox?'

Saleem looked up from the book. She suddenly wasn't as affable as she'd seemed before.

'You'd better listen to me, Phil. I'm not bullshitting you. I'm taking control of this situation and it's going to be a bumpy fucking ride.'

Her anger blew in my face like hot air from a hairdryer. Hot. Dry. She looked down at the book again. 'You've got to get stuff in proportion. You've got to do it quickly, that's all I'm saying. And it won't be easy.'

Cog jumped up on to the table next to her. He'd barely landed before she knocked him off with a vigorous swipe. He skidded as he landed on the tiles.

'You and I are going out together, right now, and we are going up on to the High Street, to the chemist's, and you are going to walk in there, straight to the counter, and in a clear, loud voice you are going to ask the assistant for a packet of extra-small condoms.'

I shook my head. I continued staring down at the tiles.

'OK, so it sounds stupid, but there's a reason behind it . . .'

'I'm not doing that.'

'It's therapeutic. Kind of like embarrassing yourself on purpose. Taking it to the limit. Forcing yourself. Taking control of embarrassing situations and so taking the sting out of them.'

Sting. Saleem. Cog stood by the kitchen door. I wanted to be where Cog was. I wanted to be Cog. I shook my head. Outside I could hear something. Footsteps, a door opening, a metallic jangle. The engine of Nancy's truck bursting into life.

Nancy. I looked up and over towards the window. Saleem was staring at me. I didn't meet her eye. And then I heard her voice whispering under the growl of the truck. Lower than the truck and growlier. She said, 'And you care about this place, and you care about Nancy, but you don't have the guts to do anything. You won't speak up. You won't even do that. That one small thing. And I'd give up my fucking body, and Doug'd give up his fucking soul. But you, you won't give anything.'

Saleem threw the book down onto my lap, picked up her stick, left me. I heard the front door slam. Outside I heard female voices. And whispering.

RAY WAS ON HIS third pint by the time I'd arrived at The Fox. He was perched on a stool by the bar. The pub wasn't too full, although Ray's enough of a man to fill any room. His arms are giant leeks, white leeks tipped with two artichoke paws, a full fist of fingers which he wiggles and he waggles to great dramatic effect.

I pulled up a stool for myself. Ray inspected my hand.

'Did Nancy do that?'

'No.'

'Saleem?'

'Let me just say something, Ray.'

He looked up, surprised by my determined tone. 'What?'

I thought for a moment. 'I just think we've got to make a real effort to keep Doug calm. Especially over the next couple of days.'

'OK.'

I smiled. It was so easy with Ray. And I said, 'I don't think we should involve Saleem too much in the park's affairs either.'

Ray suddenly looked uneasy, he fidgeted on his stool. 'Saleem's quite involved,' he said, 'already.'

'Well she doesn't need to be any more involved, that's all I'm saying.'

'No,' Ray took a sip of his beer.

'Doug's doing fine.'

Ray took another sip. He smacked his lips. 'You're right,' he said. He ordered me a pint, paid, passed it over. As he passed it I said, almost casually, almost incidentally, 'And the Chinaman . . .'

'Wu.'

'You know about him?'

Ray knew. He knew. Ray, it turned out, knew more than I'd thought. Ray, it turned out, had served as a confidant, a gatherer of scraps, an unobservant observer.

People feel they can trust Ray. They trust his gormlessness, his softness, his delicious, harmless squelchiness.

People mention things to Ray and they know that no judgement will be forthcoming, no private reckoning will take place in the cavern of Ray's brain, no stern moral hypothesis will be formulated and delivered. Ray is a sponge. Ray is natural, is, above all other things (and how could it be otherwise, really?), *himself*.

Something dawned on me. A kind of shame. No one tells me stuff. No one tells me anything. Not of their own accord. My head is so full of other things, of myself, of itself, that no one ever bothers telling me anything else.

'No one told me this stuff, Ray,' I said at one point, during a conversational hiatus. 'No one mentioned any of this to me.'

'You're lucky,' Ray answered blithely. 'You've got your own business going on. You've got,' he paused for greater emphasis, 'you've got a *secret life*, up there,' he tapped his skull.

'And you don't?'

He grinned, 'I've got all the outside stuff. That's plenty.'

By Ray's fourth pint I wasn't worried any more, not shy to be spoken to, not conscious of his gaze. Ray's eyes were watery, wandering; tadpoles in the jelly of his face. 'You want to know about Wu?' he asked. 'Well, if you want to know about Wu, then first you have to know about Doug and Mercy and the Anniversary Dinner.'

'I do?'

He nodded. 'You see, I don't understand all this business myself. It's only that Saleem said something and then Doug mentioned something else. It's not like anything fits together in any way. Nothing like that. But I keep picking up this information and slotting it away . . .'

'But Wu . . . ?'

'Remember three weeks ago? Before Doug moved in with Saleem? Before all this weird stuff? Doug and Mercy's thirtieth wedding anniversary. That's where it started . . .'

'Mercy and the diarrhoea, Saleem said something . . .'

Ray nodded. 'That's the one. Just listen,' he said. 'You won't hardly believe it.'

And slowly, slowly, with commendable precision, Ray rolled open his canvas and covered it with colour. And each stroke was perfect, each touch, each piece of his narrative fitted, each portion, each serving, so neat and geometrical, *every* element, a balance. Like he was neatly laying squares of turf down for a brand new lawn.

'Picture it,' Ray said, his eyes sparkling, 'Friday night, three weeks ago. Italian restaurant. La Bruschetta on Green Lanes. Doug's all dressed up for dinner. Jacket, tie. Mercy's wearing a new dress. Doug's been busy all day working on the accounts for the park. Things are tight. The budget's stretching thin . . . yeah, well, who cares, because they're out for a special night together. Thirty years! That's something worth celebrating.

'Now here's the important part, right, pay attention. Doug is perfectly happy. Four words: *Doug is perfectly happy!* He's got other things on his mind, naturally, other pressures: work, the park, money, their gas boiler might be on the blink . . . yeah, well, but everything's fine, and the waiter comes over to their table and they order their starters.

'Mercy has Parma ham. Great. Doug's about to have the same – he always follows Mercy's lead in culinary matters, that's just the way it is between them – and then his eye swerves, he looks down the menu, and his gaze settles on the words "prawn cocktail". He thinks: what the hell. I'm thirty years married. Time for something new. Prawn cocktail.

'Doug looks up at the waiter and he says "Prawn cocktail, please." And Mercy stares at him with a strange expression on her face. He stares back at her. "What's up?" he says. "Doug, what made you choose that prawn cocktail?" He gives it some thought. He says, "Do I need a reason?" She shrugs.

'They order the rest of their meal, their drinks, and off the waiter goes. Fine. Except Doug can't help noticing that Mercy's expression is a little bit brighter, a little bit tighter.

'The starters arrive. Doug digs in. Mercy's staring at his prawns. She's not touched her ham yet. She says, "Doug, why did you order that prawn cocktail when you know we never have prawns?" Doug puts down his fork. He says, "Now what? What's the big problem with the prawns?" Mercy says, "Remember our very first date?" Doug gives it some thought. He remembers. Mercy says, "Well, on that occasion I had prawns." Doug is flummoxed. So what? And he turns his mind back to that very first date.

'And the truth is – and he remembers it – that he didn't much like Mercy when he first met her. Not for any particular reason, but there was no spark between them, not on his side, at least, and he firmly believes in a spark. He's romantic like that, although you'd be hard pressed to imagine it now.

'Anyway, he remembers their first date, thirty years ago. Remembers it clearly, how, at the beginning, on their way to the restaurant, things were really dragging, and he was wondering why he agreed to go, and he was thinking about how his parents knew Mercy's parents and how Mercy's brother was at the same cricket club, all this stuff.

'And then Doug remembers, with a smile, how it happened, during the meal, how something peculiar, something completely unexpected happened. They were on their second course, they'd been talking, and suddenly, out of the blue, he saw that Mercy was brighter than he'd thought, and sparky, and nervous, and she had this restlessness, this vivacity. And the candle on the table flickered its light on her and she was beautiful. Beautiful.

'In that instant, Doug knew that there was a spark. Right there, in his heart. And she wasn't pushy, she wasn't slow, she wasn't any of the things he'd thought she was. She was fine, jumpy, mysterious; a thoroughbred.

'Doug remembered. *Thirty years!* He grinned to himself. He picked up his spoon. Mercy was glaring. He put down his spoon. Now what? What's the problem? "I hate prawns, Doug," Mercy mutters. "That very first date we went on, I had prawns as a starter and they nearly ruined everything."

'Well you can imagine, Doug is staring at her like she's crazy. "I mean it, Doug," she says. "I had some prawns and they gave me the quickest and the worst and the strongest dose of food poisoning I've ever had. How I sat through that meal I'll never know. My stomach was a volcano, my head was on fire. I could barely hold my fork."

'Bang! Suddenly Doug's mind is clicking and whirring, turning over and everything's playing back in slow motion. And he realizes, it dawns on him, it strikes him that Mercy is not the woman he thought she was. She wasn't the woman he fell in love with. He fell in love with – and this is the best part or the worst part according to how you look at it – he fell in love with a small dose of *staphi cocci*. That's bacteria, incidentally.

'You see, Mercy wasn't that vivacious woman, that flighty, peachy, jumpy thoroughbred. She was a boring person with a gastric disorder. But Doug hadn't seen it. He'd duped himself. He'd sold himself down the river. Bang! Just like that. Doug had built his house on sand. Doug had been living a lie. It was over. That was it. He moved out of their home that very same night.'

Ray rested his head on the bar, sideways, and stared at me. I was gawping.

'Ray,' I said, 'I've never heard such a pile of absolute garbage.'

Ray was unfazed. 'Later I saw Mercy,' he said, 'and she was sobbing her eyes out because Doug had told her she was never the person he thought she was. She just didn't get it, and I didn't get it either. I told her so. I said, "He's having a brainstorm. Men sometimes go funny at fifty." She said, "Women go funny too but they don't make such a song and dance about it." I said, "Fair enough." That's all I could say.'

'Is there anything else?'

Ray sighed. 'Well, Saleem thinks the problem is longer term. The big vegetables in the greenhouse. His obsession with getting the bandstand built. Wu. She thinks Doug's having all these weird thoughts about religion and truth and culture and the Mercy thing's just a part of it. She says she hears him talking to himself at night, having whole conversations all on his own. She says Doug's been muttering stuff to her about how events all go in a circle and that everything inside has to come outside and that all actions should be true actions and direct actions. He's private and secretive but also evangelical. You'd think it'd be hard to be all these things at once but Doug seems to manage it.

'Anyhow, Saleem says that if he talks to anyone for a period longer than five minutes then it becomes extremely apparent that he's very disturbed indeed. Very disturbed. She said he can't go to the meeting on Friday because it'll be as plain as her face that he's as mad as a hatter. We'll lose the tender.'

'Forget about Saleem, Ray,' I said, 'Doug might be thinking a lot of strange things but it hasn't affected us directly yet. I'm sure we can sort out the business with Nancy during the two weeks she's working out her notice. He'll come around. And there's no reason for us to believe that the meeting won't be just fine. It's all a question of keeping things in proportion.

'And if what Doug says is true, and things do move in a circle, then maybe Doug will get back to how he used to be eventually. Maybe even quite soon if everything stays calm.'

Ray sighed again, even deeper this time. 'It's true, then,' he determined, out of nowhere, 'what Saleem said about you being a man of integrity.'

'What?'

Ray sighed again. 'I might have some crisps,' he muttered, and then, 'Maybe you're right. Maybe we should just bide our time and keep things in proportion. And maybe Doug's right too, about the circle and everything coming back to where it started. You never know. You can't tell with life, can you? What's around the next corner?'

Ray finished his drink with a flourish and ordered three packets of smoky bacon.

I TESTED OUT the physical viability of my damaged hand during my walk home from the pub. First off, I tried bending the fingers with the aid of my undamaged hand, then I tried bending them without assistance, next I tried to form them into a kind of half-fist, and finally I pulled out Dr John Sledge's *I'm Not Angry, I'm Hurting* from my jacket pocket and tested whether I could fold my fingers round it and bear its weight. After performing this final task with some ease I decided that maybe things weren't as bad in dextral terms as they'd initially seemed.

Home is the ground floor of a nice house on Broomfield Road which has been converted into two self-contained flats. The road runs adjacent to the park on its southern perimeter. The flat used to belong to my grandmother and now it belongs to me. Consequently, it has a dusty old chintz and velvet feel to it, but is spartan too, like the home of someone in two minds about the nature and possibilities of interior decor. And although by instinct I'm a small, shy, dozy creature, happy holed up, solitary, contained, in fact I get claustrophobic inside and prefer a place where there is no roof, only sky, and a high sky at that.

I held Dr John Sledge in my hand and I swung my arm. I sniffed the tea-towel, which was still damp, but drier now, and musty, robust, sassy with the tang of sweat. Using my good hand, I felt inside my pocket for my keys. And then I saw her. On my doorstep.

Saleem was glaring. 'Where the hell have you been? I've been round here twice. I've been waiting for absolutely bloody hours.'

Saleem, incongruously, on my doormat. Was she a figment? A fragment? An ugly spectre? An invasive sylph? A sprite?

I tested out my voice. It was steady. 'What are you doing here?'

She carried right on scowling. 'We've got to talk. Now.'

I was tired, suddenly, 'Can't it wait? Would you mind?'

She shook her head. 'It can't wait. Open the door. Let me inside. I'm freezing.'

It was a warm night. I didn't want to open the door. If I let her in she might never leave, might take up residence, squat, like she did in the park keeper's house. She had that adhesive, that sticky quality which wouldn't come out in the wash.

'You're pissed,' she muttered, watching as I fumbled with my keys.

'I had three pints and I'm perfectly sober.'

'Great in a fucking crisis. First thing you do is reach for the bottle.'

I took my keys out. 'There's no crisis and I'm not drunk.'

'Let me smell your breath.' Uninvited, unexpected, she pushed her face into mine, sniffed, grinned and then took this opportunity to bite me, sharply, impishly on the nose.

'Oh Christ.' Why did she do that? Her tongue was a cattle prod. She was a ball of venom, slobbering on me.

She cackled. 'Open up. Make me wait out here any longer and I'll fuck you up the arse with my stump. And remember,' she added, 'I've been standing all the while on only one sure limb, which is twice as tiring.' She knocked my shins with her stick.

She has that capacity to offend, Saleem, to hurt, mortally. I hate that in her. I'd like to hurt her back but I just don't have it in me. I'd like to injure her, knock the other leg out from under her, just once.

I opened the door. She pushed past me and bounded into the kitchen, pulled wide the oven door and switched the gas on full.

'What're you doing?'

'Gassing myself. What d'you think? I'm cold. Give me a match.'

'If you want to light it then use the ignition.'

'I want a match. I'm cold. Give me a bloody match right now or else.'

She was cold-blooded. An amber mamba. I gave her the match and said, 'Switch it off first. Don't just . . .'

Floooom! A gust of blue flame bellowed out of the oven. Saleem didn't move or shirk. 'Yeah! I love that.'

She stared at the flame for a while, grinning, while it filled her irises and made them yellower. Then she snatched her eyes away, blinked, pulled out a chair and sat down.

'OK,' she said, 'So you don't know why I'm here, do you? Maybe you think I've come to appraise your living quarters. I've never even been in your house before. You never invited me.' She looked around the kitchen. 'Yeah, not bad. If things go wrong at the park after Friday I could easily make a den for myself here. Wouldn't take too much adjusting.'

She smiled, apparently well satisfied with this pronouncement, waiting, now, for a response.

I didn't respond. I said, 'What's the problem?'

'Make me a cuppa.'

'It's late.'

'Go on, I'm freezing.'

'It's nearly midnight. I want to go to bed, if you don't mind.'

'Make me a cuppa and then I'll come with you.'

'I haven't got any milk.'

'Fine.' She stood up, picked up her stick from the table. 'Let's fuck.'

My temples throbbed. I took one deep breath and then another. 'Why are you here Saleem?'

She grinned at me, dug her hand into the pocket of the large denim jacket she was wearing and pulled out a sheet of paper.

'See this?' She passed it to me. I took it with my good hand. 'Nancy left it out for Doug on the kitchen table. It's from the nursery in Southend she visited today.'

'So?'

'Well read it, stupid.'

I inspected it.

'Look at it,' she said, excitedly. 'Privet!'

She nudged me between my ribs with her elbow.

'Privet!' she exclaimed, yet again. 'And all the while I'd been thinking *private*. Doug's been going on about being *private*, but I'd got it all wrong, see? He meant privet.'

Saleem had lost it.

'No I don't see.'

I did see, however, that Doug had ordered literally a ton of the stuff. He'd spent a fortune on it. Three hundred pounds which I was certain the park didn't possess.

Saleem eyed me inquisitively. 'And there I was,' she said, 'thinking that the park was broke and that you could all barely afford to put petrol in the mower.'

'It's nothing,' I said, calmly. 'I already had an inkling about this.' My words sounded half-formed.

Saleem snorted, 'Phil, you're so bloody transparent. Like a square of polythene.'

I folded up the receipt and handed it back to her.

'Privet, private,' she continued, speculatively, 'one letter different.'

'I can't dispute that.'

She pushed her skinny face up close to mine, 'Doug's going to do something very stupid, and he's going to do it soon, and it's going to screw everything up.'

If I'd stepped back at this point I'd have ended up in the oven. Warm air against the back of my legs was already making me prickle.

'And where would you be without the park, huh? And where would I be? If someone new takes over the tender they'd be bound to evict me. They wouldn't care about my *history* with the place. Not strangers.'

'It won't come to that.'

She drew even closer, 'It might. It just might.'

And I felt something strange, in my midriff. Saleem's finger. It had threaded its way through a gap in my shirt, between the buttons, and was poking, sharply, pointedly, into my navel. Then it rotated, like I was a clockwork mouse and she was winding me up.

'I must just quickly tell you,' she whispered, 'the way I see it. It's like this, right: we've all been surfing, on the water's surface, on top of a wave, sure-footed, and time has passed fairly comfortably, but now, all of a sudden, we've fallen off our boards and into the ocean. We're swallowing water, it's icy cold, it's wet, it's salty, and when we come up for air, it feels different. Very different. Not like the air we were surfing in before. Better. And every breath, every breath . . .'

I pushed her away. 'Stop that.'

She stared at her finger for a moment, sniffed it, and then placed it in her mouth, sucked it, winked, removed it and said loudly, 'Grab this opportunity and make the most of it.'

'What opportunity?'

'OK, so fine,' she was suddenly businesslike, 'I said this afternoon that I was the one to change things. But now . . .' She shrugged. 'I'm entrusting all this shit to you, handing it all over. For the time being.' She grabbed my arm. 'Wanna take me now or wait till morning?

'Handing what over?'

'You look knackered,' she added, letting go of my arm, her top lip curling. 'Better wait.'

She grabbed her stick and bounded out.

Thursday

SLEEP CAME AND WENT like a slug crawling over my belly. I woke at five and lay in bed, still half-dressed. I had two unusual bed-mates. Firstly, the tea-towel, which had loosened itself from my wrist and had journeyed up my arm until it found a niche around my shoulder, under my armpit.

Secondly, incongruously, Dr John Sledge's book, which was lying on the pillow next to my head. I appraised its redness. I prodded it with my nose. I put out a hand, gingerly, picked it up, opened its pages and blinked at it. *You can't see the world through anyone else's eyes,* Dr Sledge said, *only your own. There's nothing wrong with being who you are. But let's try to make sure that you like who you are. Let's be sure that you like yourself. Because if you don't like yourself, how do you expect anyone else to like you? And if you don't know yourself, how can you expect anyone else to want to know you?*

I looked to the top of the page. It said, Chapter Two: 'Knowing Yourself'. I closed the book and inspected my bad hand. It was bruised, had the dominant colours of a fine Red Oak Leaf lettuce. Purple and red and a darkish blue. Green on its edges and a slurried yellow.

I lay back and tried to think about things. I had a lot to digest. But sometimes digesting isn't as easy, as natural a process as it might be. You see, I have the kind of brain that doesn't link things too well. Admittedly, I was the recipient of a whole, big, scruffy bundle of information, but most of it was words and feelings and hearsay, and these things mean little to me, mean nothing to me until I can see the proof of them with my own two eyes.

A wholesaler might answer in the affirmative when I ask whether the hollyhock seedlings I've just purchased are all a single colour, but when they grow, when they flower, only then can I be truly sure. And it's not suspicion or cynicism that makes me this way. I'm just stupid and dumb like a dozy mongrel. I do things and I do things and I believe things when I see them with my own eyes. That's when. Only then.

I've got some camomile tea that I made myself, that I grew myself, that I drink at night sometimes or to relax me. I got up and drank a cup. It tasted like a bundle of hay. I pulled on my shoes and I walked outside, still feeling like I had a whole farmyard on my tongue.

It was early. I was earlier than usual. I wanted to check up on a couple of things, iron out hitches, smooth stuff over. I wanted to make sure that nothing bad could happen, to try to keep Doug padded up for the day in a soft swab of cotton wool. It felt necessary.

The park wasn't open yet. I unlocked one of the gates with my key and went in. It was getting light, like the sky was slowly growing accustomed to having the sun spill out all its pale guts on to it. No clouds, only a roof in the heavens the grey-white colour of spittle.

It was so quiet, and the quiet was like a kiss. Soft and gentle, and all the plants were waking up in the sure caress of this silence, yawning and stretching and swallowing the dew. Even here, even in the city, this little green heart was pumping and throbbing and murmuring.

I followed the path to the barn. I paused for a second, stared over at Nancy's truck which was parked where it had been the previous afternoon. Everything was still. I went into the barn and pulled out some tools: a fork, a hoe, a small trowel, and headed off in the direction of the damaged flower bed. But I reached something else before I reached the bed, someone else. Wu. In a corner, filling the path between a rhododendron and the herb garden.

Wu. Dancing, just like I'd been told. In his loose robes, with his leg in the air, moving slowly up and around, he looked like a gannet, a heron, the topmost trumpet of a white lily, touched by the wind and bending its neck, swooning.

I stopped in my tracks. My hand gave a little twitch, like it remembered, like its damaged flesh had a memory. Wu hadn't seen me, or at least gave no indication of having seen me but continued with his tiny movements, began painting slow, splendid letters in the air with his hands, packed the air with his palms, shifted it, organized it. Air, only air.

I turned back on myself, slipped through the rockery, past the lake, over and around, and ended up, after this small diversion, where I wanted to be. Facing my ruined bed, my back to Doug's greenhouse.

What was it that made me turn? The sound of a door hinge squeaking? Something metallic which wasn't the close, clinking sound of the tools I was holding? Nothing like that. A little message. An inkling.

And I did turn. What made me turn? And I saw that the door was ajar. The greenhouse door. This was the first sign. The door was ajar. It made me shudder, the idea of the door being left open, the warm air escaping. I dropped my tools and walked over. I could smell something. Rich soil, compost. Sap.

I pulled the door wide and walked in, checking the temperature gauge to my left, immediately, out of instinct. Cog whisked around my ankles and made me shudder again.

I looked around me. It was terrible. Everything was up and out and overturned. Mud and dirt and water. Wretched vegetables – those giant things, those protein-pumped, overlarge, swollen creatures – scratched and hacked and bruised and bleeding, tossed and chopped and kicked around. On the floor. Corpses, partially buried. Ruined. A massacre.

My mind worked in its own natural way. I didn't think of vandals, only of Doug, that someone hated Doug very badly or that Doug hated himself very badly. A stupid group of thoughts, like my mind was a collection of dried flowers, ornate and complex, but not as good as the real thing, the fresh thing, not at all.

I moved from the greenhouse and went outside again, closing the door behind me, securing it. What did this *mean*? How could I know what it meant until I could see what it meant with my own two eyes? And in the distance, beyond the herb garden, behind the rhododendron, I saw the slightest, whitest, spitefullest little figure. I saw him.

When did I pick up the hoe? I don't remember. Only Wu. I saw him and I wondered idly, was he mad or was he only different? Was he mad or only different? Then I was next to him. I saw him. Wu. Wu's eyes, full of the sky. I saw his eyes. I saw myself in them. And I thought . . . so all this had been going on? This mess, this madman, Doug and everything? All this had been going on even while everything else carried on too, the spring, the summer, the showers, the flowers?

Suddenly Nancy was next to me. 'Phil.'

'What have you done?'

I couldn't see Nancy, I was looking at Wu, I was speaking to Wu. I glared at him. He didn't seem in the least bit concerned. Very slowly, very slowly, he brought his arms and his legs down from the sky and into a kind of repose.

'Huh?'

'Do you know what you've done? Do you know?'

Wu seemed nonplussed. 'You want me to answer your questions? Huh? Yes. No. Yes. No. Huh?'

I was holding the hoe, horizontally. I gripped it. I didn't even stop to wonder what Nancy was doing. Why she was here.

Wu took several, small steps towards me and then stopped. He then took another small step forward. I braced myself.

'Give me that,' he said, pointing at the hoe.

'Give it to me, Phil,' Nancy said, because she was there, right next to me, and she took hold of the hoe and pulled it from me. But Wu was still moving, like I still had the hoe and he had every intention of taking it away from me. Slowly, he pushed the flat of his palm forwards, towards me, as though nudging a book or a drink or a flower in my direction. Closer and closer. I watched it, dazed, dazzled, and then it touched me. This slow hand hit me like a hammer in my chest. Until . . . yes! I was flying through the air, like a pancake or an omelette, twirling – a stingray – whirling and twisting. Up and up.

What a revelation! It wasn't at all dramatic. Not in the least how it should have been. His hand had been soft and then stronger than anything. And now I was flying, and I had time to think about all kinds of stuff, to notice that the holly still needed pruning, to remember how muddy Nancy's hands had been, to see that in the centre of the rockery there was clover. And it was flowering purply. It was far and then it was close and my nose was in it.

A while after I landed I felt a jolt. My arm was twisted, slung under me. I was winded. I felt, just a little, like sleeping.

OH, THIS WAS NICE. Kind of wet and slippery and I was moving without any effort. But, thinking about it, something was hurting, was hurting. A bump and a rucking and a grazing. A long distance away I heard a voice, a tight little voice, unfamiliar, which was saying, 'Can't force flow. Flow flows.' Flow *flows*.

Actually, the more I thought about it – and, be assured, there was no rush, no reason to rush – the more I gave it thought, the less happy I felt. My head was banging on the ground. My arm was aching, turned under me. I was being dragged. I felt mud and grass and then I felt gravel. My beard was so full of it. Bits of stone finding a home. Until, finally, I was still.

Something happened then, but I was no part of it. The gravel shifted, right up close to me, and then my face was wrapped in a warm, soft towel and a vapour darkened everything.

'Hello Phil. Hello Phil. Hello.'

'Wah?'

Shit. That was me.

I opened my eyes. Saleem had her face up close to mine and she was covered in blood – her cheek and her hand.

'Don't be shocked. I'm not hurt. This is your blood.'

'Oh.'

She wiped at her face with a piece of tissue while she said, 'Nancy's here. She dragged you in.'

Nancy materialized in front of me. 'I dragged you in. I'm really sorry. I'd never have taken the hoe away if I thought he was going to attack you. He's so powerful for a little fella. Like David Carradine in *Kung Fu*.'

'Where's Doug?'

Saleem had a bowl full of warm water and a roll of kitchen towel.

'He's upstairs. Still in bed.'

She leaned over me again and applied something damp to my cheek. 'Want to know what kind of injuries you sustained?'

'Uh, I feel OK.'

'Well, apart from the odd cut and graze, I think you broke your nose and sprained your arm. Maybe you sprained your ankle too. It's swelling out a bit.'

My ribs hurt when I inhaled. I tried to sit up, still woozy. 'What time is it?'

Nancy checked her watch, and I noticed again how dirty her hands were. Muddy hands.

'About half-seven.'

My arm did feel bad. We were in the kitchen. I was on the floor.

'I think I might like to sit on a chair.'

Nancy helped me up.

'Should we call the police?' she asked, settling me down again with a small huff of exertion.

'We can't call the police,' Saleem said quickly. 'We'd be fucking ourselves over.'

I was mystified by this response. 'Doug will probably want us to call them,' I said. 'That Chinese devil destroyed Doug's greenhouse before he assaulted me.'

Saleem expressed no surprise at this. Nancy didn't either. 'In that case,' Saleem said, 'we should really let Doug decide whether he wants to get the police involved or not. They're his vegetables, after all. And you . . .' She stared at me for a moment with an almost fond indifference. 'You'll mend.'

After a short pause she turned to Nancy and said pointedly, 'Aren't you in a hurry to unload that privet or something?'

Nancy shuffled her feet. 'I suppose so. I was just worried about Phil . . .'

'Actually,' Saleem said, 'I think we should tell Phil about where you're supposed to be going today.' Saleem turned towards me again. 'Guess where Nancy's going?'

'I don't know.'

'Tell him, Nancy.'

Nancy walked over to the sink and washed her hands. She spoke with her back to me, over her shoulder. 'Doug's got me going to Southend again for some more privet.'

'Privet? How much more?'

'Loads. And on Friday, too.'

'Did he give you any order forms?'

'Yeah.'

'Can I have a quick look at them?'

'I'll get them later. They're in the truck.'

Saleem butted in, 'D'you think you might be concussed?' she asked, purely, it seemed, out of interest, as though she and Nancy had had a small wager on this possibility. I was about to answer and then I heard a movement upstairs, a creaking.

'Doug's up,' I said, panicking, 'What shall we do? Maybe I could get to the greenhouse and tidy things up a bit if you two could try and keep him here for a while.'

I tried to stand up. I nearly managed it, but something buckled. 'I've got to start unloading,' Nancy said, sounding blank somehow, avoiding my eyes. She went out. I gazed after her, confounded.

'You can't hide things from Doug, Phil,' Saleem said calmly. 'He smells trouble at fifty paces.'

Doug was on the landing now. I could hear him. Then he was on the stairs, descending.

'Also,' Saleem added, 'I didn't want to say anything before, but in case you were determined to call the police, I'm not entirely sure that it was Wu who destroyed the greenhouse.'

'What?'

Doug was behind the door, right behind it. He was at the door. He was pressing some of his weight on to the door handle. I saw the handle move, down, up again, saw the door push inwards, towards me, and behind it . . . Doug. *Doug*. Square-chinned, resolute, hinged. Hanging on, like the door, but only just. I watched as Doug took his hand from the handle and I watched as the door closed behind him, smoothly, quietly, automatically.

Doug stood there and appraised me. He drank me in, slowly, and then he said, 'Phil, there's something hanging out of your nose. Looks like a big, raw, red caterpillar.'

He went and switched on the kettle. Saleem said, 'There's tea already in the pot.'

Doug grunted appreciatively, switched the kettle off again and took himself a mug off the mug-tree. 'I'm only telling you,' Doug added, lifting an eyebrow in my direction, 'because I'd find it difficult to eat breakfast with that thing just hanging there out of your nostril.'

Saleem handed me a piece of kitchen towel. I did the best I could. I pulled at the clot, manually at first, and the jelly came out and kept on coming like I was unravelling a dark, dense, red jelly brain through my nostril. When the jelly finally dissolved into loose blood, I blew my nose vigorously, rolled what I'd gathered into the tissue, pinched the bridge of my nose and stared up at the ceiling.

Doug was pouring himself some tea. Saleem – who was staring at me with a kind of fascinated disgust, hypnotised by the mighty clot – tore her eyes away when it had finished coming and said, 'Doug, Phil was just saying how someone broke into your greenhouse and totally wrecked everything.'

My mouth fell open. I think I stopped breathing, for a second. Doug stopped pouring.

'What did you say?'

I continued staring at the ceiling. 'Doug,' I said, 'I'm sure the damage isn't terminal. Some of the plants will be fine. It was only stupid vandals.'

Doug said nothing. He put down the teapot and walked out. I heard him slipping on his shoes in the hallway, and then I heard the front door slamming. I tried to stand up.

Saleem walked over to the sink. 'Doug's not going to be wanting his tea now,' she said, cheerfully. 'Do you want it?'

I was hot on Doug's heels, well, warm on his heels because I wasn't finding it too easy to walk. My ankle kept rolling, like

I was strolling on a ship in a high wind, up on deck, trying to keep my balance.

Outside, Nancy was standing by the rear flap of her truck, staring off into the distance, after Doug – his retreating back. She was cradling a small privet plant in her arms. As I staggered past her I said, 'Nancy, whatever you do, don't go to Southend for any more privet until I've had a word with Ray first.'

She put the tree down and trailed for a few paces behind me.

'Phil, how did he take it?'

'What?'

'Doug. What did he say?'

'He didn't say anything. Not yet, anyway.'

'He'll be all right, though?'

'This is probably the very worst thing that could've happened.'

'The very worst thing,' she parroted, speculatively, and then shouted, 'Hang on,' and sprinted off in the direction of the house. I carried on walking. After thirty seconds she was back again. She caught up with me just before the first lake.

'Here,' she panted, passing me one of Saleem's walking sticks. Saleem kept a small umbrella stand full of them just inside the front door.

Nancy handed me a stick which had a handle carved into a hare's head. It was a beautiful thing.

'Don't put too much weight on your bad leg, you'll only make it worse.'

I took the stick.

'I'm sorry,' she added, sounding it, 'about you getting hurt and Doug getting hurt.'

'It's nobody's fault.'

I twisted my hand around the hare's head.

'And don't put too much weight on your bad arm, either.'

'Thanks.' I took a few experimental steps forward. Nancy didn't walk with me. She hung back, remaining stationary.

I walked on. It was easier with the stick, but still slow. And in all honesty, I was glad of the time it took me to get to the greenhouse. I was almost glad of the pain. It was a kind of empathy. If not with Doug – he was a complex creature and I was obliged to find my own level, emotionally – then at least with his spoiled and battered vegetables.

'I'm sure the damage isn't terminal.'

Doug looked up and over, towards me. 'I think you said that earlier,' he muttered, witheringly. He was standing in the centre of the debris, inhaling the chaos.

'This shouldn't have happened,' he said, finally, 'It's all *wrong*.'

'You know, it might be possible to replant a couple of the tomatoes. Some of the radishes look all right too.'

'The tomatoes?'

Doug bent down and picked up one of the tomatoes which had detached itself from its plant. He held it in his hand like it was a cricket ball, a large cricket ball.

'You'd better get out of here,' he said, dispassionately, 'before I lose my temper.'

I was deciding whether to take his advice and leave when Doug clenched the tomato he was holding in his fist, took a couple of quick steps to build up momentum and then hurled it at me. I ducked. It flew past me, just to my left and struck glass, the pane closest to the door, striking it, splitting, shattering the glass.

Doug bent over and picked up an onion. He weighed it in his hand. 'D'you know what the worst part is?' Doug asked, still sounding as calm as anything.

I felt something warm on my top lip.

'You're bleeding,' Doug said. 'I don't want blood all over the floor in here.'

I mopped at my nose with my sleeve. The sight of blood seemed to pacify Doug again, even if he wasn't actually directly responsible for it.

'The worst part is that I must've left the door unlocked. But I know in my gut that I would never have done that. In my *gut*.'

Doug dropped the onion and walked over to the door. 'See that? No sign of a forced entry. Nothing broken.'

'Maybe they picked the lock.'

Doug bent down and stared at the lock intently, as though waiting for it to tell him something. Eventually he straightened up again and said, 'I don't think so.'

He turned his back to the door and appraised the devastation before him. 'I could swear to you that I locked that door,' he said, 'but I *can't* have. D'you know what that means, Phil? How it feels?'

I shook my head.

'It feels like I can't trust my own instincts on this one. I can't trust my own instincts. And if I can't trust my instincts, what can I trust? Who can I trust? Nothing. Nobody.'

Doug spent a moment considering his words. They seemed to please him. He crossed his arms. My nose was still bleeding.

'Red blood,' Doug said, 'Red, red, red blood.' He cleared his throat. 'There's only one way to get around this.'

I looked up, hoping Doug was about to respond rationally, *hoping*. Unfortunately his eyes were dark and clear. He uncrossed his arms. 'My instincts tell me this,' he said, 'and I shouldn't trust them because they've already lead me astray . . .' He inhaled deeply. 'You can only match this kind of gesture,' he indicated towards the mess and the mud with a grand sweep of his arm, 'you clan only match this kind of gesture with an even *bigger* gesture of your own.'

I weighed up this notion in my mind. An even bigger gesture. I didn't really get it but I knew it wouldn't necessarily be a good thing. I said, 'We could call that kind of response an escalation, Doug, and I don't know if things that go up, things that get bigger, are always . . . uh . . . good.'

Doug appreciated my insight but would have none of it. 'Nope,' he said, determinedly, 'getting bigger. That's the natural order of things . . . Clarity,' he added, 'cleanness. Big and neat. That's what I'm after.'

My nose was still bleeding and my shirt sleeves were about

as soaked as they could get. I yanked up my shirt-front and put it to use.

'Shall we start cleaning this stuff up?' I asked, through the blood and fabric.

'I don't think so,' Doug said, 'I think you should go back to the house and change your shirt. That much blood doesn't look respectable. Consider the feelings of the park users. Clean up.'

I didn't want to leave him. Something in my stomach told me not to. I said, 'I don't like to leave you alone in the middle of this mess.'

Doug opened the door for me. 'Give me a minute,' he said,' 'to be privet. I need to be privet for a moment or two. Get washed up.'

I walked past him, shuffled past him, out through the door.

Ray was in the kitchen, standing next to the oven and peering into a pan. In one hand he held the saucepan's lid, with his other chubby paw he pulled at his bottom lip, yanking it halfway down his chin.

'Ray, Did you see Saleem and Nancy yet?'

Ray – deep in his own thoughts – hadn't heard me come in. He jumped like a scalded cat and dropped the saucepan's lid when I spoke and then managed to frighten himself again with the clatter that it made. He bent down and picked it up.

'Uh, I saw Saleem. She's upstairs. She's searching through Doug's room for evidence.'

'Evidence?'

'Order forms and stuff. Receipts. I think that's what she said.' He stared at me. 'Where did all that blood come from?'

'My nose.'

'Wu got you.'

'Yes.'

'Again.'

'Yes.'

'How's Doug?'

'Not good.'

Ray fitted the lid back onto the saucepan. He stared over towards the window. 'I've got loads to do. I want to finish that gatepost this morning and I swore to Doug I'd weed the tennis courts.'

'I think Doug's got bigger things on his mind at present than the tennis courts.'

Ray scratched his beard. I added, 'I also think we should consider telling Nancy not to go to Southend today for any more privet. We both know the park can't afford it.'

Ray leaned his weight against the oven and shifted it, unintentionally, an inch closer to the wall.

'But the problem is,' I said, hoping for some kind of response, 'I don't know if we can really risk antagonising Doug any further. He's already slightly . . . overwrought.' Ray carried on scratching his beard. 'What do you think?'

Ray picked up the roll of kitchen towel and tossed it over to me. 'Have you tried pinching the top of your nose? That might stop it bleeding.'

Saleem came in clutching a folder and a bundle of papers. She threw them on to the table. 'There,' she said, 'I knew he'd started keeping some of this stuff upstairs. He's getting paranoid. Being secretive's a real symptom of it. Right, let's split this lot up between us and see what we can find.'

I looked over towards the door. 'Doug might come back here at any time.'

Saleem smiled, 'We're OK. Nancy's on lookout.'

Ray stayed over by the oven, like he didn't want any part of looking through the papers. Saleem pulled out a chair and placed herself squarely on to it. She began leafing through. 'Pull up a pew, Phil. Take the weight off your bad foot.' I remained standing, breathing into a clump of tissue.

'OK . . . OK . . .' Saleem rifled through the top few sheets. She pulled something out. 'Privet!' she announced, excitedly, 'Bingo!' She passed it over to me. I looked at it. An advance order requesting privet amounting to the sum of fifteen hundred pounds.

Saleem carried on rifling. She said, 'I don't know how the

hell he's intending to explain away this little lot tomorrow at the meeting.'

I looked over at Ray. 'Fifteen hundred pounds,' I said, miserably.

Ray shifted his weight. 'Maybe you should ring them,' he volunteered, 'and tell them we can't actually afford to pay for it.'

'Maybe.'

My head felt weightless. My head felt like the bright-faced bulb of yellow sunflower. All colour, display, no substance. I pulled out a chair and sat down.

'Saleem,' I said, gently, 'I've been thinking about what you said earlier. About Wu not destroying Doug's greenhouse. Because if Wu didn't destroy it, then who did?'

'Vandals.'

'They didn't break in. They had a key.'

'Clever vandals. You're dripping blood on the floor.'

I looked down. Cog had appeared at my feet and was nosing at the drops of blood. His little pink tongue protruded and he started to lap it up. I bent over to push him away and as I bent, my head started rolling and roaring like it was full of buzzing, like it was a fluffy bumble just about to detach itself, to fly off.

It would have flown, I'm sure it would have flown, except for the fact that at that exact moment Nancy burst into the kitchen and yanked me up. She stared into my face. 'Listen,' she said, breathless, 'that's Doug.'

Slowly, I blinked. 'Doug?' I tried to focus on her face but her eyes were everywhere. I tried to focus.

'He's taken the tractor. That's him, outside. Listen.'

Saleem stuffed the papers into the folder, threw the folder into the cutlery drawer, grabbed hold of my arm. 'Outside,' she said, 'come on.'

Actually, we must've looked quite funny, the four of us, standing there in a line, like we were preparing to be presented to the Queen in a formal ceremony. Just outside the gate, near the Ladies toilets, we had a full view of Doug, the tractor, the lakes, the greenhouses, the hill opposite, the whole damn vista.

'Where's he going?' Ray asked. 'Any ideas?'

'Maybe he's thinking about mowing the grass patch just beyond the bandstand,' I suggested. Saleem snorted. Nancy said, 'He doesn't have the mower attachment on the back.'

'Did he say anything?' Ray asked, 'to you?'

Nancy shook her head. 'Nope. Just picked up the heavy-headed axe and climbed into the tractor.'

Ray looked at me. I shrugged.

'This is it.' Saleem said. 'This is the big one.'

'How?' I asked, losing patience, almost.

'I'll bet you any amount he's going to drive that tractor straight into the greenhouse.'

The tractor trundled and grumbled, between the lakes, beyond the lakes.

'He wouldn't do that.'

'Wanna bet?' Saleem put out her hand, palm skywards.

'He wouldn't do that.'

Beyond the lakes, up the hill. I saw the tractor's rear indicator flashing right. Saleem chortled at this. 'My God,' she said, 'he's a one-off. He's fucking *crazy*.'

A sharp, right turn, a questionable gear-change. 'Ouch,' Nancy muttered. And then, a revving, a roaring, a speeding up.

'He's bending down,' Ray said, perturbed, 'not even looking where he's going.'

'I know what he's up to,' Saleem said. 'He's weighing down the accelerator with the axe-head.'

Fifteen foot to go. Ten foot, five. Doug bounced out of the tractor and landed, cat-careful, on all fours, stayed hunched for a moment, stood up. The tractor – 'I told you! I told you' Saleem cackled – slowed down for a moment, choked, stuttered, lurched, kept lurching, until CRUNCH. It hit the main glasshouse, shattering and clattering, bending metal, running, roaring, covering, collapsing. And shards fell from above, the engine cut. More collapsing, more shards, a tiny, silly tinkling, a rumble, a small, metallic burp.

Doug didn't pause to look at or appraise his handiwork. He didn't turn, he kept on walking. 'He's so cool,' Nancy whispered, 'like John Wayne or that other guy with black hair and funny eyes who's in *The Gunfighter*.'

'Gregory Peck,' Ray mumbled.

'That's the one. Yeah.'

A woman in a headscarf who had been walking her miniature collie nearby called out the dog's name harshly and then, when he didn't come to heel, put two fingers between her lips and whistled. And strangely enough, it was that whistle, that sound alone which made my legs shake and my eyes fill, not any of the others. That sound alone.

'Oh shit,' Ray said, 'Doug's heading back this way. I'm off.' Ray scarpered.

Doug was strolling back in the general direction of the house. He was wiping his hands on the seat of his trousers. He seemed extremely interested in the condition of the flowering borders. At one point, I swear it, he stopped and removed a dead flower head.

Saleem turned to me. 'Phil,' she said, gently, 'maybe you should find some rope and cordon the greenhouse off, make sure it's safe before someone gets hurt over there. We'll handle Doug. Between the two of us. Me and Nancy.'

I nodded. I turned. I went to get some rope, a canvas sack, some tape and a large, strong, natural fibred, needle-bristled brush.

It was arduous, it was risky and it took just about forever. I wondered where the hell Ray had got to. I couldn't imagine he was helping Nancy and Saleem with Doug at the house. And he certainly wasn't here, helping me, clearing away the glass and mud and metal and vegetables. More than likely he was on the tennis courts, weeding.

I was almost glad to be alone. Things were moving slowly. I was moving slowly. Like something newly born, inhabiting a fresh and different body; testing out what I could and couldn't do, establishing my limited capabilities.

Luckily the damage to the greenhouse was acute but also clearly defined. After a few hours of sweeping and chipping, of taping up sharp corners, of knocking out half-spent panes, I managed to clamber on to the tractor, clear out some of the glass, pull away the axe-head from the accelerator pedal, straighten out one of the mudguards which had bent and hit its tyre, and then switch on the ignition. Using my dodgy foot, my dodgy arm, I stuck the gears into reverse and roared on out of there.

I looked up nervously, as I reversed. I looked up at the glass ceiling and waited for a reaction, waited for it to shatter and crumble, but nothing happened. It kept its clarity.

And this was the curious part: I had so many other things on my mind – so much to keep in my head – but all the while I felt like everything was flowing. A liquid sensation. Maybe it was the blood in me, travelling through my body, blooming in my face, my cheeks, but then moving on, carrying on, *flowing*. And I should have been thinking and sorting and planning in my head, organizing, controlling, but in fact all I could think of were natural things. Concrete things. Physical substances. *Substance*. Nature. Bark, rock, soil, water.

And gradually I started thinking about water and rock. How they are the two most extreme substances, two opposite poles, and yet, and yet they can work together. They can work together and be together and live together and although they both have their own energy, their own terrible strength and power, at the same time, they do not *violate* each other. Because that's how nature moves, how it works. It cooperates. And that's how I wanted to move – no more smashing and crashing and thumping and punching, I wanted to move like the water around the rock. And that was how I *had* been moving, all along, if only I'd seen it.

'Hey, Phil.'

What was I doing? I was in the greenhouse, standing amid

the wreckage, and I was holding one of Doug's giant onions and gazing at it.

'Nice onion,' Ray said, staring at me quizzically.

I imagined how this onion was inside. Layer upon layer of clean white flesh, containing, enveloping, pure and thorough. A circle. Each layer complete and depending. Each layer sharp and moist and spotless. It was so beautiful.

'Maybe you should sit down for a minute?' Ray took the onion from me and threw it into a wheelbarrow. 'Won't be able to eat that,' he said, regretfully. 'When they get too big they taste all watery. Don't taste of anything, in fact.'

Ray led me outside. My leg and arm had both started to stiffen, and the dried blood inside my nostrils itched like crazy. I sat down for a moment on the grass verge. Ray appraised the tractor. He kicked a wheel. He cleared out some glass from under the pedals.

'Not too bad,' he said, cheerfully, 'doesn't look too bad after its big ordeal.' He stared at me again. 'You should go home for a while. Maybe put your feet up for a couple of hours.'

'Have you been back to the house yet?'

He nodded.

'How's Doug?'

Ray cleared his throat. 'Lying low.'

'What's he doing?'

'I don't know.'

'Actually . . .' I tried to straighten my thoughts out. 'This morning when I found the greenhouse all messed up and I got into that fight with Wu . . .'

'Yeah.'

'Nancy was there. She just appeared from nowhere. And it was six in the morning, a good three hours before she usually gets in for work.'

'Probably out for a run.' Ray said, distractedly, and then added, 'I just weeded the tennis courts.'

My head was throbbing. Ray climbed into the tractor and started up the engine. He pressed his foot down on the accelerator a few times and then put it into gear.

'Climb in,' he yelled. 'I'll give you a lift back to the house if you like.'

'What about this?'

I pointed towards the greenhouse. There was still plenty of work left to be done. Ray waved his giant paw at me. 'I'll park this thing in the barn and then head straight on back.'

I struggled up and clambered on to the passenger seat. I hoped the tractor's vibrating wouldn't start my nose off bleeding again. As a cautionary measure I breathed through my mouth, very gently. While I breathed, I inspected my sleeves and shirt-front which were brown and heavy with dried blood. I scratched at it softly with my thumbnail as Ray and I jerked along, between the lakes, past the museum, past the toilets, a sharp right turn and then into the barn. The fabric was scratchy and hard. Stiff and solid and starched with plasma.

I was too slow. Something was very wrong with my head. I couldn't keep up, keep pace, keep time. I stood in the courtyard for several minutes before I'd accumulated enough energy to even consider going into the house. Instead I stood staring stupidly at the rows of privet bushes, little green sentries standing to attention, properly apportioned. Sharply ranked. I stared at them for a while. Ray had gone. Everything was quiet.

I knew there was something that I should be thinking but I couldn't think it. What was it? Did the privet need watering? I felt the base of one of the pots. Dry, but not too bad. I thought about fetching the hose and giving them a spray. But that wasn't it. I looked around me. There was something else. A *lack*. A space. Something empty. And then it struck me. Nancy. The truck. Gone. Both gone. I turned and headed into the house.

'Saleem? Doug?'

I pushed open the kitchen door. The air smelled damp and sweet and strange. The windows were covered in condensation. On the table, laid out, stretched out, was Cog. On his side. He didn't look his normal self. He wasn't allowed, generally, to sit on the table or to lie on it. I put out my hand to touch him, to nudge him.

'Leave him!'

Saleem was behind me. Then she was next to me and then in front of me. She grabbed hold of Cog and he lay limp as lettuce in her arms. A substantial dishcloth. Boneless.

'What's wrong? What's up with the cat?'

Saleem looked hot and ragged. 'He's dead, stupid.'

'Dead?'

I put out my hand to touch him. Saleem jerked him away, out of reach.

'Don't do that!'

'Why not?'

'It's a bit bloody late to start showing him affection now, Phil. It's not like you ever gave a toss about him when he was alive.'

This was honestly the last thing I could have expected. The cat dead. This hadn't been part of the picture. It didn't connect to anything. I stared at Saleem. 'What happened to him?'

'He died.'

'Just like that? He just died? He's not especially old. Not for a cat.'

Cog seemed irresistible, all limp. I reached out my hand again, just to touch, and this seemed to enrage Saleem. She was spitting angry.

'Phil! Just stop it! You are starting to piss me off so badly. I mean the cat's dead and only now do you start giving a shit about it. That's bloody typical of you. Absolutely bloody typical. And I'm under enormous pressure too. I am. I am! And no one gives a shit about me.' Saleem threw Cog on to the table, tossed aside her stick, yanked out a chair, sat down and burst into tears.

I wished I could die. Just die. Lie down with Cog on the table and expire. Saleem's face was wet and glossy and extremely snotty.

Eventually I said, 'Do you want me to bury him?'

She shrugged sulkily.

'There's an empty flower bed at the back of the house. I could put him in there easily enough.' She shrugged again. 'Only,' I said, nervously, 'I hardly think Nancy or Doug would appreciate seeing him dead. Not just at the moment. They're both quite fond of him. So you and I could bury him and just pretend this hadn't happened for a couple of days.'

Saleem wiped her face on the tablecloth. 'OK,' she said, eventually, 'Go dig a hole. I'll bring him out in five minutes' time.'

I nodded. 'By the way,' I said, 'where is Nancy?'

'Dig the fucking hole, Phil.'

I went. I dug.

So it wasn't much of a burial. I dug the hole. Not too deep because I found it hard to hold the spade and hard to balance and the soil seemed unusually hard, too. True to her word, after five minutes Saleem appeared holding Cog. Her face was dry and clear and she seemed, to all intents and purposes, perfectly cheerful again.

I stood aside. I wondered if I should say anything or whether Saleem herself wanted to say a few words.

'Is that it?' Saleem asked, staring at the hole. 'Sure it's deep enough?'

'I hope so.'

'Fine.' She hopped forward, held Cog over the hole and unceremoniously dropped him in.

'Cover him,' she said and watched as I pushed over the soil. She sniffed her hands. 'Christ,' she said, 'I reckon he's already started stinking. My hands smell like old urine.'

I completed the job in silence. Saleem watched me. She made me feel self-conscious. To distract her I said, 'Where's Doug? In bed?'

'What makes you say that?'

'I just wondered where he was. I wondered how he was.'

'He's gone.'

I froze. 'Gone? Where?'

'I don't know. He just said, "I've had enough. I'm going." I asked him if he'd be back for the meeting tomorrow and he said, "Bugger the meeting." '

'Doug actually said that?'

'Yes.'

'I can't believe he'd say that.'

Saleem's mouth began to tighten at its corners. 'He said it.'

'Did he say where he was going?'

'Nope.'

'D'you think he went back to Mercy's?'

'I shouldn't think so.'

I walked to the barn to put the spade away. As I walked I tried to think where Doug would go. I couldn't imagine him going anywhere. This was his place. He wouldn't leave this place.

I decided to try and ring him at Mercy's. I was standing in the hallway, dialing, when Saleem confronted me.

'Who are you ringing?'

'Mercy.'

'What for?'

'To see if Doug's there.'

Saleem slammed down her hand and cut me off.

'That 's stupid,' she said. 'You don't want to get Mercy all worked up.'

I put down the receiver. 'Fine,' I said. 'I know he'll be back tomorrow anyway. He wouldn't miss the meeting. Not for anything.'

Saleem eyed me. 'Just the same . . .'

'What?'

'Couldn't do any harm for you to acquaint yourself with the details of the park business, just in case he doesn't.'

'He will.'

'I'm willing to bet he might not.'

'He will. I know how he is.'

'Even so . . .' Saleem had a couple of folders under her arm, 'best acquaint yourself.'

I inhaled deeply. I didn't take the folders. I said, 'You know full well that I can't go to the meeting. That's Doug's job.'

Saleem was growing impatient. 'What will it take,' she asked me, 'to make you realize that you are the only person who can go? It's up to you. Doug isn't coming back. I *know* that. OK? He isn't coming back. It's up to you.'

'Then we'll cancel the meeting.'

'We can't cancel it. Doug's cancelled it twice already. All the details, correspondence, everything, are in here. In the folders. Just *take* them.'

I shook my head. I knew Doug. He was the backbone. An organism couldn't function – couldn't walk or crawl or anything – without a backbone. 'He's coming back,' I said, 'that's all I know.'

Saleem was silent for a minute. Then she said, 'Did you read that book like I told you to? Dr John Sledge. Did you read it?'

'Doug's coming back.'

Saleem pushed her face up very close to mine. 'Phil,' she said gently, 'you saw what Doug did this morning. He took the fucking tractor and he drove it into the greenhouse. You saw him do that, didn't you? With your own two eyes.'

She was right in my face, I side-stepped. She side-stepped. I backed my way into the kitchen. Something was boiling. The air was full of steam. Smelled sweet and ugly.

Saleem followed me into the kitchen. She dumped the folders down on to the table and she went to open a window. I watched her. I took a slow step over towards the door.

'Stay where you are.' She turned. 'I have something to tell you. Something important.' We had the whole table between us.

She sighed. 'OK, so I'd hoped to keep it from you so that you wouldn't get all worked up about it and spoil our chances at the meeting tomorrow . . .' I opened my mouth to speak, but she said, 'Don't say it, Phil. Doug won't be back for the meeting tomorrow. He *won't* be, and I'll tell you why.'

It was still too wet and too warm. I put my hands out and rested them on the back of a chair. I leaned on the chair. On the sideboard were a bundle of papers. On the top of these, a newspaper. It was the previous day's *Guardian*.

'Remember this?' Saleem showed me the *Guardian*. I frowned back at her. 'You know when you came in, before, and I was kind of overwrought?'

I nodded. I think I did.

'Well to be honest with you, I don't give a shit about that fucking cat, and I'm sure you're aware of that fact.'

I nodded again. She pulled out a chair and sat down. She said, 'I'll give it to you straight, Phil.'

The chair was creaking under my weight. I was sweating. Or was I covered in condensation? A pan on the oven was boiling. Water and steam and water and steam.

'Right,' Saleem said, 'now just listen. Nancy was really angry with Doug for sacking her yesterday. I tried to convince her last night that you and Ray would make sure she'd be all right. I told her you'd stand up for her against Doug. Well, unfortunately, she wasn't convinced. She was angry with Doug. She went and destroyed his greenhouse this morning. I suppose she just didn't have any faith in the two of you. And she loves this place as much as we do. You might not believe it, Phil but she does. Anyway, after Doug smashed up the tractor and everything she realized how stupid she'd been. Petty and everything. What a big mistake she'd made. So when Doug got back here she told him what she'd done and she told him she'd done it. I guess her timing wasn't up to much, well, she's already proved that quite conclusively, if her driving is anything to go by.

'Anyhow, Doug literally went wild. He felt terribly betrayed. He was yelling and throwing his fists about and he said he'd destroy the whole damn park. I mean he was just crazy. Even I was scared. Nancy was scared too. She ran to the truck, got out her gun – actually it's more like a starting pistol, I think she uses it when she goes motorcross racing or something – and Doug stopped dead in his tracks, but not for long. After a second Doug lunged at her. Nancy's tough, though. She stepped back, tried to get away, but found herself up flat against the back of her truck. She couldn't step back any further. And Doug was getting closer. And then . . . and then . . .'

Saleem's eyes were as large and round as two plates spinning on the end of two sticks. 'And then she just, kind of, shot him. In the foot. I think it was his foot because he staggered and jumped around on one leg for a while.

'Nancy yanked down the tail of her truck and pushed him inside. I mean it took literally five seconds. Doug was still distracted and slightly off balance. Then she closed the back gate. Doug was locked in there. I tried to ask her what she thought she was doing but it all happened so quickly. She just said, "He won't do this to us. He's not going to bully us any more. I'm taking him away. I'm going to keep him locked in there until he sees sense. As long as it takes." Then she jumped into her cab, started up the engine and drove off. And that was that.'

I stared at the window, the point just behind Saleem's right shoulder. Drips of condensation were making patterns on its surface. I wondered what the patterns meant.

'Say something.'

I shook my head. My wet head. I couldn't believe Nancy would behave so stupidly. I closed my eyes. I opened my eyes. The drips on the window spelled the word *muddy*. I blinked. It was gone. I said, 'Nancy wouldn't do something as stupid as that.'

'But you would say that, wouldn't you?'

'What?'

Saleem's lips were thin and white. 'Yeah. You know what I mean.'

She had lost me, finally.

'Saleem, I don't know what you're talking about.'

She leaned her elbows on the table. Her small breasts were squeezed together between her arms. 'Say that again, go on.'

'Say what?'

'My name.'

Saleem. *Saleem*. I couldn't say it. When I said her name it felt like a mouthful of unripe elderberries. On my palate. In my throat.

'Look,' I said, 'I just don't understand why Nancy . . . I need to have it explained again.'

Saleem started to smile. She was a different person, suddenly. She cocked her head to one side. 'I've been giving this some thought,' she said, 'and I don't think it's really a question of understanding, but more an issue of . . . of managing.'

'How?'

'Because it isn't such a bad thing that Doug's out of harm's way for a while. If Nancy keeps him until Friday then you can go to the meeting and everything can take its course after that. Once we're secure. The rest doesn't matter.'

'But what about Nancy?'

Saleem shrugged. 'She'll cope.'

'And Doug?'

'He'll be fine. He just needs a little time away from this place. A little distance.'

'I can't go to the meeting.' I nearly choked saying it. Just saying it was bad enough.

'You have to.'

'I couldn't do it. Doug handles that kind of thing. That's the whole point of him.'

'Let me put it this way,' Saleem said, grinning, 'either you go to the meeting or I'm going to call the police and tell them what I've told you and that will fuck up Nancy very badly indeed. And after I fuck up Nancy I'm going to think of a way to fuck you up.'

'Nancy's in trouble no matter what you do.'

'Who's in trouble?'

'What do you mean?'

'Nancy. Nancy. Whenever you say her stupid name your cheeks go red.'

'That's ridiculous.'

'That's fighting talk.'

'It's not.'

'You're making me angry, Phil.'

'I'm not. I'm only trying to understand what's gong on.'

'Some hope, lard-arse.' Saleem jumped up, tossed the paper over towards me, grinned, and scuttled out.

I stared down at the paper. Outlined in blue ink, two headlines. My eyes turned immediately to the second headline. The second headline said: 100-DAY PROTEST.

I read it again, re-acquainted myself with the story of how Mr Peter Hawes had locked himself inside his roadside café. As a protest. Surely it was different though, I decided, surely it was very different to *lock yourself*. Locking yourself was quite the opposite of *being locked*, forcibly.

I tried to picture Doug, being locked, in my mind, but I couldn't picture it. Doug. Where was he? I couldn't picture him. Not at all. Where was he? Doug? Where was he? Suddenly my brain was empty. I knew it, then. Doug was gone. Yes, Doug was lost. Lost.

I found Ray in the greenhouse. 'Ray,' I said, 'things are a mess.'

'Let's go sit on the bench.'

It was Ray's favourite bench, under a yellow laburnum. We sat down.

'OK,' Ray said, 'what needs to be done?' He plucked a couple of seeds from the branches overhead and cracked them open.

'Leave those alone, Ray. They're poisonous.'

He dropped the seeds and wiped his hands on his overalls.

I stared at him for a moment. I wondered what kinds of things were going on in his head. I said, 'So you know about Nancy and Doug?' Ray inspected his fingernails. 'Then why didn't you tell me earlier?'

Ray's jowls descended. He scratched his nose. He said, 'This never would've happened if it wasn't for Nancy's eye.'

'Nancy's eye?'

Ray nodded. 'She lost the use of it in a motorcross accident. Before Christmas. Her right eye. That's why she keeps having accidents. She thinks if she loses this job she won't ever work again. I kind of knew for a while but I hoped it'd sort itself out. I mean, she was desperate, you know?'

Things were shifting. Shifting and moving. 'Ray,' I said, almost cracking, almost splitting like the laburnum pod between his podgy fingers. 'Ray,' I said, 'don't tell me anything else. Let's just concentrate on these three things. One, we need to find Doug. Two, we need to sort things out between Doug and Nancy. Three, we need to make sure that the meeting on Friday passes off all right.'

'And the Chinaman?'

I blinked. 'Best leave him well alone.'

'And Saleem?'

'Saleem?' I almost choked. Ray leaned back, locked his hands over his belly. The bench creaked.

And I looked at Ray, and I looked at my shirt, and I looked at my hands and I looked at my feet. And I looked up. This park. This park was my place and now it had been stolen.

This park, even yesterday, was only soil and plants and weather. A sum of its simple constituent parts. Now it was people and thoughts and concoction. It had been violated. Or else, like Saleem had said, there are events and then there are interpretations of events. I was removed. I was always removed. The park was never mine after all. I was in my head and I was out of it.

I had been plucked like a weed.

MY FOOT WAS SORE but I was walking anyway. I needed to re-acquaint myself. Re-acquaint myself. To look. To touch. To reaffirm how it was that I felt about this place. To get it back. I should have talked to Ray, I should have seen what Ray had to say, but I just didn't, I just couldn't.

This is a physical world. Everything's out there and you can touch it if you want to. You can touch it if you doubt it. Just stretch out your hands and your fingers.

I was walking around the park's perimeter. I was going to feel and identify every single object and particle that I had contributed to this place. I was going to see myself, my face and features in every cowering flower, in every bird and every bud.

In the scented garden where I'd planted the pinks and the jasmine, I swung out my arm and rubbed my hand into lavender. I pinched some mint between my thumb and forefinger, then dabbed my finger on to my tongue. I could taste this place. I could touch it. I could smell this place. I could see it.

I kept on walking. Through the wild part where the squirrels dart. Through the adventure playground where the children run and bound and kid around.

Then I doubled back. To the right, past the ornamental pond. I'd filled that pond. I'd emptied it. I'd cleared out the sweet wrappers and the coins and the cans.

Up and along. The stones I was walking on. The loose gravel. I had laid down that gravel. With these two hands.

And up and up the hill. The giant oak. I had pruned that oak. A large rose bed near the fence. I had chosen those roses. Yellow roses and apricot roses. I had sprayed those roses, I had watered and fed them.

At the hill's crest I found the silver birch and the poplar. I knew how the bark of each tree felt on the calloused palms of my hands and also, and also, on the softer lid of each fist; that bare little space between my fist and my wrist.

And the grass. I had cut it. And the daisies. I had cut them too. And the weeds. I had plucked them out.

Where was the sun? I looked up for it, into the sky. I turned on the spot and tried to see it. It was behind the giant cedar, tucked like a lost ball in its branches. How late was it? The sun made me blink, I closed my eyes and it stayed nestled inside my lids, glaring balefully into my head.

I sat down. My face was damp with sweat. I licked my lips and it was like my tongue had been dipped in the Adriatic. My eyes were still closed but the sun was fading now, flickering inside me.

I put down my hands flat on to the grass. I could feel the soil through the grass. I dug my nails into it.

Doug. Why had the feel of this soil stopped meaning enough? Doug wanted things to be bigger. He wanted something universal. He wanted the colour of the peonies, the height of the pampas grass, the smell of the honeysuckle to mean something. And did it mean something? And should it?

I opened my eyes. Doug had slipped in, into my head. Doug and his doings, Saleem and her words, Nancy and her muddy hands, Ray and his *insight*, all of these things were pulling me away from what I should be thinking about, from what I should be believing in. The soil. The sun. The shade. The bright glow of the buttercup.

I turned and looked down at the park below me, all its parts fitting together. And my nose was itching and my eyes were smarting and something or someone was knocking on the inside of my skull. Knock, knock. Knock, knock. Trying to attract my attention.

And how was I feeling? How was I doing? What was I thinking? Who did I believe? Oh *Christ*. I'm so sick of this head. So sick of this head. I'm sick of it. I am. Sick.

I sat on the grass, on the slope. I wanted to be simple, a natural part of the landscape but my mind wouldn't let me. I stretched out my legs. I pulled up my trouser and inspected my ankle. It had swollen out of the top of my sock. It had swelled like pale, prime dough out of my shoe and was glooping over my laces. It was pale as cooked fish-flesh, though, and felt numb when I pinched it.

I rolled up my sleeve and inspected my arm. It still had its bruises, but now it was bent too, curved in the strangest places like a finely crafted piece of metal piping. Some new, pinky marks were dawdling up near my elbow. My shoulder smarted a little. I picked out some of the dry blood from my nostrils. That, at least, was satisfying.

While I picked I looked down at the park. Dumbly, dutifully. I looked through the trees, the tall grass, past the roses, the flower beds, the pond. And there, sitting next to the pond, I could have sworn I saw a cat. A big tabby, licking its tail.

Could I trust my eyes? I clambered up and started to walk, down the hill. The slope made me trot, made me jog. At the bottom of the slope I carried on jogging: through the trees, the flower beds, up to the water.

Cog rolled on to his back and offered me his belly. I squatted down, panting. I rubbed it. As I rubbed a small sprinkle of mud and dust rose and fell. Then Cog stood up and sauntered off, his little jaunty bollocks to the rear, neat and well balanced like a sprig of cherries.

It was then that I decided to be someone else. Seeing the cat, like that, resurrected. It was so curious. Could I be someone else? Temporarily? Could I be someone else, altogether?

I crawled over to the edge of the pond. I saw my face in it. My face looked different. Swollen at its gills, wild-eyed. My cheeks were scratched like I'd had a tangle with a fistful of thorns.

Who was I? Who could I be? I didn't care. I'd be anyone. Anyone at all. I'd even forgo the thrill of being someone else so long as I was not my self. Was it possible?

Yes. I could be. I could be un-Phil. Out-of-Phil. Un-fool-Philled. Yes.

And the process was a simple one. To scrape out a gap in my gut like the pond. Water in the middle. Rock on the edges. Water flowing. Rock, holding in, containing, not hurting. This sublime pool inside me and a chalk-empty mind. No thought, only pure action. No doubt, only purpose. The three Ps. Park (my heart), Pond (my gut), Purpose (alone).

Park, pond, purpose.

Park, pond, purpose.

Park, pond, porpoise.

My brain rattled like a chickpea inside my skull.

THERE WAS BLOOD on the courtyard. Was it Doug's or was it mine? Some stains near the privet. An unsightly little brown rivulet. Only sap, I told myself, just red, not green.

I pushed at the front door but it would not open. It had been locked from inside. I rang the bell. After a short wait, Saleem answered.

'What?'

'Can I come inside for a moment?'

'No. I'm busy. I'm cleaning. I've washed the kitchen floor. I don't want your muddy footprints all over it.'

I didn't baulk or shirk. I was empty-Phil. She couldn't touch me. 'I just saw the cat, Saleem.'

'So?'

I didn't hesitate, not for a second. 'I just saw the cat by the pond, large as life. You said he was dead.'

'So what's the big deal?'

'We just buried him.'

Saleem raised her eyebrows. 'So?'

'You said that the cat was dead and so we buried him.'

She scratched her nose, 'As I recall, I never actually said we should bury the cat. That wasn't my idea.'

Everything flowing. I told myself, everything flows. 'Saleem, you said the cat was dead.'

'I might've said that the cat was *tired*. I might conceivably have said that.'

She was either very funny or she was mad. Or else she was truly evil and she wanted to hurt me. She could kill with one flash of her eye. She smelled of pepper. She was wearing a wellington boot, a pair of old overalls, the spare leg tied up, fastened with a safety pin but still dangling.

Pool, pond, purpose, I told myself. That wasn't right. It didn't work. It didn't flow, not properly. The serene lake in my gut began leaking. Saleem was filling my stomach with lies. Her tongue was a spade and she shovelled them out, out of her mouth and into my ears. Her tongue was heaped with falsehood and fallacy.

Saleem was about to close the door when I stopped her with my hand. And very bravely, very proudly I said, 'You're just like an owner with a ball.'

'What?' She scowled at me.

'You know, when an owner throws a ball for his dog and the dog goes and fetches the ball and brings it back? And after a while the owner gets bored of the throwing and the retrieving so he pretends to throw the ball and he doesn't actually throw it, but the dog's so stupid that it runs for what it thinks is the ball anyway. Even though there's nothing there. Just thin air.'

She carried on scowling, 'You've got it wrong,' she said. 'You mean the boy who cried wolf. That's the fable.'

I shook my head. My brain rattled. 'No. Not that story. This is a different one. In this story, the next time the owner throws the ball he does actually throw it and the dog still appears to have faith in him because he runs just as readily, except, this time, when the dog returns with the ball and the owner reaches out his hand to take the ball away, this time, the dog won't hand it over. He clamps his jaws together. He won't give it up. He's making his feelings clear about the little deception of earlier. That's all.'

Saleem's expression turned from derision to perplexity. 'Phil,' she said, 'I think you might be a little concussed. You're babbling.'

I was sad again and vulnerable again but I was still determined. 'No. I'm making perfect sense.'

'You're talking shit, Phil. It sounds like perfect sense to you because your head has taken a knocking, but in fact it's only drivel. Trust me on this one. Wait a minute.'

Saleem closed the door and left me on the doorstep for a short duration. When she reappeared she was clutching a couple of folders, a carrier bag and her front door keys.

'I'm going to take you home.'

'I don't want to go home. I want to talk to Ray.'

'I can't think Ray'll want to talk to you right now. You're nonsensical. Come on. Home. Walk with me.'

Saleem grabbed hold of my bad arm and she yanked it. It felt like it might snap. It groaned, the way a big ship groans and whines when it's being launched for the very first time. I gave in and staggered along beside her.

'We've got to calm that brain of yours down a little bit,' she said, as she walked. 'This place is like a sodding war zone.'

'You don't see the plants and the grass and the trees fighting,' I said, trying to get back my previous state of equilibrium, 'only people.'

'Say another stupid thing like that,' Saleem whispered, 'and I'll put my fucking fist in your mouth.'

I'd imagined things would feel better horizontal but I was wrong. I was flat on my back, on my sofa. My feet and ankles were slung up and over the arm. Saleem had insisted that I lie this way. It was extremely uncomfortable. Saleem herself was in my kitchen, cooking.

'I'm going to feed you and feed you,' she yelled through the kitchen's open doorway, 'till your stuffed up like a rooster.'

After ten minutes she came through holding a tray. On the tray was a plate which was full of a brown, glutinous substance, slightly fried. 'Sit up and eat this shit.'

I sat up, dutifully. 'What is it?'

'It's brain food.'

'Aren't you having any?'

'Only enough there for one serving, you lucky devil.'

Saleem handed me the plate and a fork. I sliced into the brown stuff and swallowed a mouthful. It had a meaty, metallic taste to it. I ate another mouthful. I chewed briefly and swallowed. 'Is this liver?' I asked, forking up some more.

Saleem grinned, 'Nope.'

'It tastes like liver.'

Saleem scratched the tip of her stump and hopped over to peruse a photograph on the mantelpiece of my dead aunt with my dead grandparents posing on the beach at Southend.

'Remember this morning?' she asked, her back to me, 'when you got dragged in by Nancy and your nose started bleeding?'

'Yes.'

'Remember when Doug came down and you had that giant piece of jelly dangling from your nose?'

'Yes.'

'At the time if kind of reminded me of black pudding. While I watched you pull it out I wondered how it would taste if it was gently fried.'

I stopped chewing. I put down my plate and hobbled into the kitchen. I threw up into the sink. I turned on the tap and washed the mush I'd produced down the plug-hole. I poured myself a glass of water and returned to the living room.

Saleem was still staring at the picture. 'But then it dawned on me,' she said, as though there hadn't been any hiatus in our conversation, 'that black pudding is a mixture of pig's blood and fat. Plain blood, if heated, would probably just disintegrate. The fat'd be the thing that would hold it together.'

I stared at her. I said, 'You are a very sick, very cruel person.'

She turned and smiled. 'Cool, calm, confident,' she said. 'The three Cs, remember?'

I sat down and pressed my glass of water up against my hot head.

'Events,' she added, 'and how you choose to *interpret* events. Two totally different kettles of fish, like I told you.' I said nothing. 'You've got a whole lot of work to do in that department, Phil. You're too bloody suggestible. And you always seem determined to think the very worst of other people. I mean, I've come into your home and I've fried you the kidneys I was intending to cook for my own dinner. A selfless act. But still you manage to convince yourself that I mean you harm. Is that an entirely acceptable, a reasonable way to be thinking?'

I held my glass of water in front of me and stared at it.

'You are the exact same person,' I said, 'who got me to bury a live cat in the garden a few hours ago.' Before she could respond I added, 'And Doug drove his tractor into the greenhouse. Then he threatened Nancy. And Nancy, Nancy wrecked Doug's vegetables and then shot Doug in the foot with a starting pistol before kidnapping him in the back of her truck.'

I looked up and over my glass and stared into Saleem's eyes. 'And you think I've been hasty in judging everyone? You really think I'm always determined to see the worst in people?'

Saleem grimaced. 'Your problem is that you don't think a person has any right to be more complicated than a fern or a bloody chrysanthemum. People live much more complicated lives than plants, Phil.'

'I don't think that way at all. Not at all.'

'Yes, you do.'

'No, I don't.'

'Christ, you've become argumentative since you bumped your head. Let's hope this'll mean that you're extremely persuasive and forthright at the meeting tomorrow.'

I lay down on the sofa again. I was tired now. I closed my eyes. Saleem came and stood over me. She said, 'Finish your kidneys. You need some energy. You've got to take a good look at those files. You've got to assimilate all the receipts and the documents.'

'I don't want the kidneys. I don't care about the files.'

Although my eyes were tightly shut I could feel Saleem right up close to me. When she next spoke I felt her breath on my ear and on my cheek.

'Are you telling me,' she whispered, 'that the park means so little to you that this, the tiniest of sacrifices, is too much for you to make? The possibility of even the smallest bit of effort and discomfort are enough to make you abandon everything? Everyone?'

But it wasn't that. The park meant too much, not too little. How could I be held responsible for something that I loved so completely? 'Find Doug and let him go,' I said, somewhat unreasonably. 'Let Ray go,' I added, 'or go yourself if you feel that strongly about it. I don't care who goes. I won't go.'

Saleem was silent for so long that I opened one of my eyes and peeped out at her to check that she was still there. She was there. The air was bare with glare and stare. She was there.

'And you dare to tell me,' she gurgled, finding her voice, at last, locating it in the guttural regions of her lower throat, 'and you *dare* to suggest to me that I wouldn't sacrifice everything for something that I loved?'

'That's not what I was saying at all.'

'You dare to suggest that?'

Suddenly fearful, I said, 'It's a question of caring too much, not too little, that's what I'm saying. It's all right if someone else destroys the one thing you love most in the world but its a terrible thing if you destroy it yourself. No feeling could be worse than that.'

'You're wrong.' Saleem was still gurgling. 'You're wrong, Phil. What you can't see is that it's better to destroy the thing you love than to have it snatched away from you. I've learned that lesson and Doug's learned that lesson. Even Nancy's learned it. But not you.'

I shook my head. She ignored my shaking.

'When they told me they were refurbishing the museum and turning it into a crèche and a café,' she murmured, lethally, 'when they told me they wouldn't be needing a curator any more, I didn't just walk away.' I opened my eyes again. She grinned. 'I didn't just walk away. I lost my leg in that fire. And after the fire, no one could take away the books and the pictures and the papers. No one could take them away. And look where I locked them . . .' Saleem patted her left breast with her right hand. 'My heart. And that's a very tight, very dark, very *secure* place.'

I stared at her blankly. She stood up. 'Finish your kidneys,' she said, and then she picked up her stick and left me.

I RAN A WARM BATH and soaked every bit of me in it. I stuck my head underwater and breathed the water in through my nose, swallowed some of it, blew the rest of it out, full of soil and muck and flaking red residue.

After the bath I had hoped to feel bolder, but I didn't. I looked in the mirror and saw the same hairy, scared creature staring straight back at me.

In my bedroom I pulled on a clean shirt and some trousers. I pulled out my suit too, my funeral suit, from the back of the wardrobe, and laid it flat across the bed. My funeral suit. Whose funeral? I put the suit away again.

Still on the pillow lay Dr John Sledge's *I'm Not Angry, I'm Hurting*. I picked it up. I opened it. At the top of the page was a heading in bold lettering. It said: WHAT HAVE YOU GOT TO LOSE?

> Everything or nothing? Think about it for a moment. Give this question some serious thought, and once you have thought about it, think about this:
>
> (1) If you've got A LOT to lose, then why take the risk of losing it? If you've got A LOT to lose then you've got something worth fighting for.
>
> (2) If you've got NOTHING to lose, then why delay? Act today. What possible harm could it do you? Things can only get better. You've got NOTHING to lose and everything to gain.
>
> Repeat after me, out loud, 'I've got nothing to fear but fear itself.' Again, 'I've got nothing to fear but fear itself.' Feeling better? Well done. Why am I congratulating you? I'll tell you why. I'm congratulating you because you are on the road to healing yourself. It's a wonderful journey. Come, travel with me.

I shut the book, turned it over and stared at the photograph of Dr John Sledge on the back of it. Dr Sledge was younger than I imagined. He had a head like a pumpkin. He exuded a kind of ghastly, glistening rude health. He had a mole in between his nose and his top lip. He was smiling broadly and he had perfect teeth. Out loud I said it. 'Dr Sledge,' I said, 'if you came and sat down next to me on a train I'd change compartments.'

I brewed some coffee. I ate three pieces of bread and butter. While I ate I considered the things I had yet to do. Some strimming by the rose garden, the hydrangeas needed cutting back. I'd noticed some of the rubbish bins by the tennis courts were full. What else? Nothing else.

I searched for my keys, found them, picked up a jumper from the back of a chair because the air outside had turned nippy. As I picked up the jumper I knocked the files which Saleem had balanced precariously on the edge of the kitchen table. I swore. The top one fell and the bottom one followed. Their paper guts scattered across the floor. And as I picked up each sheet I told myself: See this? All this writing and planning and calculating? This is the business, this stuff. The park, well that's something altogether different. They are two different entities. Altogether separate.

But the paper was covered in Doug's close hand. Doug's figures and letters. I couldn't help but see Doug in these papers. I picked them up. Some had doodles on them, inkspots, drops of tea, bits of crumb. Some were crumpled, others pristine. Some were stuck together. I tried to pull these apart as a tribute to Doug and then there, before me, the most incredible thing happened.

The paper unfolded. Several sheets had been stuck together with Sellotape, hinged together on purpose. I unfolded, one piece and two pieces, three pieces, four, and beheld the most perfect, most detailed, accurate and lovely sketch, in green and red pen – mad colours – of the park: all its parts, but something new, too.

In gorgeous detail, a little maze. A magical thing. A heart-shaped maze with a waterfall at its centre. Ornate statues in dead ends, occasional arches and trellises, and honeysuckle. Spy-glasses and sunflowers and poppies growing through the privet. Concrete frogs peeping out from corners and pheasants stalking with glass tails.

And at last, I saw Doug. I saw Doug. My hands started shaking, my eyes filled, because at last I saw Doug. He was right there in front of me. He was not lost any more.

I FORGOT ABOUT ALL those other tasks. Instead I stared at Doug's plans for what seemed like an eternity. Of course he's mad, I told myself. Of course he is. And when I told myself that Doug was mad it sounded in my ears like the grandest kind of compliment, an accolade, the sweetest benediction.

Once I'd familiarized myself thoroughly with every detail of Doug's crazy plan, I read through the other stuff too. I put the receipts into some semblance of order, I calculated how much we'd spent over the last year and on what, and how much we'd saved by frugal management. I tried to work out whether we could claim for the damage to the greenhouse under our present system of insurance. And then I went out.

I went out and I walked for a very long time. Things needed sorting and I wasn't entirely sure who was going to sort them. Was I going to sort them? Could I?

I walked for a very long time and eventually I found myself in Southgate and I was outside an all-night chemist and then I was inside and standing by the counter.

'Can I help you?' He was a young man with ginger hair and brown eyes. He wore a white lab coat and glasses. I said, 'I want a packet of condoms please. Extra small.'

Slightly surprised, he pointed to my left. 'Over there, on the counter. We have several varieties. All sizes.'

I said, 'Only sometimes it's hard to find the extra small ones because . . . they're extra small.' My face was a fire engine.

'I'll help you look, shall I, sir?'

Cool, calm, collected. Breathe one, breathe two, breathe three. 'That's kind of you. Thanks.'

My voice was going. I sounded Scottish, to myself; vowels crawling out from all corners of my mouth like crabs.

He rummaged for a while and produced three different packets.

'Three types. Any preference?'

'Any. All. I'll take all three. Thank you.'

'I'll pop them in a bag for you, shall I, sir?'

'Grand. Thanks.'

'There we go.'

'Thanks. Very much.'

You see, the problem is a very simple one, really. It's all a question of wanting – not just wanting, but *needing*, like something categorical. Needing to be a part of a landscape. It's about belonging to a place and wanting to belong and not knowing whether other people will even let you get around to *feeling* like you belong.

It's more than that, more even than that. It's like wanting to be an *actual*, a *physical* part of the landscape.

Animals do it. A bird belongs to the sky and the trees just as much as the trees and the sky themselves belong. No one questions – no one thinks to question – whether the worm a bird plucks from the soil is rightfully his. How could a berry belong anywhere else but in a starling's gut? No one doubts it.

But people. Where do we fit in? How can we fit in? How do we know that we fit and who can we ask? And some people will always feel like they fit and try to make others feel like they don't. And others won't ever fit or feel like they fit, will never, ever feel that way.

All these thoughts, every single one of them, were my technique for avoiding stuff that was happening, that would happen. And I wouldn't stop it. I couldn't stop it.

I'd asked for the condoms, hadn't I? Saleem was right. Maybe the only way to stop being embarrassed was to no longer avoid it. To search it out, to try – even – to enjoy it. To embrace it.

I walked for a very long time and then I got on a bus and ended up in Enfield outside an all-night chemist. And then I was inside the chemist and I was telling the assistant – a small, dark woman with a silver moustache – I've got crabs. Do you have anything for crabs? Are there many different varieties of crab? What are mine like? I don't know. Little ginger things, tiny things.

I caught another bus, stayed on it, ended up in Wood Green. A young woman was in the chemist's, an attractive young woman with red lips and black eyes.

Cool, calm, confident.

'I want some tampons for my mother. It's an emergency.'

'Any particular kind? There are several varieties.' She pointed.

'Which are the good ones?'

'Tampax, Li-lets. They're all OK.'

'Regular, medium-flow, light-flow? Oh God.'

'Why don't you get regular. That's a fairly safe bet.'

'Is it?'

'I think so.'

'She didn't say.'

'Well, it's entirely up to you.'

'Maybe she'd prefer one of those padded things.'

'A towel.'

'Yes, maybe a trowel.'

'Towel.'

'Pardon?'

'You said "trowel".'

'Oh, sorry.'

'You might be better off in a hardware store.' She was laughing.

'Sorry. You probably think I'm an idiot.'

'It doesn't matter what I think. Your mother's the one who's having the crisis.'

'I'm the one having a crisis.'

'Know the feeling.'

'You do?

'Sure.'

'I'll have the regular tampons. You're right.'

'Fine.'

She grabbed them and bagged them. I paid for them.

'You've done the rounds tonight,' she said, pointing at the other two bags I was holding, smiling.

I was beyond blushing. Hot and red and hot and red and

hot and hot and hot and red. It didn't matter any more. Things were too bad. I shook my head, 'I'm just a wanker.'

'Right. Fine.' She shrugged and laughed.

'Thanks.'

'It was nothing.'

Almost ten o'clock. I stood by the bus stop, blinded by the fluorescent lights from the Shopping City, bemused by the concrete everywhere, the red-brick, glass, plastic, all those other city things. I imagined the soil underneath the shopping complex, flattened down hard and close by the weight of the city above; crushed, compacted, useless, like the core of a bad molar. And the city's breath, flowing in and out of its rotting mouth, warm with fumes and dark and stinking.

No buses, not for a while. I started walking. I had a blister on the side of my foot. My shoes weren't the problem, only the fact that I was placing my bad foot and ankle differently when I hobbled and so making the leather rub.

Past Top Rank Bingo, past Wood Green Tube Station, past the bus garage, past the town hall, past the church and on and along. I'd seen teeth on the pavement outside The Tottenham once – a pub painted in pastel shades but its bland colour was deceptive – so crossed over before I reached it, to the other side where Fagin's Talk of the Town Nightspot was bumping and grinding, its disco lights bleaching and bloodying the pavement, its music leaking out too, into the night air.

If I hadn't crossed over I wouldn't have seen it. If my foot hadn't been smarting I wouldn't have paused to adjust my shoe. But I did stop and I did see it. Parked down the side of Fagin's, half in the shade, half lit by a streetlight, a Daf Roadrunner, white, in good condition, Truck of the Year in God knows when.

I went and took a closer look. Could I remember the registration? I couldn't remember it. I almost walked away and then I noticed the front indicator, on the left. It had been smashed.

I ran to the back door and tried to open it. Locked, I knocked on the tailgate. No sound. I pressed my ear up close to its cool metal and held my breath, but nothing was audible from within.

Fagin's. Legendary Nightspot of North London. Above the entrance, a snot-green, life-sized, brass statue of Fagin himself – a skinny, untrustworthy looking character in a stetson, guitar slung across his shoulder, holding up two fingers in a weak-limbed sign of peace.

I didn't want to go in but I went in anyway. Five pounds on the door. Red strobes lit up and picked out a small gaggle of people nestled inside intimate, velvet-coated cubicles. No Nancy. A clutch of characters were cradling their drinks by the bar. No Nancy. Three people were on the dance floor, clumping gracelessly, careful not to make eye contact with each other or with me while their mouths silently worked on the lyrics to the song that was playing. *Ain't no stopping us now. We're on the move! Ain't no stopping us now. We're in the groove!*

I squinted around me, looking for Nancy but not seeing her. I described her in some detail to the barman. He was giving most of his attention to changing the optic on a bottle of Malibu. When I persisted he shrugged and shook his head. 'I only just came on my shift, mate.'

I bought a drink but didn't drink it. I left it on the bar and headed for the exit, past the toilets and the cloakroom and the coat-check girl. I stopped in my tracks and doubled back. 'Excuse me,' I said, and described Nancy to her. The girl winked. 'Have you got a ticket?'

'Pardon?'

'A ticket.' She put out her hand and grinned. She had a tight, high ponytail on the top of her head which made her look like a pineapple, and wide-spaced teeth. She was a Martian.

'I don't have a ticket.'

The girl was still grinning. She said, 'Well, the policy is that if you want to collect something then you have to exchange a ticket for it. I mean, you could be anybody. How am I supposed to tell that the item in question is actually yours?'

Using her thumb, she indicated over her shoulder to where a small collection of summer jackets were hung on numbered metal hangers. I stared at the coats blankly.

The girl tossed her head and her hair nearly took out my eye. 'Not there, stupid! On the floor.'

I looked down. Huddled in an ungainly heap against the wall, half covered in a denim jacket, apparently sleeping – eyes shut – but still making the kind of quiet retching noises a cat makes after it's devoured a gutful of grass: Nancy.

'How long has she been there?'

'Since she got pissed and passed out by the bar.'

'Is she all right?'

'What do you reckon, Einstein?'

The girl unlocked the kiosk and beckoned me inside. 'Take her away with you before she chucks up in here.'

'Nancy?' I crouched down next to her and touched her shoulder. 'Nancy? Wake up.'

Very slowly, Nancy opened her right eye and stared at me.

'Nancy, it's me. Phil.'

Not a glimmer of recognition. The coat-check girl came and stood beside me. I said, 'I don't think she even knows who I am.'

The girl stared intently into Nancy's face. 'Nah, she'll be OK, it's her bad eye, that's all. The right one. She just can't see you from that side.' She nudged Nancy's shoulder, 'Come on, you. It's home time.'

Nancy had been blind in one eye since before Christmas and this was the first time I'd actually noticed, and yet Pineapple Head had observed and digested it seemingly in a matter of moments. I stared up at her with new regard. 'How did you know? About her eye, I mean.'

The girl adjusted her ponytail and said, 'I noticed when she checked in her coat. I put the ticket down on the counter, just to the right of her and she didn't seem to see it.'

I stared deep into Nancy's right eye and saw that it was pure and glassy. And I suddenly felt almost tearful. That dead right eye gave me the strangest sensation – like my feelings, my feelings and fact, *fact*, were two totally separate things. My feelings and fact. I was deluded.

My mind turned to Doug and what he'd said in the greenhouse that morning. *If you can't trust your instincts, what can you trust?* I stared down at Nancy. What is there to a person, after all, beyond how they feel? What are human beings apart from little bundles of feelings and apprehensions and misapprehensions?

Nancy started wheezing more violently.

'Out!' the coat-check girl yelled, 'before she hurls. Quick!'

'Nancy.' I shook her shoulder, harder this time, 'Hey, Nancy, wake up.'

Very slowly, very gradually, Nancy opened her other eye. Wide and then wider.

'Phil!' she mumbled, speaking like her tongue had trebled in size and was working on inhabiting the whole of her head. Her right eye stared through me, the left eye skittered and slid around.

'Hello Nancy. Where's Doug?'

She turned her head, 'Doug? Where?'

'Yes.'

She eyed me expectantly. I stared back, for a moment, before it dawned on me that she wasn't intent on telling but on waiting for an answer. I said, 'Isn't he still in your truck?'

'I'm sorry,' Nancy muttered, woozily, 'all the veg-e-ta-bles.' After a short pause she added, 'Boom! Just like Gregory Peck. Boom!' She cackled and made pathetic little mushroom-shaped cloud pictures in the air with her hands.

I peered up at the coat-check girl again. 'Do you remember by any chance whether she arrived here alone or with someone else? A man.' The coat-check girl was no longer feeling quite as cooperative as before. 'She could've come in with seventeen eunuchs and a Jack Russell for all I care. I want her out of here.'

Nancy's eyes were closing again. 'Come on,' I said, and grabbed hold of her arm. I tried to tug her up but wasn't strong enough.

'Out of my way, you twat,' the coat-check girl clucked, pushing me aside, bending from the knee, lifting Nancy up with apparent ease and draping her across her shoulder. 'I'll take her down the corridor to the public phone and then it's up to you,' she declared tartly, and led the way.

The cab driver stared at Nancy and said, 'If she spews in my car I'll make you lick up every last drop of it.'

I gave him Ray's address and then spent the entire journey staring at Nancy's mouth and her throat, waiting for her to retch, waiting to catch any liquid in my cupped hands or in the flaps of my shirt-front.

Nancy didn't seem to know what she was doing or where she was going. She lay across my lap and panted like an old dog pants when the sun has risen to its midday height and the shade he was lying in has crept a short distance away, but he's too old and too tired to drag his stiff bones back into it. She panted in just that way, but thank God she did not retch. I still tried talking, though. 'Doug,' I kept asking, 'where did you put him? Is he still in your truck? Was he bleeding?' 'Mine's a Bacardi,' she rasped, 'with coke and ice.'

Once we'd arrived, the driver didn't want to help me with Nancy but he didn't have much choice. She had to be moved and I wasn't man enough to move her. He dumped her on Ray's doormat. She grinned up at him, gratefully, while he overcharged me.

Ray answered the door wearing an old striped night-shirt that reached just below his knees. He looked like a waxen and buttery Wee-Willie-Winkie.

'So you found Nancy, then,' he said, sounding not the slightest bit surprised, picking her up and tossing her like a bag of compost over his shoulder. I followed him upstairs, into his flat. He threw her face down on to his sofa. She pushed her nose into a pillow and wheezed.

'How about Doug?' Ray asked, 'Did you find him too?'

'Nope.'

He looked down at Nancy. 'Did she tell you anything?'

'Too drunk. I found her truck. I banged on the back of it but I got the feeling Doug wasn't in there. It has a certain kind of echo when it's empty.'

'So,' Ray inspected the palms of his hands, 'either she dumped him somewhere or she took him to hospital . . .'

'Or else . . .'

'What?'

'Or else she never took him in the first place.'

Ray didn't seem impressed by this line of reasoning. He said, 'Then why would she have taken her truck and gone and got herself so drunk that she could hardly string a sentence together?'

I shook my head. 'I don't know. Maybe she was ashamed. She wrecked the greenhouse. I'm positive of that.'

'And maybe,' Ray added, catching on to the whys and wherefores of speculation, 'maybe Saleem did tell Doug after all, after she'd promised not to, about Nancy being blind in her eye.'

It was feasible, but I couldn't help wondering what Saleem would have to gain from that particular line of action. I told Ray as much. Ray stared at me, wide-eyed.

'You, of course,' he said.

'Me?'

'She likes you.'

'Nancy likes *me*?'

Ray cackled at this. When he laughed he tensed his belly and his night-shirt lifted to reveal the top of his dimpled knees. 'Not Nancy, Saleem!'

'Saleem?'

'Yep.'

My chin dropped. 'You don't know that.'

'I know it.'

'She hates me.'

'She hates everybody, but she hates you with a special kind of, uh, intensity.' Ray was proud of these four fancy syllables. He would have worn them on his lapel as a badge if it had been possible.

I said, 'I think that just means that she hates me more than other people, not that she . . .' I couldn't say it, no way. 'Not that she . . . hates me any less.'

Ray shrugged. 'I didn't mean to step over the mark,' he said, 'I just thought it might have had something to do with this particular situation.'

He nodded over towards Nancy. 'She thinks you don't like her,' he added, off the top of his head.

'Nancy?'

'No! Saleem!' He laughed.

'She thinks I don't like her? Why would she think that?'

'I don't know. She just does.'

'How do you know?'

'Just little things.'

'Like what?'

'Well . . .' Ray thought about it for a while, 'she thinks she makes you angry. You never pay her any attention when she talks to you. You just get, kind of, huffy.'

'Huffy?'

'Yeah.'

I scratched my head. Why was I having this conversation? It was so embarrassing and I was embracing that embarrassment, but Ray plainly didn't know what he was talking about.

'Maybe we should phone Mercy,' Ray said, changing tack suddenly, 'and see if Doug's there. Or maybe I should ring around some of the hospitals in the area and see if he's been checked in.'

'We wouldn't want to ring Mercy and make her worry unnecessarily,' I said, and then realized that Saleem had said the very same thing earlier that afternoon. 'I'm sure Doug's capable of looking after himself. I don't think Nancy could have done anything too terrible to him. We'll just have to wait until she sobers up a bit and see what she says then.'

'And what about the meeting?'

'Hopefully Doug will have turned up by the morning.'

'And what if he's crackers?'

'We'll work something out.'

Nancy started snoring. Her mouth vibrated into the pillow.

'She's got her own built-in muffler, there,' Ray said, smiling, and added, 'By the way, I don't think she's a bad person at heart. I don't think she'd've wrecked the greenhouse without someone else putting her up to it.'

'Well, I didn't,' I said, somewhat stupidly.

'Neither did I,' Ray said quickly. 'And Doug wouldn't have. And the Chinaman . . .'

'Forget about him.'

'Yeah.'

We stared at each other in silence for a moment, then Ray showed me out.

RAY LIVES ON a strange street. Actually it's a road, Avondale Road, and his flat is next door to the house where Stevie Smith, the poet, used to live. I checked my watch. Eleven twenty-two. Now what?

Stevie Smith, as far as I know, was Palmers Green's most famous inhabitant, ever. The house she had lived in – a plain and undistinguished place – was rendered exceptional only by the cobalt-blue plaque on its wall. I stared at the plaque but it was too dark to read it properly.

And I didn't know much about Stevie except that she lived with her aunt and dressed like a little girl when she was old and that she drank a bit too much because she was lonely, sometimes. And one other thing: she was loyal. She had lived in Palmers Green her whole life. On this street. Sometimes she went riding in the parks, or walking in them. And she had loved this place; strange, lonely old Stevie, she had loved this place, just like I do. Just like Doug does. Just like Ray and Nancy. Just like Saleem.

'Where's Doug?'

Saleem had Cog under her arm. She didn't look like she was expecting me. She was wearing a dirty vest and some cut-off jeans. 'What the fuck are you doing here?'

'I saw the light was on.'

'So?' She held Cog under her arm like he was a hot water bottle.

'Doug. Where is he? Do you know where he is? Is he inside? Is he upstairs?'

'What kind of a stupid question is that? Nancy's got him. I already told you.'

'I've seen Nancy. He wasn't with her.'

'What did she tell you?'

'Nothing. She was drunk.'

Saleem licked her lips. 'She's such a slut. She deserved to be fired.'

'That's not what you were saying earlier.'

'Maybe I changed my mind. It's a woman's prerogative.'

'Did you tell Doug?'

'What?'

'About Nancy's eye.'

'Of course not. But I'll certainly consider telling him if you don't go to that meeting tomorrow.'

'No,' I said, 'you won't tell Doug.'

Saleem tightened her grip on Cog, who had started to writhe and to wriggle. Her arm was a vice around his midriff. When she tightened her grip, a little squeak of protest shot out of him.

'Why not?' Saleem asked, slitting her eyes. 'Nancy's expendable.'

'I'll tell you why not. If you tell Doug about Nancy's eye, I'll tell Doug about the fact that you burned the museum down. I'll tell Doug and anyone else who'll listen that it was arson, not an accident after all.'

'I don't think you'd do that.'

'Try me.'

Saleem was silent for a minute and then she said, 'Actually, why don't you come in for a while? We should talk this over. I've only just brewed some tea.'

She pulled the door wide. I hesitated. 'Look,' she said, suddenly, 'of course I wouldn't tell Doug about Nancy. I'm just trying to make sure that you'll go tomorrow, that's all. I have no real problem with Nancy. See?'

Maybe she knew I wasn't keen to come in. She turned and let go of the front door so that I had to catch it to stop it from closing in my face and by the time I'd pushed it wide again she had already disappeared into the kitchen. I closed the door behind me and followed her in. She was holding two cups full of steaming tea. She offered me one. 'Herbal,' she said, 'peppermint. Sit down.'

I sat down. Saleem took a sip of her tea. 'I suppose you saw the maze,' she said, 'in among the receipts and things.'

'Yes.'

'He ordered all that privet and he hasn't even got planning permission. He knows full well that they'd refuse. I don't think we could accuse Enfield Borough of being all that imaginative.'

'I suppose not.' I sipped my tea. It was horrible. Too strong and not peppermint. Fennel, more like.

'I must say,' she added, pulling out a chair for herself, 'I'm very impressed by your loyalty to Nancy. Very impressed.' She fixed me in her steely gaze and smiled. I drank some more tea. I looked down into my cup and then drank more still.

Breathe one, I thought. Breathe two. Breath three.

'I wonder,' Saleem said, then didn't add anything. I wondered what Saleem was wondering but I didn't ask because I was certain that it would be something bad or something cruel. My tea was hot but I drained my cup and put it down decisively.

'Right,' I said, but didn't stand up like I'd intended to.

'I wonder,' Saleem said again, reaching down to stroke Cog, 'I wonder whether you actually *would* tell Doug about the museum. I mean, it's not as though they could prove anything, really. It was so long ago.' She smiled. 'And I was so very, very careful.'

She was still stroking the cat, so I chanced it. 'You lost your leg,' I said, 'you couldn't have been that careful.'

She ignored me. 'I'm not at all intimidated,' she said, 'by your little threat to tell on me. Not at all. I'm only interested in whether you would tell.' She straightened up and stared at me, then added, eventually, 'And I actually think you would, too.'

My mouth went dry. I said, 'Nancy's tough, but she can't defend herself against someone like you.'

Saleem shrugged. 'There's no need for her to defend herself. I have nothing against Nancy. This is between you and me.'

I yawned. It seemed such an inappropriate response to what she was saying, but I simply couldn't help myself.

'Hope I'm not boring you.'

I yawned again. My mouth felt drier still.

'I don't know why,' Saleem said, very quietly it seemed, 'but I always think that when you confide in a person, when you give them a present of something private that's hidden away in your heart, well, then that's like a kind of bond between you, a link. And if someone threatens to break that bond . . .' She whistled under her breath. 'What could be worse than that, Phil? What crime could be worse than that?'

I would have answered, I had plenty to say on this matter and on other related matters, too, but when I tried to move my mouth it wouldn't move. I stared at Saleem for a little while. She stared back at me. Then my head fell slowly forward on to the table. I stared at the grain in the tablecloth for a long, long time. It was the oddest sensation, seeing the rest of Thursday trickle away and sensing Saleem moving around in the kitchen like a dark, hard, sharp arachnid.

Friday

FIRST THING I remember: a musky, dusky, single-limbed bundle of badness was sitting on my lap with a razor. I couldn't do anything. Had I been asleep? I guessed I must've been. I felt very heavy. Could've been her weight on me.

'Hello Phil,' she said, when I opened my eyes, and then carried on touching my skin with the blade.

'Usually,' she said, 'I use this razor under my arms. See?' She lifted her arm. I saw the pores under her armpit, close up like little craters. 'Nearly finished,' she sighed, lowering her arm and wiping off a spot of foam from the blade and on to the vest she was wearing. 'Hot,' she said, 'isn't it?'

I wondered how long we'd been having this conversation. Might've been hours.

'There!' Saleem threw the razor on to the table and dried her hands on her vest, then lifted up the front of the vest and rubbed my face with it. I sensed her breasts against my shoulder. I couldn't feel them, but I sensed them, soft. Soft.

When she'd finished wiping me she pulled back for a moment and stared. 'You know, you're quite a dandy, really.'

I stared back, blankly.

She shifted on my lap, sat sideways, one leg dangling down, the other, truncated, stiff and horizontal like the erect, docked tail of a pointer.

'It's nice,' she said, casually, 'to have a bit of company.'

'Feel this?' she asked, a moment later. I felt nothing. I tried to shake my head. I blinked.

'What's that mean? Yes? No? Feel this?' she asked again. I stared straight ahead. I felt nothing.

'Only,' she said, slightly preoccupied, 'you've got an erection. Either that or . . .' She shifted on my lap. 'Either that or you've got the keys to the main gates in your pocket. Do you happen to know off-hand if you have those on you?'

I tried to nod, couldn't.

'The ones with the big, wooden . . .' she guffawed, 'the big, wooden key-ring? Hang on.'

She dug her hands into my pockets. She removed some small change, an old tartan handkerchief, a couple of till receipts.

'No keys,' she said, smiling. From the other pocket she removed my wallet. She opened it, looked inside and, finding nothing of interest, tossed it down on to the table. 'Right,' she said, 'do you want me to kiss you?'

I remained frozen. She moved up close to my face. Her arms wound around me. She closed her eyes and caught my top lip between her teeth, then let go with her teeth and held my lip between her two lips. Her breath tasted of germoline and bubblegum. Sweet and antiseptic.

She opened her eyes. 'Your face,' she said, 'is very swollen. You look like an apple that's been peeled and soaked in water. Kind of bloated.'

She licked my cheek like a cat with a tight tongue. In my ear she whispered, 'Why do you hate me? What did I ever do? You evil son of a fucking bitch.'

She unwound an arm from around my neck. 'I'm undoing your trousers.' More wriggling. 'I've taken off my knickers. See?' She held a pair of old, skinny black flannel briefs in front of me, then dropped them. 'Apparently,' she grinned, turning to face me, 'you're drugged and heavy and dumb and kind of numb, but one tiny little part of you is still awake, has a mind and a motivation all of its own. Life's a killer like that,' she added, 'isn't it? Full of those wicked, bitter, little surprises.'

She pulled off her vest. I could see her shoulders and her shoulder-blades. My mind was caught up in a debate with itself about whether I would like to be feeling something or whether I preferred not to feel. I could not feel. I could not.

Saleem kissed my lips again. 'That's right,' she muttered, 'move your hands just that way.'

My hands? What was I missing?

'I'm kidding you,' she smirked. 'Your hands aren't moving.'

Her face, close up, seemed damp. When I listened, I could hear a pan boiling on the oven and the air was full of steam. Saleem nudged my cheek with her nose. 'One moment,' she whispered, and pulled herself up, both her hands pushing on my shoulders, and then one hand let go, for a second, before she lowered herself down again, but slowly this time, her face puckering with something like spite but not quite. She sighed. 'This is a good kind,' she whispered, 'a sweet kind of revenge.'

I wished I could feel something. Anything. Only my eyes and my lips. She kissed my lips and then sucked the air out of me. She rose and she fell. The simplest, the slightest of movements: she was a small lake, lapping away in her own time, rolling and riding with her own regular momentum. Gentle waves, rising, falling. Tiny sighs like gusts on the water.

The chair was rocking. I stared at her face. Her eyes were closed. She was smiling. She had nice teeth. I hadn't noticed before what good teeth she had. She leaned back a bit. If I looked down I could see her breasts. I looked up again. I looked down again. What could I feel? A tingling in my chin and in my neck.

She leaned in closer and bit the side of my throat with her fine teeth. I could feel it. I felt something. Her hair tangled around my ears. Her hands touched my shoulders, lightly, and then my chest. She pulled at the buttons on my shirt. I could feel my shoulders, and just below, I was sure I felt something.

While she undid my buttons she whispered into my ears. 'Is this hurting? As bad as I want it to? You evil, loyal, Nancy-loving little fuck.' She pulled her head around and stared into my eyes. 'Is it?'

I was sure I could have answered, but I remained as stiff as if I couldn't answer. I could feel my ribs and my belly. I could feel them. She pushed her hands down on to my hips. I felt her hands. They prickled on me like itchy peaches.

Her breathing quickened. She rose and she fell. I could feel my belly. I could feel below my belly. Oh, I wanted to feel her so badly! Her eyes were closed and if I shifted my neck slightly I could see her breasts which were lifting as she was breathing, and shimmering wetly. I watched as a drop of perspiration swooped and shot from her chin to her stomach. I wanted to catch it on my lip.

Her eyes were still shut as she pushed herself up close. I could feel her so softly against me. She kissed my lips and she was smiling when she drew away, and she was very glisteny as she pulled back and as she opened her eyes.

I could feel something. Oh Christ! Something dark and strong and hot and tight and urgent as anything. The chair was still rocking. I could feel something.

She froze. She was glaring, all of a sudden. She stared at me. She had stopped moving. 'It's no fucking good,' she said, savagely. 'Fucking Nancy! Nancy! I don't believe it. You'd fuck me over just for Nancy. That bitch. Fuck it.' She pushed herself up. Oh, that was too bad. That was too, too bad. 'Fuck Nancy! Fuck her! Fuck you! Fuck you both.'

She hopped over to the oven, picked up a saucepan, hit herself hard on the side of her head with it.

'Ow!' she yelled, staggering, and then hitting the table, gathering speed, all the time, until, finally, with the swiftest and the smartest backhand I'd ever witnessed, she hit me. *Bop.*

I WAS GOING to stay quiet this time. I was going to give no indication – absolutely none – that I was awake. The lights were off, which was a good sign. I was lying on the kitchen floor, slightly curved, arched like a banana with my head resting on the bunched up tablecloth and with Cog looped around me, like a fur muffler across my neck.

If I looked up I could see through the blind. The sky was lighter than pure dark. 3 a.m.? 4 a.m.? I held my breath to see if I could hear anything. Cog's stomach rumbled and then he yawned. I slowly raised my arm and lifted him off me.

I sat up. My foot touched something metallic which shifted and clattered. I froze. I squinted. It was the saucepan that Saleem had hit me with. I put the hand to the side of my head. My head felt odd. My whole face felt odd. I rubbed my hands up and down it and it was like someone else's face. Soft and bare and rubbery. Altogether different.

I turned my mind back. I touched my face again. I almost panicked. Who was I? It was dark. Who was I? I stood up. I looked around me. I had to see myself.

Everything ached. Into the hallway. Up the stairs. I needed a mirror. The bathroom was the first door to the left on the landing. I pushed the door wide and slid inside. I closed the door and switched on the light. I blinked. Oh my Christ.

My face was bare and clean and neat as a cauliflower. Bruised florets above my eye and on my cheek. My eyebrows had gone. My hairline had been cut back by three inches so that I looked like a Franciscan monk or Henry VIII or Coco the Clown in a wind tunnel.

I was so angry. Saleem had wanted me to go to the meeting and I had been coming round to the idea, I had been seriously considering it, actually contemplating it – I told myself, I believed myself – and now this. How could I go looking this way? Had she no faith in me? I was angry. It was a stupid feeling. I was angry as hell.

Where was she? I tried the first door to my left. An empty

room. Second door. A cupboard. Third door. Shower unit. The right-hand side. The first door. I pushed it open.

Doug. It was dark and Doug was darker but I saw him, lying on a double bed, arm hanging off the side of it, mouth open, eyes open, staring up at the ceiling. I almost withdrew but something stopped me.

'Doug?'

He didn't move.

'Doug?'

I stepped up closer. One step, two steps. Closer still. I stood over him.

'Doug?'

I touched his shoulder. He felt cold. I looked into his eyes. They didn't focus.

'Doug?'

I touched his cheek. Waxy. I put my hand next to his mouth. No air. I pulled the blanket up to his chin. I shuddered.

'Doug?'

I backed out of the room, quietly, slowly.

The next door along. I tried it. Saleem's room. She was on her bed too, curled up like a squirrel under the sheets. I opened my mouth to say her name but I didn't say anything. I squatted down next to her. The side of her face was bruised where she'd hit herself. Her bottom lip stuck out like she was sulking with sleep.

I leaned forward, barely breathing, and I don't know what I was planning to do. Maybe I was intending to get right up close to her ear and then to shout in it, to scare her, to start to pay her back for all the bad things she'd done. Perhaps not.

In fact I drew close and I found myself touching her cheek with the tips of my fingers. She opened her eyes. 'Climb in,' she said, dopily. 'Come on.'

I pulled off my shirt. I pulled off my trousers. I pulled up the sheet and climbed in. Under the sheet she was as warm as baked bread. She curled around me and pressed her nose to my neck. I touched her hair with one hand. With the other I touched her hip and her thigh and her left breast which was like moss only softer. She crawled around me, like I was an old sofa and she was settling herself comfortably.

She kissed me. I kissed her. I counted the bumps on her spine with my index finger, pushing the skin on her back and feeling it slide. She took hold of my hand and guided it down, between her legs, and then lower, to her lost leg, to where it stopped. The scar tissue had left it as fragile as a petal. Just like a plant, I thought, when it's been pruned back in autumn. And I drew my hand up her leg again. And I kissed her.

'Fuck Nancy.' I said, feeling her moving.

'Fuck me,' she said, and almost started laughing. And I would have, but I kept thinking about Doug and whether I'd dreamed him.

'Doug's dead,' I said, finding a place to fit myself.

'He's not dead,' she sighed, 'only sleeping.'

'I don't think so,' I sighed back. 'He isn't breathing.'

'What?'

I said nothing. I carried on moving.

'What?'

She pushed me off and sat up. 'Why the hell didn't you tell me before?'

The light shone down brightly and rudely. Saleem was wearing my shirt. I wore my trousers, hastily pulled on. I buttoned up the fly as I watched her.

'Oh God,' she said, 'you're right. He doesn't seem to be breathing. Can you feel a pulse? Do you know where to look for one?'

I drew closer to the bed. 'His eyes. Open like that,' I said, squeamishly, 'that's what struck me as wrong, first off.'

'His pulse!' she yelled furiously, 'where is it?'

I grabbed hold of Doug's wrist. I stuck my thumb across it and pressed down hard.

'I don't feel anything,' I said, 'but I'm probably not doing it right. What did you give him?'

'Same stuff you had.'

She was slapping his face now, gently and then harder.

'What stuff?'

'Tea, stupid.'

'Tea? Where from?'

'I made it. Boiled it.'

'Boiled what?'

'You know, that stuff. You told me about it.'

'Stop hitting him. If he's dead it won't be helping matters. If he comes to, he'll be livid.'

She turned and glared, 'D'you have any better suggestions?'

'What kind of tea was it?'

'I can't remember the name. You pointed it out to me. You told me to boil the root.'

Things started slotting into place.

'A plant? And you gave it to me too?'

She grunted her affirmation. She had her ear next to Doug's lips.

'Why did you give it to me?'

'You fucked me off. It was only temper. I regret it in retrospect.'

'I could've been dead too.'

'You only had a cupful.'

'What did Doug have?'

'Since this morning? Two pints.'

'How did you get him to drink it?'

'Told him the first lot was brandy. He knocked it straight back. Second lot I fed him through a straw.'

'Maybe he choked. You shouldn't have done that.'

Saleem looked up at me. 'What shall we do if we've killed him?'

'We? We've killed him? I haven't been anywhere near him.'

Her mouth turned down at its corners. 'Great one. Who was it told me about the plant? You did. I wouldn't mind, but you came in here, saw Doug was distressed and your only course of action was to creep into my room to try and cop off with me. That in itself is tantamount to bloody manslaughter.'

I stared back at her. 'You are truly a vixen,' I said, stunned.

Her face slowly crumpled, as readily as a fistful of tissue paper. She flung herself across Doug's chest. 'Oh Christ!' she said, 'and I really love Doug.'

I went and sat down on the other side of the bed. I said, 'I didn't know you loved Doug.'

'Of course I do,' she muttered, through tears and through mucus. 'Why else would I have gone to all this trouble?'

'For yourself,' I said.

She pulled her head up and stared at me. 'To think,' she said, 'to think I was going to let you fuck me. My God.'

I stared back at her. 'You poisoned me, you lied to me, you shaved my eyebrows off, you hit me with a saucepan.'

Saleem sniffed. She appraised me. She said, 'You have such a negative approach to things.'

'Where did you get the plant from?'

'Inside the museum. The plant which grew from my leg. I thought it was a sign.'

'The grenadilla.'

'The passion flower.' She nodded.

'Didn't you stop and think about how strong the stuff was? After you boiled it?'

'Of course I did,' she scowled. 'I tried it out on the cat.'

'The cat.' I smiled.

'What are you smiling at?'

'The cat,' I said. 'Remember?'

'What?' She was losing her temper again.

'You thought you'd killed the cat.'

'So?'

I decided to tell her. 'OK,' I said, 'I'll admit it. I felt Doug's pulse. And he blinked.'

'What?'

'While you were sobbing just now he blinked.'

Her eyes were round as two full moons. 'He blinked? He blinked, you fucker, and you didn't tell me?' She lunged at me. I stood up. I was very proud of myself, suddenly. I was avenged.

Saleem was looking around her for some kind of weapon.

'Let's hope,' I said quickly, 'that Doug comes to in time for the meeting.'

Saleem had grabbed hold of the bedside light and was trying to yank the plug out of the wall by its cord. It wouldn't come, thankfully.

'Doug's not dead,' I said, resolutely, 'which is something to be pleased about, surely.' She stopped yanking for a moment. 'And you love Doug,' I said, 'apparently, so you should be ecstatic.'

'Get stuffed.'

Saleem put down the lamp and stared into Doug's face. 'He's still out cold,' she said and then peered up at me. 'I knew you wouldn't go to the meeting. I knew it. That's why I got so angry.'

I was indignant. I said, 'I was seriously considering going.'

'Bollocks.'

'Before you shaved my eyebrows off.'

'Bollocks you were. I knew you wouldn't. You don't have the guts.'

I shrugged. There seemed little point responding. I said, 'May I have my shirt back, please?'

'Why?'

'I want to go home now. I'm tired.'

Saleem left the room. I sat down on the bed again and looked at Doug. He was still fast asleep but his eyes remained open. I considered trying to pull down the lids, gently. I leaned over him.

'What are you doing?'

Saleem stood in the doorway, dressed in her vest and some knickers. The sight of her strange, pale stump almost made me smile. There was something so special about it. Something neat and extraordinary. She tossed me my shirt and I pulled it on.

'You won't believe it,' I said, determining to carry on embarrassing myself, if needs be for the rest of my whole stupid life, 'but I love Doug too.'

'You don't.'

'I do.'

'How?'

'What do you mean?'

'How do you love him?'

I shrugged. I said, 'He's great.'

Her eyebrows rose. I added. 'I mean great, like Julius Caesar or someone. Napoleon. A giant personality.'

'I'll tell you what he is,' Saleem said sourly. 'He's an unholy pain in the fucking arse and he's half-mad.'

'I know.' I stared into Doug's dead eyes. 'He's everything.'

'Come downstairs.' She beckoned me from the doorway.

'Why?'

'I can't talk properly in here with Doug lying there.'

I stood up. I followed Saleem to the top of the stairs. She didn't have a stick with her and refused the arm I offered. Instead she sat on the top step and then bumped down on her bottom. I remembered doing just that when I was small. As she bumped down and I followed her, I said, 'How did Nancy get involved in all this?'

'Fucking Nancy,' she grumbled.

'I'm only interested.'

'Christ, you're so pleased with yourself all of a sudden.'

Am I? I wondered. I couldn't think why I should be.

Saleem reached the bottom of the stairs and pulled herself up on the banister. I saw from the rear that her bottom was pink with friction. She hopped into the kitchen. She went and turned on the kettle.

'I'm going to have a boiled egg,' she said, and set about preparing it.

I sat down at the table. The sun was thinking about coming up. My hand was still swollen. My ankle looked horrible, bright and red like the skin might crack and blister.

Saleem pulled out a chair for herself. 'OK,' she said, licking some margarine from her thumb, 'so you think I'm a shit. And yes, I did kind of twist Nancy's arm. The point is, though,' she turned as the kettle boiled but didn't move to make some tea. I stood up instead and made some coffee.

'The point is, right, when I heard about Nancy's eye from

Ray it seemed like too good an opportunity to miss. Shall I tell you why?'

'Why?'

'Because it's all just crap. Ray might've noticed about Nancy's eye before the rest of us, but what he doesn't realize is that Nancy's perfectly within her rights to drive with only one eye.'

'How do you know that?'

'I thought it best to find out the details before I set about blackmailing her. I phoned the Department of Transport.'

Saleem smirked. 'And I'll tell you something else. If you check out the damage on the truck and the receipts for the repairs on the other accidents she's had, it turns out that all the smashes were on the *left* hand side of the truck.'

'What does that mean?'

'She's over-compensating, stupid. Her eye isn't the problem at all. The problem is that she's so het-up about the eye that she's driving badly by trying to overcompensate for it. She's so paranoid about the possibility of losing her job that she didn't even think to find out whether it was ever a problem in the first place.'

'So it isn't?'

'Nope.'

'But you blackmailed her anyway.'

'Yep. I needed her to help me carry Doug's body upstairs, and as a decoy.' She stared at me, unrepentant. 'I told her we'd all lose everything if Doug wasn't stopped from going to the meeting. I also threatened to tell you about her eye and how she'd deceived you. I convinced her and I convinced Ray that you were a man of integrity. I told them you'd stand by Doug come hell or high water, if you believed he was in the right. Even if he was mad.'

I passed her a mug of coffee. She took the mug. 'Thanks.'

'So all of this,' I said nervously, 'has been for my benefit.'

'Yep. To prove to you that Doug was mad; you needed irrefutable proof. To corner you, to bully you, to beguile you.'

She took a gulp of her coffee and then hopped over to the oven to remove her egg. She put it on to a saucer and then hopped back to the table. She knocked it on the saucer and then started to peel it.

'I realized, though,' she said, preoccupied with the egg, 'when I left you this afternoon, that you had no intention of going to the meeting.'

'Why?'

'Why? Because you don't really love Doug. You don't understand Doug.'

'How can you say that?'

The egg was peeled now. 'How? Because if you loved Doug you'd want to go to the meeting. You'd want to help him. You wouldn't think that all the things I'd done to him were bad. You'd understand that I'm Doug's friend and so I want to protect him.'

I almost laughed at this. Saleem ignored me and took a bite of her egg.

'You think you're different,' she said, chewing and swallowing, 'but you aren't different at all, you only feel different on the inside. But me and Doug, we just can't help it. People think we're different because we are, physically. We're a different colour. Doesn't matter how much you do. It doesn't fucking matter how much you care. You won't fit. People won't let you. Even if you find the most perfect landscape and it's yours. Even then.'

I stared at her, flummoxed.

'You're a part of this place,' she said. 'No one doubts it.'

'Doug's a part of it too. So are you.'

She carried on eating her egg in silence. Eventually she said, 'How you feel and fact, Phil. Two entirely different matters.'

I tried to work out which was worse: feeling different but fitting in or being different but feeling in your heart like you should fit but not quite fitting. Which was worse? Stupid question.

Saleem finished her egg. She sucked her fingers clean. Istared at her. 'Would you have told on Nancy?' I asked, eventually.

She shrugged. 'Dunno. I like to think I'm capable of anything.' She licked her lips and added, 'We're back to Nancy again, I see.'

'No,' I said, 'I was only thinking about what you were saying earlier, before you drugged me.'

'What was I saying?'

'About how you have a responsibility to someone once you know their secrets.'

She sighed, 'Screw it. We're going to lose everything anyway.'

'You really think so?'

'I know it.'

'Where will you go?'

'Who cares? This is the only place I fit.'

'And Doug?'

'He's everything, he's everywhere. Poor fucker.'

We sat in silence for a while. 'OK,' I said, 'I'll go to the meeting. I don't know why I made such a fuss about going in the first place.'

I thought of my funeral suit, hanging up in my wardrobe. My heart contracted.

'We've got nothing to lose,' I added, thinking, at the same time, about the herb garden and the ornamental pond, the ducks, the geese.

'I'll wait and see,' Saleem said, showing a laudable lack of faith in me. 'I'll believe you've actually gone only when I see it with these two eyes.'

She pointed. We were both silent for a while. Upstairs I could hear Cog walking down the passageway. Saleem looked up at the ceiling.

'The cat,' I said.

She shook her head, 'He's on my lap.'

'Doug!' I exclaimed, feeling something slither down my spine.

We both listened. Doug was dragging himself up the corridor and into the bathroom.

'What time is it?'

Saleem knocked the cat off her lap, leaned back on her chair and stared at the clock on the cooker. 'Six fifteen.'

'When's the meeting?'

'Nine sharp.'

Upstairs I heard the taps turning.

'What's he doing?'

'Having a wash. Maybe a bath. He usually gets up at about this time. Just shows you. He was comatose an hour ago. He's so bloody determined. That's what happens when your mind starts to turn.'

I was suddenly frightened. I said, guiltily, 'I don't suppose you could give him some more tea?'

She shook her head. 'I'm not risking it.' She smiled at me. 'So now what, Phil? Any suggestions?'

My head was empty.

'There's a heavy chest of drawers,' she said, softly, 'in my bedroom. You could push it up against the bathroom door. Jam him in.'

My heart began beating. 'I'm very weak,' I said, nervously. 'My hand and my foot.'

'It's up to you.'

'He'll go mad.'

'He's mad already. It'll only be like more of the same. And anyway,' she added, 'he'll still be kind of slow and fuzzy, like you were when you first woke up.'

I remembered and began blushing. 'Fine,' I said.

The drawers were heavy. I couldn't get any grip with my bad hand and I couldn't get any thrust with my bad foot. After five minutes I'd got them to the doorway of Saleem's room. I paused a moment to get my breath back. While I paused the bathroom door – directly opposite – opened and out came Doug, still steaming from his bath and wrapped in a towel. He looked lidded and dopy. He paused in the hallway and appraised me.

'Phil,' he said, eventually, groping for my name. *Feel.*

I froze. My heart stopped and then it started up again. 'Hi Doug.'

He stared at the chest of drawers. 'What's going on?'

'Nothing. I'm helping Saleem move some furniture.'

'You look different,' he mumbled and scratched his head, like he couldn't quite believe he wasn't just imagining me. I took a deep breath.

'Actually,' I said, thinking on my feet, speaking quickly, 'I think you cut yourself shaving. On your cheek. It's bleeding.'

'Yeah?' Doug put his hand to his cheek, blinking with the effort this afforded him.

'You'd better go and check in the mirror.'

Doug slowly turned and went back into the bathroom.

'Is it bad?' I asked, 'It might've just been a nick.'

Doug didn't reply straight off. I bounded over the drawers, pushed the bathroom door to, bounced back again and gave them a mighty shove. A deep breath and then another shove. During the second shove Doug tried to open the door but the door only pushed ajar by five inches before I gave the drawers a third great heave and knocked it shut.

I waited for a minute, in silence, breathing heavily, sweating. After a minute, Doug said, 'Phil, I have a beard. I haven't shaved with a razor in fifteen years.' His voice sounded muffled through the wood. Thick-grained and oaky. He tried the door. Another minute. 'Phil,' he said, 'what's the problem?' I felt my heart swoop. Doug tried the door again, more aggressively this time.

With impeccable timing, Saleem appeared at the end of the corridor. She put her finger to her lips. I realized my mouth was open. What had I been intending to say? I closed it. She slid past me and into her room then came out dragging an old camp bed. She put her lips next to my ear and whispered, 'If we prop this between the drawers and the wall there's no way he'll be able to get the door open.'

I took hold of the bed and did as she'd said. Doug was silent for a moment. I guessed he was intent on listening for any noises outside. Then I heard him curse under his breath before he launched a full-blown attack on the door. The door shook. I stepped back, shocked by his sudden vigour.

'It'll hold,' Saleem whispered, apparently unfazed. 'It's an old house. The doors are solid and so are the frames.'

She grabbed my hand and pulled me away to the top of the stairs. Doug was still raging in that small, square room with all the conviction of a wild boar in a balsa-wood crate.

'Ignore him,' Saleem said, calmly, 'Here's the plan. You go home now and get yourself something to eat and have a wash. Get changed into your suit. Catch the number 29 bus into Enfield. The Council offices are a short walk from the market place. You've been there before, haven't you? You know the address?'

I nodded.

'Good. Get there for nine and don't be late. Tell them that Doug's got flu and we didn't want to cancel again. Tell them you've got a roundworm and that's why you've lost some hair and your face is such a mess. Bullshit them about the privet. Don't forget the files and the accounts.'

Doug was still banging against the door and yelling now.

'What if I screw up?'

She grinned. 'If you screw up, I'll tell Doug that you locked him in there on purpose. When he gets out he'll hunt you down and kill you.'

'He knows I locked him in there,' I said, trembling. 'He came out while I was shifting the drawers and I had to speak to him. He *knows* I locked him in. Oh Christ,' I said desperately, 'why did I do it?'

Saleem's grin slipped for a moment and then rose up again and regained control of her face. 'We'll tell him he dreamed it. I'll say I was moving my room around and halfway through I went out to buy a bottle of furniture polish so I didn't hear him yelling.'

'D'you think that'll work?'

'No. Sod him, though. Keeping this place going is our top priority.'

I stared at her, sweating and frantic and suddenly suspicious. I said, 'I thought we were doing this for Doug.'

Saleem scowled. 'We have a whole series of priorities, Phil. Like a set of balls which you have to keep juggling. You can only keep a certain number in the air at any one time.'

Doug was baying at the bathroom door. It sounded like he was biting at the paintwork. I was frightened.

'And afterwards,' I said, terrified, 'who's going to let him out of there?'

Saleem sniffed, put her head to one side, thought for a moment. 'We'll toss for it. Now fuck off.'

BY RIGHTS I should have expected him, but it still came as a surprise to come across him standing on one small foot next to the giant yellow broom. Wu. I wished he'd stay in one place and then I could have been sure to avoid that area. A quiet corner where no one would see him and he, in turn, could see no one.

He was in his own world. I stood, out of sight, behind a silver birch, and I watched him. Just like Doug had. He was so beautiful. I couldn't help myself. Doug was right, of course. He was so much a part of the landscape. Taking what he wanted from his surroundings. Digesting the good things, rejecting the bad things. A part of the universe and yet entirely himself. Flowing. Needing nothing, owning everything.

Was that what Doug craved? Was that what I wanted? And Saleem? I didn't think so. We were all smaller. Wanted to hold something. A small space. A small holding. And the smaller the holding, the harder to hold. The smaller, the harder.

I slipped my arms around the tree and clung to it, until it was time to let go.

MY FUNERAL SUIT. The files. Enfield. An office. Four men and me.

It was hard, to start off with, so instead of evading and avoiding – my normal course of action – I embarrassed myself on purpose. Straight away. Up front. I gave myself a proper reason. I said, 'Sorry about the way I look. I developed an allergy to a new type of weedkiller we're using.'

They stared at me, smiled, and then they stopped staring.

'I'm sorry Doug couldn't make it,' I added. 'I'm a poor second best but he has the flu and didn't want to risk spreading it.'

Two of them nodded, the third one stared out of the window (in a world of his own), the fourth was inspecting the files.

'Things have been tight,' I said, preparing to mention the deficit, to discuss the privet, the insurance.

'Actually,' the man with the folder looked up, 'actually, Phil, there's something we need to talk about.'

My heart sank and then, miraculously, it rallied. I resolved, that instant, in a flash of fizzy sweetness, of white-blindness, to tell them about Doug's maze. To tell them. Was it insanity? Doug's crazy plan. I owed him, I decided.

I opened my mouth to speak but someone else spoke first.

'We've had an idea,' the second man said, 'and we aren't sure how you'll take to it, or Doug either for that matter.'

I wanted to tell them so badly. I needed to tell them. I wanted them to see how beautiful Doug's vision was, how complete.

'Crazy golf,' the first man said, and then nudged the third man who was still looking out of the window.

'Crazy golf,' the third man parroted, 'Nine holes. Nothing too big. Family fun and all that.'

The fourth man closed the folder. 'Crazy golf,' he said. 'That's what we've been planning.'

He unfolded a detailed map of the park and laid it out on the table in front of me. He opened up my heart on the table and performed careless surgery on it with the tip of his pencil. 'Right there,' he pointed, 'in that little gap. What do you think?'

HERE'S THE STRANGE PART. I felt odd before, like I was weird and my weirdness was an awful secret just waiting to be discovered. And yet now that I was actually weird – shaved and hairless, bald and bare – now that I was actually weird I found that I didn't really care. No point thinking about it. I was that thing I'd most dreaded being. I was that thing. And frankly, it didn't matter. Not an iota.

I climbed off the bus and walked down Green Lanes, took a right turn on to Aldermans Hill, took a left through the park gates. I was home. I looked around me. What did I see?

I saw litter, I saw weeds, I saw dogshit. If I squinted, in the distance, I could see the crazy golf course. It was there already. Families putting, children dripping their cornets on to the artificial turf, the rubber flooring a bright synthetic colour. I could see it already, a clot in the centre of this little green heart.

I walked towards the house. On the way I passed Ray, securing some climbing roses on to their trellis. He didn't see me. I walked on further and I saw Nancy. She was reversing her truck into the courtyard, her face drawn-up and hung-over. She didn't see me. I turned and headed up the steps, pushed open the door, walked inside the house, into the kitchen.

Doug sat at the kitchen table cradling a mug of Lemsip between his two hands. We stared at each other. I shrivelled.

'Don't ask me,' he said, finally, his voice as deep as the lowest note on a fine, French horn, 'don't ask me how I got here.'

I said nothing. I didn't dare ask.

'So, Phil,' he said, quite affable, 'you went to my meeting.'

I gulped down some air. I nodded.

Doug gazed ruminatively into his mug of Lemsip. 'I suppose,' he said, slowly, 'I suppose I let you down baldie.'

'Pardon?'

He cleared his throat. 'I suppose I let you down badly.'

I put my hand up to my bare face, to my forehead where the hair had been hacked.

'No,' I stuttered, 'You didn't let me down.'

Doug gritted his teeth, 'I should've been there.' He paused. 'I appreciate you stepping in, though. Stepping into the breach. Because things are very *tight* at the moment.' He paused for a second, rubbed his eyes with the back of his hands. 'Very tight,' he repeated.

I nodded stupidly. I'd have agreed to anything. The truth. Lies. 'I know,' I said. Doug pulled his hands away and stared at me.

'Thank you,' he whispered, somewhat gratuitously, and carried on staring. My hackles rose. 'Thank you,' he said again, his voice all honey. My hackles rose even higher. They were ridiculously high, so high I was almost floating, suspended and smarting up close to the ceiling. Doug, I knew, was at his most dangerous when he oozed.

He spread out his hands on to the table.

'You know, life can be a bitch, Phil. And you find yourself tiptoeing through it, barely knowing where to put your feet down, and you hold on to these tiny little things, these tiny little places where you've rested your feet, these spaces. And then sometimes you start to look at these spaces, these places, to really look, and you see how tight they are. Really tight. And you begin to wonder . . .'

I gazed at him, hypnotized.

'How'd that meeting go, Phil?'

'Uh . . . fine.' I couldn't bear to tell him how this space was getting smaller. I couldn't bear to tell him about the nine holes and the artificial turf and the nominal charge and the soft-soled shoes.

'How'd it go, Phil? Did it go well or did it go baldie?'

My hand flew back to my face. 'It went OK, I think.'

'We'll talk about it later, huh?'

I nodded.

Doug's eyes were very gentle, suddenly. I was almost sick with fear. He said, 'I've had the worst head-cold, Phil. And it's been hanging around above my nose for a good while now. And I've been waiting for it to break. Just waiting . . .' Doug paused and stared at me for what seemed like an eternity. 'And then finally it broke.'

I nodded.

'It broke.'

'Right.'

'Still feel rough, though, Phil. Phil?'

'Yes?'

'Still feel rough.'

It was then that I noticed that Doug had a pair of shears on the table, right next to him, and he had been sharpening them. The blades were a bright silver. Doug took hold of the shears. He passed them from one hand to the other. He stood up, still holding them.

'Phil?'

'Yes?'

'Want a cuddle, Phil?'

He was saccharine-voiced. He was smiling. He never smiled, not Doug, not ever. He was going to kill me. I was certain. He would kill me. The shears were sharp enough. I deserved it. He held out his arms. The shears were high and steady in his right hand.

Slowly, stiffly, I approached him. I drew close and then closer. I tucked myself, wincing, into his arms. He chuckled and clucked and then he patted me on the back. He held me.

'The tractor,' he said eventually, 'is it still in the barn?'

I choked as I spoke. 'The tractor? I think so.'

'Good. Good.'

He was as gentle as snow. He squeezed me. I waited for the stab of the blade. He squeezed me again and then let go. Without another word, he drained his Lemsip and then calmly padded out. Out of the kitchen, out of the house.

I was shaking. I took a deep breath and I followed him. Saleem was on the doorstep. She grinned. 'You're pale as pastry. How was he?'

I shuddered, 'I don't really know.'

'And the meeting?'

'The meeting?' I struggled to remember.

The tractor's engine burst into life, its roar reverberated inside the barn. The gears were hacked from neutral and into reverse. Saleem, I realized, was staring up at me. My mind was in the barn. My brain was vibrating.

'You won't shake him, Phil,' she said, gently, 'And you won't shake me.'

What did she mean? She always meant something. She didn't waste words. She was purposeful.

The tractor swung out of the barn, indicated right and then left, straight after.

I said, 'He had some shears on him and I think he picked up a length of hose. Maybe he's thinking about cutting back the big border on the east side.'

'Nah.'

We followed behind at a slow pace. There seemed no reason to rush. As we walked I said, 'You know, I think Doug's right after all about everything going in a circle.'

'Bollocks.'

We walked down and past the burnt-out museum.

'He is right,' I said, growing ever more certain, watching as the tractor turned right and picked up speed.

'Ten pounds,' Saleem whispered, reverently, 'ten pounds says he goes straight into the ornamental pond.'

I put my hand into my pocket. 'Ten pounds he doesn't.'

The tractor veered boldly towards the pond.

'He's my hero,' Saleem said. 'He's off his fucking head.'

And the tractor drew closer to the pond. And the ducks and the geese were waggling their tails and getting nervous. Some stood up. A couple honked and hissed. Doug's hand waved regally from the tractor. He applied his brakes.

'Told you,' I said, cheering up suddenly, forgetting about the crazy golf and the litter and the dog mess and all that other business. 'Told you,' I said, 'he's slowing right down.'

Doug slowed down to a trundle but he didn't stop. Not quite. Instead, very slowly, very carefully, he eased the tractor into the pond: front wheels, back wheels, drove for a few seconds and then stalled.

Saleem showed me the palm of her hand. 'What did I tell you?'

Doug climbed out of the cab, holding his shears and with a length of green hose curled around his arm like a python. He waded through the pond, climbed up and out the other side, turned, waved again, holding the shears aloft, and then carried straight on walking.

Just for an instant, less than a second, Saleem's outstretched palm sagged. 'What's he doing?'

'More to the point,' I said, 'what's he *thinking*?'

'Easy enough,' Saleem smirked, her palm coming back up and flattening out again. 'He's thinking about how badly and how thoroughly he's going to fuck us all over.'

Her face sagged and then it tightened. She cackled. I turned, amazed, and watched her laughing. Then I found myself laughing. She made me laugh. The simple way she sliced through things. The wonderful way that she hissed and she slithered.

And up until that point, I'll admit it, I had been wound up, halted, blocked, but then my mind did something so curious. It flew backwards, it turned, it clicked over – like one of those calendars that each day clicks over a page – and I saw Doug, in that instant, so clearly, so thoroughly.

I saw Doug as many things; pure and bright and full of light. I saw Doug as many things, in all his incarnations; and he was an insect, an egg, a pearl, an onion, a giant onion, many-layered. He was a jewel and a flower and a beautiful, bright yellow bird. He was all these things. He was everything. Doug was God and God was doG and Evil was dEvil and Devil was liveD, was *livid*, red, angry, emergent, emergency, was 999, was 666. I saw them, so clearly. I saw all these things.

And the park was my soul. And I would not leave this place. Soul. Soil. I would not. I could not. I could not leave this place.

It was then that the eye was like the
ear, and the ear like the nose, and the nose like the mouth: for they were all one and the same. The mind was in rapture, the form dissolved, and the bones and flesh all thawed away; and I did not know how the frame supported itself and what the feet were treading upon. I gave myself away to the wind, eastward or westward, like leaves of a tree.

Lieh-tzu

Nicola Barker

lives and works in east London. She was the winner of the David Higham Prize for Fiction and joint winner of the Macmillan Silver Pen Award for *Love Your Enemies*, her first collection of stories. Her second story collection, *Heading Inland*, received the John Llewellyn Rhys/*Mail on Sunday* Prize. Her novel *Wide Open* won the IMPAC Prize in 2000. Her most recent novel is the critically acclaimed *Behindlings*. She has been selected as one of Granta's Best Young British Novelists of the decade.

REVERSED FORECAST

is a novel of gambling and allergies, music and dogs, set in some of London's less scenic locations. Chance meetings result in the unlikeliest of couples – and there's always the risk that it could all work out disastrously. But, as Ruby, the story's soft-centred heroine, observes: 'Losing, that's the whole point of the gamble.'

Praise for Nicola Barker:

'She writes of the comic and sometimes sinister surrealism of ordinary people's lives, and the results are books to make you wince, gasp and laugh at loud.' *Independent On Sunday*

'Like Mike Leigh, Barker chronicles the dark underlay beneath the beige shag-pile of suburban life.' *Sunday Telegraph*

'Her novels inhabit the same world as Gary Larson's "Far Side" cartoons: at once comic, dark, surreal and oddly plausible. The diversity of Barker's imagination is stunning; her language, witty and exact.' *Observer*

'*Reversed Forecast* is an imaginative lowlife tale, told with acuteness and verve.' *Literary Review*

'*Reversed Forecast* is beautifully rendered – well written, clear and revelatory.' *The Times*

'Barker is adept at manipulating a complicated group of characters, knitting their lives together adroitly and watching them interconnect.' *Daily Mail*

NICOLA BARKER

Reversed Forecast

Flamingo
An Imprint of HarperCollins*Publishers*

By the same author

Love Your Enemies
Small Holdings
Heading Inland
Wide Open
Five Miles from Outer Hope
Behindlings
The Three Button Trick

Flamingo
An imprint of HarperCollins*Publishers*
77–85 Fulham Palace Road,
Hammersmith, London W6 8JB

Flamingo is a registered trade mark of
HarperCollins*Publishers* Limited

www.**fire**and**water**.com

Published by Flamingo 2003
9 8 7 6 5 4 3 2 1

Previously published in paperback by Faber and Faber Ltd 1995
First published in Great Britain by Faber and Faber Ltd 1994

ISBN 0 00 716399 1

Set in Palatino

Printed and bound in Great Britain by Clays Ltd, St Ives plc

For Ben Thompson,
who's always liked a bit of a flutter

ONE

At night she breathed through her mouth, which would have been fine, if unerotic, except for the fact that her loose lips and sagging tongue spilled out copious quantities of saliva on to her pillow. Sometimes she woke up in the morning to find that the side of her mouth and chin, as well as portions of her lower cheek, had become damp and chapped from her sloppy expulsions.

She slept on her stomach – her breasts, soft pillows; her face, crushed against the bedclothes, misshapen by sleep, like the face of a pug, a boxer or a pekinese: inelegant but charming.

This morning – a Saturday – too, too early; she slept and she dreamed. In her dream she saw the wings of a large black bird. Some people are frightened by wings, she thought. And feathers. Some people are afraid of moths. The way they flutter. This fear – she didn't know the word for it – a nameless fear.

One instant the bird was at her shoulder, but the next it was outside her window, holding on to the sill with its strong claws, tapping, tapping.

Christ! she thought, suddenly feeling her body, her face, crashing into consciousness. Something *is* there at the window.

Ruby turned over and tried to open her eyes, both still gummed up with remnants of liquid eye-liner and mascara. She lifted a warm hand to wipe them clear, but this rapid movement, the whiteness of motion from her bleached hair, her pale skin, made the bird – if indeed it was a bird – fall from the sill, as though shot by an arrow of whiteness, a white lightning. When her eyes could properly focus, all she could see through her tiny bedroom window was a pinkish hue, reflected from wall to wall on the buildings outside – diluted light like a weak pink gin. She sniffed, still thinking of the bird. 'It was probably only a pigeon,'

she said, calming herself, then she opened her eyes wider, registered the reddish atmosphere outside and muttered, 'Bugger. It's going to rain.'

She turned over, relaxed, opened her mouth to inhale, and in a single breath was gone.

It didn't rain immediately. Several miles away a small dark woman stood alone on an open piece of roof-scape. She was still, rooted, like a tree, but her leaves were feathers, which quivered and vibrated in the slow, smouldering, morning light. The mass of birds on her outstretched arms were shrill, excitable, ecstatic, and called, *'Sylvia! Sylvia! Sylvia!'*

They were heavy, but Sylvia waited, remaining benign and impassive until one, last bird had arrived. It landed on her shoulder, gently brushing her cheek with its great black wing.

'Hello,' she said quietly, her voice low and rasping. 'I could see you coming from miles away. A minute ago you were only a tiny speck on the horizon.'

'Cor!' it replied, tipping its head, fixing her with a single, black eye.

She grinned and then dropped her arms, feeling the weight of many birds instantly lift, turning her head, hearing the whirrrr of their wings as she watched them ascend.

At ten-forty-five, Ruby ran across Wardour Street and made her way down towards the main bulk of the Berwick Street fruit market. Here she bought a bag of apples and smiled hello to various stallholders. She was late for work, but didn't seem concerned. From the far end of the market her peroxide hair was clearly visible amongst the bright cuts and smashes of different fruits – the casualty of colour.

To any incidental observer, standing attentive at the end of the market, watching out for motorbike couriers, the wasps, the fruit skins, Ruby painted a diverting picture.

She's bold, she's tall. When the men on the market call her a Big Girl, and they do, she spits out her tongue. Her short, unruly, badly bleached hair initially distracts attention from her

large, red lips and black-lined eyes. She never tans, but she does wear tinted make-up to stop her skin from looking too pale, too insipid. She has a long nose which is rounded at the tip – not snub – and which suffers the indignity of a slight dent in the middle. She has a big but good body and her clothes are fashionable but not showy. (This is no place to be showy. Soho is cheap-showy.) She has green eyes and five hooped earrings in each ear. Until recently her nose was pierced too. On the palm of her right hand she has a tattoo, which depicts, somewhat clumsily, a small, blue bird in flight. This doesn't irritate her too much now – she tries not to regret things from the past – although sometimes it surprises her when she puts out her hand in shops to receive change.

Occasionally, as she walks, the market men send teasing whistles in her direction, which make her smile, check her tights and pull down her skirt. Her skirts are usually short but not excessively so, because her legs, although long, are also thick and muscular. If asked what part of her body she hated most, she would probably slap her thighs. She is resolutely curvy: a pear-shaped peach.

Close up, in focus, beyond the hair, the nose, the thighs, hides another essential, unmistakable, uncosmetic detail. It reveals itself physically, although it is not physical. It shows itself in her half-smiling, bright red, cherry lips. In her eyes, which see everything, are concerned with every small detail. You can hear it in her flat, soft voice. You can tell by the way she holds her arms, loose at her sides, informal and approachable. It hits you. It hurts you.

The main thing about Ruby is that she's obviously, unashamedly, determinedly *nice*.

Nice? And what does that mean?

One word. She laughs at it. *Trouble*.

Dawn was heaving a limp body through the shop doorway and swearing for all she was worth. Ruby paused and watched, unable to gain access while Dawn pushed and shoved. When Dawn paused for a second to draw breath, Ruby asked, 'What's

he done wrong? He's just drunk. Leave the poor sod.'

Dawn frowned. 'Grab his feet will you?'

Ruby ignored her. 'What's he done?'

Dawn stepped over him and tried another angle, pulling now instead of pushing. He moved a couple more inches.

'He stinks. He's smelling out the fucking shop and he's putting off the punters.'

Ruby peered into the shop. It was empty. But what did that prove? It was still early. She bent over and perused the man's face more closely. She recognized him.

'I've taken bets off him before. He's not doing any harm. Can't you just leave him?'

'No.'

Ruby crouched down and tentatively nudged the man's shoulder. 'Come on, stand up and get out before she drags you out.'

He half-turned his head and grunted. His eyes were unfocused and he was drooling. She was uncertain what to do. Her impulse was to leave him alone, but Dawn was still pulling his feet from the other end. One of his shoes came off and she threw it into the street. It landed in a puddle next to the flower stall.

'Go on, Dawn, just leave him. It's still wet outside and he doesn't really smell.'

Dawn wasn't convinced. 'I've rolled him this far,' she said, 'and I'm not stopping here.'

The man began a half-hearted attempt to drag himself back into the shop, but collapsed after a couple of seconds. Ruby stood up, sighed, stepped over his body and left Dawn to it.

Jason, the manager, smiled at her through the glass partition and then stood up to unlock the door. He said, 'There's no stopping Dawn once she gets going.'

Ruby grimaced. She took off her coat and went into the back kitchen to make a cup of tea.

'Tea, Jason?'

'I only refuse blows.'

She plugged in the kettle. After a minute Dawn wandered in.

'Tea, Dawn?'

'Nah, I'm on the One-Cals today.' She opened the fridge and took out a can.

Ruby watched her. 'Were you early?'

She shrugged. 'Ten minutes. Jason was late. He'd only just opened up anyway.'

'I overslept again. I feel like hell.'

'You look like shit.'

Dawn opened her drink and flounced out, smirking.

Ruby waited for the kettle to boil. She felt bad about the dosser. When things like that happened they could undermine her whole day, and things like that happened all the time. She felt as though she hadn't had enough sleep, had a slight headache and wasn't happy at the notion of spending yet another day sitting by her till taking bets, helping Dawn with the clues in her crossword puzzle book.

The only positive aspect to working on a Saturday was the morning coverage of dog racing from Hackney. Sometimes, when she had a day off during the week, she worked as a kennel maid at the Hackney track, parading the dogs before their races and putting them into their traps. It was a good way of earning extra cash, and when Hackney was covered in the shops she had some familiarity with the dogs, the track and the personalities that worked there. It was, at least, a diversion.

The kettle came to the boil and switched itself off. She made the teas and strolled back into the shop just in time to see one of the punters – who was he? not a regular – approach the counter and smash his head into the glass partition next to the pay-out where Dawn had stationed herself and her can of One-Cal.

Ruby had long speculated whether the partition – which extended from the till to the ceiling with only a three-inch gap through which punters could push their betting slips and money – was glass or a type of reinforced plastic. This mystery was immediately resolved. The entire screen, whose purpose was to protect the working section of the shop (but chiefly the money), exploded into motion. It cracked, shattered and fell in a mixture of large random chunks and tiny, pebble-shaped splinters both inwards and outwards.

Ruby slammed down her hot drinks on Jason's desk and raised her arms over her head, protecting her eyes with her hands.

Jason had half-risen from his swivel chair, which spun behind him like a waltzer. A few of the smaller fragments of glass showered the back of his desk and nestled into the curls of his hair and moustache.

Initially, Dawn had thrown both hands forward, as if to catch the entire partition in her arms, but was now drawing them in again to protect her face and neck from the larger pieces which were descending from above.

Vincent (not a punter, not a regular; merely, for the time being, an aggressor) pulled his head back from the impact of the blow while his face composed itself into a violent snarl, which Ruby felt, in all probability, anticipated further damage. His forehead was cut directly below the hairline and blood was already pouring down to his eyebrows, through the funnel of his frown and on to the bridge of his nose.

After the few seconds of initial shock, Vincent began to scream obscenities at the three people standing behind the betting counter. By now his face was almost entirely awash with blood. Some of it ran on to his lips and into his mouth. He spat it out as he shouted, spraying out rude blood like an aerosol.

Jason ignored his yells and dialled the police. Ruby lowered her arms and glanced sideways at Dawn to check that she was all right. Then she turned towards Vincent. 'We're fine, but your head's all split.' Vincent squinted at her, surprised at being spoken to.

Jason placed his hand over the mouthpiece of the phone. 'Is anyone hurt? Dawn? Does he have a gun?'

Dawn shook her head. Small pieces of glass rattled down on to the carpet. She stood up. 'I don't think he's got a gun. He's too bloody stupid. If he'd had any brains, he'd have worked out that the side door's still open. He could've come straight in.'

She adjusted the collar on her blouse and then stalked off to the toilet.

Vincent had lost his initial impetus. Blood was streaming into his eyes. The first few punters of the morning were coming into

the shop and standing around in clusters by the door. Jason picked up his keys and tossed them to Ruby. She caught them and made her way around the counter, encouraging everyone outside. 'Sorry. Looks like you're all going to have to find somewhere else to spend your money this morning.'

She grinned to herself. They were bound to close up for the day, and if she could get out quickly, she might be able to make it down to Hackney Wick in time for the second race. They always needed help on a Saturday.

When she closed the door she didn't lock it. Instead she walked over to Vincent and said quietly, 'Why don't you get out now while he's still on the phone? He's called the police and they'll be here any minute.'

Vincent glared at her. He looked like a red gargoyle. 'I don't need any favours from you.'

'Suit yourself.'

She walked back around the counter and into the kitchen, where she moistened one of the cleaner tea-towels in hot water, wrung it out, then returned to the shop and threw it at him. Vincent caught the towel and sank his face into it. Jason had finished with the police and was now deep in conversation with his area manager.

When Vincent lifted his head from the towel, Ruby noted that his face was square-shaped, with generous features but smallish eyes. It was a Celtic face – pale skin, reddish-brown lashes, stubble and brows – but his accent wasn't Irish or Scottish, only rough and vaguely rural. He was of medium build and stocky. Solid, she thought. And stupid. Like a ginger tom. She said, 'Some of our other shops don't have glass screens any more. Maybe you could go into one of those next time.'

He leaned up against the counter and appraised her. 'I was supposed to be meeting someone in here this morning, but I fell over him outside. He was lying in a pile of old fruit and cardboard. They told me on the stalls that you'd thrown him out.'

I didn't even do it, she thought; only let it happen.

'I didn't do it. Someone else did,' she said.

He blotted the towel against his forehead. 'Did you bother to take his pulse? Did you check he wasn't having a fit?'

Her eyes widened. 'He wasn't, was he?'

Vincent smiled. 'Who's to say?'

'He wasn't, was he?'

'Fuck you.'

The police arrived, pushed through the door and strolled in.

Ruby held out her hand to Vincent. 'My name's Ruby. I'll try to explain things if you like.'

Vincent slapped the damp, bloodied tea-towel down on her outstretched palm and said calmly, 'You'll pay for this.'

She backed off but was not afraid. She was tough enough. He was shorter than her by a couple of inches.

Oh yeah, she thought, walking back into the kitchen to make some more tea. Just another bad dream.

He left cuffed, but quietly.

TWO

When younger, Sylvia had been something of a diversion, a novelty, an idiosyncracy – eccentric but endearing. Now she's just a problem. And she knows it. She knows it well, but she doesn't care.

The general consensus on talent is that it is something that everybody appreciates, something that people want to share. Talent is just another commodity. No matter how obscure the talent may be, it's powerful, it's positive, it's something good.

Sylvia is nineteen. She thinks that she understands most things, and the things she doesn't understand she knows are of no interest to her. When she was fifteen she looked up the word 'talent' in her dictionary and saw that its origin was in the Greek *talanton*. The rough definition of this particular word was 'a weight'.

Talent, she decided, isn't always a good thing. It can't be. She pictured it as a weight around her neck, something heavy, choking and burdensome. She remembered Bette Davis in *Whatever Happened to Baby Jane?*

Sylvia is very ill, and it's all because of the birds. She suffers from a rare condition known as Bird Fanciers' Lung. This condition is caused by excessive contact with birds, their feathers and their dirt. Eventually you get allergic. Eventually it can kill you.

The first time Sylvia suffered symptoms of this rare disease was at the age of thirteen.

The birds had always loved her, she was always the apple of their beady eyes, but when she reached puberty (she reached it late and never seemed to get over the shock) the birds just couldn't resist her. She became a magnet for their tiny, fragile, feathery bodies. They simply couldn't bear to keep away.

And Sylvia grew to love them.

Her relationship with the birds isn't a silly or a dramatic one. She can't talk 'bird' for example; she certainly isn't a Dr Dolittle.

This makes her talent somewhat redundant. She can't put on a show with the birds – a circus show or a freak show. It is simply that they love her and she has grown to love them. Possibly the attraction is just hormonal – hormones are complex things – but possibly not.

Steven John had wasted a good part of the morning driving up and down Mare Street, Hackney, trying to locate the relevant turn off for Jubilee Road. He didn't know the area well and his sense of direction was abysmal. He'd tried perusing an old, dog-eared copy of the *A to Z*, but had been unable to work out which way up to hold it, which was left and which was right. Eventually he had managed, through sheer coincidence, to find the right road, the correct building and a handy parking space. The space, he thought; that at least must be a good omen.

Before getting out of his car he straightened his lapels and adjusted his collar.

He looked smart. His clothes were always of a high quality – hand cut – but slightly loud. He had a problem with colour. His suits were invariably too beige or too blue or too black. He usually wore a tie, a silk tie, and today was no exception. Peeking out from the inside pocket of his jacket was a gold-plated Parker pen and matching pencil. He found some difficulty in forming the letters correctly in real ink but preferred the classic charm of an ink pen to the bald, cheap brashness of its modern-day equivalent, the Biro. Biros, in his book, had no style and no class.

Steven John has always believed that the little things in life count. Sometimes he thinks that they count more than the big things. This small, almost mediocre philosophy of life is part of the reason why, in his own eyes, he has always been such an absolute failure. He feels insecure, lacks confidence and is devoid of panache. Even his name – this cuts him to the quick – is like two Christian names jammed gracelessly together. Of course it's a name that could easily be imagined on the front page of

Variety magazine. The kind of name someone on the cabaret circuit might have. The kind of someone who makes a break in the chorus of a West End musical. Probably homosexual.

It was as a consequence of his belief in the importance of detail that Steven resolved, at an early age, to gravitate towards the world of showbiz management. He was not made of the stuff of stardom, he knew this full well, but he was a pretender, a trier, a people person.

He sees himself as a fighter, an endurer, someone who battles manfully against all odds. The fact that he battles, suffers and invariably loses is incidental. He makes a living. Some people, he often thinks, correctly, can't even do that.

He entered the block of flats and, on discovering no lifts, began to climb the stairs. On reaching the third floor he became aware of a strong, musty flavour in the atmosphere – a smell akin to damp, but stronger. The brickwork was newly painted and the hallways seemed clean and well maintained. He put a hand to his throat and wished he was fitter, that his lean body was more athletic, so he wouldn't be compelled to breathe in this nastiness so deeply, so completely. He cleared his throat, although this didn't help matters, then continued his ascent.

The smell grew stronger as he reached the fifth floor. Restraining an impulse to sneeze, he raised his fist and rapped gently on the door of the top flat, which was painted a bright, fresh evergreen.

Within seconds the door was pulled open and Steven beheld Samantha, who was looking absolutely radiant and whose first response to his restrained nod of greeting was to smile and say, 'We thought you'd gone and stood us up.'

She took hold of his hand and shook it. Steven appreciated this small touch.

'Come in, we're just having breakfast. We were waiting for you, but it got so late we've already started.'

Her face was like a punch, a slap. She was so perfect that it set his teeth on edge. Like a madonna, a princess. Radiating something – an inexplicable serenity – from her black hair and her black eyes. Everything about her just so. A terrifying

neatness, a rightness. Her lips, a cupid's bow; her lashes, so long that he could have plucked them and used them to string a viola.

He forgot to say anything. He could have apologized for his lateness, but he found it impossible to contain anything else in his mind during that instant but her face – the glow of her. Words melted and turned into honey.

She led him through the flat. He followed, still numbed by her. If you had a relationship with a girl like this, he thought, you'd spend all your time trying to find some one thing wrong with her, and when you found it you'd be devastated.

Sam turned to say something to Steven as she led him along the corridor, and caught him staring at her bottom. She forgave him his indiscretion immediately, expecting no better than this from your average man. Steven blushed and continued to stumble down the corridor behind her, keeping his eyes to himself.

The flat was bright, clean and well decorated, but it stank. Steven couldn't understand the smell. He was momentarily worried that the smell might be his fault, and furtively checked the base of his shoes before following Sam into the kitchen.

The kitchen was painted a meticulous white and filled with red utensils. Sitting at a large red table in the centre of the room was Sam's mother, Brera, who was thirty-eight, had long auburn hair, fine features and slightly jutting teeth. She beckoned Steven towards the table without standing up. He found her grandly matriarchal.

The table was set with butter, jam, percolated coffee and a half-eaten plate of hot croissants. Steven noticed four settings and hesitated over where to sit. 'You've not gone to all this trouble on my account?'

Sam sat down on the chair to his left. 'Of course we have.'

She picked up a croissant and ripped it in two with her fingers. Steven sat down and nervously unfolded his napkin.

Brera poured him a cup of coffee. 'You're over an hour late, which is hardly an auspicious start.'

Sam grinned. 'Ignore her, she's only trying to frighten you.'

Steven felt daunted by these two women, both so vibrant and

voracious. So different. A black daughter, a white mother. Could you get more different than that? He picked up his coffee and placed it close to his nose so that its steamy aroma would cut out the smell of the flat which was starting to make him feel nauseous. He looked at Brera over the rim of his cup and said, 'I'm very pleased you agreed to meet up with me like this. When I saw the two of you last week at the Bull and Gate I was bowled over. It's not often you see two such attractive women on stage together who can actually sing, I mean really sing, let alone write their own music.'

Neither woman seemed especially impressed by this. Sam reached over for the coffee jug, scattering bits of pastry across the table in the process. She said, 'We've got lots of ideas, if that's what you mean.'

She poured her coffee and then licked her fingers clean. Steven watched her small pink tongue darting in and out of her mouth. It reminded him of a lizard's tongue or a hamster's. That's odd, he thought. I've never even seen a hamster's tongue before. He wondered why she had to talk, why she couldn't just sit. Just sit.

Brera said, 'Sam's in charge of this venture. She imagines everything, how we should be and so forth. She's fussy.'

Sam nodded. 'I am.'

Steven laced his fingers together. 'I can deal with that.'

'We've got a fairly pure vision. It's complex, but we can discuss all the details later.' Brera picked up a croissant and then spooned on some jam. 'We're bullies. We don't like being told what to do.'

Sam added, 'We've already decided that we won't put up with too many changes musically. We like doing some of our own stuff, well, my sister's stuff. We know it's eccentric . . .'

Steven began to look sceptical, but he kept in mind the fact that his latest client, a snooker player, had recently thrown in the towel to go back to his day job. He said, 'Obviously, the fact that you don't just do cover versions stands in your favour. Although my ideal image of the two of you is more as a mother-and-daughter soul and country duo. I prefer the country songs to the new-wave stuff.'

Sam mouthed the words 'new wave' at Brera and smiled. Steven was insulted. He thought, five years ago the term new wave was perfectly respectable.

Brera frowned at Sam and then said, 'Of course we'd be willing to consider some new songs for the act, so long as we don't lose all our own stuff.'

Sam leaned towards him and whispered, 'You think our own songs are crap, don't you?'

Before he could think how to respond she added, 'Well, that's OK, we think so too, sometimes. The problem is that they aren't written according to the standard musical scale.'

Brera interrupted. 'It's complicated, that's all.' Then she added, 'Don't worry, you'll soon get the hang of us.'

Steven was struggling to keep up. He said, 'So you both want me to manage you?' They nodded.

He felt as though he was missing out on something crucial, was bemused, but threw caution to the wind and said, 'Then I'd be delighted to.'

He held out his hand to Brera. Brera hesitated for a moment before taking it. She had the strong yellow nails of a long-time guitar plucker. After pressing his fingers for a second she let go and picked up the plate of croissants. 'Take one. They're nearly cold.'

Sam laughed. 'They *are* cold.'

Steven was secretly irritated that this courteous gesture on Brera's part had deprived him of the opportunity of shaking Sam's hand again. Sam didn't seem to care though. She was sipping her coffee and looking over at Brera as though they were sharing some kind of private joke. He hoped emphatically that he wasn't it.

Sylvia had been asked by both Sam and Brera to attend the breakfast meeting. She had agreed to go. 'After all,' they'd said, 'whatever the outcome, it's bound to affect you.'

She had agreed to go but had never had any real intention of attending, although this didn't dissuade her from standing outside the kitchen and listening to the on-going conversation

inside. Occasionally she was forced to scamper back to her room to stifle her coughing, which was dry, hacking, and came in short bursts every few minutes.

She had watched Steven get out of his car and walk towards their block of flats from her window, and had disliked him, on principle, instantaneously. What she overheard from outside the kitchen didn't improve this opinion.

She was glad that she had kept out of the way. She was sure that her presence at the breakfast table would have spoilt the success of any joint venture.

Why should I care anyway? she thought furiously. I have my own bloody life.

She sat down on her bed and stared blankly at the carpet. She felt constricted. Things kept changing. Things always changed.

A sparrow flew in and landed on her shoulder. The pigeons cooed.

THREE

'How long have you been waiting?'

The policeman glanced at his watch. 'Five minutes.'

Ruby found him moderately attractive, for a policeman. He was tall but thin and had a deep dimple in either cheek and in his chin.

'I've come about the bail,' he said, stepping out of the doorway so she could get to her door.

'Why?' she said. 'What did I do?'

He smiled at this. While he smiled, it dawned on her. 'For *him*? You must be joking. He expects me to pay his bail?'

'He told me that you were the closest he had to a relative.'

Ruby's startled expression made him laugh out loud.

'You're just a sadist,' she said, 'in a bloody police uniform.'

'In case you wondered, I got your address from your manager. He said this was a company flat.'

Ruby felt around in the pocket of her jacket for her keys. 'I'm not paying his bail. I don't even know him.'

'That's up to you. He's got no money of his own.'

She put her key into the lock. 'I never even met him before today.'

'You must've made a good impression.'

'How much is it, anyway?'

'Two hundred.'

She pushed the door open. 'He can sing for it. You can tell him that.'

'I will.'

'Is that all?'

He nodded.

'Thanks, then.'

She stepped inside, then turned. 'Where is he exactly?'

'The local nick.' He began to grin. 'You're going to pay it, aren't you?'

'Even I,' she said firmly, 'am not quite that stupid,' and closed the door behind her.

Two hundred, she thought, climbing the stairs. He's crazy.

She'd almost reached the top when she heard the doorbell chime inside her flat. She swore, turned round, and walked back down again to answer it. Outside, instead of the policeman, whom she'd half-expected, was her friend Pablo. Everyone preferred to call him Toro. She didn't know why. He was holding two bottles of cheap lemon vodka. Ruby took a bottle from him and inspected the label. 'What's wrong with Martini or a crate of lager?'

Toro smiled, his cheeks bunched up and the pressure of them squeezed his eyes into almonds. 'I saw you at Hackney,' he said, 'on television.'

'Yeah?' She turned and started to walk upstairs again. 'Where? In Ladbrokes? How did I look?'

He slammed the front door and followed her. 'Completely beautiful.'

'Thanks.'

Once inside, Ruby took off her jacket and slung it over the back of the sofa, then flung herself into an armchair and scraped her heels across the floor to pull off her shoes. She wriggled her stockinged toes and said, 'Maybe I should grow my toenails and paint them, then I could wear sandals and my feet wouldn't sweat as much.'

Toro looked slightly disgusted. 'Why was the shop closed this morning?'

She didn't answer immediately, so he searched for the volume percentage of alcohol on the label of one of the bottles he was holding.

Ruby's flat was comfortable but shoddy. It consisted of a small sitting-room and adjoining kitchen, with an old Baby Belling, a sink and a fridge, a tiny bathroom and a small box-shaped bedroom. The walls were painted a uniform creamy yellow which gave the place a distinctly institutional feel. The furniture

was old but solid. Ruby had few homely or ornamental possessions, but a lot of clothes and records. The records lined one wall of the sitting-room and items of clothing, clumps of accessories and numerous pairs of boots and shoes had been tossed about with general disregard. The room was dusty.

Toro unscrewed the top of a vodka bottle and asked for some glasses. Ruby picked up a couple of dirty mugs and went to the sink to give them a wash. She couldn't find a clean tea-towel to dry them with so used a bathroom towel instead. Toro grimaced at them. 'The mouth of these mugs is too thick.'

'Not mouth, lip. You should know. You're the wine waiter.'

She banged the mugs on to the floor next to his feet and sat down again while he poured. He half-filled both mugs and then handed her one. She took a sip, pulled a face, but said nothing. Two hundred quid, she thought.

Toro was over fifty and poorly though smartly dressed in a grey suit and old shirt. He was small and slightly overweight, with dark black hair, greased back, and sallow cheeks. His eyes were hooded, red, but lively. She'd never seen him clean-shaven, but often smelled aftershave on him – a whiff of cinnamon and spearmint. He worked in a restaurant, but spent most of his time gambling.

Ruby told him about Vincent and he listened intently. She concluded, 'I've never even met him before, but now he expects me to fork out two hundred in bail money.'

'That Dawn's a bitch.'

Ruby wasn't receptive to this. She didn't want to feel implicated. Even so, she said, 'I've still got the money I won on the National. I've got at least two hundred left. I wanted to use it for something sensible, to invest it . . . I dunno.'

Toro bent over and screwed the top back on the bottle. 'You were lucky for me this morning. I bet on the two dogs you were with at Hackney. Won both times.'

He indicated the two bottles with a smile. Ruby smiled too; not at him, but to herself.

'They were Donald Sheldon's dogs,' she said. 'He came over and had a chat. He said he'd offer me a job full-time if he got the

chance. Took my number and everything. I told him I'd sooner be a trainer than a kennel-girl. Lots of women do it, you know.'

Toro chuckled. He said, 'A big dog in a place like this?'

She scowled. He offered her the bottle again. She gulped down her vodka in one go and passed him her cup. While he poured she visualized Donald Sheldon. Top trainer at Hackney, she thought, remembering how he'd put his hand on her arm as he'd spoken to her. Creepy. Sexy. Too old for me, and too flash.

Toro was watching her face. 'Don't pay that bail,' he said, misinterpreting her thoughtful expression.

'What?'

'He's taking you for a fool.'

She stood up and went into the kitchen, took a coffee jar out of the cupboard, opened it and removed a bundle of notes.

'Toro,' she said, suddenly feeling lively and quite purposeful.

'What?'

'You're full of bull.'

In the bathroom, she applied a thick coat of bright red lipstick, licked her teeth to ensure it hadn't smudged on them, stared into the mirror at her own simple, stupid face, and mouthed the word *moron*.

FOUR

Sam was peering through the kitchen window, trying to see if Steven was outside yet and what kind of car he drove. Brera was clearing the table. Sam said, 'He drives an old Jag. I wonder what that means.'

Brera piled a cup on to a plate, a cup on to a plate, a cup on to a plate. Spinal column, she thought, vertebra, disc, vertebra, disc. She carried them carefully over to the sink, slipped them into the soapy water and then peered out too. 'Your problem,' she said curtly, 'is that everything always has to mean something. I like him.'

'That's simple enough,' Sam said, wondering what Brera meant exactly.

Steven was debating whether it would be possible to get an old girlfriend of his to do some promotional shots of the Goldhawk Girls. (Bad name, he thought. That'll be the first thing to go.) She wasn't professional, but she was cheap.

As he drew closer to his car, he noticed that the side mirrors had been pulled off and that the aerial had been twisted into a heart shape. 'Curse the bastard,' he muttered. 'Curse the bastard that did this.' He grabbed the aerial and tried to straighten it.

Sylvia walked out of her room and into the kitchen. 'He makes me want to spew,' she announced.

Sam and Brera were doing the washing up. They both turned to look at her.

'He liked your songs,' Sam lied. 'You should've come in and said hello.'

Sylvia removed a strand of her hair from the confines of the

pony-tail she was wearing and twisted it around her finger. 'He hated the songs. I heard him.'

Brera pulled out a chair and sat down. 'He thought they were good but unusual.'

'Don't make me laugh.'

Brera crossed her arms and stared at Sylvia as she stood in the doorway. 'Grow up.'

'I'm nineteen. That's old enough.'

For what? She didn't look nineteen. She looked twelve. Like a scruffy, ill-adapted pre-teen.

'And by the way,' she added, 'I vandalized his car.'

Brera continued to stare at her. 'You appal me.'

Sam leaned on the window-sill and peered out again. Steven was still there, yanking at his aerial.

'It's only the aerial,' she said. 'Anyway, it's an old car.'

Sylvia glared at her. 'Who asked you?'

Brera threw herself forward on to the table and banged her forehead against it. *Thump*. She did it again. *Thump*.

Sylvia was furious. 'Stop it!'

Brera stopped and straightened up. 'Are you happy now?'

'Yes!' Sylvia shouted, and the shout turned instantly into a cough, into several coughs, whooping coughs.

She couldn't breathe. She clutched her stomach and leaned against the side of the door, bent double.

Good, she thought. Punishment for everybody.

She coughed carelessly, loosely, so that the unrestrained force of her hacking might rip up her throat and bring out blood. She visualized the cough as two tiny beings playing volleyball inside her throat, passing the tickle back and forth, catching it, returning it, blocking it, holding it. If only, she thought desperately, seeing their impassive faces through her streaming eyes, if only they could enjoy my illness as much as I do.

She turned, still coughing, and staggered back down the corridor.

'Go!' Brera shouted after her. 'I'm sick of the sight of you!'

Sam began washing up again. After a minute or so she said, 'I think she feels left out.'

Brera rubbed her eyes. 'She's such a little bitch. She never does anything for herself and she resents everything we do.'

Sam ran a finger across the bubbles in the sink, watched them burst on her skin. 'She's bound to feel threatened by Steven. She might feel like she's losing us. Losing something.'

Brera's lips tightened. 'To hell with what she thinks.'

Sam glanced towards the open door and then walked over to shut it. As she turned back she said, 'Perhaps we should've explained about her to Steven. I'm sure he would've understood, and if he hadn't, then we wouldn't have wanted anything to do with him anyway.'

'You think I'm ashamed of her?'

Brera's eyes filled. Sam found the sight of her mother's imminent tears disagreeable and unsettling. I shouldn't feel that way though, she decided, and tried not to. She pulled off a piece of kitchen roll and handed it to her. Brera blew her nose and then looked up. Her eyes were bloodshot.

'I'm frightened, that's all. I want to protect her.' Her eyes exuded tears: large, fat tears like transparent slugs, slithering down her face. 'She's such a little shit.'

Sam watched the tears. If I taste one, she thought, then everything will be all right. She put out her hand and brushed a tear from Brera's chin on to her finger, then let it fall from her finger on to the end of her tongue.

'She'll be fine,' she said.

FIVE

Vincent had been staring at his hands with unswerving concentration for almost five hours. During this time there had been no perceptible change in their appearance.

After his initial statement to the two police officers – 'I fell over. I banged my head' – a short period of speculation about bail payments and a perfunctory medical check, he had refused to involve himself in any further interaction. This hadn't really worked to his advantage, but he hadn't honestly expected it to.

Within the previous couple of weeks he had been detained on two occasions and charged on one of these for breach of the peace. He was hardly a novice in the cells, and, as such, no one paid him much attention.

While he stared at his hands his mind ran over a variety of subjects. *Larson. Arson. Willie Carson.* Occasionally he slumped into an unthinking daze, but when he came to and refocused on his dirty nails, fingers and the pale hair on the back of his knuckles, his mind raced on with as much enthusiasm as if it had never paused. *Blood in my nostrils, dried blood, like paint.*

He often lost all track of time. His life was a strange mixture of time-using (demonstration) and time-wasting (remonstration).

He has many opinions, his own opinions, and he has many faults. The chief one is intolerance. He sees himself as an anarchic bob-a-job man – doing favours, splitting hairs, trading down. Always down. He is unusual in that his intolerance and his pureness of vision haven't made him into boot-boy, a Tory or a fascist. He is the opposite of these things; is ceaselessly, peacelessly contrary.

My life. What fucking life? No life. Low life.

He has a terror of involvement, of commitment – to places, to

things. He won't be held culpable or responsible, will only represent one view: his own view. He thinks the world, everything, is stupid.

Stupid!

During the course of his twenty-nine years, he has never seen any purpose in dedicating himself to traditionally worthy or helpful occupations. He refuses to give over his considerable powers to anything specifically useful. His prime, twin attributes of determination and energy have never been expressed constructively. If they are – and of course he thinks that they are – he has a definition of 'constructive' which is all his own.

He survives on a diet of grand gestures, obnoxiousness and guile.

Only one thing blots his anarchic copy-book. It is a simple thing. He is full of love. So full of love – indiscriminate, luminous, pulsating, unremitting – that it threatens to make him weak, to make him burst, to make him give in, completely. To what, though? He doesn't know.

The strange thing about love, Vincent decided, studying the white flecks on the pink moons of his nails, is that it starts off as one thing, and comes out as something altogether different.

His arresting officer pushed open the cell door and walked in. 'Your bail's been settled.'

I love this man, Vincent thought, but it'll come out some other way.

He looked up from his hands. 'Fucking bail. What a joke.'

'Yeah, very funny.'

He stood up. 'Can I go?'

'Sign a couple of papers and you're a free man, for the time being, anyway. So long as you don't behave like a lunatic again before your court case.'

Vincent smiled. 'Well, that's hardly too much to ask for, is it now?'

When he caught sight of Ruby she was leaning against the reception desk reading a pamphlet about the police cadets. She looked up as the door swung back and slammed behind him. He thought, My God, she's a push-over. The best kind of girl.

He pulled on his canvas jacket and said, 'You can get me something to eat if you like.'

Ruby picked up the pamphlet and stuffed it into her pocket. 'I don't think so.'

His eyes, she noticed, were like two blue marbles. He adjusted the collar on his jacket, grinned at her and strolled outside. Ruby nodded to the constable behind the reception desk and followed him.

She stepped into the afternoon sunlight and saw him disappearing into a burger bar over the road. She crossed cautiously and followed him in. He beckoned to her from the counter. 'How about buying me a burger and a drink?'

'Why should I?'

'Because you're loaded.'

She scowled at him. 'How did you work that one out?'

'I want a burger, a Coke and some chips.'

The counter girl flinched at the mention of the word 'chip' and then looked to Ruby for her order. Ruby sighed. 'I'll have a medium coffee please, with cream.'

Vincent sauntered off and took possession of a plastic table next to the window. Ruby paid, and while she waited for the order, counted the remaining small coins in her purse. Vincent was sitting at the table and running his fingers over the cut on his hairline. The cut stretched across a bluish lump and glimmered like a red mouth. Ruby supposed that he must have been given a stitch, although it didn't look like it from where she was standing.

Her order arrived. She picked up her tray and made her way to the table. Vincent looked up at her. 'I haven't eaten all day.'

She sat down, removed her coffee and then pushed the tray towards him. She felt light-headed.

'Your hands aren't very clean. I don't think you should touch that cut. It might get infected.'

He shrugged. 'I've had worse. It's given me one hell of a headache, though. I could do with a proper drink.'

'Maybe you're concussed. What did the doctor say?'

'I don't know. Some crap. I might get gangrene of the brain.'

He was joking. Ruby gently removed the lid from her polystyrene cup. You've already got it, mate, she thought.

He noticed the tattoo on her hand. 'What's that? A name? A bird?'

'A swallow. I did it when I was seventeen.'

He wiped some ketchup from the side of his mouth with the back of his hand. 'Let's see.'

She opened her palm and showed him.

'You did it yourself?'

She nodded. 'Pen and a pin.'

'Ouch.'

She sipped her coffee. 'What did you tell the police?'

'I told them I tripped.'

'Did they believe you?'

'No.'

'Was your friend all right? The epileptic.'

'I only met him once before.'

'What do you mean?'

'He wasn't my friend.'

Ruby tried to understand this, but had trouble doing so.

'Was he an epileptic?'

'Might be. He didn't say he wasn't.'

'He was unconscious.'

'Exactly.'

She said, 'You're not from London, are you?'

'Why?'

'You don't sound like you are.'

'Nope.'

'Where are you staying?'

He thought for a while. 'Wembley.'

'Really?'

'On someone's floor. Before that I was in Amsterdam. Squatting.'

She visualized him, squatting, in a field full of tulips. A windmill.

He was eating his fries and his fingers were greasy. He said, 'In case you're wondering, I'm not naturally a violent person.'

She smiled at this. She could see no reason to deny being violent unless you actually were violent. He noticed her smile and was indignant. 'Give me some credit.'

'Two hundred quid,' she answered, 'that should do you.'

He continued to eat in silence. Eventually she said, 'Will I get it back?'

He thought about this for a while. 'You shouldn't have paid it.'

'I thought I'd get it back.'

He offered her one of his fries and she shook her head.

'What were you planning to do with it?'

She shrugged. 'I dunno. Save it.'

He squinted at her. 'Well, saving it isn't doing anything.'

'I was going to do something.'

'What?'

She tried to think. 'Something. An investment. I don't want to discuss it.'

'Why not?'

'It's private.'

'You could give it to charity.'

'Haven't I already?'

He gulped down his Coke and then licked his teeth. 'It's kind of like . . .' he said thoughtfully, 'I'm your investment.'

He was pleased by this. He couldn't imagine a worse investment. And I'm me, he thought. Fuck only knows how she feels about it. He chuckled to himself.

She drank some more of her coffee. With her free hand she felt underneath the table, touched something soft, instinctively stuck her nail into it and then realized that it was chewing gum. She quickly withdrew her hand. The table was a startlingly bright yellow. All along its edge were melt marks, brown stains from cigarettes.

'I was going to invest it properly,' she said, after a pause, 'in a small business.'

'Two hundred,' he said. 'That'll get you a long way.'

'I was intending to.'

'I bet you were.'

She glared at him. She dealt with men like him every day at

work. One day, she knew for sure, she would do something constructive and she wouldn't have to deal with men like him any more.

She turned and looked out of the window, into the street. She saw pigeons, people, grey buildings. This city, everything in it, including me, is a big lump of grey muck, she thought.

'I've got a headache now,' he said. 'Do you live near here?'

'Why?' She stared at him again.

'I only wondered.'

'Why?'

'I just need to put my head down for half an hour.'

She started to laugh. I'm pissed, she thought. I'd rather die than invite him home.

Eventually she said, 'You think I'm a bloody push-over.'

'You are.'

She was.

Sylvia's room always seemed dark, although it had no curtains and the windows were usually open. The walls, which had once been white, were now a shabby grey. Bits of wallpaper hung in strips where the birds had ripped at it to secure lining for their nests.

No attempt had been made to clear up the splatterings of dirt left by the birds on the floor, or at the bases of the thirty or so perches which had been erected on three of the four walls. Here it had formed into small, pointed, pyramidic piles.

The perches varied in size and were nailed to the wall in a series of regimented lines. They were fixed at four heights, some ten or so inches from the floor, others only inches from the ceiling. They encroached on the room, making it seem much closer and smaller than it actually was. About a quarter of the perches had been enlarged and built into perfunctory nesting boxes, although the birds rarely hatched their eggs or brought up their young within the room's perimeter.

Pushed up against the only clear wall was Sylvia's bed. The duvet was a dark green colour, stained intermittently by whitish bird droppings. There was little else in the room except for a

large, grey trunk at the foot of her bed in which she kept all her clothes and the few other personal possessions that she valued.

The room was rarely quiet. The air was constantly full of the sound of vibrating wings, of bird argument and intrigue, and underneath each sound, humming at the very bottom, the purring, cooing, singing of the pigeons.

Wild birds are not naturally aromatic creatures, but the consequence of a large number of them inhabiting an enclosed space was that the room smelled something like a chicken coop. It was a strong and all-pervasive smell which was gradually taking over the top few floors of the block. During fine weather – in the heat – the smell expanded and could be detected over an even wider area.

Sylvia was oblivious to the smell. Since she rarely ventured out of the flat, it never struck her as out of the ordinary. Sometimes she noticed it when she travelled back indoors from her dawn vantage point on the roof, but even then it smelled like something good and reliable, a heavy, dusty, musty familiarity.

She knew that the dirt, the smell and the feathers were bad for her. Often she tasted this in her mouth after she had coughed. When she suffered from an asthma attack she would use her inhaler and hide under her duvet, somehow believing that the air under here was cleaner, free of the cloying thickness.

During the long, solitary periods spent in her room, Sylvia usually sat on the trunk at the foot of her bed with her legs drawn up and her chin resting on her knees.

She did very little, but was skinny. Her face was not thin, though. It was round and her cheeks were pouched and protuberant. Her father was a Cypriot. She had never met him, never mentioned him. Her mouth and nose were heavy and her lids and lips were thick and rich. Her eyes were a bright deep green: ironic cat's eyes.

Most people – apart from those who were expert in such matters – presumed her to be retarded. Yet it always grew increasingly difficult (with familiarity) to pinpoint exactly how this was. She was numerate, literate, articulate. Only her will was retarded. She couldn't quite do anything. She couldn't quite

want anything. She had no real desire, except to be left alone. She didn't even really want the birds that much, but she perceived them as though they existed in a different realm of being, a realm of necessity, of inevitability.

Earlier on, Brera had supposed that external stimuli might renew Sylvia's vigour, her will. She had tried psychotherapy, counselling, family therapy. But nothing had worked. Nothing encroached. She remained aloof.

Sometimes Sylvia sat in her room and with a great deal of effort tried to summarize her life, to get her head around its totality. Whenever she did this, she could think only of nothing. Of a vacuum. The enormity of this vacuum terrified her. So instead she fixed things in terms of the birds, in a feathery cycle of birth, youth, age, death. This meant that after a time she couldn't actually do without them. They were her.

Straight after the argument she had regretted it. Steven John didn't really matter, she knew that. He didn't threaten her. He couldn't change things.

She sat on her trunk, pressed her chin into her knees and thought, I want them to leave me. I want things to be quieter and simpler. If they deserted me, if they grew tired of me, I could sit here for ever. I wouldn't have to try any more and that would be good. I think that would be good.

She knew it.

SIX

Because he had forced himself to await a precise time before calling on her, Steven felt almost as though a previous arrangement had been made for this meeting. He felt confident. He waited for her to say something as he stuck his thumb into his belt and grinned.

Ruby squinted out at Steven through the half-light, her expression a mixture of impatience and exhaustion. 'Oh God.'

His expression sank from cheerful to jowlful. 'I'm pleased to see you too,' he said.

He watched as she pushed her hand through her hair. He thought, She's still wearing too much make-up and her skirt is too tight. Paradoxically, these familiar flaws made him feel inexplicably fond.

'Can I come in?'

'Um.' She thought about this for a moment. 'Why don't we go out for a drink? I can run up and fetch my coat.'

'And put some shoes on.' He pointed to her stockinged feet.

'Yeah.' She turned. 'Wait here.'

He ignored this and followed her, up the stairs and into her flat.

Her jacket was slung over the arm of a chair. She grabbed it and frantically looked around for her shoes. He stood in the doorway and appraised the room, wondering what it could be that she was so keen to conceal. Someone was in the bathroom. He could hear a tap running. She pulled on a pair of boots. 'That's Toro,' she said, 'washing his face.'

'Why?'

'He's drunk. He won on a couple of races this morning.'

Steven stared at the bathroom door, waiting for it to open.

She checked in her pocket for her keys. 'Right, let's go.'

'Don't you want to tell him?'

'What?'

'That you're going out.'

She stood in front of him, awkwardly, her eyes unblinking, hiding something. 'No.'

He looked not at her but over her shoulder.

'How about that person on the floor?'

'Who?'

She turned. 'Oh. Him. He's fine.'

Vincent lay on his back, spread-eagled across the carpet, his head hidden from view behind the sofa.

'Is he sleeping or what?'

She sighed. 'It's not a problem.'

Before he could respond to this she said, 'How do you manage to always make me feel so bloody guilty?'

He shrugged. He just had that knack. They both knew the reason. He disapproved of her. He liked her, but he thought her capable of behaving, at times, stupidly and carelessly. She allowed her life to become sordid. He found this hateful.

He walked over to where Vincent lay. 'Who is he? Do I know him?'

'No.'

'Is he all right?'

'I think so. He passed out.'

'When?'

'Five minutes ago.'

'His head's disgusting.'

'He did it this morning.'

'He must be concussed. Has he been drinking?'

She smiled, unhappy. 'He got shit-faced with Toro. One minute he was chatting away, the next, pop! Flat out.'

'Is he breathing?'

Ruby stepped across Vincent's prone body and lifted one of his eyelids to reveal the white of his eye. 'He's out cold.'

She stood up again.

'You aren't just going to leave him there?'

'Yes, I am.'

Some things she'd always disliked about Steven. He liked order and he didn't often do dirty or grubby things. She believed that he thought them, but he wouldn't do them, wouldn't let them happen. So he disapproved of her for letting them happen. And I do, she thought, I really do.

Toro staggered out of the bathroom, barely acknowledging them both, stumbled into the living-room and sat down on the sofa.

'I'll meet you in the pub,' Steven said, his tone measured. 'The Blue Posts.'

'Right. Give me five minutes.'

There's a line, he thought, heading down the stairs, a fine line between being soft and being stupid. She can't see it.

It was a moral flaw. He believed this. But morality didn't interest him, only manners.

Ruby wandered into her bedroom to find a blanket. After a short, fruitless search she pulled one from her bed and carried it into the sitting-room. She wondered whether it was preferable to let Toro stay or to make him go home, but by the time she'd returned with the blanket that decision had already been made. Toro was stretched out on the sofa, covered in his coat, fast asleep and snoring.

She looked down at her wrist-watch. It was only eight-thirty. She made her way over to where Vincent lay and covered him with the blanket. She touched his hand, which felt stiff and cold, so she knelt down next to his head and put her ear close to his mouth. His breath touched her ear and tickled it.

She turned her head to stare at him. His face was tense, even in sleep. He was frowning. She inspected the skin on his cheeks very closely: the pores, the paleness and the small, reddish bristles of his beard. Her eyes were drawn to the bump on his forehead which now appeared much angrier and tighter than before, and the cut, much purpler. A few of the hairs in his fringe had bent down into the mouth of the cut. She repressed the desire to move them, to pull them out, in case this should wake him.

She moved back a fraction, still staring. He looked gruff but intelligent. He seemed troubled. She thought, I wonder what he

does? She had a suspicion that he didn't do anything.

She frowned and then pulled the blanket up and tucked it around his chin.

Steven had already bought her a drink.

'Thanks.'

She took it from him and sipped it. She had known him for six months. He was her oldest friend in London. He'd lived in London all his life. He was an expert at it. She'd arrived six months previously from Sheffield. They'd met at night-school on a photography course.

'Would you do me some photos?' he said.

She grimaced.

They'd bought a camera together, during their single month of intimacy. She'd kept it. He liked borrowing it. Borrowing her. Will he ask about Vincent? she wondered. Will he moan about Toro? Steven knew Toro of old and hated him. Not so much hates, she decided, just doesn't have the time.

'If we arrange it for Tuesday,' he said, 'that'd be good. Four, half-four.'

The ceiling, she noted, was stained beige with smoke. In centuries to come, she thought, scientists will find this ceiling and they'll have the equipment to analyse the smoke, to tell something about the lives of every single person that ever exhaled in this pub.

Ruby. Unnatural blonde. Never wore matching underwear. A push-over.

'Hang on,' he said, 'make it five, to be on the safe side.'

Steven. Big hands. Nice face. Small ears. Gives Ruby a hard time.

Steven wrote down the address. 'They're called Sam and Brera. Brera's Irish. You'll like them.'

He handed her the slip of paper. 'Don't lose it.'

She frowned at him.

'Yeah, well, I know how you are.'

She recognized several people in the pub. Punters. Where do they get their money from? she wondered. Not from me. Losing's the whole point of a gamble.

'Be professional,' he said, slightly embarrassed to be asking. 'Take the tripod and everything. Also, this might sound stupid, but, well, try and ignore the smell.'

She tried to remember the last time she'd had a bath. Last night? Yesterday morning?

'Did Toro go?'

She shook her head. Here it comes, here it comes. I'm stupid, I'm useless.

As he spoke she wove a fantasy out of different parts of the pub's decor: the colour of the liquor in the bottles, the texture of the barman's starched, white shirt. In this fantasy, she was very rich, she did what she liked. No one told her what to do.

SEVEN

Vincent opened his eyes. Black. He turned his head to try to look around him. It was then that he realized that he had no head. He didn't attempt to confirm or deny this possibility by touching his face. He said, 'If I have no head, how can I touch my face?' and then, 'God, my voice sounds strange. Where's it coming from? My armpit? My arse?' Wouldn't be the first time, he thought.

After a moment's consideration he said, 'Why am I talking out loud? Maybe I'm not talking at all. Maybe all this darkness is only inside me. Fuck.'

He staggered to his feet and banged his leg against the stereo. It rattled. The room wasn't completely dark, but even so, he still had some trouble locating objects and moving without collision.

He veered away from the stereo and smacked into the back of the chair. He paused and stared fixedly in front of him, making out the blurred shape of the sofa and a lump on it which seemed like a sleeping figure. Slowly he recalled Toro, although he had forgotten his name. Shortly after he remembered that he was in Ruby's flat. I did it! he thought. That was a result.

He made his way towards the left-hand side of the sofa, moved around it and located the small kitchen work surface with his right hand. He felt blindly for the sink, turned on the tap, then fixed his lips to the bright, white stream of water that poured from it. He drank for a few seconds and felt the water rush through his mouth and throat to his stomach and then through his temples where it banged and pounded.

His head rematerialized. It began to hurt. He touched it and it felt hot. His hand discovered the lump on his hairline and it surprised him. He touched the lump again, very gently, then muttered, 'How come I saw the water when I couldn't see hardly anything else? I must be able to see everything.'

He looked around him again and immediately the room was quite clear.

He decided to go and study his lump more closely in the bathroom, although he couldn't remember exactly where it was. He didn't relish the prospect of stumbling into Ruby's bedroom.

Luckily both doors were ajar. Vincent couldn't resist the temptation to peer around the door into Ruby's room, and when he did was surprised to see that it was empty.

Suddenly he felt an intense urge to urinate. He grabbed at the buttons on his trousers and rushed to the toilet. He produced very little liquid and felt vaguely dissatisfied, but before he was able to locate this dissatisfaction, a blast of nausea hit his throat and threw him forward, towards the toilet bowl. In a matter of seconds he had reproduced mashed burger, sloshy fries, a substance not unlike popcorn – my spleen, he thought – and a mouthful of phlegm.

He was shaking. He was desperate. He crawled into Ruby's room and climbed on to her bed. The blankets were in a state of disarray. He forgot to remove his shoes.

Brera ate a yoghurt in front of the television and worried about Sylvia. She had gone out a few hours earlier and had not yet returned.

It was eight-thirty. Brera rarely went out on a Saturday night. She had rarely gone out any night before the Goldhawk Girls. Sam, however, was excessively sociable.

When Sam was away, Sylvia and Brera would sit in front of the television and watch whatever was on in companionable silence. Sylvia didn't actually watch. She always kept her eyes closed. Brera supposed that this was because she had no interest in television, but the truth was that Sylvia had become too sensitive. She could either listen or watch, but she couldn't manage both. She couldn't cope with the noise of television – the conflict of voices, music, slogans – while taking in its speedy visual menu of flashing colours, signs and faces. It overwhelmed her, but she realized that she and Brera had little else in common except the television – sitting in front of it, together.

Brera picked a raspberry pip from between her teeth. She knew that Sylvia's trip out was a form of protest, but she didn't want to consider Sylvia's motivation too fully, couldn't risk feeling implicated.

Instead of wondering why she'd gone, she wondered where she'd gone. This seemed an altogether simpler proposition.

The act of walking with purpose and the elimination of her usual close environment made Sylvia's inhalation easier and reduced her coughing. She was in the process of considering this fact when, just after six-thirty, she made her way briskly down to the canal. She intended to follow it to Victoria Park. She fancied seeing the ducks.

On Saturday evenings the canal was usually chock-a-block with fishermen. Each sat in a solitary daze, focusing only on the water. Each resented the presence of others, resented the casual purposelessness of the average stroller.

Sylvia kept her head down on her way to the canal, through the complex assortment of streets that led from the flat to the water's edge. But it was dusk, a quiet time. Most people were at home by now. Most birds were thinking about roosting.

She reached the canal in good time, but before following its curvaceous route to the park, she paused on its brink and stared at herself in the black, polluted water. Her face shimmered as a tiny fish swam under the surface and breathed a bubble of oxygen to the top.

The canal was silent and eerie. For the first time since leaving the flat she felt fully a sense of the hugeness of her environment. She envied the birds their more acute understanding of space, their capacity to fill it and use it.

She turned and began to walk. Her eyes watched her own feet, the beginning of each step and its completion. The pathway was covered in a golden gravel substance which threw up a light dust in front of her and behind her. The old sandals she wore gave it access and she felt it settle between her toes.

The rhythm of walking calmed her. It made her mind empty itself of all things except the single task of consuming distance.

The birds were rarely a problem when she walked at this time of day. Had it been earlier, they might have flocked, massed and pestered her, but in the late afternoon they were dozy and dazy. Just the same, she thought it best to move rapidly, quietly and to stare at her feet.

When she had covered a good three-quarters of the route, her concentration was interrupted by a small group of boys who were hunched in a bundle by the edge of the river. One of them was passing a fishing net to and fro in the water. As she walked by, the boy with the net looked up and stared at her. He was a mean-faced child of eight or ten – thin, petulant and aggressive. Sylvia sensed him watching her. She walked until she was directly adjacent to him and then caught his eye. This was foolish. He grinned and said, 'You've got a face like a pig. You look like a monkey. You're stupid.'

She continued walking, her eyes returning to the ground. She sensed the other boys staring at her too, their eyes making the skin on her back crawl. One of them (larger than the others) said, 'She's from a funny farm. She's an old woman. She's got no tits.'

The other boys laughed in unison and then pored over the net to see if anything was caught in its mesh.

Sylvia flinched but did not falter. She walked on determinedly, reached the park and entered it through its grand wrought-iron gates. The benches in the park had been painted an ostentatious blue and gold. She sat down on one which was close to the lake. Everything felt too big. She stared at the lake through a tangle of hair that had formed into a long fringe over the top half of her face.

A tiny finch fluttered down from a nearby tree, landing on the back of the bench, only a few inches from her. Sylvia noticed the bird, but did not move her head or body towards it, only her eyes. They stared at one another and then Sylvia's eyes returned to the lake, which looked still and grey-green. Its surface was dotted with pieces of white fleecy down – feathery remnants. She wondered absent-mindedly whether the geese had been fighting or moulting.

The finch pecked at her T-shirt, trying to procure himself a

strand of fabric. Sylvia offered him her index finger. He jumped on to it. She felt the tiny weight of him and watched the breeze ruffle the millionfold feathers on his chest. His feet were scratchy and dry. They itched the eczema on her hands. She moved him closer to her face and whispered, 'Hello Dry-foot. Hello Dry-foot.'

The bird blinked, cocked his head and then reached up and grabbed hold of a single strand of her hair. He jerked it from her scalp. Sylvia laughed, and the sound of her voice propelled him skyward.

The park was quiet. Fifteen yards to her left she noticed a young girl and a woman standing by the lake's edge. The girl was eating a sandwich. She looked about five years old. The woman, who Sylvia presumed to be the child's mother, bent down to talk to her and then walked away. Sylvia decided that she must be going to the seafood stall on the park's perimeter. She frowned and thought, That girl looks too young to be left alone. Everything's big. There are so many possibilities. None of them good.

Her attention was distracted by a tatty flotilla of Canada geese who were gradually making their way towards the edge of the lake. She stood up, pushed some hair behind her ears and strolled over to them. They crowded around the bank as Sylvia squatted down and smiled at them. A couple of them honked their admiration. She reached out a slow hand and rubbed the edges of the closest bird's beak. This was a form of caress that most birds usually understood.

As she petted the geese Sylvia noticed that the girl was moving towards her. She was small and skinny with wide blue eyes and yellow curls. She sidled up to Sylvia with her sandwich in one hand and a fold of her skirt in the other, which she pulled and twisted with tiny fingers.

Some of the geese turned their heads to stare at her. One or two backed away, but a couple of them noticed the bread in her hand. Sylvia saw the bread too. She stood up and looked down at the child. On her sandwich was a mixture of cheese and luncheon meat. She said, 'Birds like cheese. It's full of fat which is good for them.'

The girl gazed at Sylvia and gave a small laugh. She seemed too young to make conversation so Sylvia stood in silence for a few seconds and stared at the geese and the water. The girl let go of her skirt and tossed a piece of cheese from her sandwich on to the ground by her feet. It landed at least half a metre from the edge of the lake. One of the geese stretched out its neck to try to reach the cheese, but it was too far away. Sylvia frowned. 'If you're going to feed them, then place the cheese closer. They won't bite.'

The girl looked up. Her face seemed very tiny to Sylvia, and yet everything about it was adult, especially its expression, which was puffy and petulant. Even so, it was a child's face. She looked straight into Sylvia's eyes and said, 'Why should I?'

Sylvia paused and contemplated this question. 'Because you have to treat other animals with respect. If you don't, then they won't respect you.'

The girl moved forward slightly and pushed the cheese closer to the edge of the lake with her toe. As she did this, the pressure from her shoe covered the cheese with sand and dirt. Nevertheless, the goose reached for it again, stretching its neck thinly across the bank and opening its beak to try to grasp the cheese. But before it could do so, the little girl had lifted up one of her feet and had kicked at the gravel and dirt in front of her, blinding the goose with a spray of soil and stones.

It only took an instant. Before she knew what she was doing, Sylvia had grabbed hold of the girl and had thrown her, arms waving, legs kicking, into the lake. When it was done, she thought, Maybe she can't swim. What if the lake is deeper than it seems?

But it was too late. She was running.

She didn't turn back to look at the lake or the geese or the girl. She thought she heard screaming, but by then she was right by the park gates and on her way home. Not a scream, she decided, panting already, struggling to breathe. Not a scream, but the call of a crow.

EIGHT

Ruby unlocked the door and automatically reached out her hand for the light switch. She stopped herself just in time, feeling the switch with the tip of her finger but applying no pressure. Instead she paused in the doorway for a moment in order to adjust her eyesight to the room's darkness. After a few seconds she could make out the shape of a figure on the couch – Toro, still snoring – and she could also see, if she stood on tip-toe, beyond the sofa, where Vincent's blanket was bundled up into a deceptively large pile.

Very gently she closed the door behind her. She fancied a cup of coffee but didn't want to wake her guests, so she settled for a glass of water and then padded quietly into the bathroom.

It smelled. She closed the door and switched on the light. She was positive that the smell was of vomit, but could see no sign of it. She inspected the toilet bowl, which looked clean, but squirted some bleach down there for good measure.

After completing her ablutions, she switched off the bathroom light and made her way blindly into her bedroom. Before she closed the door she felt under the handle on both sides for the keyholes, located the key on the other side, took it out, pushed it in on her side, pulled the door to and locked it.

The small window in her bedroom let in just enough light. She pulled off her clothes and hunted around on the floor for something suitable to wear. Eventually she found a large T-shirt which she put on and pulled down.

She climbed into bed. Her blankets were rucked up and jumbled. She put out a hand to pull one over and then gasped as she touched something warm and bristly.

There lay Vincent in a state of irritable semi-wakefulness. He opened one eye and stared at her. 'Get your hands off my neck.'

She sprang out of bed. 'Christ! I locked myself in here and you're in here already.'

He pulled himself up on to his elbows, thought about saying something, opened his mouth to say it, but no words came out, only liquid.

Ruby was almost sick herself, but not in sympathy, not exactly.

'Get out of my bloody bed! You could be anybody!'

'I am anybody.'

He rolled over, stood up and staggered towards the door clutching his stomach. He pulled at the door handle with his free hand but it wouldn't open, so he threw up against it, then fell to his knees and inspected his handiwork.

'That's my kidney, liquidized.'

Ruby snatched a cardigan from the floor and wrapped it around her.

He groaned, 'You really think I intend taking advantage of you when I'm crippled by some kind of chronic gastric disorder?'

She pushed past him and switched on the light. They both blinked. Ruby's eyes adjusted. Vincent's wouldn't focus. He removed a hand from his gut long enough to touch his forehead and then clutched his stomach again, leaning forward. Ruby, fearing more mess, looked around for something he could vomit into, but didn't have a rubbish bin in the room or anything like a bowl or bag. Instead she grabbed hold of an old broken guitar without strings that was leaning against the wall. She thrust it towards him. 'Don't you dare be sick on the floor again.'

Vincent stared at the guitar. 'If you're expecting me to vomit into a musical instrument, I'd prefer a trumpet.'

He leaned even further forward and put a hand across his mouth, speaking through his fingers, 'Just open the door.'

She dumped the guitar, turned the key in the lock and pulled the door wide. He crawled through, and, after a moment's hesitation, dragged himself into the bathroom. Ruby glanced over at her bed and saw that his vomit was a particularly strange colour: a harsh taramasalata pink.

When Vincent crawled back out of the bathroom a short while later, he paused in the doorway and watched as Ruby stuffed all

affected linen into a refuse bag. She scowled at him. 'This pink stuff is like something you'd serve with crackers.'

She went and found a cloth in the kitchen and began to scrub at the door and the carpet. Vincent made no attempt to help her or to arrange himself comfortably. Instead he lay in a clumsy heap next to the wall.

She walked over to inspect him. He looked pale and sweaty. She prodded him with her toe.

'Are you asleep? The floor's rock hard.'

She touched his hand. It was wet.

She went into the living-room and leaned over the back of the sofa. 'Toro? Wake up.'

He grunted. 'You think I could sleep through that?'

She kicked at the back of the sofa. 'You got him pissed in the first place. Come and give me a hand.'

He sat up, rubbed his eyes. 'It smells like a hospital.'

She picked up the blanket from the floor and moved back towards the bedroom. 'Dettol. I cleaned everything.'

He followed her, lounged in the doorway and stared down at Vincent. 'Leave him. He's OK.'

She remade her bed. 'Lift him up. I've half a mind to call a doctor.'

Toro bent over and grabbed hold of Vincent's shoulders, then dragged him towards the bed, rucking up the carpet. They lifted him together and dumped him down on the blankets. He emitted a loud groan as his head hit the pillow. She arranged a couple of sheets over him, then perched on the edge of the bed and felt his forehead. Soaking. His lips were dry though. She peered up at Toro who was standing, looking bleary, feeling his own forehead.

'What's your game?' she said.

'What's the time?'

'Eleven-ish.' She looked down at Vincent. 'He couldn't throw up while he was asleep could he, and choke on it?'

Toro shrugged and went to find his coat. She heard the kitchen tap running, and then, a few seconds later, the front door closing. She looked down at Vincent. 'Fancy joining him?'

The room seemed very bright. She stood up, strolled into the living-room to check that the latch was down on the front door, then returned to the bedroom and switched off the light. The darkness soothed her eyes. She sat next to Vincent on the edge of her bed and stared at him. His eyes were flitting around under his eyelids. She said quietly, 'Are you dreaming? Do you want some tea? An ambulance?'

She yawned and looked over towards the window, bringing her legs up on to the bed and leaning her back against the headboard. The streets were still lively. Outside she could hear people talking and laughing. Inside everything was silent. She pulled one of the blankets over slightly so that it covered the top of her knees and thought, Isn't it strange how a place can be both noisy and quiet at the same time?

NINE

Samantha stayed out all Saturday night and returned to the flat shortly after midday on Sunday. The intervening time had been spent with her latest flame, Connor, who was tall, with a curtain of long brown hair that swung across his face, a slim body and smooth skin. They had known each other for several weeks. They had met at a charity benefit in Kentish Town. Connor had been performing with the main band, his own band, Stirsign. He was a drummer, and he sang too, in a scrappy, scraping, tuneless voice.

Sam had laughed at him from the side of the stage. She thought he looked ridiculous, smashing away at his drum-kit, bare-chested, his hair a mess, flying everywhere, his neck craning upwards towards an artfully placed microphone.

He spotted her immediately. She was the only girl there who found him funny. Girls didn't usually. When he'd introduced himself, later on, she'd said that she'd never come across a drummer who also sang. Connor had then proceeded to list every singing drummer he could think of. The way he saw it, the longer the list was, the longer she'd stay and talk.

'I just remembered, the drummer with Teenage Fanclub sings sometimes, and there was a band called Blyth Power a while ago whose drummer was the main vocalist, like me.'

Sam had smiled up at him, taking in every visible detail of his face through the silk-screen of her lashes. His voice was sexy, she decided, vaguely American, his tongue embracing a kind of cultured Southern twang. She appreciated the fact that he was self-assured. Confident men were the only kind she ever bothered with. Less brash, less aggressive men took one look and ran a mile.

She had been a late developer in the game of love. It was a game. Love was a diversion, but not an interest.

Men had never been at a premium in the Hackney flat. Her father, a Somalian student, a law student, had left home when she was three. In the long term she'd decided that this was a good thing. She had no silly expectations or preconceptions. She was beyond all that. Men couldn't disappoint her and they couldn't rule her.

Initially she had been too shy to push herself forward, preferring instead to think about things, to theorize and rationalize. But eventually she had learned to assert, if not herself, then a good approximation of herself – she always saved something, kept something back, which was the secret with men – and had learned how to flatter and to flirt. Love could be fun. You could get something out of it: sex or attention or ideas.

Connor had stared down at Sam's lips as he spoke to her, focusing on these instead of her eyes. 'What do you do? I don't want to bore you to death with talk of singing drummers all night.'

Sam smiled. 'I'm a singer too. A different kind of singer.'

An exotic singer, he thought, her hair drawn back, scraped back like a seal's. 'How different?'

'I sing in a band with my mother. We played the Bull and Gate last week.'

He grinned when she mentioned the venue, then said, 'I've never met anyone who played in a band with their mother before.'

'You have now.'

He asked her what kind of music they played but she didn't answer.

'It's more than that,' she said, finishing her drink. 'It's more complicated.'

'How?'

He liked her. But he only wanted small talk. That was his way. That was the whole point of flirting. He had a suspicion, though, that she was the kind of girl who didn't need to flirt.

She cleared her throat. 'Language is symbolic.' He flinched. She didn't notice. 'In other words, language represents things. And the way I see it, sexual representations work in the same way. I'll give you an example . . .'

He was watching her lips, not her eyes, watching how her teeth appeared and disappeared. Her teeth, the white crest of her mouth's pink wave. Rolling and rolling.

'Father and son. If I say that, it has positive associations. Hierarchy, order, calm, a kind of quiet power . . .'

He didn't care what she said. She was exquisite. He would agree and agree.

'But mother and daughter. I can say it, over and over, but it doesn't work as a symbol. It has no power.' She looked up at him. 'Are you following me?'

He nodded.

'Freud said daughters hate their mothers because all a daughter really wants is to have sex with her father. Mothers get in the way.'

Connor laughed. 'He really thought that?'

She nodded. 'But I'm not very interested in why symbols work the way they do, only in subverting them. I want to change them. I mean, there's such power between women. Mother and daughter. It should mean something. It does mean something, it just doesn't work at a symbolic level. And that's what I want to do, with the band. To help to create a new, positive, popular stereotype.'

As she spoke she saw Connor's face sag. She thought, I've blown my chances. He thinks I'm boring or strident or both.

When her lips stopped moving, Connor pushed his hair out of his eyes and asked, 'What does your mother think about all this?'

Sam grinned. 'She likes singing. She's always played the guitar. In fact she was in a girl group herself as a kid. She came over here from Dublin as a teenager in a band.'

He smiled at her. 'You're lucky. My mum has no fashion sense and she listens to Val Doonican.'

Sam laughed. 'Well, my mum wears Levis and she likes the Ronettes.'

Brera and Sam had always been close. Sam loved Brera because she was tolerant and quiescent and never pushy or judgemental. Brera loved Sam but often worried about her, even though she rarely articulated these worries. Instead she confided to Sam

her fears and concerns about Sylvia. Sylvia, her younger daughter, was, after all, her problem child. Sam had her flaws too, and Brera saw them, but she chose to hold her tongue.

In fact Brera thought Sam slept around too much. She couldn't understand her daughter's promiscuity. Sam had ideas about things which she was forever discussing. Brera acknowledged the ideas but ignored them. She thought, Sam needs to need a man. She just doesn't know it yet.

Sam and Connor arrived at the Hackney flat shortly after midday on Sunday. Although Brera sometimes found the situation with Sylvia difficult where strangers were concerned, Sam was entirely devoid of any sense of embarrassment. She had explained the situation fully to Connor shortly after their first night together. He had been confused but intrigued. He remained intrigued as Sam unlocked the door to the flat and invited him inside. The smell was pungent but tolerable. He'd had an aunt who kept chickens. It was comparable.

Brera was sitting on the living-room sofa watching *The Waltons*. She smiled up at them when they came in. 'Hi,' she said, 'I'll make you both something to eat when this finishes.'

Connor had been told that Brera was Irish, but, even so, was unprepared for her pinkness, her whiteness, the red of her hair. Sam was so different. And her sister? How many colours in one family? What did it mean? It had to mean something.

Sam linked her arm through Connor's and led him to her bedroom. She closed the door, pushed him up against it and put her arms around his neck. They kissed. She slid a hand under his T-shirt. He pulled away. 'The house seems so quiet.'

'You want some music on?'

Connor could hear someone coughing. He looked around the room, which was small but colourful. Above the bed was a large poster of the Judds. He walked over to it. 'I guess the Judds must be a big influence on you. The mother-and-daughter thing. The mother is really beautiful. They could be sisters.'

He sat down on Sam's bed. Sam took off her jumper and her shoes. She put them in a small wardrobe next to the door.

'I love the Judds, but sometimes I think they're a little bit too perfect, too polished.'

She bent down and pressed the play button on her tape recorder.

Connor frowned, failing to recognize the music. 'Who is this?'

Before Sam could answer, Brera had pushed open the door and had carried in a tray with two cups of tea and a plate of sandwiches. She said, 'It's Laverne Baker. Jackie Wilson's in the background. I hope you like garlic cheese.'

Connor was too surprised to respond. Sam looked unruffled. She put out her hands to take the tray.

Brera walked back towards the door. 'Steven phoned. He said he'd lined up a photographer for Tuesday.'

Sam offered Connor his mug of tea. 'That was quick.'

Brera nodded and closed the door behind her.

'Who's Steven?'

Sam picked up one of the sandwiches. 'Our new manager. We only met him yesterday.'

'You didn't tell me you were getting a manager.'

'Mum likes him. He's OK.'

Connor put down his mug and lay back on the bed. He stared up at the ceiling. She's so bloody secretive, he thought. Saves secrets like sweets. Eats them in private.

Sam moved to the end of the bed and pulled off his boots. He looked around the room again from his new vantage point and then held out his arms to her. 'Let's get this over with before your mother comes back in with lemonade and biscuits.'

Brera knocked on Sylvia's door and waited for her to answer. After a minute or so and a certain amount of scuffling and fluttering, Sylvia opened the door several inches and peered out.

'What?'

Brera offered her a mug of tea and a plate of sandwiches. Sylvia slid her hand through the crack and took the tea. 'I'm not hungry.'

'You should eat. I haven't even seen you since yesterday night when you went out. Where did you go?'

'Nowhere.'

Brera resisted the temptation to shove her foot into the crack in the door. Instead she said quickly, 'Sam's got her new friend around. Did you hear them come in?'

'No.'

'He's in a band too. They've been on television. He's called Connor. Sounds a bit American.'

Sylvia's face disappeared for a moment and then returned. 'I'll have a sandwich. Only one, though. Thanks.'

Her hand darted out and took a sandwich. Brera smiled. Sylvia nodded and then closed the door. Brera swallowed down her irritation. She went into the living-room, picked up her guitar and started to sing 'A Pair of Brown Eyes', strumming along in time.

Connor was mid-way through removing his trousers when he heard the conversation commence between Brera and Sylvia. He thought, I can't sustain an erection with those two chatting away like they're in the same room.

He pulled his trousers back on and did up the buttons. Sam groaned, exasperated, from her position on the bed and grabbed hold of her T-shirt. 'Why don't we go back to your flat? It was you who wanted to come here in the first place.'

Connor had half an ear on the conversation in the hallway. He turned down the music on the tape recorder and said, 'I didn't mean for us to come here for sex. I just wanted to meet everybody.'

He listened to their voices again. 'Your sister's voice is so hoarse. She sounds like Rod Stewart. Does she sing?'

Sam laughed. 'What do you think? She writes a weird kind of music. Like jazz but less tuneful. That's her contribution to things. She likes doing it. It's kind of methodical. She's hardly even got a speaking voice, though, let alone a singing one.'

As she spoke, Sam put on her T-shirt and picked up a book from her bedside table.

Connor moved a few steps closer to the door. He heard Brera mention his name.

Sam said tiredly, 'It's her allergy. If she tries to sing or shout her voice disappears altogether.'

'It sounds amazing, though, really distinctive.'

Sam looked up at him. 'The only reason she talks that way is because she's gradually choking herself. It's a slow process of strangulation.'

Connor felt foolish for being so enthusiastic. He turned towards her and changed the subject. 'What's that you're reading?'

She turned the page. 'Something about Hélène Cixous. She's this brilliant French intellectual. I've read all her stuff, but it's difficult. She's very controversial. She won't even call herself a feminist because feminism's too bourgeois.'

Connor looked down at the plate on the floor. 'What sort of cheese did your mother say this was?'

Sylvia sat on the end of her bed and drank her tea. The weather was turning. The day had started off warm and sticky. Now the sky was clouding over, was grey, heavy, lowering. The birds – at least a hundred or so – had flown inside as a consequence, in anticipation of the storm to come. They lined the walls of Sylvia's room, chattering and bickering. Several bounced to and fro across the carpet, scratching, preening and flapping their wings.

Sylvia thought, Above the bird noise I can hear Sam talking with that man. What are they discussing? What are they doing?

Sometimes she imagined what it would be like to have a male companion, but she couldn't really conceive of herself doing the things that normal women did. She couldn't imagine herself wanting the things that normal women wanted. She tried to feel pride in her abnormality, but she often felt as though her abnormality had become the only normal thing about her, the only relevant thing.

She sat on the end of her bed and drained the cup of its last few drops of tea. As she swallowed her tea, the incident in the park popped into her mind. The tea turned into dirty water in her mouth. She tried to swallow in air as the tea went down but she could not. She gagged on the liquid and it choked her. She

imagined herself in the lake, with the mud and the slime and the tin cans. She imagined that she was the young girl and that she could not swim. She did not feel remorse, just fear. She wished that she could tie a tourniquet around her imagination, a piece of strong rope or cloth that could effectively cut off all dangerous ideas and fanciful notions, stop the flow of her thoughts from streaming, frothing, flooding and overwhelming her.

She could hear Brera singing in the living-room with her guitar. She tried to concentrate on this sound and to block out everything else. Then she heard Sam's voice. Sam had been laughing and talking before, but now she too had started to sing. Her voice toned in with Brera's perfectly. Brera sang in a higher register with a Celtic twang. Sam sounded very low and clear, like a soft, brown thrush – intense and lyrical.

She heard Sam emerge from her room and walk towards Brera's voice, still singing herself. She rolled her eyes towards the ceiling. They infuriated her. She found them unbearably smug and confident, like nuns or traffic wardens – self-assured and immensely self-motivated. Pure.

She inspected the eczema on her hands and wrists. The skin here was bumpy and itchy, some of it moist and shiny. She pulled off a scab which covered the tender flesh that linked the space between her finger and thumb. Her eyes watered. She enjoyed this strum of pain, lost herself in it and savoured its tone.

Suddenly she saw the little girl's face in the chafed and pinky pattern of her flesh, imagined for a second how the cold water would have felt entering her nose and throat, covering her eyes.

The sound of Connor's hesitant tread in the hallway distracted her. She stopped breathing for a moment and listened out for the slight noises he made, her head to one side, eyes closed. He had a light tread. Must be thin, she thought. His step seemed tentative, well-meaning, self-conscious. She heard him enter the living-room and began breathing again. The air she drew into her lungs felt dry and coarse. It rattled in her throat. She coughed for a short while then swallowed down a mouthful of phlegm.

Connor was singing now too. He was doing a comic version of

Dolly Parton's 'Love is like a Butterfly', in a low, brash voice. She could hear the two women laughing. She put her hands over her ears, imagined that her hands were like shells, and the noise of the blood, the compressed air in her ears, the wail in her head, was really the sea. She stood on a bone-pale beach. It was an airless place.

TEN

Ruby awoke to the sound of the telephone ringing. She opened her eyes and tried to pull herself up straight. She'd been slumped over sideways on to her bedside table. Her face felt strange, like warm wax that had set overnight into a distorted, lopsided shape. Her neck ached, even her tongue ached and her body felt, in its entirety, distinctly askew.

Vincent was there. Ugh! She looked at him. A horrible face. Dirty. Phlegm, mucus, special smells. Blood, dried. Everything inside spilling out.

His face was a solid bruise. He was a car accident, still jumbled. She had no clear impression of him. Not mentally, not visually. It was bright in her room, a yellow-white brightness, reflecting unkindly off him.

She sprang out of bed to answer the ringing. She was still wearing her cardigan, which she pulled close around her, and her T-shirt, which she noticed had coffee stains down the front.

The telephone – it had a long extension cord – was situated in the centre of the draining-board next to the sink. She picked up the receiver. 'Yeah? Ruby here.'

She licked a finger and applied it, somewhat hopelessly, to the stain.

'You sound rough.'

She didn't recognize the voice. 'Hold on.'

She put down the receiver, turned on the cold tap and stuck her head under it, inhaling sharply as the water gushed over her hair, into her ears and down her neck. She turned it off and shook her head, like a dog after a dip, then picked up the receiver again. 'Hi.'

She felt the water dripping down her back and her face. Eventually a voice said, 'Hello, Ruby?'

'Yeah.'

'Donald Sheldon. Is it too early?'

'I've been up ages,' she lied. He'd never phoned her before.

He said, 'Actually, I'd like to see you. This afternoon if it's possible.'

'Oh. OK.'

'There's a café near Seven Sisters tube.' He described its precise location. 'We could meet twelve-ish.'

Twelve was too early.

'Yeah, that's fine. Seven Sisters. Twelve-ish.'

'See you then.'

She put down the receiver and walked into the bathroom to look for a towel. She found one slung over the edge of the bath and wrapped up her dripping hair in it before putting the plug in the bath and turning on the taps.

Back in her bedroom, she rooted out a pair of jeans, a black vest and some clean underwear. Vincent lay across the bed, his legs spread, his feet dangling off the end. His arms, she noticed, now held a pillow over his face. She said, 'I wouldn't do that. Someone might be tempted to press down on it.'

He said nothing.

She returned to the bathroom. While she undressed, she debated how soon it would be acceptable to ask him to leave. She tested the water with her hand, climbed in, then lay back and relaxed, staring abstractly beyond her breasts, her knees, her toes, at the taps and the steam from the water.

Vincent felt like a caterpillar changing into a butterfly. That inbetween stage. A pupa. His skin, hard, semi-impervious; himself, inside, withered and formless.

He was not himself. His head bumped and pumped. The light, the morning, scorched him.

During the night he had awoken, he didn't know what time, and had found a girl, a stranger, next to him. Her hip near his chin. Wool, scratching; cold skin. He had pressed his forehead against her thigh. It had cooled him.

And now it was morning. He needed something. Had

to stretch his body – that crumpled thing – his mind, his tongue.

Ruby picked up a bar of soap and started to build up a lather. What does Sheldon want? she wondered. What does he want from me? Her toes curled at the prospect. She stared at them and thought, Why am I doing that with my feet?

Vincent stood on the other side of the bathroom door with his hand on the handle. He shouted, 'You could've told me you were having a bath.'

Ruby dropped the soap and covered her breasts. 'Don't you dare come in.'

'I have no intention of coming in,' he said scathingly. After a pause he added, 'Why the hell did you bring me here? I've had the worst time.'

She gasped at this, her expression a picture, and shouted, 'I didn't bring you here.'

'Well, I didn't get here on my own.'

His voice sounded muffled, further away now. 'Do you always live like this?'

She stood up, indignant, and stepped out of the bath. 'Like what?'

Silence, then, 'Forget it.'

'Like what?'

She grabbed a towel, wrapped it around her and pulled open the door. 'Live like what?'

He was standing in the kitchen, looking inside one of her cupboards. He glanced at her, in the towel. 'For a minute there,' he said, grinning, 'I thought you were a natural blonde. But it's only foam.'

She yanked the towel straight. With his cut, his pale, white face, the bruises, the suggestion of a black eye, he looked like Frankenstein's monster. But he didn't frighten her. She said calmly, 'Get out of my flat.'

He grimaced. 'Some hospitality. I have a migraine and all you can do is shout.'

'Yeah?' She smiled. 'Well, I think you should go.'

She returned to the bathroom, closed the door, dropped her towel.

He said, 'I have a blotch. I'm going blind. You expect me to go when I can't even see straight?'

She stared at the bath. 'Well, whose fault is that?'

She picked up her towel and started to dry herself. She heard the cupboard close.

'Yours. You shouldn't have paid my bail.'

She rubbed herself vigorously.

'And lunch. I only get migraines from gherkins.'

'What?'

'An allergy.'

She laughed. She was glad that he had an allergy.

He listened to her laughing. Smiled at it. He liked her flat. It was central. He sat down on the sofa, picked up one of the empty vodka bottles, sniffed the neck of it and winced.

Eventually she emerged, fully dressed, made up, her teeth brushed and her hair gelled.

'I made you some tea.' He held out a mug to her.

She took it from him. 'Aren't you having any?'

He shook his head. 'Couldn't keep it down.'

'Did you try?'

'I had some water.'

She sipped the tea. It was luke-warm. 'How are you feeling?'

He shrugged.

'What are you going to do?'

He shrugged again.

'Will you go home? Are you up to it?'

He cleared his throat. 'May I use your bathroom?'

'Of course you can.'

Once he'd closed the door she shouted, 'I'm going out in a minute. Should I trust you here alone?'

'I wouldn't.'

She put down her mug of tea. 'Only a trustworthy person would've said that.'

'Think what you like.'

'I will.'

She picked up her keys. She was insured. She needed a new stereo, anyway.

Donald Sheldon – self-appointed king of Hackney Wick – was a short, squat man with thick, wavy hair and skin the colour of roasted peanuts. He was drinking a foamy coffee and wore an expensive business suit. Ruby was nervous, had thought too much about meeting him.

'Am I late?'

He shrugged. 'Ten minutes. Coffee?'

She nodded. 'Thanks.'

He manœuvred himself out from behind the table and strolled over to the counter. Ruby watched him. She regularly saw him down at the track. He trained mainly at Hackney, but she was well informed that he ran his dogs wherever he could. She'd often seen him interviewed on SIS, the racing channel.

He returned to the table, carrying her coffee, holding on to its saucer. She looked down at his hands and saw that he wore rings on most fingers but none that seemed like a wedding ring. He sat down again. 'I've seen you at Hackney a lot. You obviously enjoy the sport.'

She nodded.

'How old do you think I am?'

This question surprised her. She stared at his face, his thick hair, his good tan. She wanted to flatter him. 'Forty, forty-two.'

He smiled. 'Forty-eight. I've been racing dogs since I was fourteen.'

'Thirty-four years.'

'I first went to Hackney when I was five, with my dad. You might get to meet him later.'

She stared at him, bemused, wondering where his dad fitted into the equation.

He smiled fondly, but more to himself than at her. 'My dad got me my first dog. He helped pay for it by putting his every last penny on Pigalle Wonder in the 1958 London Cup. A great champion: big, but well balanced. Really handsome.'

Ruby put her teaspoon in her coffee and stirred away some of

the foam. She felt obliged to say something but couldn't think what, so she just said, 'Betting on the dogs is a bit of a lottery.'

Don looked irritated. 'I tell you, the only important thing you need to do to win at the dogs, Ruby, is to rely on honest thinking.'

She liked the way he'd used her name. She looked into his face. Did he want to employ her or to fuck her? Either way, she was flattered. He was saying, 'Racing isn't just about speed.'

He paused. 'Do you know what it is that makes a good dog?'

Ruby focused on her coffee and tried to think. Eventually she said, 'Speed and intelligence, mainly.'

He shook his head. 'Racing is all about negotiating bends. To negotiate a bend you need balance, coordination and muscular control. But it's more than that. A dog must have the will to win. It has to have that primitive urge. Some dogs will always be chasers or chuckers. A dog must know how to place itself. It's got to be crafty.'

She looked at his hands as he spoke. Brown, clean hands. What did he want? What was he doing?

He said, 'I didn't know anything when I got my first dog.'

An image shot into her mind of how Donald Sheldon would look naked. She visualized him with an all-over tan and pinky-brown genitals. Not too much body hair. His stomach, slightly saggy, and his breasts.

He said, 'All this is leading somewhere.'

'Is it?'

Of course. He looked at her, grinned, then said, 'And I think I have a good idea where you want it to lead.'

His voice sounded suggestive, arrogant, even sensual. He was old. Not that old. She inhaled deeply and stared straight into his eyes. He picked up a fork and shook it for emphasis, 'I'm willing to sell you that dog.'

'Dog?'

'The one we discussed.'

'Discussed?' Ruby wanted to rewind this conversation in order to try to make sense of it.

He dropped the fork, laced his fingers together and leaned

forward. 'She's trained. She's in good form. I mean, she's out of season now and she's in good nick. She's registered. She has a race or two lined up at Hackney, but after that it'd be your business.'

He was trying to sell her something! Donald Sheldon!

I would never, she thought, holding in her gut, I would never have had sex with him. Never.

He added, 'It must be about her fourteenth week since she was in season. She's probably got a bit rusty while she was rested, but that's only natural.'

Ruby tried desperately to remember what she had said to him, how this situation had developed. Had he confused her with someone else? I didn't even want a job, she thought furiously. Not that kind of job.

He frowned. 'She's put on weight, but bitches often do, even if they haven't been mated. Her current grading figure isn't very encouraging, but I'd be giving her to you for nine hundred.'

She said carefully, 'To be honest, cash-flow is a bit of a problem for me at the moment.'

She wanted to laugh in his face. It was all so stupid.

He shrugged. 'I wouldn't want the money straight off. A week would do. Six days. If we shook on it now you could take her immediately.'

He was squinting with sincerity. He sincerely thought he was doing her a favour. If he'd employed her, if he'd fucked her, he would've worn that same expression. But he was selling her something.

Selling her something.

She had to admire him.

He waited.

It was her turn. To do. What?

She took the easiest option, as was her nature.

She nodded and shook his hand. His skin was warm and dry.

He stood up. 'The dog's down at the kennels. Here . . .' He handed her his card, which she took and inspected.

'My dad'll be there for most of the afternoon. He's expecting you.'

'Thanks.'

'I'm not doing you any favours. I've had very little luck with this particular bitch. But you expressed an interest and now she's yours.'

Ruby tried to smile as she placed his card in the front pocket of her jeans. He turned to go. She watched him as he walked between the tables and up to the door. He pushed it, it swung outwards and he stepped outside.

She raised her eyes to the ceiling and noticed a large fan up there, turning rapidly.

Which particular bitch? When had she spoken to him at the track? Had he been holding a dog at the time? Had she been holding one? Had she expressed an interest?

She felt hot. The fan's rapid movements were making her feel queasy. She pulled off her jacket and walked outside. It was hot here too. Things were fuzzy. She blinked, unable to tell whether this fuzziness was caused by heat, a heat-wave shimmering on the Sunday roads, or by movements behind her eyes, inside her.

Vincent pottered around the flat, feeling no particular urge to leave. He tried to assess Ruby on the basis of her personal possessions, but there was little of interest to look at apart from her record collection and her underwear. The record collection was impressive.

His headache was now a dumb whine at the back of his skull, but tolerable. He found an old Kraftwerk album and put it on – turning down the volume slightly – then wandered about, acclimatizing, inspecting things.

He had a bath. It felt like ages since he'd had a proper wash. He picked up Ruby's soap and sniffed it. It wasn't strongly perfumed – smelled like Palmolive – so he used it freely, grinning to himself, imagining which parts of Ruby's body it had lathered. The warmth of the water, the rubbing, the foam, gave him a slight erection. He stared at it for a while with a terse and serious expression, then burst out laughing. It bobbed down in the water, submissive again, mournful and flaccid.

After drying himself, he went into the kitchen, still naked, did

the washing up and then returned to the bathroom, where he picked up his clothes, dressed and surveyed himself in the mirror. His whole forehead was a pinky-purple colour. This bruising reached down to either side of his eyes. One eye was black. He inspected the cut more thoroughly. Most of the bump had gone down, but several strands of hair were caught inside the mouth of the gash. He pulled at them, very gently, wincing as some of them came out. He pulled a few more and then gave up, concerned that he might bring back his headache.

He returned to the kitchen and inspected the cupboards to see what food Ruby had in. Tinned stuff, dried stuff. He'd cook something.

While some beans were soaking he tidied up the living-room and then moved into Ruby's bedroom. Her carpet was knee-deep in pieces of clothing. He kicked these into a large pile and then sorted out what was clean and what was dirty. He sniffed, looked, fondled.

He liked it here. He'd stay for a while, but he wouldn't ask. If you asked, people said no. Even soft people. Eventually.

Ruby pressed the buzzer and listened out for barking, but could hear none. The building was a mixture of grandeur and delapidation. It was built in a square around a tarmacked courtyard. The entrance was barred by a large, black, metal gate.

After several minutes a tiny old man staggered across the courtyard towards her. He looked like Mr Punch, all nose and chin with eyes like sultanas. He reached the gate, puffed out, and gazed through it at her. 'You've come to get the bitch?'

Ruby nodded and said, 'I've seen you at Hackney before, haven't I?'

'Could've, but I'm usually at Walthamstow.'

He started to unlock the gate before adding, 'That bitch of yours wouldn't run on the Walthamstow track for love nor bloody money. They've got a McGee hare there. You familiar with it?'

Ruby frowned. 'It's smaller, isn't it?'

'Smaller than the Outside Sumner and doesn't make so much

noise. Stupid bitch wouldn't run for it. Trap opened and she didn't come out. Nice grass track but she wouldn't have any of it.' He shook his head. 'Racing manager was about ready to kill me. Punters weren't happy either. There again, she was still a novice, so she probably only had about fifty quid on her.'

He pulled the gate open. Ruby stepped inside and he closed it behind her, then turned and led the way across the tarmac. She followed him, watching the back of his yellowy kennel coat, into the main building, through an unprepossessing passageway, which smelled of detergent and dog, and into a large, square, brightly lit kitchen.

He pointed towards the big pine table that filled the centre of the room. 'Sit down while I go get her. I'll bring her registration booklet too.'

Ruby sat down and rested her elbows on the table. The room felt airless, she felt aimless. Why was she here? She thought, I won't think anything. Not anything. Nothing.

When he returned, she said, 'Don didn't get around to telling me your name.'

He grinned. False teeth. As straight as a die. 'Stanley. Stan. I'm seventy-four and he still has me working a seven-day week.'

Ruby pushed herself back on her chair and peered over at the dog. Stan was holding a lead and the bitch stood at the end of it, looking tense. She couldn't help thinking how large the animal seemed. Not fat, just big.

Stan leaned against the table and got his breath back. The dog stood still, not pulling on her leash, but managing to look on edge, padding from foot to foot. He stared down at her. 'I like black bitches. This one's related to Dolores Rocket. Won the Derby. Won the Puppy Oaks too, twenty-odd years ago.'

He jerked the lead and brought the dog's head up. Her face was skinny, scraggy and strangely petulant.

'I'll get a muzzle on her.'

'Do you have to?'

'She'll chase anything if she feels the urge.'

'Anything but the McGee hare, eh?'

Stan fitted the muzzle over the dog's face. 'Well, they've all got

coursing in their blood, but these dogs . . .' He slapped her lightly on her rump and she stiffened her legs to take the slap. 'These dogs were bred from strains of dogs that didn't so much care what they chased, they'd run for anything.'

He brought the bitch around the table and handed Ruby her lead. Ruby hesitated and then took it. She felt a dart of terror in her chest that started between her breasts and shot up to her throat. She tried to swallow it, to keep it under.

Stan looked down at her for a moment, then said conspiratorially, 'How much is he asking for?'

Ruby felt the leather of the lead between her finger and her thumb. 'Nine hundred.' When she said it, it meant nothing.

He burst out laughing. 'I'll tell him you'll give him seven. He had her down at Swaffham in Norfolk on Friday. Check her toes.'

Ruby picked up the dog's right foot. The pads all seemed fine. She picked up the left and he interrupted her, taking hold of the paw himself and parting the front pads. 'Third pad's slightly swollen.'

'Is that a problem?'

She knew it was. I know all this, she thought, I know this stuff.

'I'll tell Don you thought it was.'

She smiled gratefully and stroked the dog's back. 'How did she do at Swaffham? I didn't even know Don raced in that part of the country.'

'How do you think she did?'

He passed Ruby the registration booklet. She opened it. *Little Buttercup. Black bitch* . . . When she was born, where, the names of her parents, the size of the litter. Physical description. Tiny details. Times of her races, places. *Swaffham* – the latest entry.

'Sixth.'

'She's got a race lined up at Hackney on Thursday. You'd better have a chat with the racing manager, though. He's not happy with this bitch. Did Don tell you she's in the E grade? Her actual running time at 525 yards was 30.40 on her last night out.'

Ruby verified this in the booklet. It wasn't a good time.

'Just the same,' he added, noting her expression, 'there's

nothing wrong with her physically. The toe's no problem. You've obviously got a good eye. She's a fine-looking bitch.'

Suddenly, at last, she remembered. A month ago, Hackney Wick, the traps were loaded. Six dogs. The hare, starting, the squeal of it. Some dogs, barking, whining. And then. She remembered it. Her trap. Number six. A tail, sticking out through the bars at the front.

'She turned around!' Ruby said. 'In the trap. She turned around in the trap, and I thought . . .' Ruby had thought, That's only logical. She turned around because that's the direction the hare's coming from. And Don was furious. He said . . . and I said . . . and he said . . . and I said, 'But she's a fine-looking bitch.'

Stan was staring at her, nervously.

'Sorry,' she said, almost laughing with relief, 'I just thought of something.'

'Don didn't say what you were planning to do with her.'

'I don't know. He said she had a couple of races lined up.'

'One race on Thursday.'

Ruby was thinking now, planning. 'I'd better get a licence.'

He stared at her blankly. 'She's not your only dog?'

'My first.' She liked this idea. She'd been sloppy, before, admittedly.

'Have you got kennels?'

'No.' She said this with great certainty, as though only saying it this way would mean it didn't matter.

'You won't get a licence then. Not without proper kennels. Anyway, when the racing manager at Hackney finds out Don isn't training her any more, he'll drop her from the card. If she doesn't get a place in her next race, he'll drop her for the season anyway.'

Ruby stared at the dog. The dog's expression was docile but furtive.

'You,' she said, with sudden fondness.

The dog licked her lips. Her whiskers stuck out of her cheeks – silver against her black fur – like needles in a pincushion.

After a while Ruby said, 'There's no law against being too keen.'

'There should be, though.'

Stan leaned against the table. 'You could run her at an independent track and you wouldn't even need a licence. Swaffham's a permit track. You could run her there for fifty quid. Or you could even breed from her.'

'I could,' she said. 'I could, but I don't want to.' She was making decisions now. She could make them. 'I want to run her at Hackney.'

'You can't.'

'I can run her on Thursday.'

'He'll drop her if he finds out Don's sold her.'

'What if she got a place?'

He laughed. 'She won't.'

'But what if she did?'

'He'll drop her anyway.'

'She deserves a chance.'

Stan thought about this, looked unconvinced, but said, 'If I come down on the day, and anyone asks, you can say you're with me.'

Ruby smiled. 'I've got plans for her.'

Stan stuck his hands deep into his pockets. 'You'll find out soon enough she's got plans of her own.'

Vincent scowled at the dog. 'Where did that come from?'

Ruby closed the door behind her and unclipped Buttercup's lead from her collar.

'She's a bitch. I just bought her.'

'Why?'

She sat down. 'I don't know.'

He stared at the dog as she walked around the room, sniffing furniture and poking her nose into corners.

'Black's a good colour. She matches everything,' he said.

'Yeah. I really needed to hear that.'

'I made dinner.'

'I thought you'd be gone.'

'Sorry to disappoint you.'

He went into the kitchen and dished up the food he'd prepared.

'Don't give any to the dog.'

'I wasn't planning to.'

'She's on a diet.'

Ruby took the plate he handed her and started eating. Tuna, rice, sweetcorn, beans. The dog smelled the food and walked over. She sat next to Ruby, staring at the plate, her tail making a slight swishing sound against the carpet.

'Does she bite?'

'I don't think so.'

'Why's she wearing that muzzle?'

Ruby closed her eyes, stopped chewing and swallowed. 'At Tottenham Court Road tube she chased a woman wearing a fur-trimmed jacket up the escalator.'

He laughed. 'Did she get her?'

'She caught her but she didn't bite her. She was wearing her muzzle.'

'You should've had her on a lead.'

Ruby dropped her fork and showed him her hand. 'Leather burns.'

She continued eating. 'This is nice.'

'I trained as a chef. In Dublin. They had a big dog track there. Shelbourne Park. I went once but I never won a penny.'

'There are always plenty of jobs for chefs up west. Imagine what you could earn. You could pay me back in no time.'

'I don't think so.'

He stood up and went to turn over the record he'd been listening to earlier, then ran some water into a pan and put it down on the floor for the dog.

'Can she drink through that muzzle?'

'Yeah.'

He returned to the sofa, noting Ruby's miserable expression. 'I get the feeling you didn't really think this through.'

'Story of my life.'

She continued eating, then added, 'But there was a great moment back then when it really did seem like a good idea.'

'She'll chew this flat to pieces.'

'I'll keep her muzzled.'

'What will you do with her when you're at work?'

The dog, suddenly, inexplicably, started to bark. Vincent jumped and dropped a forkful of rice on to his lap. He scooped it up with his fingers and crammed it into his mouth. Ruby craned her neck and stared over the back of the sofa towards Buttercup, who was still standing next to her bowl of water.

'What's up?'

She called out her name but the dog didn't respond, so she put down her plate and walked over to her, squatted down next to her and tried to attract her attention. The dog continued to bark, loudly, bouncing forward on her front paws. Ruby tried to force her to sit by pushing down her rump but the dog wouldn't oblige. She tried talking sternly and then, finally, shouting.

Vincent put down his plate and walked over. 'What's she barking at?'

'I don't know. She was fine when she came in.'

The dog fell silent. They both stared at her, surprised. Then, after a five-second hiatus, she started up again.

Ruby swore.

'If the bloody neighbours find out I've got a dog, I'll be evicted.'

'Follow her eyes.'

'Why?'

She peered into Buttercup's face. The dog's eyes were glazed and purposeful. Her breath was bad.

Vincent bounded over to the stereo and lifted the stylus. The dog stopped barking. He dropped it again. She barked.

'She doesn't like Kraftwerk, so she's barking at the speakers.'

He squatted down, took the record off and threw it on the floor, then put another one on.

Ruby's eyes widened. 'Be careful. You'll scratch them.'

He turned the volume up and waited for a song to start. As soon as it did, so did the dog. He laughed and switched it off. 'She doesn't like Inner City either.'

He took out a Ray Charles album and slung it on. It began to play. The dog cocked her head, listened intently and then sat down.

'Look at her! She's an old crooner.'

He was preparing to change the record yet again when Ruby crawled over to the socket in the wall and pulled out the plug. She glared at him, still on her hands and knees. 'If you've scratched any of my records you can pay me for them.'

'I won't scratch them.'

'I bet you already have.'

He picked up one and inspected the vinyl. Ruby squatted down next to the dog and stroked her. She said, 'She's all upset. Her heart's beating like crazy.' After a few seconds she added, 'You can tell everything you need to know about a dog's condition when you stroke it. She's got strong, wide shoulders, a good, firm back . . .'

I'll get him to stay, she thought, at least for tomorrow. He can look after her while I'm out, until she gets used to this place. He can take her to Hyde Park.

She continued to stroke the dog, who rested her chin on the carpet and closed her eyes.

Vincent watched this. He realized something. They wouldn't get around to sex now. That's what the dog meant. He hadn't really considered sex, planned it, wanted it. Even so.

He snapped the record he was holding in half. It was a sharp, clean break. They both stared at him: Ruby, the dog.

'You're going to replace that record.'

He smiled. Of course he would. He studied the two halves to see what it was.

Ruby picked up the dog's lead and attached it to her collar.

'Where are you going? You haven't finished eating yet.'

She ignored him, pulled on her jacket, checked for her keys and then opened the door. He was a bastard. She wanted to punch him. She stepped out into the hallway, the dog at her heels.

He stood up. 'If anywhere's open,' he shouted after her, 'You're completely out of milk.'

ELEVEN

There was a painting in the living-room, a portrait, that Connor especially hated. 'That's her,' he said, when he first showed Sam around his flat, 'Sarah. I share this place with her.'

Sam liked the painting. It was creepy. A female nude. Lips, russet nipples, ribs.

'Does she really look like that?'

He laughed. 'She thinks she does. She's so vain. You'll meet her.'

'Where is she?'

'Los Angeles for a month. Helping to research a book on the paranormal.'

Sam was fascinated. 'Para-normal. Not normal.'

'She's a researcher.'

'And you don't like her?'

The flat, she could tell, was the site, the centre, of subtle guerilla warfare. A picture; a wall-hanging; garish, orange hessian curtains. All Sarah's contributions. Sam grew accustomed to spotting her in objects. Teapots, candles, cosmetics in the bathroom.

Connor claimed to be an aesthete. He said he hated clutter. But his bedroom, his territory, was full of musical flotsam: a drum-kit, African bongos, symbols, a tambourine. His records, his stereo.

Sam couldn't learn much here, though. In the living-room, she inspected the bookshelves.

'Henry James?'

'Hers.'

'Kurt Vonnegut?'

'Mine.'

'*Psychoanalysis: the Impossible Profession*?'

'Hers.'

'Dead Babies?'

'Mine.'

'Skinhead Escapes?'

'Mine.'

She picked this book up. It was a cheap, trashy novella. She didn't like it. She found it distasteful. 'I wouldn't want to own something like this.'

'It'll probably be worth a fair bit in a few years' time.'

'It's exploitative.'

He nodded. 'But sometimes that kind of stuff can be interesting.'

'Oh.'

She put the book back on the shelf.

Connor. He was interested in everything. She'd learned this very quickly. He was pragmatic. And what was she? Idealistic. Full of ideals.

Connor's problem, the way she saw it, was that he was interested in too much. He was funny and gentle, but he was fascinated by stupid, sometimes even bad, things.

'My parents,' Connor explained, 'rented this place to Sarah while I was at college. She's always been here.'

Sam liked her. I've been living with this woman, she thought, learning all about her.

It was early morning. Connor was still asleep. She'd risen to get herself a drink of water. On her way back to bed she paused in front of the painting. Bones, white flesh, red hair, red eyes. It was hung on the wall adjacent to Sarah's room. Connor, she thought, is still sleeping. She touched the door handle, shuddered, pressed it down. Pushed.

Inside, the curtains were drawn. The bedspread was patchwork. She could smell patchouli oil. On the dressing-table, however, she noticed bottles of what appeared to be more sophisticated scent. She walked over and picked up a bottle of Rive Gauche, tentatively sprayed it into the air and sniffed. Next to the bed – she sat down and inspected it – was a book of women's erotica. She opened it. Marilyn French. Anaïs Nin. She

started to read, struggling in the half-light to focus on its ant-black print.

'Hello.'

Samantha gave a start, almost dropping the book and the perfume. A tall, very thin woman stood in the doorway, grinning sardonically. She had bright, hennaed hair and a gaunt, striking face. In her hand she held a suitcase.

'What are you reading?'

'You must be Sarah.'

Sam stood up and quickly put the perfume back down on the dresser. 'I shouldn't be in here.'

Sarah walked into the room, threw her suitcase down on the bed, strolled over to the window and drew the curtains.

'What were you reading?'

'Angela Carter.'

'Were you enjoying it?'

Sam nodded.

'You must be Connor's new friend.'

Sam didn't much like this description of herself, but nodded again.

Sarah stared at her. Sam wore only a dressing-gown with nothing underneath. She tightened the belt self-consciously.

'That picture,' she said, confused and embarrassed, 'in the living-room. It does look just like you.'

Sarah laughed at this. 'Connor's been telling you about my monumental ego.'

'No. I didn't mean that.'

'The print is by Schiele. He's very famous. He painted male nudes too.'

She opened her suitcase and peered at its jumbled contents.

'How was Los Angeles?'

'OK. I was working. Do you work?'

'I'm a singer.'

'Not with Connor's group?'

'No. I'm in a band with my mother.'

'That's a novelty.'

She started to unpack. 'I'd rather strangle my mother than sing with her.'

Sam closed the book she was holding and put it down on the dressing-table.

'You can borrow that if you like.'

'Thanks.' She picked it up again.

'Angela Carter,' Sarah said, frowning. 'You like her?'

Sam nodded.

'The way I see it,' Sarah said, pulling out some clothes and shoving them into a wicker washing-basket at the foot of her bed, 'there are two types of women. Those who think we're the same as men, and those who think we're different. Equal, obviously, but different.'

Sam was delighted. A proper conversation! Connor's idea of animated chat was a discussion of the intricacies of Gram Parson's fretwork.

'Which type are you?' she asked.

'The first. But I don't know about Angela Carter, and that makes me suspicious.'

'I like her,' Sam said, 'I like that difference. Whatever it is.'

Sarah considered this for a moment and then said, 'Maybe because you're culturally different, you have a looser approach to questions of gender.'

'Culture doesn't come into it,' Sam said, vaguely defensive. 'I might be a different colour, but I still know that sex is more complicated than race.'

Sarah continued to unpack. She took some magazines from her case, some papers and a notepad.

'Connor,' she said, smiling, 'must find you a challenge.'

'How?'

'Politically.'

Sam tried to understand this. 'It's not politics I'm interested in. It's something more subtle.'

'Subtle?' She laughed. 'You think Connor's up to that?'

Sam stared at her. How could she respond?

Connor appeared in the doorway and saved her. 'Hello,' he said, nodding at Sarah. 'So you got back in one piece?'

'I landed at five.'

He turned to Sam. 'I wondered where you'd got to.'

He hitched up the sheet he was holding around his hips.

Sam moved towards the door. 'I suppose I'd better leave you to it.'

Sarah nodded. 'But keep the book as long as you like.'

Sam thanked her, tucking the book under her arm.

Back in his room, Connor yanked off the sheet and climbed into bed. 'I heard what she was saying. She'd have eaten you alive.'

'I don't think so.'

'No?'

'But I felt really stupid.'

'That's ridiculous.'

Sam paused for a moment and then said, 'Why don't you like her?'

He puffed up his pillow. 'I wouldn't mind her if I didn't have to live with her.'

'She's abrasive.'

'Yeah.'

'Threatening.'

'What?'

'Maybe because she's clever.'

'Opinionated.'

'Because she's a feminist.'

He rubbed his face with his hands. 'So are you.'

'You just don't like aggressive women.'

'That's stupid.'

'If she was a man, you wouldn't mind her.'

'I don't like aggressive men either.'

He turned over, on to his side, making room for her in the bed. She hadn't yet decided whether she wanted to join him when the doorbell rang. He sat up. 'We're rehearsing this morning.'

'But what about Sarah?'

He frowned. 'What about her?'

'She's been awake half the night. You can't practise now.'

He smiled. 'Can't I?'

'Bastard.'

He stood up. Unexpectedly, the sight of his thin, naked body aroused her. She put out her hand and touched his back. He turned, smiled, moved closer. She whispered, 'Let's have sex.'

Outside she could hear Sarah answering the door, sounds in the living-room, male voices.

He stroked her hair. 'No rubbers. You wouldn't want me to re-use one.'

He bent over to pick up some shorts. She hit him across his rump with a tambourine and said tartly, 'You don't need a condom to give head.'

As she reached consciousness, Brera rolled over and focused dozily on her alarm clock. Nine-thirty. It was Monday. She signed on every Monday. Every Monday at nine. She sat up. She was late. Something was wrong. Something was missing. Suddenly she knew. Sylvia! Sylvia always wakes me!

She sprang out of bed, then froze, barely breathing, listening intently. At first she could hear nothing. Then she heard a noise, the faintest of sounds: a desperate, rattling, guttural wheezing.

She sprinted into the hallway. Sylvia's bedroom door was closed. She didn't knock, she flew in. Sylvia was on the floor, clutching her throat, in her own stranglehold, tossing and turning.

The room was full of birds. When Brera ran in they left their perches and filled the air – there must have been sixty of them – aiming upwards, towards the ceiling, in a feathery whirlwind. She found them terrifying, but she kept her wits, fell to her knees and grabbed hold of Sylvia, whose face was a whitey-purple colour, her lips flecked with foam. She took hold of her shoulders, slid her hands firmly under her armpits and dragged her out.

She lay her down flat, in the hallway, and dashed back into the bedroom. She searched around on the floor for a few seconds, then looked on the bed and finally found what she was hunting for on top of Sylvia's grey trunk: her inhaler. She snatched hold of it, kept her head low (the birds were still flying, calling, panicking) and ran out, slamming the door behind her.

Sylvia had begun to jerk and convulse. Brera pushed the inhaler between her lips. 'Exhale and then breathe this in. Exhale!'

Sylvia turned her face away. Brera jammed Sylvia's head between her knees and forced the inhaler into her mouth again, even deeper this time. She pressed it, and it pumped its fumes into her.

'Breathe it in! Breathe it in, you stupid thing!'

The inhaler had little or no effect. Brera began to panic.

'Sam? Where is she?'

She closed her eyes for a moment and tried to think what Sam would do, then pulled Sylvia along the hallway and into the living-room. This was an airy room. She dragged her towards the door that led out on to the roof, wrenched the door open. 'It's fresh air. Breathe it in. Go on!'

Sylvia's body was shuddering and gyrating. Brera hauled her on to the roof, out into the open air. She felt the cold tarmac on her bare feet and knees. She opened Sylvia's lips, inhaled deeply herself and then attempted mouth to mouth, placing her hands on Sylvia's ribs to see whether they expanded with the air she was providing. Nothing happened. Her convulsions had lessened, but this wasn't necessarily a good sign. Brera noticed that Sylvia's face was wet and thought, Why is she sweating so much?, then realized that she had soaked Sylvia's face with her own tears.

'The inhaler!'

She ran back into the house, through the living-room and into the hall. It was still on the floor. She picked it up and headed outside again. As she passed through the door on to the roof she shrieked.

Sylvia's body was seething and twitching. Twenty or thirty birds were sitting on her, covering her, smothering her. Brera threw herself at them, shouting, crying, and they ascended, together, like a funeral shroud, a brown feather blanket.

Sylvia's face was marked with large, red blotches. Brera took hold of her head and rammed the inhaler between her lips, but her teeth were clenched together now and grinding. She tried to

prise her jaw open but she wasn't strong enough. Instead she gathered her up in her arms, lifted her and, staggering, carried her through to the living-room. She dumped her on the couch, picked up the phone, dialled 999 and waited.

'Ambulance. Emergency. Jubilee Road, Hackney. Flat 9. Asthma. Please, quickly.'

She slammed down the receiver. What if they took too long? She had to get Sam.

She scrabbled among the pieces of paper next to the phone, hoping Sam had written Connor's number down. She saw a number written in Sam's hand and dialled it.

'Hello?'

It was Steven's number.

'Hi. Steven here.'

She thought her head was about to explode. She couldn't stop crying.

'Have you got a car? Where are you?'

'Who is this?'

'Brera. Please! Where are you?'

'I'm . . .'

'Are you near here? Are you near Hackney?'

'I . . . not far away. I'm at Liverpool Street. This is my mobile phone.'

Brera could hardly speak. 'Please come here. My daughter . . . I've phoned an ambulance but it might take too long. Please come.'

She dropped the receiver and ran back over to Sylvia. Sylvia was now limp, her eyes were closed and her head was lolling to one side. Brera lifted up her T-shirt and started to rub her chest. Sylvia's eyes opened slightly. She whispered, 'I'm not going anywhere.'

Brera felt as if a firework had gone off inside her mouth. 'You can bloody talk! You can bloody talk you little vixen and that's all you can say! You can talk and that's all you can say! Christ! Say something. No. Don't say anything. Just breathe!'

She stopped rubbing, ran out on to the roof, picked up the inhaler and sprinted back inside with it. She rammed it between

Sylvia's lips and pressed it three or four times. Most of the gas escaped through the sides of her mouth. Her head lolled. Brera tried it several more times and then, once again, attempted mouth to mouth.

It seemed like an age before she heard the buzzer sound. She ran to the entry-phone and pressed the button next to it, shoved the front door wide open to ease access and then ran to get Sylvia. She pulled down her T-shirt and tried to pick her up.

There was no ambulance, only Steven. He jogged up the stairs, through the flat, into the living-room. He was breathless and frightened, not so much by the possibility of facing something horrible (like a bloody injury, for example, a broken limb) as by the fear that he might not prove up to coping with it. He was prepared to see Sam, cut, bruised, maimed, electrocuted, but instead all he saw as he ran in was Brera, her face red, her hair red, wearing only a blue and white striped night-shirt, trying to pick up the prostrate body of a girl he had never seen before.

Brera glanced over her shoulder and saw, with horror, that it was only Steven. 'Oh God! I thought you were an ambulance. What good can you do? It's been at least fifteen minutes since I phoned.'

Steven moved swiftly over to Brera's side and helped her to lift the girl. He picked her up easily and held her in his arms. 'Shall I carry her downstairs? I can take you to casualty in my car, but you'll have to tell me where it is.'

The girl he held was trembling and wheezing. Her face was purple. He felt a wave of dizzyness at the prospect of carrying this sick creature, this sick thing, in his arms. She felt so light.

Brera completely lost control. She stood stiffly, blinking, saying nothing, clenching and unclenching her fists.

'Come on, let's go! Get a coat, or come as you are. I need you to give me directions.'

He turned and carried Sylvia towards the door. Brera ran after him. 'If we pass the ambulance on the way we can stop it.'

They reached the door and then all hell broke loose. Sylvia's body, previously slack and pliant, exploded out of Steven's arms like a firecracker.

'Let go of me!'

Steven tried to grab hold of her. Sylvia wasn't strong enough to resist, but she angled her body on the floor, against the two walls and the door, in such a way as to make moving her virtually impossible. When he tried to lunge at her, she kicked out at him, used her elbows and her nails.

He drew back. 'What's wrong with her? What is this?'

Brera ignored him, threw herself at Sylvia and landed on top of her, using all the force of her weight to subdue her. Steven looked on in amazement. He thought it possible that Brera might crush the girl completely, might certainly break a bone or a rib. He said, 'Don't hurt her . . . don't . . .'

Brera's weight curtailed Sylvia's thrashing. Her head collapsed to one side. Steven noticed, when this happened, that her nose was bleeding. The blood was dark. The sight of it appalled him.

Brera could hear noises on the stairs. Seconds later, two ambulancemen arrived carrying a stretcher. One of them had a bag and a syringe. Brera lifted herself. 'She's having an asthma attack but she won't leave the building. She's . . .'

No words for it. What was she?

The ambulanceman with the syringe said, 'Take her in and lay her down on a sofa.'

Brera scrambled up and grabbed hold of Sylvia's arms. Steven held her legs, and between them they carried her back to the sofa and dropped her on to it. Her body felt heavy, a dead weight. Her face was still purple, her lips were white and her teeth were chattering.

The ambulanceman filled his syringe, pulled up her sleeve, stuck it into her arm and emptied it. He then refilled the syringe and did the same thing again. 'What set this off? Some kind of allergy?'

Brera nodded.

'She should be hospitalized but I don't want to risk upsetting her any further,' he said.

'Maybe you could sedate her?'

'Too risky on top of the stuff I've just given her.'

Sylvia was moving her head from side to side. 'Just . . . bloody . . . leave me.'

He laughed. 'She can talk, but she can't breathe.' He peered into her face. 'How do you feel? Better yet?'

She didn't respond.

'How about we take you to hospital now? You'll be fine there.'

Sylvia's body, which had begun to relax, stiffened up again.

He opened his bag and took out an inhaler. He showed it to Brera. 'How much of this stuff has she had?'

'I don't know. A lot. But it didn't seem like she was breathing it in.'

'This close environment's setting her off. The weather especially. We have a nebulizer in the ambulance. It'll have to do her for the time being.'

Brera nodded. 'She had one before. If I keep her still for a few days and make her stay quiet . . .'

She leaned over the back of the sofa and spoke to Sylvia directly. 'You'll do as I say or I'll drag you to the hospital myself.'

Sylvia ignored her. The ambulanceman had refilled his syringe. He showed it to her. 'How are you feeling? Better? Do you want any more of this?'

She scowled up at him. Her face was still pale but less blotchy. Brera moved towards him, keen to help, feeling woefully inadequate for her earlier lack of competence. 'Can I do anything?'

'Make yourself a cup of tea.'

She nodded, chastened.

Steven said, 'I'll make the tea. I know where the kitchen is.'

Brera stared at Steven, looked at him as if she had only just realized that he was there, that it was *him*. She felt as if everyone was trying to make her feel useless, as though, in some way, this entire situation was her responsibility; Sylvia – her indomitable will, her obstinacy – had nothing whatsoever to do with it.

The ambulanceman felt Sylvia's pulse. 'Her heart's almost back to normal. She'll wheeze badly for a few days. She'll probably be very weak.'

He looked over at Brera. 'How old is she? Thirteen? Fourteen?'

'Nineteen. She just looks younger.'

'You'll have to be firm with her.'

She nodded, extremely resentful but incapable of expressing it. She wanted them all to go, then she would slap her, she could strangle her.

Of course she knew that she would do neither of these things. A cool bath and a packet of biscuits, she decided. They would have to suffice.

After carrying up the nebulizer, they set about rearranging the living-room furniture, pushing Sylvia, on the sofa, up against a wall so that the nebulizer could be placed next to a socket. As they worked a small congregation of birds accumulated on the window-sill. The door to the roof was still open and letting a cool breeze into the room; two or three birds were in the doorway. Brera, hawk-eyed, noticed them. She slammed the door and drew the curtains.

It was dark now. Sylvia turned her head and muttered something.

Brera moved closer, placing her ear next to Sylvia's lips. 'What?'

'Open the curtains.'

She frowned. 'Sorry?'

'Open the bloody curtains!'

Brera smiled. 'Open them yourself.'

Sylvia tried to move but she was too weak. She tried to speak again, but the ambulanceman gently placed the nebulizer mask across her nose and mouth. She stared at him, livid. What was he doing? He had gagged her. She closed her eyes. If she'd had the energy, she would have stopped breathing just to irritate him.

Later, after they'd gone, Brera sat in the kitchen with Steven and tried to explain. But Steven kept interjecting, to comment, to express sympathy and amazement.

When he was seventeen Steven had read the book *Sybil*, about a girl who'd had fourteen personalities. He'd also seen the film starring Sally Field. He said, 'This is twice as interesting as *Sybil*. You should write a story about it. Sell it.'

Brera frowned. 'This isn't like that. It isn't even very interesting. Only stupid. Stupid and sad.'

Steven was surprised by the ferocity in her voice. He said, 'Of course it's sad. I thought she was going to die back then. Just die as I stood there, holding her.'

Brera smiled at him, gently, wishing she owned a small firearm.

In the morning, bright and early, Ruby had taken the dog out for a long walk, down through Leicester Square, to the Embankment and along the river. This was now almost a habit, she decided, was already becoming one: last night, this morning. Thinking, walking. Couldn't be bad.

When she arrived back at the flat, Vincent was still stretched out on the sofa, half-asleep. She pulled open the curtains. He groaned. 'How early is it?'

She consulted her watch. 'Nine-forty-five. I'm working ten till six.'

He sat up. Ruby noticed that he was wearing a shirt. He was slightly chubby. His stomach protruded and his navel stuck out too, like a white cherry on an iced cup-cake.

'Why tell me that?'

'What?'

'Where you're going to be and how long.'

He yawned, not really expecting an answer.

She picked up a large, aluminium pan from the draining-board, rinsed it out and then threw some Weetabix, water and milk into it. This mixture she mashed up with a fork and then put down on the floor for the dog.

'Will you eat anything?' he asked, meaning by this that he would, that he wanted some coffee.

'I bought a cup of tea earlier.'

'You haven't chucked me out yet,' he said, secretly pleased, 'because you need me to stay.'

'Yeah?'

She watched the dog eating. She said, 'I don't want you feeding her or losing her. I'll put her muzzle on when she's finished her breakfast.'

He lay back down again, stretched out, pulled up his blanket. He debated whether he minded being indispensable, and decided that he didn't mind, on this particular occasion.

'You will be careful?'

'I will be.'

'There's dark glasses and a baseball hat in the bedroom. Unisex. In case you feel self-conscious.' How would he look without that mess on his face? She smiled to herself. Less colourful.

'Fine.'

'Don't step on her paws. I haven't paid for them yet.'

'So long as she doesn't step on mine.'

'I've paid for yours.'

'Ha!'

He waved at her. She completed her chores, patted the dog and left some spare keys in a prominent position.

When she'd gone, Vincent stared over the top of the sofa at Buttercup, who was sauntering around the kitchen area, sniffing the tiles through her muzzle. He whistled to her. She popped her head around the edge of the units and stared at him, obliging but sullen. He whistled again. She sat down.

He threw off his blankets and went into the bathroom for a pee. The dog followed him and watched from the doorway. Vincent flushed the toilet and then rinsed his face and hands in the sink. He stared at his wounds in the mirror and then debated whether to use Ruby's toothbrush, but didn't. Instead he ate some toothpaste, swallowed the foam and stepped over Buttercup, who was now lounging on her side, blocking the bathroom doorway.

He strolled into Ruby's bedroom and looked around for the hat and glasses she had mentioned. Eventually he found them, stuck on top of her wardrobe. He put them on and wandered into the living-room. The dog was now lying on the sofa.

He considered whether it was appropriate to play-wrestle with a greyhound. She seemed rather large. Just as he was forming an opinion on this issue the telephone rang. He answered it. 'Yes?'

There was a pause. It was Steven.

'This is Ruby's flat,' Vincent said smartly, 'but she's not here.' As he spoke, he picked up the packet of Weetabix, took one out and ate it dry.

'She's at work?'

Vincent's mouth was full. There was a short pause and then Steven said, 'I met you, didn't I? The other night.'

Vincent couldn't remember. Dreamworld, he thought, Dreamland.

'Will you just tell her that it's off tomorrow. There's been a hitch, so it's off.'

'Fine.'

'You will tell her?'

'Yes. Fine.'

He chewed on the cereal, his mouth a cement-mixer, turning, churning, his brain, already, he decided, a cool block of concrete.

Steven hung up. He turned and stared over at Sylvia, who was lying on the couch, almost obscured by darkness, wheezing.

Eventually he said, 'I'm Steven, by the way, if you can hear me.'

Sylvia said nothing. She felt absolutely miserable. She just kept thinking, They all patronize me. Why won't they leave me? I wish I was strong enough to chuck a chair at this fool. Even a pillow, but a pillow isn't hard enough. I couldn't aim properly anyway. It's too dark. And she felt so tired.

Connor had agreed to rehearse without the use of amplifiers. Sam and Sarah were sitting in the kitchen discussing Sarah's work.

Sarah was shouting above the noise, 'Men have always linked the female sex with a kind of irrationality. Hysteria is perceived as something entirely feminine. Doctors used to think that when a woman became hysterical her womb rose into her throat and became jammed there. Men get hysterical all the time but we just don't use the same words to describe their anger. Of course it's exactly the same anger. Sensitivity, hypersensitivity, mysticism, magic. These are all things that marginalize us. But women

pretend to enjoy the margins. It's a kind of control through a lack of control, if you see what I mean. We're responsible for our own contradictions.'

In the next room, Connor started to drum in earnest, then to sing. Sam stuck a finger in each ear. Sarah followed suit. They grinned at each other, dumbly.

Ruby was sitting on the sofa watching *This is Your Life* and waiting impatiently for Vincent to return with the dog. She'd been rattling around in the flat for an hour or so, aimless, like a pea in a tin can. She was trying not to worry over his whereabouts, and took reassurance from the fact that his shirt was still on the floor. It smelled – she noticed when she sniffed it – of sweat and vomit.

When he let himself in she said, 'I tried to phone you earlier this morning but you'd gone already.'

This sounded like an accusation, but he didn't let it bother him. He felt a general sense of well-being, was pleased, in fact, to see Ruby, although he was uncertain why. He smiled at her. 'I've been exercising this dog all day. I haven't rested for a single minute.'

There was something speculative and unfinished about his speech. She said, 'I only asked you to look after her,' and made a kissing noise at the dog, patting her lap to encourage her over. Buttercup strolled across and sat down next to Ruby, sniffing at her legs through the muzzle. She had a strangely replete air about her.

'You didn't feed her, did you?'

Vincent shook his head, taking a rucksack off his shoulder and slinging it on the floor. 'She chewed a cigarette butt, only she didn't swallow it.'

'You've been drinking.'

He ignored her. 'What'll you feed her tonight?'

Ruby stroked the dog between her ears. 'She should be eating a special high-fibre diet. Stuff called Beta-Racer. I couldn't find any, though, so I got her some normal dog food instead.'

Vincent sat down on the sofa next to her. She stared at his profile. 'Your bruises are still bad.'

He nodded and then stretched out his legs and pushed his hands into the pockets of his jeans. He pulled out a handful of notes. 'Here.'

She took the notes and counted them: Two tens and four twenties. 'What's this? Where did you get it?'

He leaned forward and stroked the dog. Ruby noticed with some alarm how natural this gesture looked. She couldn't help thinking how useful the dog was, as an excuse, as a reason to ignore everything.

'Did you borrow it?'

'I won it in a bet, in a pub.'

She rolled the notes up into a tight wad. 'It's illegal to bet with people you don't know in pubs. You can get arrested for it.'

He smiled. 'I'd fucking burp and they'd have me for noise pollution.'

Her eyes returned to the television screen. 'I'm just telling you.'

After a short pause he said, 'You'll be needing some new sunglasses.'

'You lost them?'

He shook his head.

'You broke them?'

'No. I ate them.'

She focused on his face. 'You ate them?'

He nodded. 'For a bet.'

'I bought those on the Kings Road. I liked them.'

'I only ate the lenses. The frame was still intact, but I couldn't see any point in bringing that back.'

'You'll be ill again.'

'I won't. I vomited them up straight away.'

'You hate vomiting.'

'I hate a lot of things, but I still do most of them.'

The money. She felt it in her hand. What was he after?

They both stared at the television for a while. Eventually she said, 'You didn't do anything special with the hat, then?'

He picked up his bag. The hat was squeezed into one of the front compartments. He pulled it out and tossed it at her. It

landed on her lap and she stared at it without moving. He pulled open the main flap of the rucksack, took out a record from the back and passed it to her. She took it from him and pulled the corners of the cover straight where they had become bent in the course of his journey. Ray Charles. It wasn't new.

'This is a completely different record. Thanks, anyway.'

He located his toothbrush in his bag and sprang up. 'I'm just going to brush my teeth.'

She handed him the roll of notes. 'Stick these into the coffee jar in the cupboard above the sink.'

After he'd done as she'd instructed he went into the bathroom.

She wondered where the rucksack had come from. What exactly had he been doing all day? The dog looked all right. Tired, though. She picked up one of her paws. The pads looked fine.

Vincent returned and sat back down on the sofa. 'What's this about?' He was holding the registration booklet.

'Bad news.'

'Why?'

'Read it.'

Inside he found a betting slip; on it, some notes. 'I wrote those today,' she said, 'in a spare moment.'

'Is she any good at racing?'

'She came in the first three during her maiden race, which I think is good. But she's raced badly since.'

'How many races?' He looked at the book.

'Too many. She could race well if she felt like it, but she doesn't seem to want to.'

He inspected her betting slip. 'What's this mean?'

'Things that might help. I listed them.' She pointed. 'That says "weight".'

'She needs to lose a few pounds? Well, that's straightforward enough.' He battled to read on: 'Hurdles, handicap, distance and positioning.'

'She hasn't raced over hurdles before. I thought she might be good at it.'

He frowned. 'If she can't be bothered running in a normal race, how's making her jump things going to help?'

'It's complicated.'

She stood up and went into the kitchen, opened a bag of dog biscuits and tipped them on to a plate.

Vincent was still reading her notes. 'What does handicap mean?'

She picked up a can opener and stuck it into the top of a tin. 'Sometimes she interferes with other dogs. That's a really bad sign. Greyhounds aren't bred to be aggressive. Bitches especially. So if you have a greyhound that snaps at other dogs – even though it's usually only because of friendliness or boredom – the racing manager gets really upset about it.'

'I asked about the handicap.'

'Well, if she ran in a handicap race her trap would be at the front. Because she's crap they'd give her a head start.'

'And so?'

'When she's released she'd have the advantage of a few extra seconds on her side. She'd be able to see the hare without being put off by other dogs.'

'You've written "positioning" here in capital letters.'

'Yep. It's connected.'

She mashed up the meat from the tin with the biscuits, put the bowl down for the dog and took off the muzzle. 'I bought two bits of fish on the market this afternoon. Maybe you could make dinner?'

'I know that some dogs run wide and some run close to the fence.'

'The rails.' She grinned.

Vincent caught her expression. 'Well, fuck you!'

She walked back over and sat down again. 'OK.'

He pushed his toothbrush behind his ear, as if it were a pen, and folded his arms.

'There are six traps. The first four traps are chosen in a kind of draw. The first trap is usually the best trap for most dogs because the distance that dog ends up running is much shorter, I mean, if it stays close to the rails.'

'Why?'

'Think about it. The dogs run an oval course. The inside of an

oval is going to be a shorter distance than the outside. Anyway, if a dog is a good railer and a fast trapper and it's in trap one, it'll be hard to beat. In the bookies, if anyone's going to bet in forecast doubles, most punters will bet the combination one and six. They're the two best traps.'

'Why six, then? The dog in that trap'd be running the longest distance.'

Ruby nodded. 'True. The two outside traps, five and six, aren't included in the draw. Dogs that are well-known wide runners are always given the outside traps to save on injuries.'

He was frowning again. Ruby jumped up and hunted around for a pen and some paper. She found a small red pen and the back of an electricity bill. She sat down and drew a large oval and then six small boxes on the oval which she numbered one to six, then moved up closer to Vincent to show him what she was doing. He felt her leg touching his, could smell her hair.

'If a wide runner was placed in any of the four inside tracks, he'd come powering out when the trap opened and go shooting towards the hare, smacking into several other dogs in the process. The speed they go, he'd probably end up hurting either himself or one of the other runners. What it comes down to is the fact that a wide runner will always chase the hare.'

'Hold on . . .' He was confused. 'So if they're all chasing the hare, what about the railer, the dog in trap one?'

She smiled. 'Dogs are like people. They do stuff for different reasons. The strains of dogs from which most of today's greyhounds are bred were strains that just ran for the sake of it. They'll chase anything. For a railer, it's more the running than the chasing that excites them. If a dog is a good railer, then it isn't that bothered about catching the hare. It's canny. It knows how to win a race.'

'So,' Vincent took the pen off her and pointed it at the two boxes numbered five and six, 'what about these dogs? They're just stupid?'

'Nope. The distance around the track is longer from these two traps, but at the same time they've got much more room to really stretch out. Racing's all about negotiating bends. A dog that's

railing has a much tighter bend to negotiate, and the other dogs will be crowding him more. But the wide runner can really stride out and he's less likely to be bumped.'

Vincent rubbed his forehead. Ruby noticed. 'It gets even more complicated when you try and think how your own animal fits into the whole thing.'

Buttercup had finished her dinner and was now lying across the kitchen tiles. Vincent turned his head and stared at her. 'What sort of a runner is she?'

Ruby took hold of the registration booklet, opened it, pointed. 'That there is the first race she ran. Her time . . .' She ran her finger down the column, calculating out loud. 'She was at least five or six seconds faster in that race than in any of her others.'

'Which trap?'

'Two. Which makes you think she's going to be a railer, but in fact I know she runs fairly wide. She's never been in traps five or six, but they've run her in all the others and she hasn't done anything.'

Vincent was staring at Ruby's ear as she spoke. He said, 'Did you have all those holes made in your ear at the same time?'

'What?'

She frowned at him. He scratched his nose. 'If you think about it, there's no point in considering this stuff tactically unless you've actually seen the race.'

She closed the book. 'And how d'you work that one out?'

'Well, a race isn't only about how one dog performs.'

'But I'm only interested in one dog.'

'I'm saying that a race isn't about how one dog performs, it's about how six dogs perform. Maybe she is a wide runner.'

'So why her best performance from trap two?'

'Well, maybe in that race she came out of the trap faster than the other dogs to her right, was able to see the hare, unhindered, and move outside before the other dogs overtook her.'

Ruby thought about this. 'I don't think she's a particularly fast trapper, which means she doesn't usually come out of the trap all that quickly.'

She threw the book down and stood up. 'I'd better get dinner on.'

'So what's the plan?'

'Fish.'

'Not for dinner, for the dog.'

He stretched out his arms across the back of the sofa; his fingers nearly reached her as she leaned on the arm. 'You've written out your lists and you said she's got a race on Thursday.'

Ruby stared at her finger-nails. She was wearing a transparent polish that made them shine, but they still looked ragged.

He said, 'I think we should take her down to the track right now and experiment.'

'How? What good would that do?'

'You've got to offer her some kind of incentive.'

'Like what?'

'Greyhound racing originated with coursing, didn't it? Dogs chasing live hares?'

'In Ireland.'

'She's probably just bored. She isn't stimulated, so she won't perform.'

Ruby shook her head. 'I was telling you how these strains of dogs chase anything. Usually they'll run after anything because that's how they're bred.'

'So?'

She thought for a moment. 'In coursing I know for a fact that dogs never interfere with each other.'

'Why's that?'

'Lots of reasons.'

Vincent grinned. 'Deviants are always more intelligent, so they get bored more easily.'

Ruby considered this for a while. Eventually she said, 'We can't just go down to the track. They might have speedway on tonight. Anyway, I'm tired and she's just eaten.'

'In the morning, then.'

She stood up. 'I suppose I could phone and ask if it's all right to take her down early.'

'If we get there for eight, you'd have a full two hours before work.'

Ruby went to the phone and picked up the receiver. She didn't feel very enthusiastic herself, but any enthusiasm, from any source, no matter how misplaced, was better than none at all. She was about to dial and then stopped.

'Why all this sudden interest in the dog? I didn't know you even liked dogs.'

He was staring at the television. 'I don't. But I do like plans.'

Ideas. To have an idea, he thought. To think and to do. What could be better?

She stared suspiciously at the back of his head before dialling. He was full of shit.

Sam sipped her lager and waved a hand in front of her face. Someone nearby was smoking and holding their cigarette too close. She shouted, 'Well, everything's relative, isn't it? I mean, your position is always going to be affected by where you stand, who you are and your sex.'

She couldn't help thinking how smart Sarah looked. Her hair was drawn back away from her face and she wore very little make-up, except for black liquid eye-liner on her top lids and some mascara which made her eyes look enormous. Sam couldn't believe she'd managed to persuade her to come along tonight. She felt honoured.

Sarah put her lips close to Sam's ear: 'Yeah, that's fair enough, but sometimes that sort of argument gets you out of everything, if you see what I mean. Relativism's often just an excuse for not committing.'

She was stopped, mid-flow, by someone pushing past her who tipped up her drink. It spilled down her shirt and drenched her breasts. She swore and tried to wring it out ineffectually with one hand. 'It's too bloody full in here,' she shouted, 'and it's too LOUD.'

Sam grabbed hold of her arm and steered her towards the nearest exit. 'It shouldn't stain if you give it a quick rub down.'

Sarah indicated the stage with her hand. 'Won't Connor be on soon? It's been at least half an hour since the last lot played.'

'They'll be doing loads of songs. I don't think we're obliged to see every one.'

Sam threaded a route around the bar, towards the ladies' toilets.

Inside were two or three women. It was cramped, even in here. Sam turned on the warm tap at one of the sinks and beckoned Sarah over. 'Splash some water over it. There's some liquid soap if you want it. Then hold it under the hand dryer.'

Sarah tried to bend over the sink. 'It's right down the front. I'll end up even wetter this way.'

Outside Sam could hear the taped music stop and a loud cheer as people waited for the imminent arrival of the band on-stage. She said, 'I've always really hated this place, but it must be exciting to play here. Connor's played here loads.'

She walked to the door and opened it, standing on tip-toe to try to see the stage. But the crowds were too dense and her angle too oblique. The three women who had been in the toilet repairing their make-up and brushing their hair pushed past her. Sarah shouted from inside, 'What's happening?'

She walked back in. 'They've come on. I can't see them, though, only hear them.'

Sarah cocked her head to one side and listened. 'I can just hear a kind of roaring noise. Is it them or the toilet cistern?'

Sam grinned. 'You must be so glad you came.'

Outside there was more cheering.

'What are they called again?'

Sam watched with surprise as Sarah unbuttoned her shirt and took it off.

'Stirsign.'

She held it under the tap, lathering it with soap and then rinsing it.

Sam watched her. 'D'you want me to stand guard at the door?'

'Not when the band's just come on. It's perfectly private in here.'

She wrung out the shirt and then stuck it under the hand dryer.

Sam couldn't help staring at Sarah's body, which was pale, angular and extremely thin. She wore a turquoise bra which efficiently cupped her small, neat breasts. Sam thought her too thin, as though if she moved too sharply or quickly her bones might push through the skin and show themselves, bursting out like little daggers.

Sam touched Sarah's shirt to see how quickly it was drying. 'It's still soaking. The dryer isn't very efficient.'

Sarah misconstrued the source of Sam's concern. 'Look, why don't you go on out? I wouldn't want you to miss anything.'

Sam shook her head. 'I can see him any time. Anyway, it's too crowded out there.'

'What's your star sign?'

'Guess.'

'Aquarius or Gemini.'

'Neither: Pisces, but I am a water sign, if that's what you're getting at.'

Sarah smiled at this. 'I'm a fire sign. We're incompatible.'

Sam was about to reply when the door swung open and two women came in. She noticed them staring at Sarah's bare skin and exchanging glances. One of them went into a cubicle while the other fluffed up her hair with her hands, watching Sarah in the mirror. Sam felt compromised, but couldn't understand why.

'D'you want me to hold it under for a while?'

Sarah, apparently oblivious, handed the shirt over. 'Thanks.'

She picked up her lager and took a sip of it. Sam held the shirt under the dryer. It felt soft.

The second girl came out of the cubicle, washed her hands and then held them, dripping, limply in front of her.

'Oh, sorry.'

Sam turned and was about to step sideways. But Sarah said, 'Don't worry,' pushed her firmly up against the dryer and kissed her, fully.

Sarah's lips felt delicate and her breath tasted of lager and another flavour: garlic or liquorice. Sam felt Sarah's tongue, like a mollusc, a foreign thing, curving up along the inside of her lips.

She felt her hands, she was sure she felt them, touching her breasts, soft on her breasts. The dryer pushed out warm air, the weight of them both reactivating its mechanism.

Just as suddenly, Sarah withdrew. She was laughing. 'They've gone. We frightened the shit out of them. Give me my shirt and I'll put it on.'

Sam handed her the shirt. 'Why did you do that?'

Sarah slipped it on and began to fasten the buttons. 'It was the highlight of their evening.'

She peered at herself in the mirror, wiped the corners of her lips with her thumb and forefinger, smiled and then pushed the door open, holding it ajar for Sam. 'Come on.'

Sam didn't pause to check her own reflection. *Her stomach.* How did it feel? As if she'd just been told the lemonade she'd been drinking was actually turpentine. A kind of horror. Confusion? No. A pure feeling without fixed meaning.

Sarah led the way, pushing past people at the back, moving gradually forwards. Near the front, everyone was dancing. Several people were stage diving.

Sam shouted over the noise, 'If we get too close we'll get thrown about. Everyone's pushing.'

Sarah launched herself into the middle of the fray. Sam opted to stay back, craning her neck, trying to see Connor. Eventually she could see him, banging away at his drum-kit, hair in his face, T-shirt still on but soaking wet.

I want to feel part of this, she thought. She wanted to, but suddenly she felt removed from everything. Lonely. Alone. The drum, the beat, the sound it made, reminded her. Of what?

She was twelve years old and Sylvia was asking her if she could borrow her skipping rope. The music – she couldn't escape it, but she could block it – came in waves. It reminded her of the rope: swinging round and round, whizzing, whirring and slapping the ground.

Sylvia had borrowed it. Sam heard the rope turning: vicious, unstoppable, cyclical. She watched Sylvia's feet as she jumped, inefficiently shod in a pair of old, soft, blue canvas deck shoes.

Sylvia counted as she jumped, 'One, two, three, four . . .' By the time she'd reached fifty, her feet had grown heavier, faltering. She stopped on fifty-four, without grace, clumsily tangled, her breathing laboured.

On the ground, surrounding her, their necks and wings broken, were five or six birds. Injured by the rope. Killed by the rope.

Sylvia fell to her knees and gathered them up with her hands, her breath turning into jerky tears.

Sam had watched coldly, thinking, Will I ever love anything that much?

Her heart contracted and the feeling she experienced was not so much love as jealousy.

Steven spent the evening watching *Sophie's Choice* on video. During any especially tedious or gut-wrenching moments he cast an eye, somewhat apathetically, over the latest edition of *The Stage*.

Steven loved Meryl Streep. If asked to explain this adoration, he'd say that he loved the way that she was never shrewish. She was so dignified. She could be angry – he thought she did Angry extremely well – but she was never vulgar. She didn't forget herself, her dignity.

Sometimes he'd masturbate as he watched her on screen. She was so aloof, and that in itself was sexy. But after he'd finished – when he'd cleared away the tissues and washed his hands – he'd always feel an intense pang of self-disgust.

He'd been staring at one particular page of *The Stage* for several minutes, reading but not reading, when something caught his eye and caused him to blink, pick up the paper and stare at it more intently. The focus of his attention was a small but nicely written obituary towards the bottom of the page. He read it, re-read it.

Sylvia watched Brera talking on the phone. She watched but she didn't listen. She'd been using the nebulizer since the morning, and its vapours had been opening her bronchial tubes, releasing the hostage air in her lungs, and then escaping; travelling

onwards, upwards, making her brain smart, glisten, pulsate, making colours painfully clear, and smells . . . but she couldn't smell anything, she just knew that everything was clearer, magnified, extended, elongated. Her senses were ecstatically jumbled.

Brera was sitting close by, talking on the phone but also staring at Sylvia, thinking, It's not so much that she can't breathe, more that she doesn't want to breathe. She's happier not breathing.

She focused on Sylvia's face. Her lips were moving, she was muttering, and whenever the mask fell from her nose and mouth, Brera could hear disjointed pieces of conversation. She struggled to keep her attention focused on Steven.

Inside Sylvia's head facts and images were floating, connecting, disconnecting. She said, 'I can see these conversations taking place, everywhere, but really the conversation is the same one. It's the same conversation.'

She saw herself in a place full of bright lights and a bright girl with white hair was saying something about ideas.

'You say you like ideas? What does that mean?'

A voice responded. It came from nowhere, but it was a harsh voice, full of emphasis: 'Ideas alter things, form things, change things unilaterally. They can be modified, disciplined, controlled. I see stuff. Life. I see life and it's only a mishmash of facts, thoughts, images, pictures. But everything crystallizes in my head, forms doctrine, produces its own clear meaning. My mind works that way.'

Sylvia couldn't understand this at all. The girl seemed to be having difficulty too, but she said, 'Life is more jumbled than you think. Caring about things should be enough. Even if you can only manage to care about one thing. You have to understand what it is to be good. Not so much what you can make of life, but what you can give to it.'

Sylvia wasn't bothered any more, but the dialogue continued anyway. 'That's an idea, though! It's just that you can't be bothered to take it any further, to politicize. It's just sloppy thinking.'

Sylvia could taste the word *politicize* on her tongue. Its rough

edges, its sharpness. She had no feelings either way – towards it or against it – she could only taste it.

The white voice was saying, 'I never take things further because that's how you get into trouble. Once you accept one thing, you end up accepting loads of stuff, half of which you don't really understand. When things get too big, they get out of your control. You start off by thinking that you're being good, but you end up finding out that ideas have a life of their own. They can turn bad, can make you bad and you don't even know it.'

The hard face, the hard voice, laughed. This laughter tickled Sylvia. It had its own particular charm, this laugh, like snuff, or the smell of fruity pipe tobacco. 'But I want to get into trouble! Don't you? Why not get into trouble? You're naive. You know it too, and you think that your naivety makes you good, but in fact all it makes you is easy to manipulate.'

'Manipulate? Who by?'

'By me. By anyone and everyone.'

Sylvia felt herself being sucked away and thrown between the stars, but the stars were on the ceiling, were, in fact, just one star: a bright bulb peeking through a wicker shade. The roof was white. Now she heard something else, but it was the same thing she had heard before. A familiar voice, but a different place, in a sea of orange and roughness: 'I'm like you. I like to think about things, to be open to every influence and then to make up my mind. But sometimes, sometimes it becomes impossible to make up your mind because the information, the information . . . books, paper, pens, books, films, paper, pens . . .'

Sylvia digested the word *information* and it made her want to burp. The voice said 'information' almost as though it had not said that word at all but had said 'sex' – with a mixture of desire and dread. 'Sometimes you end up finding out too much. Reading, discovering and uncovering.'

Sylvia wanted to locate the other half of this conversation, thought for one awful second that she herself was expected to provide it. Luckily this was not so. The voice came, the rebuttal. It was a loving voice, wheedling and whining: 'You don't have to

digest everything, to crystallize it. Why can't you just open yourself up to things, be open to things and let that be an end in itself? I guess that's a sort of, a kind of . . .' The voice hesitated. 'I was going to say "liberalism", but I don't want to involve myself in all that.'

The first voice sounded sad: 'That's just it. You have to involve yourself, otherwise you can't give anything.'

'I want peace and freedom.'

'Clichés.'

'Why?'

'Because those things don't mean anything when you say them.'

Sylvia picked up the word *mean* and juggled with it. She thought, Everything has meaning. I'm in a sea of it. Swimming in it, drowning.

The voices came together in her head and each voice she tried to simplify by making it into a shape. The harsh voice became a square, the white voice an arrow, the familiar voice was a circle . . . A fifth voice emerged, strident, sensual, suggestive, feminine. It said, 'I don't want truth. Ideas get lost in truth. Truth is stupid. Take any letter away from it and it becomes stupid. *Trut. Thur. Hutt. Ruth*. It's just a word. It's just another word and words stand for very little unless you use them sensibly and with rigour. I only want truth if I can use it. I want to rebuild the world with my own ideas, selectively.'

This voice contained all of the other shapes. It was a star. It throbbed. For a horrible moment Sylvia thought that this was in fact her voice, her own voice, but then she realized that she didn't believe anything that this voice was saying. She mistrusted it. She had no voice herself.

Ideas flooded the room and she floated on them. One idea was that every story was one story, everything boiled down into one single narrative. Every thought, idea, commentary, fiction, was travelling towards a single meaning. She tried to find this meaning but it was hopeless. It was too big. It was nothing. That one meaning might have to be God, she decided, which would be like a defeat.

She found herself in a cave. She remembered reading *A Passage to India* (where did that come from?) and the sequence in the caves, with the echo, when every noise that was made, that could be made, every noise was reduced to nothing, a hauntingly meaningless echo, a jolt, a thud.

A song became a thud, a poem became a thud, a prayer became a thud, a sneeze, a thud, science, thud, beauty, thud, glory, thud, love, thud, God . . . And so . . .

She sighed. The mask fell from her face and she, in turn, fell from dreaming to sleeping.

Brera put down the phone and walked over to Sylvia. She picked up the mask, folded it and turned off the nebulizer at the plug. The air smelled high and vaporous. She stared down at her sleeping daughter, then slowly, hollowly, said out loud the worst word she could think of: 'Cunt.'

She regretted this instantly. 'Sam would have something to say about why I chose that word,' she muttered. 'I'm too old to swear.'

It didn't even make her feel better. It just sounded foolish.

TWELVE

Connor woke Sam by kissing her ribs and her belly, by dampening her hips with tiny, sharp licks and bites.

Unfortunately, as Sam awoke, instead of finding this luxurious introduction to wakefulness pleasurable and erotic, she had to restrain the impulse to slap Connor with the back of her hand, to swat him.

'Did we argue last night?' she asked.

Connor's tongue stopped what it was doing and he straightened up, placing his head next to hers on the pillow. He stared at her, but she didn't catch his expression because she was looking up at the ceiling.

'I don't think we did. I was drunk. I remember Sarah droning on about something.'

'What's the time?'

She could smell his hair, which, although it looked ragged and uncombed, was soft on her shoulder and smelled of smoke from the night before.

'I dunno. Eight? Eight-thirty?'

She sat bolt upright. 'I promised Brera I'd be home early today. We're going shopping.'

Connor grinned. 'Oh yeah?'

She looked down at him. 'You can't come.'

'Why?' He pretended to be hurt.

'Because I'm going with Brera.'

'Sounds weird when you call her by her name.'

He reached down and pinched her knee, then let his hand slip up and along the inside of her thigh. She leaned over, pecked his cheek and jumped out of bed. 'Actually, I would invite you to come, but I know you've got an interview at lunchtime.'

'Which leaves me four hours to think of something interesting to say.'

'You think that's long enough?'

He laughed and threw a pillow at her, but she ducked and padded through to the kitchen.

Sarah was lounging against the kitchen cabinets waiting for the kettle to boil, wearing a short, multi-coloured bathrobe. Her long thin legs protruded from the robe, untanned. As she leaned over, Sam could see the curve of her breast and her tiny, pink nipple. Sarah's red hair had fallen across her face, half covering it.

'Hello.'

Sarah turned, straightened herself, and pulled a handful of curls behind her ear. 'I'm totally knackered. Jet lag.'

She yawned with neat precision, like a cat.

'Making coffee?' Sam asked.

'Tea.'

Sam walked over to the kettle and turned it off at the plug before it had a chance to boil for too long.

'Mine's white, if you're making. I like it insipid.'

Sam busied herself locating cups and finding a tea-bag. She wasn't sure if she felt a tension between them. She thought, Maybe it's just because she isn't dressed. She's so sluttish, the way she lounges about. No make-up, her face all gaunt and white.

'Do you have any plans for today?' She poured water on to Sarah's tea-bag.

Sarah shrugged, noncommital. 'You?'

'I've got to go shopping with my mother. We're having some photos taken this afternoon.'

Sarah's face brightened. 'Can I come?'

'It'll be very dull.'

'Go on. It'll be a laugh. I can meet your mother. That'd be interesting.'

Sam finished making the two coffees. 'I'll phone and ask once I've taken this in to Connor.'

Sarah poured some extra milk into her tea. 'I hope he appreciates you running around after him like this.'

Sam said nothing, only smiled as she carried the cup carefully out of the kitchen.

Connor reached out for the cup. Sam perched on the edge of the bed and handed it to him. 'Can I use the phone?'

'Sure.'

He pulled himself up into a sitting position, careful not to spill anything.

'Sarah wants to come shopping.'

He frowned. 'Why?'

'I don't know. She said she thought it'd be fun.'

'Amusing. I bet she said she thought it'd be amusing. That's the kind of thing she'd say.'

'She said she thought it'd be a laugh.'

He brushed some hair out of his eyes. 'Will she be going back to the flat in Hackney with you?'

'Does it matter?'

He seemed to think that it did.

'Have you told her about Sylvia?' Her name felt strange on his tongue, as though it implied a familiarity that didn't in fact exist.

'No. Why? Should I discuss my sister with everyone? I'm sure you don't make a habit of discussing your family at length with every new person you meet.'

'I'm just saying that you hardly know her.'

Sam stared at him, irritated. 'I hardly knew you once and it wasn't a problem.'

Connor put his cup of coffee on the carpet and lay back down in bed. How can I feel jealous? he thought. Of *her*. Christ.

'I'm tired,' he said, sullenly.

'Fine.' She stood up. 'You're being pathetic.'

He didn't answer. She pulled on her clothes, picked up her coat, which was slung over the door handle, and closed the door gently behind her.

Sarah was getting dressed in her bedroom. The door was slightly ajar. Sam called through: 'I'm ready to go when you are.'

Sarah appeared in the doorway wearing an old-fashioned,

yellow shirtwaister, black tights and flat black shoes. Her hair was tied back with a yellow scarf. She wore no make-up.

'That didn't take long. The dress is great.'

'Did you phone your mother?'

Sam shook her head. 'No, but I shouldn't think she'll be bothered.'

Sam followed Sarah out of the flat. 'I didn't mention my sister before, did I?'

'No. She sing too?'

'Not much. We let her write some of our music.'

Sarah slammed the front door. 'Yeah?'

'She suffers from a kind of disability.'

'Really?'

Sam stepped out into the street. 'She's afflicted.'

'An affliction?' Sarah smiled. 'Sounds biblical.'

As soon as he heard the front door slam, Connor sat up in bed and looked frantically around his bedroom, trying to locate something – anything – that Sam might have left behind. Eventually his eyes settled on a small, white, cotton bra which was slung over the cymbal on his drum-kit. He went and picked it up, then folded it carefully so that it would fit into the fist of one hand. He smiled to himself, feeling its softness, then stopped smiling and tried to bring to mind exactly what it was that had passed between them.

Vincent led the way down to Berwick Street. He was bossy this morning and full of purpose. 'I'm sure I saw a butcher's down here.'

Ruby nodded. 'There's a few of them. They all open early. Supply hotels and stuff.'

'This one.'

They went inside. Vincent smiled at the butcher, who stared at him coldly, taking in, in one glance, the cut on his forehead and his crumpled shirt.

'I want a whole rabbit.'

'Skinned?'

'No, whole. Ears, fur, everything.'

The butcher disappeared into the rear of the shop. When he had gone Vincent turned to Ruby: 'I used to do this trick with dead rabbits when I was a kid. I'll show you later.'

She imagined him as a child – exactly the same, only smaller. She wondered what he was up to, but didn't really care. She'd given up on things, temporarily. He'd had that effect on her.

Outside again, he said, 'We want to head for Oxford Street.'

'Fine. We can catch the bus from Oxford Circus.'

Oxford Street was quiet at this hour. Vincent stopped walking and leaned against a rubbish bin. They stood in silence together.

'Now what?'

'Shut up and listen.'

She waited mutely for several minutes but nothing happened. The dog began to grow impatient and pulled on her lead. She was about to complain when Vincent said, 'I can hear something. Can you hear it? The dog can.'

Ruby looked down at Buttercup and as she looked she began to hear something: a strange kind of clattering and banging, a hollow noise, a repetitive thuddering-shuddering. Like thunder. Like an earthquake. She stared down the street, towards Oxford Circus and gasped.

A sea of horses. So huge. A glorious plague of them. Filling the city, exploding its damp, grey glass and granite, its rubble, its tarmac. Shattering the city with the gloss of fur, of muscle. Steam; ears, nostrils, quivering; eyes, black, whites rolling; tassels; tails. The smell of them. Their froth, their breath, their foam. Saddle leather. Sweet wax.

This was beauty. Like a knife twisting in her stomach. They passed her by, three abreast, on and on and on. Until the last, like water trickling down a plug hole, suddenly gone. Like a drum that stops beating. Beating.

'It's a fascist thing, really.'

'What?' She could still hardly breathe.

'That feeling.'

Her eyes were full of tears. He had given her this moment, had handed it to her. She said, 'Don't say anything else. You'll ruin it.'

He laughed at her – she was such a fool – and walked down to Oxford Circus, still laughing.

They stood on the track.

'What's the plan, then?'

He looked around him. 'Give me a minute.' Then added, 'Let's walk her for a while.'

'Great idea.'

He scowled at her, but they started walking. Vincent had been full of ideas the night before, full of plans and schemes, all of which had suddenly dissolved.

Ruby was saying, 'Either they feel the urge or they don't.'

'Where's the hare?'

She stood still and glanced around the perimeter of the track. 'If we carry on walking we're bound to come across it.'

They walked past the traps, six metal boxes, neatly numbered, which had been pushed off the sandy track and on to the grass verge.

'How come the traps aren't on the track?'

'They're mobile. Think about it. If they left the traps on the track after a race had started, the dogs'd run into them on the last bend.'

'Can we push them out?'

They pushed them out together. Vincent wanted to put Buttercup into one.

Ruby opened trap six and helped her inside. Vincent walked around to the front and peered in at her. He could see her pointed nose and her eyes. 'She looks pretty bored from this end.'

Ruby crossed her arms. 'She's bound to. She can't hear the hare or anything.'

'Can we run her now?'

'No. I'd have to ask the groundsman to operate the hare and I don't fancy doing that.'

She opened the trap, pulled the dog out and put her lead back on. 'The hare's over there. Can you see it?'

Vincent looked in the direction she had indicated. 'That orange

and white thing? It's like a balloon. No wonder she can't be bothered chasing it.'

He walked over and inspected it more closely, then took his rabbit out of the plastic bag, holding it aloft in his left hand, pushing the hare manually along its runner with his right, so that it made the requisite clattering noise.

The dog's ears pricked up and she pulled on her leash. Ruby held her back. Vincent continued pushing and after several steps he broke into a slow trot. The dog began to bark and pulled on her lead so hard that Ruby had to hold on to it with both hands.

'She's pulling my arms off.'

Vincent carried on jogging but shouted over his shoulder, 'Keep her until I tell you, then let her come, but let her pull you.'

The dog was riding up on to her back legs, still barking. Twenty yards on, he shouted, 'Come on, then!'

Ruby allowed the dog to pull her along, slowly at first, but after several steps she could no longer control her and moved faster, and then faster still. Eventually she was running after Vincent and the dog was loping in slow but effortless bounds. Vincent stopped the hare just beyond the finishing line, about sixty yards from its original position.

He was breathless. He tossed his brown rabbit across the artificial hare and waited for Ruby and the dog to catch up.

'What shall I do?' Ruby was hurtling towards him.

'Let her have it.'

She couldn't do otherwise. The dog jerked out of her hands, almost pulling her arm from its socket, charged at the rabbit and did her best to grab hold of it through her muzzle. She managed, somehow, to snatch it off the hare and shook it, swinging her head violently from side to side. The fur on the rabbit's hindquarters started to rip and the red flesh gaped through. Vincent, exhausted, was roaring with laughter. Ruby was bent double, trying to catch her breath, feeling the palm of her hand burning from the pull of the leash.

'Don't let her eat the bloody thing!'

He took hold of her lead and pulled on it. The dog held on to the rabbit and growled at him.

Ruby grinned, still panting. 'You're never going to get that off her.'

'You try and grab it.'

He was facing the dog, pulling her towards him. The collar had ridden up on her neck and was stuck behind her ears. Her head was down low, close to the ground. She growled again.

'D'you think I'm mad?'

'Come and take the lead then.'

She obliged him. He moved closer to the dog, circling her, bent down slowly and then lunged at the rabbit. She snarled, still holding on, and jumped forwards, towards Ruby, altering Ruby's centre of gravity and toppling her over. As she fell she let go of the lead. The dog dashed away, carrying the rabbit with her.

'Are you all right?'

She sat up, slightly winded, and tried to dust herself off. He offered her his hand. Her first impulse was to spit on it, but she reached out and took hold of it.

Ruby apologized for being late, and was about to explain about the state of her clothes when the area manager, Tom Croft, emerged from the kitchen carrying a bundle of notes through from the safe. He had yellow hair and a long, soft chin.

'So you finally made it?'

'I just told Jason . . .'

'What are you wearing?'

She said nothing. He stared at her coolly. 'You think this job is so difficult? There are plenty of others who could manage to do it, come in on time and dress properly.'

He pointed towards the till closest to where she was standing. 'I suggest you get some work done.'

Ruby sat down at the till and was about to give it a routine check when a punter came up for a bet. She rang it on, took the money and thanked him. When he'd gone, she took out the larger notes and counted them.

'Jason, this is a tenner short. Did you put in a float this morning?'

Jason was about to say something when Croft interrupted: 'I've been using that till myself all morning. It was fine when you sat down there two minutes ago.'

'Well, it's not fine now and I've only taken one small bet.'

'Are you sure that's all you've taken?'

'What?'

She noticed that Jason was blushing. Croft said, 'You've signed on. You should've checked the till first. The loss of that money is now your responsibility.'

He pulled on his jacket. 'I want you properly dressed next time I see you and I want you in on time.'

He strolled out.

As soon as he was gone she turned on Jason. 'I don't believe this! He practically called me a thief.'

'At least he didn't give you a formal warning.'

'That isn't the point. Where's Dawn?'

'I dunno. Not here yet.'

'If I'd been ten minutes later, I'd have missed him too.'

Jason smiled grimly. 'Knowing your luck, he'd have waited.'

'Oh yeah?'

She pulled off her sweatshirt and sat down. 'What bloody luck?'

Already Sarah could smell something strange. Her olfactory senses were incredibly refined. Her gut was stimulated not so much by sight as by sound and by smell. It churned as this new, unexpected aroma entered her nostrils and gained access to her interior. When she inhaled a good or a bad smell she sometimes felt as though she were actually eating it. Aromas were like foods but were less physically complex, like a kind of dispersed matter. When she inhaled them they invaded her, filled her and travelled through her system.

She tried to think of something else. 'What's your mother called again?'

'Brera.'

'Weird name.'

'It's Irish.'

'Nice name.'

'Yeah.'

'Don't the lifts work?'

'There aren't any. It's only five floors.'

By the fifth floor, Sarah was breathing so heavily that she couldn't smell anything.

Sam opened the door and ushered Sarah inside. It was dark. They walked down the passageway and into the living-room. Sam was about to switch on the light, but then resisted and strolled over towards the window instead, intending to draw the curtains. She bumped into an armchair. The furniture had been moved around. She grabbed hold of a curtain and was just about to yank it open when she heard Brera's voice.

'Leave those.'

She paused.

'Don't open the curtains. Sylvia's on the sofa. She's had a bad attack.'

Sam squinted around her in the half-light. 'Well, she's not there now.'

'Damn!'

Brera turned and headed towards Sylvia's bedroom. Earlier she had taken the precaution of locking the door. She tried the handle. It was still locked. She peered into Sam's bedroom but this room was also empty. She turned towards the bathroom. She tried the door but the bolt inside had been shot across.

'Sylvia?'

No reply.

'The window's jammed in there. You won't get it open.'

She heard a quiet, scraping noise, like the sound of soft sandpaper against wood. Then she realized that this was actually Sylvia's voice.

'I know that.'

'Come out, then.'

'Later.'

She could hear the gentle wheezing of Sylvia's breath.

'What're you doing?'

Sylvia's voice was raw but censorious. 'I'm having a crap, all right?'

Brera scowled and turned to see Sam and Sarah, standing directly behind her. Sarah was smirking.

'Who's this?'

'Sarah.'

Brera felt ridiculous.

In the kitchen, she filled the kettle, plugged it in and turned it on. 'She nearly died yesterday.'

This was her excuse.

Sam sat down but said nothing. This irritated Brera, who could still visualize the horror of the day before: Sylvia's blotchy face and clenched teeth, the *sounds* she made.

Sarah was leaning against the door, one hand on the handle, pushing it up and down. After a while Sam said, 'She seems fine now.'

Brera dropped her voice: 'Not really. She can hardly walk. Hardly breathe. I decided it'd be best if we cancelled the photographer. That was all sorted and then Steven phoned last night . . .'

'Why are you whispering?'

Brera put a finger to her lips. 'He phoned last night and said he'd managed to organize a small club tour. Only about ten dates, but it starts almost immediately. Some singer dropped out at the last minute. Irish pubs and clubs. Mainly in the north.'

They all turned as they heard the toilet flush, and, after a short duration, the slow sound of the bathroom door being unbolted.

Sylvia staggered back to the living-room. It took her several minutes. She sat down on the sofa and tried to calm herself. She felt terrible, but this sick feeling, this illness, was paradoxically reassuring. It was simpler than everything else. There was something intimate and familiar about it. She smiled to herself and thought, Sickness is like a boyfriend.

She stopped smiling and frowned. That morning she had awoken and her mind had been full of one thing, one word. The word was *virus*. She couldn't stop thinking about it. Virus! The idea of it had stuck with her. She thought, Life is about man

battling with the virus. The virus is like a force, but something so simple, so destructive. And man, in all his complexity, can't beat it. He can't beat the virus.

The thought of this made her skin crawl, but it made her feel gratified too and strangely calm.

Ruby's bad start had infected her entire day. She'd argued with several customers, had broken the printing mechanism on her till before the biggest race of the afternoon, had spilled tea over one of Dawn's magazines and had dropped the sugar bowl on the floor in the kitchen.

As she climbed the stairs up to her flat, the sugar on the soles of her trainers made an irritating gritty noise against the linoleum.

Almost at the landing, she met a neighbour: a small, mousy-haired girl who wore John Lennon glasses and baggy trousers. She was on her way down. She stopped Ruby as she moved past her, taking hold of the sleeve of her sweatshirt: 'Ruby, is there an animal of some kind in your flat?'

Ruby almost smiled. Vincent, she thought, but said, 'A dog.'

'Terry was sniffing around earlier. You'd best get rid of it.'

Terry was the caretaker.

'Hell. That's all I need.'

She took out her keys and unlocked the door to her flat. She could hear music inside. She couldn't place it, though. As she opened the door she listened more attentively.

Vincent was standing in the kitchen wielding a large bread knife.

'What're you doing?'

She walked over to the stereo and turned the volume down.

'Dinner.' He grinned at her. 'Watch this.'

He bent down low, disappearing from sight behind the work surface. After several seconds he raised his arm, bringing his right hand into view. On it, cleverly reassembled in macabre puppet form, was the tattered rabbit skin. He bounced it along the counter, waving the rabbit's paws and nodding its head.

Ruby covered her mouth with her hand. 'That's disgusting.'

The rabbit clapped its paws and then bowed.

She felt queasy. 'Get rid of it. It's horrible.'

Vincent stood up, the rabbit still covering his hand, and strolled towards her.

She took a step backwards. 'Keep it away from me.'

She moved behind the armchair.

'For God's sake, it's only a piece of fur.'

She tried to distract him. 'Where's the dog?'

'The rabbit ate her.'

He moved around the armchair. Ruby continued to back away. 'Is she in the bedroom?'

'Might be.'

'Something's burning.'

'Onions. They aren't burning.'

Ruby stepped up against the sofa and then toppled on to it. Vincent bent over towards her, holding the rabbit only inches from her face and clapping its paws together as if intending to grab hold of her nose. She yelled and tried to escape sideways, but Vincent was too quick for her. He grabbed her arm with his free hand and pushed her flat on to the sofa. She struggled, but he held her hips down with his knee and moved his free hand to her shoulder.

'Get lost!'

Her face was scarlet. She was perfectly serious. Vincent was laughing.

He said, 'I won't put it in your face, honestly.'

Instead he pulled up her sweatshirt and stuck the rabbit between her breasts. This time Ruby screamed. She pushed Vincent's hand and knee away and ripped at her sweatshirt. Vincent rolled off her and on to the floor, roaring.

Ruby could feel the sticky fur and skin of the rabbit against her bare flesh, but she couldn't bear to pull it out with her hands. Instead she pulled off her sweatshirt and watched disgustedly as the rabbit fell to the floor. Vincent put out his arm to reach for it, but she kicked it away and then kicked him in the stomach.

'Fuck!'

He grabbed her foot and twisted it, bringing her down heavily

on top of him. He was winded but still gasping with laughter. Ruby tried to scramble to her feet, but he stuck one of her arms behind her back and held it painfully in this position.

Her face was pressed into his shoulder. She bit him in the soft flesh between his shoulder-blade and his armpit. He swore and then tossed her over on to her back and straddled her stomach.

At this point it dawned on him that she was wearing no shirt, only a black bra. Her pale skin underneath it felt like candle wax.

She said, 'I could really hurt you if I chose to, but I choose not to.'

He laughed. 'You think so?'

He touched the place where she had bitten him. 'I bet you pierced the skin.'

She stared at his hand. It was caked with dry blood from the rabbit. He looked at it and smiled. 'Rabbit blood.'

She wondered whether he intended to lean over and kiss her. She thought, It'd take so little effort to kiss me now. He will kiss me.

But he didn't. He put his hands on the floor, either side of her, and pushed himself up. She thought, He doesn't even want to.

She lifted her foot and kicked him squarely between the thighs.

He yelled. His legs buckled and his expression lost all traces of merriment. She scrambled to her feet, pushed him over sideways and used all her weight and strength to hold him down.

His face was pale. She smiled dryly to herself, pinning his arms to the floor with her knees.

Gradually he regained some of his colour. She leaned over him. He opened his eyes and looked into her face. She stared back at him, still holding him down firmly, although he offered no opposition. She moved slowly and deliberately closer to his face and then kissed his nose, his lips. These were small kisses, soft kisses, her lips puckered loosely as though she were about to suck a lychee.

He turned his head away. 'Don't do that. Don't touch me.'

She pulled back.

'Where's the dog?'

'In the bedroom.'

'Right.'

She stood up and looked around for her sweatshirt. It was slung over the arm of the sofa. She grabbed it and held it to her chest as she walked over to her bedroom. Opening the door, she said, 'Those onions still smell like they're burning.'

He sat up. 'How was work?'

'I had a terrible day.'

She went into her room. 'And I've got to go out now.'

'Where?'

He scrambled to his feet and went into the kitchen.

'To take some photos. I won't have time to eat.'

'It'll keep.'

Scowling, he turned off the oven.

Ruby closed her bedroom door and leaned up against it. She felt sick.

The dog was stretched out on her bed. She opened a lazy eye and perused Ruby with it. Her tail thumped gently against the pillow. Ruby walked to her cupboard and searched for something special to wear. She wanted to look good. She had been insulted.

At the back of her wardrobe was a cotton dress, plainly cut, flattering but not too short. She took it out and inspected it. It was black with a thin white band around the neck and hem.

She pulled it over her head and put her arms through the armholes, but before she pulled it down, she yanked off her trainers and stepped out of her jeans, spat on her hand and rubbed it between her breasts to eliminate any final traces of the rabbit, then adjusted the dress and looked around for a pair of sheer black tights. She found some, checked them for holes and then sat down on the bed to pull them on. As she eased them over her feet and stretched them up her calves she thought, Does he hate me now? Does he think I'm easy?

She hated that word.

Did she like him? She remembered Sunday and the incident with Donald Sheldon. On Sunday I convinced myself that I liked Don Sheldon and I've never fancied him.

She stood up and pulled the tights over her bottom and thighs, settling the elastic comfortably around her waist. Would I have had sex with Vincent? Yes? What did he mean, 'Don't touch me'? What does that mean?

Shoes.

She searched for a specific pair of high-heeled black shoes. She found them under her bed and slipped them on, then stared down at her feet and thought, How can I fancy him?

All she could think of was that moment, on Saturday, when she had walked into the burger bar and he had been standing by the counter. It was a random moment, but the thought of it seemed to satisfy her in some way – nothing specific about the moment, but the moment itself.

She liked his carelessness.

She marched to the door and opened it. Vincent was leaning against the oven. He hadn't moved. He stared at her. She felt her insides swelling.

'What's up?' He asked this aggressively, defensively.

She glared at him, not understanding what he meant. She said, 'I'm in a hurry.'

She turned and went into the bathroom, inspected her face in the mirror and picked up her make-up bag.

Vincent called through from outside, 'I'll get the dog ready.'

'Why?'

'We'll come too.'

She didn't want him to come, but said, 'The camera stuff is under my bed, in a black case. It's all there. Get the dog muzzled.'

He popped his head around the bathroom door. 'I like that dress.'

'You're welcome to borrow it.'

She turned back to the mirror and reapplied her lipstick. She thought, *Don't touch me*? Jesus.

Sam walked through to the living-room. It was dark and stuffy in here. She perched on the arm of the sofa, inspected the nebulizer and then the top of Sylvia's head, which was all but

covered by a blanket. She could hear her breathing rattling underneath it.

'You must be boiling under there.'

Sylvia moved slightly.

'Sounds like you had a bad attack yesterday.'

No movement.

'Mum was telling me how you went out on Saturday night and that you've been strange ever since.'

Sylvia's body stiffened. Sam noticed. That's odd, she thought.

'Was someone rude to you?'

Sylvia pulled the blanket away from her face. 'Who's that girl?'

'Sarah? She's a nurse. She's going to look after you while Mum and I go away for a few days.'

'She's no nurse.'

'No, she's just a friend.'

'You're going away, though.'

'We've been offered a small tour, but Mum isn't keen to leave you, especially now you're so sick.'

Sylvia tucked the blanket more tightly around her chin.

Sam changed tack. 'Your breathing sounds terrible, like the noise a balloon makes when you let go of it and the air speeds out. Like a whistle. Have you tried the nebulizer?'

'Last night. A bit this morning.'

'You'll be on steroids again if you're not careful.'

'I won't be.'

Sam paused for a moment and then said, 'What about your room?'

Sylvia turned, suddenly attentive. 'Can you get the key?'

'I don't know. Maybe.'

'How?'

'If you act reasonably over this tour thing, I'll try and talk her round. Otherwise . . .' She made an expansive gesture with her hands. 'She might have you locked out here for good.'

Sylvia started to say something but the entry-phone buzzed. Sam stood up. 'That'll be Sarah. She just popped out to get some wine. I could bring you a glass if you like.'

Sylvia grimaced, turned over and pressed her face into the

back of the sofa. 'I don't want anything. Keep her away from me.'

Her throat tightened.

'I'm not being rude,' Sarah said, sipping from her glass, comfortably ensconced at the end of the table, 'but in performance terms, in any terms, it probably wouldn't occur to most people that the two of you were even related.'

Brera was infuriated by this.

'We are though,' Sam said.

Brera added, 'In a way that makes it even better. More dramatic.'

Brera didn't actually know what she was talking about. This was Sam's concern. Even so, Sarah gave her comment some consideration. 'Well, it adds another dimension, certainly.'

Sam realized – and it came almost as a shock – that she didn't like justifying herself, only explaining, only . . . not even discussing. Just talking.

She didn't want to think about being different. They were all women, after all. That united them. Colour separated her from Brera, from Sylvia, but *gender*, that was what connected them. They understood each other. Their breasts, their vaginas. Sarah too. They were all the same.

Sylvia was escaping. Had to. Get some air. She made it to the door. The front door. They hadn't locked it. Sarah's fault. She pulled it open and stared into the hallway.

Two people were there, on the doorstep, engaged in an argument. They stopped when they saw her. She was wearing only a T-shirt, knickers and socks. Her mask was attached to her nose and mouth, but the wire dangled, unplugged, across her shoulder.

Two people and a dog.

Vincent had just told Ruby about Steven's phone call. Ruby focused on Sylvia and began to say something, Sylvia simply turned her back on them, hopeless now, and started her journey back inside. She put her hand out to the wall to steady herself –

everything achingly slow – and found instead Ruby beside her, Ruby's hand steadying her, Ruby's arm and Ruby's shoulder.

Sylvia caught hold of Ruby's hand. 'What's that?'

Ruby could barely understand her growl, but said, 'It's a bird.'

'What does it mean?'

'I did it years ago.'

They shuffled inside. Vincent followed, like a porter, he thought, with the dog and the case.

Sylvia maintained her tight grip on Ruby. No one understood her here. She had to find understanding.

'Shall I put the light on?' Vincent asked in the hallway, and then, on receiving no reply, in the living-room.

Ruby settled Sylvia on the sofa. 'Best leave it off.'

Sylvia's breathing sounded like the noise a young fledgling might make, a mouse.

'You can't be either Sam or Brera.'

Vincent inspected the nebulizer. Sylvia indicated the refill bottle with her foot. He picked it up and tipped some inside where she showed him. She turned it on.

'Why are you doing that?' Ruby asked, suspicious.

'Air conditioning,' Vincent said. The smell in the flat was sickening.

Sylvia started to tell them both about the virus, still wearing her mask. Ruby sat down with her. Vincent squatted next to Ruby, closest to the machine and its expulsions.

'Several . . . jangles . . . body-part . . . layer . . . transaction . . . locomotive . . .'

They couldn't understand her. The nebulizer was steaming, producing a vapour, a heady, menthol mix. Their eyes began to stream. They were sniffing, inhaling something spectacular, the weirdest potion. After a while they were all laughing for no particular reason. Ruby was sure that she felt Vincent touching her leg, her tights, feeling her shoes. Was he really doing that? The air was so warm, so warm, and something else . . . Why was she here? She couldn't focus. She struggled to remember.

*

Sam was on her third glass of wine. Sarah was discussing a trip she'd taken to the Philippines when she was eighteen. Brera felt something soft and moist against her thigh. Wine usually made her feel this way, but inside her chest, her stomach . . .

Sam, opposite Brera, sensed something vibrating between her knees. Their eyes met. 'I think it's a dog,' Brera said, bursting out laughing. They peered under the table.

'Where on earth did you come from?'

Sam listened intently for a moment and thought that she heard mutterings from elsewhere in the flat: chanting, grunting, stifled guffaws.

In the living-room, the darkness, she found them. The atmosphere had overloaded with the scent of ripe menthol.

'How long have you all been here?'

She tried to open the door on to the roof, but of course it was locked. Instead she opened the curtains and the window.

'You must be Sam . . . or Brera.' Ruby tried to stand up. Failed.

'What are you all doing?'

'I'm supposed to be taking some photographs. Steven sent me.'

Sam walked over and switched off the nebulizer. She waved her arms around, trying to improve the circulation of air. 'It's like an opium den in here. That stuff's toxic if it isn't used properly.'

She noticed that Sylvia was holding Ruby's hand and that her mask was unplugged.

If this girl, Sylvia thought, tells Sam I was trying to escape . . .

'We knocked on the door and your friend answered,' Ruby said.

'My sister.'

This was a mistake everyone made.

Sylvia grinned, under her mask, victorious.

'I only just found out we weren't even supposed to come,' Ruby added, apologetically, 'which is a pity, really, because the light's brilliant.'

She squinted towards the window. Samantha, her back to the sun, glowed with an almost supernatural beauty.

'Are you all OK?' Sam asked, staring at the three of them. They seemed in a state of collapse, appeared limp and giggly.

Ruby pulled herself up straight. 'I feel a bit dizzy.'

'You're always doing this,' Sam said, directly to Sylvia, 'using something good and getting the worst out of it.'

'What does that mean?' Vincent wondered out loud, speaking for the first time, his voice slow and his face groggy.

Sarah strolled in with the dog trailing behind her. Vincent slapped his thigh and Buttercup trotted over. Sarah smiled at him. 'Is it yours?'

'She,' he said, with great deliberation, 'is a bitch.'

Sam said, 'If the light's so good, then maybe we should do the pictures after all.'

She didn't want to waste this opportunity. Ruby looked down, still dazed, and noticed that her dress was all rucked up. She tried to smooth it straight.

'Are you a photographer?' Sarah asked Vincent, focusing on the cut across his forehead.

'I'm her assistant.'

'What does an assistant do?'

'Assist.'

'Come with me,' Sam said. 'We can find Brera and see what she thinks.'

Ruby let go of Sylvia's hand. Sylvia's eyes filled with tears. Sam noticed. 'What's wrong?'

'The light, that's all.'

Sarah and Vincent were still talking. Sam closed the window and drew the curtains again.

In Sam's bedroom, clothes were strewn across the bed. 'Something plain is probably best,' Ruby said.

Sam felt irritable, but she wasn't sure why. It wasn't clothes. Nothing cosmetic.

'My sister really took a shine to you.'

'She liked the tattoo on my hand. She wouldn't let go of me after she'd seen it.'

Like something I saw in a dream, Ruby thought, that girl, this smell, this feeling.

She couldn't stop staring at Sam. She was like an angel. 'You'd

look good in anything,' she said. 'A bin-bag with a piece of string as a belt.'

Sam smiled as she pulled on a plain white shirt and a black skirt.

'Where have you come from?'

'Soho.'

'A studio?'

'I live there.'

'Sounds glamorous.'

Ruby laughed. 'Hardly. I like it here better. It's near to the track where I race my dog.'

Sam could hear Sarah laughing in the kitchen. She felt disgruntled, but she wasn't sure why. She picked up some eye-liner and applied it carefully.

'Well, the light's still fantastic,' Ruby said, trying to sound like she knew what this meant. Brera and Sam both held their guitars under their arms like machine guns. Ruby couldn't be bothered with the tripod. She took out her camera and tried to focus it.

'Sing something.'

They began to strum 'Jesus Don't Want Me for a Sunbeam'. Connor had taught them this tune on Sunday.

Ruby felt tipsy. Was the film in? Did she need a flash? The air, at least, was clearer out here. She inhaled deeply and then started to shoot.

She had no particular talent for photography. She worked on the premise that the more film she used, the more likely it would be that a clutch of snaps would turn out decently. Brera wore a long, grey, smock-like dress, her red hair loose. Ruby focused on her. It was easy. They did a song by Captain Beefheart.

Where was Vincent? She didn't care. But where was he?

Sam said, 'I've half a mind to call Sarah out. She mentioned earlier that she'd like to hear us.'

Brera began playing again. This time, a strange song, a song without a middle, an end, a chorus. Ruby was dazed by it. She was still frizzy. Her mouth – inside – felt gluey and sticky. The song started up, flew off and didn't come back. Like modern

art, she thought. She'd never been able to understand that either.

After they'd finished, Sam said, 'Sylvia wrote it.'

Sarah popped her head out, around the door, and shaded her eyes against the sunlight. 'I could hear you all the way through in the kitchen just then,' she said. 'I thought it was a cat fight.'

'Things can still be interesting,' Ruby interjected quickly, 'even if you don't understand them.'

Sam started playing something else. Sarah stepped outside and lounged against the brickwork.

Inside, Sylvia prepared a mental salad with all the voices in the flat. Sarah, she decided, was a radish. A small, round, purple thing; fibrous. She took out a sharp knife and sliced Sarah in half and then into quarters. She poked the knife into her again and again and again. Until, eventually, she was only pulp.

Back in the kitchen, Brera volunteered to make Ruby some coffee. Ruby sat at the table, putting film into containers, removing lenses and packing things away. The others were still outside. Vincent had been helping himself to the wine and had become, unexpectedly, positively garrulous.

'You must have photographed lots of people,' Brera said, smiling.

'Some.'

'It wasn't too formal, which was great.'

The dog trotted in and sat down next to Ruby. Ruby stroked her. Brera leaned against the sink. 'Sam said she'd never seen Sylvia so friendly with a stranger before. She's not generally so tactile.'

'She seems very weak.'

'She's ill.'

'I like her.'

'Where do you live?'

'Sam asked me that. In Soho. In a flat. It's much smaller than this.'

'Is it nice?'

Ruby shrugged and continued stroking.

'Does Steven pay you much for taking pictures?'

'If he likes them. I hope he will. I need the money.'

'Sam said you raced the dog.'

'At Hackney Wick. Just down the road.'

'Do you like this flat?'

Ruby frowned. 'It's nice.'

'The dog likes it.'

Brera, Ruby decided, was barking mad.

'You must think I'm mad,' Brera said, pulling out a chair and sitting down. 'I'm not mad, but I've just had a mad idea.'

That's how it starts, though, Ruby thought. Mad ideas, doing mad things, *being* mad.

In the pub, facing an interviewer, a small tape recorder and a bottle of Newcastle Brown, Connor had felt the need to blow his nose. He put his hand in his pocket to pull out a handkerchief but instead, accidentally, pulled out Sam's brassière.

Small, white, soft.

This, he thought, is a real rock cliché.

Afterwards, though, whenever he spoke, whatever he said, he could think only of Sam. His mind was full of her. Where she was going. What she was doing.

Brera's idea was that Ruby should move into Jubilee Road with the dog for an initial period of two weeks while the Goldhawk Girls went on tour. Brera assured her that she would keep in constant contact and that Ruby would receive a percentage of their earnings for her services. Sam strolled in to get a clean glass and Brera filled her in. She was enthusiastic. She said, 'We could give you twenty-five per cent. Sylvia would have to get her cut too. It should end up being a reasonable amount.'

Ruby agreed that the money would be useful. 'But the problem is . . .' She cleared her throat. 'The real problem is that you don't even know me and I don't even know Sylvia.'

Brera shrugged. 'I think we could trust you. Sylvia's an adult. She doesn't need constant attention.'

Ruby felt as though Sam and Brera presumed some kind of

awareness on her part about Sylvia's particular circumstances, but in fact she couldn't make any sense at all of the situation. Her brain was swamped with images – her own inky, blue tattoo; a retchingly acrid smell that pervaded every corner of the flat; Sylvia herself, white, acerbic, wheezing; the dark rooms; the nebulizer.

'I don't know.'

'We're near the track,' Sam offered helpfully.

'True.'

She didn't know whether to tell them that she worked full-time, just in case Steven had told them something himself that she'd be obliged to contradict. Eventually she said, 'How about you discuss this with Steven first?'

Brera nodded. 'We'd have to ask him for some kind of reference.'

They were still in the kitchen, three of them now, sitting around the table. Ruby stood up and placed her mug in the sink. 'You could get Steven to ring me later. You could mention the idea to Sylvia as well and see how she reacts.'

Vincent came in, holding the dog by her collar. 'I just took her out for a pee.'

'We're going now, anyway.'

Sam stood up too. 'Where's Sarah?'

He grabbed the dog's lead. 'I heard her talking to your sister.'

Sam had been smiling, but her smile disappeared. She was starting to wish she'd kept Sarah all to herself. Connor, it turned out, could be right about some things.

Sarah pulled up a chair next to the sofa. Sylvia was under her blanket.

'Hi. I'm Sarah, Sam's friend. We haven't been properly introduced yet. I saw you earlier.'

Sylvia didn't reply.

'I heard you chatting to Vincent just now.'

Nothing.

Sarah thought Sylvia was just like a child. If you wanted her to do something, she wouldn't do it. She was simply contrary. This

was her way of asserting herself. She wouldn't conform. She was outside things. Sarah understood this, wanted to let Sylvia know that she understood. She started talking. And she talked.

'I read *The Female Eunuch* years ago, and when I got to the part about feeling pride in your own femininity, I discovered something very disturbing about myself.'

Silence.

'Greer said that if you aren't ashamed of being a woman, then it should be possible to dip your finger into your vagina, during your period, to immerse your finger in menstrual blood and then to put that finger into your mouth without any feelings of disgust.'

Nothing.

'I tried it. I tried it, but I just couldn't do it. I tried for years, every month, and each time I failed I felt so bloody guilty.'

Sylvia shifted under the blanket. Sarah noticed and took this to be a positive sign.

'Then it dawned on me that the only reason I felt disgusted was because of a natural fastidiousness. I suddenly thought, How the hell does Greer get off on telling me how to feel about my sense of self? I know how I feel.'

Under the blanket Sylvia put a furtive hand between her legs.

'Setting tests is a kind of masculine construct. If something doesn't come naturally, then, quite simply, it isn't natural.'

Sylvia drew back her blankets and, in the darkness, held something aloft between her finger and thumb. Sarah squinted through the half-light and saw that Sylvia was holding a used tampon, dangling it by its string as though it were a small, live mouse.

Sarah felt her gorge rise. Sylvia stuck the tampon between her teeth – like a short, fat, pink cheroot – closed her lips and sucked.

Sarah could hear the cotton wool squeaking against her teeth.

Ruby was locked in her bathroom, bathed in a red light, developing the photographs. Outside she could hear Vincent clattering around.

They'd begun arguing on the bus during the ride home. She'd

made the mistake of mentioning Brera's scheme to him. She hadn't thought it would prove all that contentious. It wasn't as though he even appeared to have any kind of objection to the scheme itself. At one point, though, when she'd said, 'Maybe one day I'll get to rent a proper house with a garden and all that stuff,' he'd said, 'You're a shithead.'

'Thanks.'

Vincent and the dog were on the sofa together, watching television, when Ruby finally emerged from the bathroom, smelling of chemicals.

'D'you want to see the pictures?'

He put out his hand. She passed one copy of each of the prints to him.

Something smelled good in the kitchen. She walked over and peered into a pan on the stove. 'What's this?'

'It's probably ruined by now.'

'Can I have some?'

Vincent held up one of the prints. 'I've been thinking about money.'

'What?' She had expected a comment on the quality of her work.

'I said . . .' He perused the print as he held it aloft. 'Brera's eyes are skew.'

'Are they?'

Ruby walked across and peered at the photo over his shoulder. 'It's just that she's singing and focusing on the camera at the same time. Sam looks fantastic. Those lashes.'

'She's like a racehorse.'

'How's that?'

'A painting in the National Gallery.'

She grinned. 'Very poetic.'

He handed back the pictures. She slid them carefully into an envelope.

'You could make some money you know, get the money you need for the dog, and you wouldn't even have to do anything.'

'Oh yeah?'

'Sit down.'

She sat on the sofa, pushing the dog's legs over, lifting them and arranging them across her lap.

'Shall I give you some advice?'

Blue, blue eyes, he had. She frowned. 'Is it sensible to take advice from someone who doesn't give a damn about anything?'

'Yes, if it's good advice.'

And the funny thing is, she thought, I know exactly what kind of advice it will be.

The dog's nose was touching his thigh. This meant that the two of them were touching, were linked, indirectly.

'You handle a fortune every day. And if you think about it, it isn't even as though the money belongs anywhere.'

'It doesn't belong to me, that's for sure.'

'You owe a fair amount.'

She knew this. And that he owed her.

'You are owed,' he said, with great certainty.

'So what?'

'Listen to me.' He leaned closer. 'Between the two of us we could make money without actually even taking anything.'

She was so tired, all of a sudden.

He outlined his plan.

'No.'

'Why not?'

'It's stupid.'

'It's not stupid.'

'No.'

He had rejected her, that afternoon, in this very room. She would deny him whatever she could. For any reason. She would deny him.

THIRTEEN

Sylvia stood by the window. The curtains closed behind her.

Where do thoughts go? she wondered. They travel, in your voice, out of your body, in waves, into other people's ears. She breathed on the glass. Where do they start? A circuit connecting? With an electric buzz? A chemical reaction?

She pushed at the glass. Still weak. It wouldn't open. Sam had opened it, the day before, effortlessly. Would she smash it? She thought that she might, she considered doing it, but she didn't.

A small bird on a telephone wire. Something travelled through his feet. He vibrated. She filled him with her thoughts, and his body contained, so perfectly, the contents of her mind.

Off he flew.

He saw things. He saw the city from above and from below. He saw trees, small, like pieces of broccoli; a blade of grass, big as, bigger than, himself. A worm, on concrete. It would curl up in his stomach.

He saw many things, and many of the things he saw meant nothing: a succession of images, only registered in his tiny brain, photographed but not digested.

Each day – she saw it clearly now – so little could happen. Each day, each person, every person, yearning for only one thing. To own, to love, to keep, to do, to forget, to try.

In Soho. Do it. I will not. Do it. I will not. A pattern, like the beat of a clock, a heart. Tick *tick*, tick *tick*, tick *tick*, tick *tick*.

Sam's mind, full of Sarah. Connor's mind, full of Sam. Brera's mind, full of Sylvia. Sylvia's mind, contained so easily, flying above the city.

FOURTEEN

What the hell had happened? A day of nagging, an ugly, pointless, driven, aimless time. He didn't want to think about it. Solid things. That was better. Something solid. Thursday. Yes. Bateman Street. Yes. Ladbrokes.

He was sitting on a small, red plastic stool. He was watching the television screen. How was he feeling? Defeated? Frustrated? There was no answer to that. He wouldn't provide an answer.

Ruby. She had refused him. He worried that she lacked understanding, and therefore, as a consequence, that she also lacked imagination. She's deceptive, he thought. She looks like she doesn't care, she lives like she doesn't care, but she does care. She does. He couldn't deny that he liked her strength, but her goodness?

On the screen appeared a list of the runners for the two o'clock at Hackney.

Was it goodness or was it just stupidity? No, not stupidity, worse than that. Conservatism.

He had wanted to go to the track with her, but he wouldn't admit it. He had been forced to argue with her instead, which, everything considered, was for the best.

He had been hoping for an outside trap for Buttercup: four, five or even six, but he saw immediately that she had been drawn in trap three. He felt around in his pockets and pulled out a handful of notes. He stared at the list of runners, trying to understand the odds. Buttercup was out at twenty-five to one. The favourite, a bitch called Karen's Special, was the four-to-five odds-on favourite. The commentator for the race was saying how she'd been dropped a grade because she'd just come out of season, so she was running well below her class. She was usually a railer, but was drawn in trap four.

'Right.'

The notes he was clutching had been removed that morning from Ruby's coffee jar. This was his revenge. He reached for a pen and was still scribbling on his slip when the commentator introduced a visual survey of the animals in the race. Six small figures led six tiny dogs in coloured jackets out on to the track. He saw Ruby immediately, saw, even from this great distance, that her jacket was ill-fitting – too large, greyish – and that her hair shone out like a clump of flossy white cotton. He found himself grinning.

He watched intently as each dog was paraded in front of the camera. Ruby was third. Her expression was serious as she posed Buttercup and encouraged her to stand straight, side-on, to her best advantage. The dog's tail, Vincent was pleased to note, wagged cheerily. Ruby did not look at her best on screen. In fact she looked rough – her expression tired, almost grim, and her face heavily made-up, especially her eyes, which looked too dark somehow, too hooded.

Vincent peered around him at the other punters. Most of them were staring into space, writing on their slips or inspecting their papers. He felt a tightness in his chest. This isn't sex, he told himself, refusing to even consider the word *affection*; not sex, only excitement.

Ruby had moved on and the favourite was now showing: a lean, slight, brindle bitch.

He picked up a pen and completed his slip. Trap four. A practical choice, a sensible gamble, free of sentiment. He visited the counter and returned to his stool.

On the screen the dogs were being loaded. Ruby, he noticed, was chatting to the person handling the dog next to her and smiling. What was she saying? Did she think she'd win? What was she thinking?

He listened to the whistle of the mechanical hare.

'Hello.'

Toro stood beside him, eating a doughnut.

'Hang on.'

The hare whizzed past the traps and at that same instant the

traps opened. Vincent's eyes were glued to the third trap. Buttercup sprang out.

'Yes!'

She shot out of the trap like a bullet and veered immediately towards the hare, smashing full-on into the dog to her right. This dog (the favourite) rolled twice and pushed into the dog from the fifth trap who had come out more slowly. Buttercup stumbled, found her feet and ran on, but was then cut out of the picture as the camera followed and focused on the leading dogs from traps one, two and six, who had come out unhindered.

Vincent jerked his head sideways as though endeavouring to see beyond the screen, beyond what the camera would show.

Traps one and two were running close to the rails, six was in the picture but running wide. By the third bend, six had fallen back and Buttercup had inched her way into view, running in enormous, exhaustive bounds, on the outside, eventually running close to the six dog and then overtaking him.

'Yes!'

Vincent bounced up from his stool, forgetting about his bet, thinking only about Buttercup. 'Go on, you silly bitch!'

He was so intent on watching Buttercup's progress, her every move, her every stride, that he failed to notice as the number one dog ran across the finishing line, followed closely by trap two.

The race was over. The hare stopped.

He looked down at his slip. 'That was quick.'

Toro put out his hand for the slip, but Vincent screwed it up and threw it at one of the television screens.

'Forget it. Come on.' He took hold of Toro's arm. 'Let's get drunk.'

Stan bent over and ran his hands down the dog's back, her rump and hocks. 'Seems OK. We're in seven kinds of shit, though.'

Ruby was patting Buttercup, was so proud of her. The dog was still jerky, panting, trembling.

'Did one of the other dogs get hurt in the tumble?'

He shrugged. 'I dunno. That's not our main problem. Our problem is the racing manager. He'll have to explain why an

obvious wide runner got drawn in trap three. It's his responsibility. The punters'll be fuming, and if it looks bad for him, then it looks bad for you.'

'But it's . . .'

'His fault. Yeah, but that won't make him feel any better. It's not as though he's had any indication from her previous form.'

'No.'

'He might scratch her.'

Ruby's jaw dropped. 'He can't do that. She came third.'

She towered above Stan. He was a withered four foot nine, hunched and red-nosed. She waited for him to say something. The dog was sitting down now, panting, her paws still hot.

'Don lost a lot of money recently.'

'What?'

'Gambling. He lost a load gambling, so he sold a good dog from the kennels, and unloaded this bitch on you.'

'Well, he can't have been that desperate. I haven't even paid him yet.'

'Exactly.'

He gazed down at the dog.

Connor was in his bedroom practising on his drums and keeping up a frenetic, repetitive, hardcore beat. He stopped for an instant, flipped a drumstick into the air, caught it, and then commenced with another song. He laughed out loud, relishing the noise he was making, the tension he was releasing.

Tension?

Am I tense? Just thinking about it made him stiffen up even further, although his arms kept on banging and tapping and whipping.

Am I tense?

He was desperate to communicate with Sam. She'd been out of contact for . . . he counted the hours in time with each beat . . . fifty-one, fifty-two, fifty-three, fifty-four hours. He continued drumming, noticing how his heart had started to pump in time. One, two, three, four. One, two, three, four. Too quick, too

speedy, too swift. He was warm, not warm, hot, not hot, wet. His head was wet.

I want to stop drumming but I can't. It was too loud, too fast. Sarah will think . . . two, three, four. What would Sarah think? He didn't give a damn what Sarah thought.

He felt as though his heart was beating so rapidly now that it was actually faster than the drums: double-time. His head began to feel light, soft and airy.

Calm down, calm down, two, three, four.

Sarah flung open his bedroom door. She had knocked twice but he hadn't heard.

'Would you give it a rest for a while? My head's splitting.'

He stopped immediately, was almost grateful to her.

She glanced at his face. 'You look terrible. As white as a sheet.'

He said nothing. She disappeared. He sat still, stared at the drumsticks in his hands, debated whether to start up again, but couldn't face it. He was wound up like a watch. His palms were damp. He needed to unwind.

He stood up, stepped carefully away from the kit and walked into the living-room. Sarah was in her bedroom. He could hear her hairdrier. She can't listen, he thought. He picked up the phone.

Sylvia never answered the phone. She lay on the sofa as it rang. She didn't even bother considering who it could be. She didn't know anybody.

Brera and Sam were out shopping. Again. She stared around the dark room. So this is how it's going to be from now on? She smiled to herself.

The telephone continued to ring. She sucked her teeth.

Connor was so shocked when someone answered that he actually dropped the receiver. He picked it up in time to hear a voice say, 'No one rings for this long.'

'It's me, Connor.'

'Who?' She knew perfectly well who he was.

'I'm a friend of Sam's. Is she there?'

Sylvia put down the phone and walked to the bathroom. She washed her hands, noting how much her eczema had improved over the past couple of days. She returned to the living-room and sat down on the sofa. Connor's voice vibrated in tiny sound-waves through the air. Eventually she stood up and strolled back over.

'Look, I'm tired.'

'Where have you been?'

'Why?'

'I just wondered.'

Sylvia debated whether to answer this and then said, 'I'm locked in.'

'You are?'

'Yes.'

'Are you all right?'

She grinned to herself. 'Are you all right?'

'Why shouldn't I be?'

'Why shouldn't I be?'

Connor scowled. 'What are you doing?'

'What are you doing?'

'Look, this is silly.'

'Silly?' She smirked. 'Well, you're paying, stupid.'

'Will he be gone all night?' Ruby asked, feeling relieved, but also defeated.

Toro was drunk, leaning against Ruby's doorframe and emitting yeasty belches. He shrugged.

'Where is he?'

He shrugged.

'Fine.'

She slammed the door and then opened it again. 'Don't you have any idea?'

He shook his head.

'Didn't he even give you a message for me?'

'I gave it to you.'

Ruby watched as he turned and staggered downstairs, hanging on to the banister for support. She closed the door and sat

down on the sofa again. The dog was asleep in her bedroom, but the flat still felt empty.

'Bastard.' Her voice sounded ludicrously small.

She wanted a drink. A lager. She was peckish. A kebab. She stood up, went into the kitchen, opened the cupboard and took out her coffee jar. She took off the lid and peered inside. No money. What had he done with it?

She wasn't so much angry as hungry. She put down the jar and looked around for Vincent's rucksack. It was still on the floor next to the sofa. She frowned. Did I really think he'd gone? He wouldn't go like that.

She picked some mould off a piece of bread and put it in the toaster.

Two hours later they were still on the phone. Nothing real or significant, in conversational terms, had been achieved during this time. Connor had tried, on several occasions, to turn the subject of their conversation around to topics closer to his heart, but such attempts had proved futile. He said, 'About Sam . . .'

Sylvia cleared her throat and then cleared it again. Her throat never felt fully clear. After clearing her throat for a third time she said, 'My sister.'

'Yes.'

Connor hoped that Sylvia wouldn't go off at a tangent again. He was sick of the virus. She'd told him all about it. At inordinate length. Having a conversation with Sylvia was like blowing an egg. All the time you did it you could only think what a waste of energy it was, and sometimes the pin holes at either end would collapse and the overall effect would be entirely ruined.

Sylvia knew perfectly well that Connor only wanted to speak to her because he couldn't speak to Sam. She was obstructing him. It has also occurred to her that it was possible to do just about anything on the phone without the person at the other end having the slightest inkling. She considered some of the things that it would be possible to do and tried a few of them.

'About Sam . . .'

Sylvia didn't respond. She was inspecting the hair under her right arm while holding the phone slackly in her left.

'Is she busy at the moment?'

'How should I know?'

'Sarah told me . . .'

'Fuck her.'

'Who, Sarah?'

'Fuck her.'

'Sarah?'

'Fuck her.'

'I was told that Sam and Brera had several gigs lined up.' He'd tried to inject some enthusiasm into his voice.

'Ha!' Sylvia laughed and then coughed.

'What's so funny?'

She had just been sniffing the hair under her arm. She sniffed it again – deeply, fully – and inhaled the strong, pungent smell of old sweat. It was a horrible and yet a delicious smell.

Connor was still talking: 'I don't suppose you'd mind mentioning to her . . .'

Sylvia said, half to herself, 'Why did I put my nose there?'

'What?'

'Smell. I never noticed.'

'What?'

She stared around the room, looking for things that were aromatic. She put down the phone and muttered, 'If I didn't notice, maybe I couldn't. If I couldn't, then why did I put my nose under my arm?'

Connor sensed that all was not well at the other end. He could hear a selection of distant squawks and muffled thumps. He debated whether to hang up. Why am I speaking to this girl? Am I that fucked up over Sam?

On Tuesday when Sarah had returned home from Hackney she'd asked, 'Have you met Sylvia before?'

'Why?'

'Because she's a barbarian.'

'You don't like her?'

'She's like a big, brown, hairy man. She even speaks like a man.'

Connor had tried to imagine Sylvia as a man. He imagined Sam, but masculine. He liked the idea. Yet when he spoke to Sylvia, she didn't sound like a man at all, more like an old woman: stroppy, strained, dithering.

He wouldn't hang up. No. He held on.

Sylvia stood in the kitchen, staring into the fridge. She took out a bottle of milk and sniffed it.

'Oh my God!'

She shook her head, blinked, and then sniffed it again. 'Can I taste it? I can't taste it.'

She put it down, too frightened to try, reaching instead for a half-eaten packet of soft cheese. She pushed her face into it, covering the tip of her nose in its soft stickiness. She gasped, dropped the cheese, backed into the kitchen table, knocked over a chair and clutched at her face with both hands. She stood still, her two hands covering her nose, her breathing jerky and uncontrolled.

Connor was relieved when he heard her again.

'Hello?'

She was close to the phone, panting and hesitant. She picked up the receiver.

'Um.'

She was rubbing her nose with the flat of her palm. Her nose was now red from rubbing.

'What were you doing?'

'Nothing.'

Her response was too quick, he thought. He smiled to himself. 'You said something before . . . something about a smell.'

'I did?'

'Yes.'

'Um. Shit.'

'What?'

'Go away.'

'I heard you shouting.'

'I dropped something.'

'You know . . .' He paused for a moment. 'Today your voice sounds a whole lot better.'

She stopped rubbing her nose. She cleared her throat. It felt empty and unobstructed. She tried to clarify her thoughts, but couldn't.

'Look, don't tell anyone.'

Connor sounded thrilled: 'Don't tell them what?'

'About this. The smell. It's nothing. OK?'

'OK.'

'OK?'

'All right.'

'They're coming.'

She slammed down the phone and ran to the sofa, jumped on to it and pulled up her blanket.

'Oh no.'

It smelled awful. She took a gulp of air and then thrust her head under.

Connor listened to the dialling tone for a while and then hung up. He returned to his bedroom, closed the door and sat down on his bed. He thought, She's up to something, and, whatever it is, I'm sure Sam would appreciate knowing about it.

He lay down. She's up to something, but what the hell could it be? That girl, he decided, is a nut.

Steven was staring around the living-room. 'This place is disgusting.'

He had brought some wine. Ruby washed up a glass and a mug.

'Where's your friend?'

'Which friend?'

Steven kicked Vincent's rucksack. 'That friend.'

'Out.'

She didn't fancy explaining.

'The photos are on top of the speaker if you want to take a look.'

He picked up the envelope, opened it and sat down in the armchair. After inspecting three or four he said, 'These aren't too bad.'

She uncorked the wine, poured them both some, and then slouched across the sofa. She drained her mug in one gulp and gave herself some more. Steven opened his briefcase and slid the photos inside. 'I'll pay you later.'

'Fine.'

Ruby rolled on to her back and shut her eyes.

'Brera mentioned that you were considering staying in their flat while they do the gigs.'

'Did she?'

'You seem fed up.'

'Do I?'

'You are fed up.'

Steven cupped his wineglass between his large, pale hands. His hands dwarfed the glass. He looked like an enormous gnome handling a bubble.

'Well, if you're intending to do it, you should tell me. The first gig is on Saturday.'

He stared at her for a while. 'You seem disorganized.'

'I am.'

Ruby pulled herself up. 'Lately I feel like the top of my head's disappeared.'

His expression didn't change.

'I'm not being practical. It's my own fault.'

He opened his briefcase and took out the photos again.

'Do they really want me to stay in their flat?'

He looked up. 'I think they do. They don't seem very motivated, though. No one is, apart from me.'

'That's your job.'

'Well, if you do stay in Hackney, I'd have one less thing to worry about. I told them you were reliable.'

'What about the smell?'

'You'd get used to it quickly enough.'

'What about when I'm out at work?'

'She doesn't need nursing or guarding.'

'Brera said . . .'

'Brera's very protective, but Sylvia's independent.'

As he spoke, he remembered how she'd looked the other day when he'd picked her up and carried her to the door. How light she'd been.

*

'Sylvia's being weird.'

Sam whispered this to Brera. Brera was sitting at the kitchen table working out their finances. Sam was standing in the doorway holding a tray which held a cup of cold tea and an untouched meal.

'She wouldn't eat anything. When I asked why, she said she only wanted a glass of water.'

'Has she used her inhaler tonight?'

'I couldn't smell any vapour. I think she's up to something.'

'She's missing her birds.'

'Yeah, but it's more than that.'

'You think she's trying to stop us from going away?'

'Not necessarily. Earlier she asked when it was that we were going, as though she was actually looking forward to it.'

'Maybe she's planning to starve herself.'

'Possibly.' Sam didn't sound convinced.

'Maybe it's still to do with her trip out on Saturday. She's been strange ever since.'

'Couldn't you have a word with her?'

'She'd think I was prying.'

'Take her some water. Try and be subtle.'

Brera picked up a glass from the draining-board and ran it under the tap.

Sylvia was sitting in the dark, her legs drawn up, covered by the blanket.

'I brought you some water.'

Brera tried to discern the outline of her face in the darkness.

'Thanks.'

'Your voice sounds good.'

'Fantastic.'

'I'm being serious.'

'So am I.'

'Sam said you didn't touch your dinner.'

'Sam says put your hands in the air.' She raised both hands and waved them above her head.

'Don't be silly.'

Brera offered her the glass. 'I brought you some water.'

'Thanks.'

Sylvia took the glass. Brera watched her. 'Don't you want it?'

'Give me a minute!'

Brera sighed. 'You want to go back in your bedroom?'

'Obviously.'

'You can soon, but not yet.'

Sylvia scowled.

'Are you upset about Sam and me going away? Because you're welcome to come too, if you feel fit enough.'

'Yeah.'

'What does that mean?'

'I just want to be left alone.'

Brera sensed that she had already outstayed her welcome.

'I'll be in the kitchen, then.'

'Good.'

She turned to leave and Sylvia said, 'I'll have a bath.'

Brera was surprised. 'You had one on Monday.'

'I'll have another one.'

'I'll check the water's hot.'

When she'd gone, Sylvia inspected the glass of water. She sniffed it and then screwed up her face into an expression of intense distaste. She was thirsty. She poked out her tongue and tentatively dipped it into the glass, then quickly withdrew it. 'Soap.'

She pinched her nose between her finger and thumb, gulped down three or four mouthfuls then shook her head and blinked. 'Chemicals.'

Every glass of tap water in London had been through at least twenty other people. For a while she tried to imagine the people that this particular glassful had been through, then turned her mind to more pressing issues.

Now what? Secrets. She had a small batch of them. First, the girl in the park. Second, tasting and smelling. Third, Sam's friend. He said . . . What did he say? He said he wouldn't say anything.

She chuckled. Having secrets made her feel proud and maternal. Her gut felt full of an unspecified mystery. Like she had

a pearl inside her, forming, layer by layer. She stopped smiling.

Things must return to normal. They mustn't know. They must go.

She listened as Brera cleaned the bath and set the taps running.

FIFTEEN

What time was it? Four a.m.?

Ruby shifted in her sleep and muttered, 'I don't want this to end.'

In her dream she couldn't open her eyes. Everything was too bright, and when she tried to open her eyes – the effort involved was enormous – the light made her eyes ache, as though she were staring at the sun.

But it didn't matter. She could see perfectly clearly elsewhere, inside her head, in another compartment.

In this compartment it was dark and warm and everything smelled of wet dog. Everything felt like wet dog.

Someone was breathing. She turned to see who it was, but it was too dark.

Where am I?

Maybe . . . She tried to make sense of things. Maybe I'm out swimming. The water is hot. I'm out swimming and now I've climbed from the water on to a rock, inside a cave. The cave is warm and damp. The rock is covered in a soft, woolly seaweed.

She felt it against her skin and it made her skin tingle.

Someone was next to her. She tried to open her eyes, to stare, yet when she opened her eyes the light was too bright, so she closed them again. But this is a different dream. In this dream I can see everything.

Next to her, on the rock, was a dog – a big soggy dog. She turned her head and stared at it. Vincent! She laughed. It wasn't a dog at all. He glared at her. She realized that she was naked.

He said, 'I'm going to have to throw you in.'

His voice was so soft. Obviously the cave has made his voice softer, she thought.

He grabbed her arm. Is he wearing anything? She tried to see,

but when she opened her eyes everything was too bright. She felt him touch her breasts and then her belly. Again he said, 'I'm going to have to throw you in.'

'All right.' She giggled. Her voice sounded stupid.

He was pulling her towards the water. She wasn't afraid. She wanted him to pull her in. He was holding her arm, still holding it, but now she was holding his too. She said, 'If I go, you go.'

She sensed the water close to her feet, surrounding her feet, her shins, her calves, her knees. She tried to slide in quicker, but he held her back. She felt his skin all wet and shuddered.

When she awoke her pillow was on the floor. She reached out for it, keeping her eyes closed.

Oh no. I won't wake up from this.

Connor dragged the telephone into his bedroom. He had just made a cup of tea, tip-toeing around the flat so as not to wake anyone. Sarah had a guest. He didn't want to intrude. The telephone cord was just about long enough. He slipped it underneath his door, pushed the door shut, then sat down on the floor and drank a mouthful of his tea. He coughed. It was still too hot. He put the cup down and dialled Sam's number.

It rang several times and then she answered it. He shoved some hair behind his ear. 'So you're up?'

'Yes.'

Already – it had only been three days – it felt strange to her: his voice, his manner so familiar.

He said, 'We haven't spoken in ages.'

'How's Sarah?'

'Pretty busy. Someone stayed over.'

'Who?'

'God knows. A man.'

Sam jerked at the phone cord so hard that she almost disconnected the call.

He was irritated. He thought, What does it matter? It's only *her*.

He said, 'Sarah mentioned that you had some gigs lined up.'

'Hull on Saturday.'

She sounded half-hearted. He noticed and tried to flatter himself that he was the cause of her misery.

Sam said, 'You were in the paper today. A picture and everything.'

'I saw it.' He was pleased that she'd seen it. 'We've got a gig tomorrow too. Subterrania.'

'That's good.'

'Could I see you tonight? You left some stuff here.'

'I don't think so. Sylvia's not been well. We want to spend some time with her before we go.'

'Oh.'

'I'd better get off the phone. I don't want to wake her.'

'I hope it goes well tomorrow,' he said, sounding disconsolate.

'Thanks. See you.' She hung up.

Sylvia coughed. Sam turned. 'Did I wake you?'

'You always have to use me as an excuse. I hate it.'

'Oh. I'm sorry.'

'You both make me sick. You and Brera. You're always doing it.'

'We don't mean to.'

Sam's eyes were fully adjusted to the darkness. She could see Sylvia propped up on the sofa, surrounded by cushions.

'That's the worst part of it, though. You always mean everything you do.'

Sam went back to her room. She sat on her bed and promptly burst into tears. She kept thinking, What's going on? I can't make sense of this. I don't want to make sense of it.

Sylvia padded quietly into the hallway and listened to Sam crying. Good, she thought, that's her out of the way. She could hear Brera brushing her teeth in the bathroom.

She slipped along the passage and into the kitchen. It was so bright in here. She blinked for several seconds before she could adjust her eyes.

The paper was open on the kitchen table. She paged through it, hoping for a familiar face, an image she could recognize, but nothing sprang out at her. She turned to the front and looked for

some indication of content. She found what she was searching for and turned towards the back.

Half-way down this page was the heading STIR-FINE! and a picture. She stared at the picture, her eyes widening in surprise. He looked absolutely nothing like he sounded, nothing like she'd imagined.

She was disturbed by a movement in the hallway. She spun away from the paper towards the sink, picked up a glass and held it under the tap.

Brera walked in. 'I thought you were Sam.'

She didn't reply.

'What're you doing?'

'What does it look like?'

'What's wrong?'

'Nothing's bloody wrong!'

She banged the glass down on the draining-board and marched out. She felt dizzy. In the sunlight everything smelled so acute, so strong. Even the newspaper, like bleach and ink – a hot, savage smell.

She was so hungry but she couldn't eat. If I eat, she thought, I might give myself away.

She threw herself on to the sofa. Everything needs to be normal, she decided. She lay down flat. I'm threatened. By what? Alternatives. I must get *back* . . . the feathers, the fluttering, the catch in my throat. No senses, no sense.

She remembered Connor's face: unshaven, so dirty, all that hair, in tangles. She thought, He kept my secret. Now I owe him something. Now we owe each other something. This notion depressed her.

She coughed for a while and then spat out the phlegm from her mouth on to a tissue. Suddenly she found it hard to swallow phlegm, to do normal things.

Maybe God is punishing me for killing that little girl. Everything is getting bigger and bigger, and the bigger everything gets, the smaller I am.

She felt minuscule.

*

Vincent was strolling down Argyll Street with an open can of lager in his hand and a paper under his arm. He was happy. If you ask for anything, he was thinking, you face the possibility of someone saying yes and of someone saying no. This didn't strike him as good enough. It didn't satisfy him.

Pigeons were everywhere: oily, skinny, puffy, mottled. He kicked up his feet as he walked, as if he were striding through winter leaves.

What kind of a commitment had he made to her? Any? None?

Ruby pondered these questions as she worked the till and the pay-out. Friday was Dawn's half-day. As usual, it was busy.

Two-thirty now. Was the dog still all right? She'd nipped out at twelve and had taken her for a short stroll. She'd been going stir-crazy.

Where was he? Sod him.

Where was he, though?

There he was. She felt. Sick.

Two forty-five. He was going to do something she didn't want him to do. The bastard. She'd said no to him, over and over, but he was still here, like he'd threatened. He wore her hat and a pair of almond-shaped mirror glasses. Where did he get hold of those? He looked absurd.

Jason was busy. She checked furtively. He was filling out a stationery order.

'The whole idea,' she'd said, 'is stupid. People rip off bookmakers all the time and they always get caught.'

'Only the ones you hear about.'

'But even the ones I hear about have better ideas than yours.'

'How?'

'Well, either way I come out of it looking like I've made a mistake.'

'A small mistake. I bet you make mistakes like that all the time.'

'Not on purpose.'

*

He had chosen his horse: Origami. She'd never even heard of it. Just before the off, when it was busy, he came up and handed her his slip. A queue of punters formed behind him. Jason was giving her a hand, working the other till.

She took the slip from him. This was stupid. She'd told him she wouldn't do it. She'd said so, but now she was doing it. He'd said that he wouldn't write out the slip properly. That was part of the scheme. Only the horse's name and a two, two noughts, in the wrong box. Under pounds instead of pence.

She pushed the slip into her till, pressed a two, kept her finger on the nought button that little bit too long. God! She did it. Registered the bet, tore it in half, handed him his half. He gave her no money.

'What do you call it?' he'd asked. 'The technical name.'

'An over-ring. If your hand slips, or if you don't remember to put in the decimal point at the right time.'

'You wouldn't notice a mistake like that straight away, not if you were busy.'

'I would.'

'I bet you've done it before, though.'

'Accidentally.'

'If the horse wins, you say I gave you the two hundred. Pay your till back with part of the winnings. If I lose, say it was an over-ring.'

The swine, she thought. How many times did I tell him I wouldn't do it?

The race was off. She stood up. How long would it last? Six furlongs?

'Jason,' she said, 'I want to get a Coke.'

She walked past the safety door, through the shop and outside.

'Jason would be bound to recognize you if you came up to collect the money.'

'I'd get someone else to collect it.'

'Who? I wouldn't want anyone else involved.'

'Nobody.'

'Anyway, if I take a bet worth over fifty quid I'm supposed to notify the manager.'

'Not if you're too busy.'

'Even then.'

She picked up two crates, placed one on top of the other and sat down. It was warm here. The sun shone on her bare arms and her face.

'What's the point?'

'You could buy the dog. They treat you like shit anyway.'

'Even the thought of it makes me feel sick.'

'That's excitement.'

The crates were uncomfortable. They cut into her legs. Vincent tapped her on the shoulder. For an instant she thought he was a wasp, a hornet. She jerked away.

'I told you I didn't want to do this. I said no.'

And he'd punished her by staying away. She had been punished.

I'm not nice after all, she realized, only weak. Weak. That was an ugly word. It made her feel ugly.

'The horse won,' he said, grinning. 'At five-to-one. Origami. I chose it because my sister used to make origami swans.'

She looked up at him. 'I said I didn't want to do this.'

She couldn't see his eyes, only her own face reflected in his glasses. A weak mouth. A weak chin. A weak face.

'But you did it.'

'I'm fidelity-bonded. Do you know what that means?'

'No.'

'It means that if I ever get caught doing anything illegal, I can never work with money again. Not anywhere, ever again.'

He scowled at her. Maybe she just wasn't clever enough.

'I've earned you eight hundred pounds. The horse came in at five-to-one.'

'I don't want your money.'

'Not my money, your money.'

'I don't want the money. You have it.'

'I don't need it.'

'Then burn it.'

She stood up and walked back inside.

When she sat down again, Jason said, 'There's a bet here for two hundred. You should've told me you'd taken it before the off.'

'It was on the off. I didn't have time.'

He handed her the slip, settled, with the amount she had to pay out written in red ink at the bottom. She stacked ten bundles of hundreds into a neat pile and waited for Vincent to come back in. He didn't come.

She settled other bets, took slips, counted money, handed it over. She waited. She took a slip, counted the money, took a slip . . .

Vincent's writing. She looked up. A face she almost recognized. Not Vincent's face. She picked up the bundles she'd prepared and handed them over, two hundred short. He took the money and thanked her. The spare two hundred she moved into her till.

She knew that face. Who was he?

Fuck.

Sam noticed something strange about Sarah's complexion as soon as she met her. A roughness. A reddish, blotchy patch around her mouth, nose and on her chin.

They were at the Scala watching a matinée showing of the director's cut of *Pretty Baby*. Sarah's idea. Sam had been keen to talk, which was unfortunate.

'How's Connor?'

'Himself. Loud.'

'Have you been busy?'

'No.'

'Do you like Brooke Shields?'

'Sometimes.'

That redness. She had been kissing someone. With stubble. That would explain it.

She took the dog out, made something to eat, began packing. Only a small bag for the time being.

Vincent arrived while she was feeding the dog. He thumped on the door and then pushed it open.

'You should be careful. I walked straight in here from the street.'

She wanted to silence him for a minute so that she could yell at him, but he kept on talking.

'This small guy was sweeping the stairs. He stopped me and was asking all kinds of questions. Wanted to know about the dog.'

'The caretaker. Red hair.'

'That's him.'

He walked into the bathroom. She heard him turning on the taps. She returned to her bedroom and sat down on her bed. She listened to the sound the water made as it hit the enamel bath. She listened to laughter, conversation, arguments going on outside in the street. She listened to the noises the dog made, pushing her bowl around on the kitchen tiles with her nose.

A while later Vincent appeared in the doorway, wrapped only in a towel.

'What are you doing?'

'Packing.'

She was packed.

'You aren't really going to Hackney?'

'I said I would.'

'You should've kept that money.'

'You told me,' she said, very calmly, 'that you didn't even know that epileptic.'

'Who?'

'Don't fuck me around.'

'I actually just met him again today.'

'You set me up.'

Vincent's expression, previously churlish, became serious. 'You don't honestly think that?'

She knew it. She knew it.

What could he do with her? She had shocked him.

They were both silent for a while. She was staring down at her hands.

Eventually she looked up at him. He had dropped his towel. Her eyes widened.

'Is it just sex you want?' he said, his voice sounding flat and angry. 'Is that it?'

She wasn't surprised by this question. The only thing that surprised her was his honesty. But he was always honest. That was the problem.

'Look at me,' he said, 'I'm ridiculous.'

She did look at him. She straightened her back and crossed her arms. He didn't appear to be upset or embarrassed by her scrutiny. His skin was pink-tinged from the heat of the bath. His body was surprisingly hairy. He looked overweight. His stomach protruded. His thighs were stocky and angular. He said, 'Don't you want to laugh? Don't I make you want to laugh?'

As he spoke she was staring at his penis, which seemed unusually pale, a whitish-blue colour by comparison with the ruddy tone of the rest of his skin. His testicles were lopsided.

She stood up and unbuttoned the shirt she was wearing. 'You made me do something I didn't want to do.'

'What?'

She took off her shirt, hooked her thumbs into the black leggings she wore, pulled them down, stepped out of them, unclipped her bra, pulled down her knickers.

He noticed that her skin was a very cheap white and that her hips were fleshy and strong. Her nipples were tiny and a pale beige colour, like small round servings of coffee ice-cream.

Now what? There was something in her expression, something harsh and hostile.

He said, 'Why are you doing this?'

'I'm sick of you taking advantage. What did you do with that money?'

She was crazy for him, but he'd made her hate herself. Somehow.

He had never seen a woman strip as an act of hostility before. He wondered whether that was how she saw his body – as something offensive – when all he'd really intended was to ridicule himself.

'I let him have it. It felt like he was owed it. I don't know.'

In the same way, in the same way that he'd not wanted her to touch him, to kiss him, in that casual manner she had, that easy, accidental fashion. He didn't want to be like the dog. A mistake. He either wanted plain sex, or, plain sex, or . . . He never thought about these things. Never. He couldn't think about them.

He picked up his towel and walked out. She climbed into bed.

SIXTEEN

When Brera found Sylvia early on Saturday morning, she was huddled in an ungainly heap by her bedroom door, clutching a partially unbent coat-hanger and a fish-knife.

Brera prodded her with a slippered toe and said grimly, 'Now what? Is this how it's going to be?'

Sylvia stirred and then turned over. She opened her eyes. 'I want to go in again. We agreed, didn't we? You locked me out before and it didn't work.'

'Twice.'

Brera clearly remembered these two occasions. On the first – Sylvia had been thirteen – she'd gone on hunger strike: eight days without food before Brera relented. On the second occasion – at fifteen – after three days outside she'd sliced her arms with a kitchen knife. Brera didn't really want to dwell on either incident. This time, she'd decided, it wouldn't come to that. She said tersely, 'Are you warning me? Is that it?'

'I'm not doing anything. I can do exactly as I please.'

'Listen to your voice. It sounds so clear.'

'I don't care.'

'Have you eaten?' Brera was keen to avoid a confrontation.

'No.'

'Why aren't you eating?'

Sylvia sat up, leaned her back against the door and rapidly changed tack. 'I did eat, earlier on, before I fell asleep.'

'What did you eat?'

'Some bread. An apple. Milk.'

'That's not enough. I'll get you some cereal.'

'I'm full.'

Sylvia patted her stomach and looked off sideways. Brera found her expression shifty and devious. She's still such a child,

she thought, as she squatted down next to her and put out a hand to touch her hair. 'You know we won't go if you don't want us to. That woman, Ruby, is coming this morning at eight. Maybe you don't like her?'

'She's all right.'

'You don't really want us to go.'

Sylvia's hair felt like wire under her hand. Sylvia turned and squinted up into her face. 'You want to blame me for not wanting to go yourself. I can see straight through you. But I won't have you blaming me again. I just want . . . I only want to be left alone, that's all.'

Brera drew back her hand and stood up. 'You're going to do something stupid. I can tell.'

'I won't do anything. I just want . . .'

'I know what you want. Just give it two more days. I want you to recover properly.'

'Give me the key.' Sylvia put out her hand.

'I'll give the key to Ruby. I'll instruct her to let you in on Tuesday. That's a promise.'

'It's too long.'

'Only two days.'

Brera tried not to sound brutal. She knew that with Sylvia a fine line had to be drawn between cooperation and coercion.

Very gently Sylvia said, 'I'm lonely. Please let me in.'

'No.' Brera's voice remained sure and calm. 'Tuesday's soon enough.'

Sylvia crossed her arms. 'You always have to treat me like a child.'

'You always have to behave like one.'

'OK.' She stood up, scowling, her face reddening. 'We'll see.'

She turned and stalked away, down the corridor and into the living-room. Seconds later, Brera could hear her opening the curtains.

She called out after her, 'Are you trying to spoil things? Are you punishing me?'

After a short silence Sylvia shouted back, 'Only God can punish you.'

Brera scratched her head and then inspected her finger-nails. Eventually she said, 'You don't even believe in God, you bloody hypocrite.'

Sylvia grinned to herself, then sat down on the sofa. Why am I grinning? she wondered. I've got nothing to grin about.

There was a mustiness in the room that made her want to sneeze. She listened out to hear what Brera would do next. She crossed her fingers, hoping that she wouldn't try to bring her something to eat, then uncrossed them with a small sigh of relief as she heard her go into Sam's bedroom.

It felt strange having the curtains open. Over the past four or so days she'd spent all her time in virtual darkness. Early on she'd had trouble working out why this was so, but had felt too ill to do anything about it. Now she stared at the window, looking for her birds. Maybe they've forgotten me? If they have, I might just as well be dead.

She blinked several times, growing gradually more accustomed to the light.

When had the sun risen? Two hours, three hours earlier?

She sniffed and then sneezed. In the bright light she could see dust floating in the air: thousands of specks of it. She tried not to breathe them in, then felt light-headed, so filled her lungs. She could smell the sunlight. It smelled like a big, black oil slick – warm and oozy.

When she'd been talking to Brera, she'd been struck by how pungent her perfume was. Like dried apricots – a sweet, harsh smell. She thought, It smelled so strong as her hand touched my hair, I thought I'd gag.

The sunlight began to upset her. She debated whether to close the curtains again, but became too fearful, too frightened in case the birds had forgotten her. Several had accumulated on the window-sill – three sparrows and a starling. She couldn't be sure, though, that they wouldn't have been there anyway. She peered at them, over the arm of the sofa, too overwhelmed by the new, hot, hazy, dazy smells in the room to walk over.

Her mind switched to the night's activities: the coat-hanger

and the fish-knife. *The smell from her room!* She'd noticed it before, of course, but she hadn't realized quite how *repulsive* . . . She couldn't think about it. Too dangerous.

She lay down and closed her eyes. It was that time of day: cars full of people, driving to work, trains, tubes and buses. She could smell the exhaust fumes, like a thick, yellowy grog – a horrible, tepid, burning smell. The smell of business, of a big cigar.

If only I could hibernate. Draw in my head like a tortoise. Get into a dark cave, like a bear and simply sleep.

Two days, she thought. They won't get me this way.

Sam had overheard the conversation in the hallway. She was lying in bed. She'd been awake for several hours; had, in fact, been listening to Sylvia earlier, working away at the lock on her bedroom door.

As she lay there she wondered whether Brera was intending to talk her way out of going on the tour. At the last minute.

She tried to think about Connor, but couldn't concentrate on him, his feelings, the possibility of having hurt him.

She tried to think about Sarah, but, again, couldn't settle her thoughts.

If I loved her. Loved, she thought, still smarting, my face, my figure, all that would be wasted. And then, What a stupid way to think.

Brera tapped on Sam's door and walked in. Sam opened her eyes. 'What's wrong?'

Brera closed the door, walked over and sat down on the end of her bed.

Sam propped herself up on her elbows. Brera's hair was tied back into a scruffy pony-tail. She untied it and then massaged her scalp with the tips of her fingers. As she did this she said, 'You've been distracted lately.'

Sam was surprised that they were suddenly discussing her and not Sylvia.

'So?'

Had Brera noticed anything? Her heart felt like a sparrow – small, light, fluttering.

'You're uptight because you think I'm going to back out of the tour at the last minute.'

Sam relaxed, was relieved at her mother's lack of insightfulness. She said calmly, 'Things have a way of sorting themselves out.'

Brera stopped fiddling with her hair and started to speak again, but Sam's mind was elsewhere: I'm missing something. It's true. I'm missing something but I don't know what. Something's wrong. I'm incomplete.

She was miserable.

Brera was saying, 'There comes a time when you have to let a person take responsibility for their own life. Otherwise it's like a kind of cruelty.'

Sam listened to this string of words as though they were being spoken on the surface of a pool, above water, and she was floating, just underneath, submerged, her ears full of liquid.

Am I different? I want to be the same, but now I feel . . . separate.

This was Sarah's fault. Were men the same as women after all? Was she being like a man? Was that how she felt?

Brera was saying, 'I won't have her dying in my house. She can go and die somewhere else. She's old enough to. She's got to start being courteous.'

Sam rubbed her face. Small dots of sleep were encrusted in the corners of each eye, like tiny scraps of wheat. She picked them out and then said, 'So go and tell her.'

She felt amoral. Removed. She didn't care what happened.

Brera stood up. 'I'll get packed first.'

'Go now.'

'You're right.'

When Brera had gone, Sam lay down in bed again. She thought, I am different.

And what could be worse than that?

Sarah wasn't yet dressed. Her long legs stuck out from her dressing-gown. To Connor they looked thin and ungainly, like the limbs of a deer, but white.

'Sam's like a tiny goddess,' she said, provoking him. 'I don't believe she ever invests in anything emotionally. She's invulnerable, which means that she wants to understand things but not to feel them. She's incapable of genuine involvement.'

Connor was trying to eat his cereal. He ignored Sarah. She loved it when he ignored her. It meant that she could say anything, that she had beaten him, defeated him, had won, was winning or would win.

He picked up a cup of scalding hot coffee, holding the cup itself, not the handle. It was burning him. He continued to ignore her. She was only a parrot, chattering. How strange it is, he thought, when things that are extremes come together. He used all his energy to convince himself that what his fingers felt was a freezing sensation instead of a burning one.

Sam was perched on the edge of her bed playing the guitar. The noise she made drowned out the sound of raised voices from elsewhere in the flat. Above the guitar she could only hear a vague squawking sound, a frantic bickering, like the call of a starling.

She wore a loose pair of brown dungarees, the straps of which nestled in the crook of each arm. The front bib had tipped down too, revealing her left breast in its entirety. She knew how beautiful she must look, like this. But it gave her no joy and no comfort.

She continued to play, remembering as she strummed something that Sylvia had said about birdsong. She'd said, 'If you listen to a thrush sing, you can hear how birds use a musical scale which contains far more intervals within the octave than our scale. Our system is a kind of compromise. We cancel out all those extra tones so that we're left with a practical scale of twelve. Birds have a completely different musical language. We can listen to it, but we can't understand it. And it's only because of the way that we've chosen to transcribe music. We made it incomprehensible, on purpose. We decided.'

The doorbell rang. She stopped strumming and listened to the sudden silence in the flat. She put down her guitar.

*

Brera welcomed Ruby inside and pointed her towards an armchair in the living-room. To Ruby the flat seemed different: lighter. Doors and curtains were open. She dumped her suitcase and sat down, holding on firmly to the dog by her collar. She sensed an atmosphere. Brera wore no make-up but her cheeks were red. Sylvia seemed, if anything, even smaller than during their last encounter – anaemic, a pale yellow, her every feature like so many tucks and pleats in a piece of pastry.

Sylvia spoke: 'That dog stinks of dog.'

Sam appeared in the doorway. 'That's a tautology. Well, nearly.'

Sylvia's eyes flickered over towards her and then away.

Sam smiled at Ruby. 'Hi.'

Ruby smiled back and said, 'Are you all packed yet? Has Steven called?'

'No, but I should think he'll be here soon.'

Brera was staring out of the window, watching a small congregation of sparrows who had assembled under the eaves of the roof outside.

Sam said gently, 'We'd better get a move on.'

Brera snapped to attention. 'I'll get changed. Then I'll pack.' She turned to Ruby. 'I've scribbled down a few instructions. I left them in the kitchen on the table.'

Ruby nodded, hoping that things would be organized before nine-thirty. She couldn't afford to be late for work again.

Sam and Brera disappeared. Sylvia sat cross-legged on the sofa. As soon as Brera was out of earshot she said, 'I won't be any trouble.'

'I'm sure we'll be fine.'

Ruby felt uneasy.

'Maybe you should give the dog some water?'

Ruby stood up. 'Good idea.' She pulled the dog along the corridor, past Sylvia's room – the smell was as bad, if not worse, than on her last visit – and into the kitchen. Sam was here, making tea. She put three cups on a tray and passed a fourth one over to Ruby. Ruby took it and sat down.

When Sam had gone, she tried to convince herself that her life

was a broad expanse, a large space, like a field, which Vincent only fitted into in a very small way – on the horizon, a figure on a distant hill, a scarecrow, a small, insubstantial dot.

Sam took Sylvia a cup of tea. Sylvia motioned her to put it down a distance away, on the floor.

Sam did as she was instructed and then said, 'How many days has it been since your last asthma attack? Four? Listen to your breathing. The difference is amazing.'

Sylvia's nostrils twitched as she smelled the steam rising from the cup of tea, which stank of curdled milk, sour milk mixed up with a sharp scent of tannin. It disgusted her.

She stared up at Sam. 'The thing is,' she said, calculatedly mournful, 'I'm not happy.'

Sam couldn't help chuckling. 'Are you serious? You? Not happy? You're never happy.'

Sylvia's eyes began to water, entirely of their own accord. Everything overwhelmed her. Usually things overwhelmed her and she was passive. She *chose* to be. But this was different. She felt helpless and impotent. When she tried to speak, her voice emerged as a tiny, timorous squeak. 'No matter what I say or do, it makes no difference. No wonder I feel angry. No wonder I want to hurt myself.'

'Shut-up!' Sam moved towards her and placed a hand across her mouth, gagging her, feeling the damp warmth of her lips and saliva against her palm.

Sam's voice had sounded ferocious, but she didn't feel at all angry. Instead she felt frightened; mainly for Brera, but for herself too. Sylvia's eyes widened but she didn't move. Sam kept her hand where it was and said quietly, 'Don't ruin everything just because you know you can. Consider us. Imagine how we feel.'

She removed her hand, inspecting it for a second – as though the hand was somehow separate from her body, from herself – and then wiped it on the front of her dungarees before turning and leaving the room.

Once Sam had gone, Sylvia took hold of the bottom of her T-shirt, pulled it up and rubbed her face vigorously with it. When

she'd finished rubbing, her face was crumpled and wrinkled, as though she wanted to howl, or was howling, but without making a sound. She looked like a tiny red ant.

After a while her expression returned to normal. She whispered, 'What did she have on her hands? What sort of perfume? Like vanilla pods. Like terrible vanilla on a knife blade.'

She was calm now, outside, but inside she was wild, galled and hot with anger.

I've got to hurt them back. But hurt them without hurting myself. That's how people behave. That's what Brera wants.

She stared over towards the window, but for once the birds – on the sill, in the sky, perched on the power lines – didn't seem like everything, didn't fill her world. Suddenly she felt the need to make room for something else. To broaden her horizons.

He'd already been awoken once by the phone.

At half-past eight the doorbell rang. He staggered up from the sofa to answer it, feeling like his spine had been twisted during the course of the night into a voluptuous spiral. He held the base of his back with one hand, endeavouring to massage the offending area, while with his other hand he clutched walls, doors and banisters, trying to support himself. Eventually he reached the front door. He opened it.

Steven stood there, smartly attired in a light-green suit. His lapels were wide, and his tie too. The tie was decorated with tropical fruit: a mango, kumquats, grapes and a papaya.

Vincent gingerly put out his hand and took hold of the tie. 'You weren't obliged to wear that.'

Steven knocked his hand away. 'Has Ruby gone yet?'

Vincent tried to remember whether he'd seen Ruby or not. He shook his head. 'I've been asleep. Someone phoned her early on.'

He attempted to call to mind his earlier phone conversation. Steven, meanwhile, pushed past him and bounded upstairs. Vincent closed the door and followed him at a more genteel pace.

He walked into the flat and closed the door behind him. Steven emerged from the bedroom. 'Some of her things are gone.'

Vincent scratched his head. 'Someone phoned this morning. What's the time?'

Steven checked his watch. 'Eight-thirty.'

'Don.'

'Who?'

'The man who phoned. Don. He said it was important. Will you be seeing her?'

'I hope so.'

'Good.' Vincent sat down on the sofa. 'You can tell her, then.'

Steven appraised Vincent from above. He inspected the cut on his hairline. After a few moments he said, 'I suppose this means you won't be seeing her again.'

'Ruby?' Vincent thought for a second. 'Probably.'

Steven couldn't tell whether this 'probably' meant yes or no. To try to ascertain which, he said, 'How long were you planning to stay here?'

Vincent rubbed his forehead. His fingers followed the path of his scar, his scab. Steven winced as he watched this, worrying that he might try to pull the scab off. He did try, but the cut was still too new.

Steven didn't like the idea that Vincent might be planning to stay on in the flat indefinitely. 'Doesn't it bother you that she's gone?'

Vincent yawned. 'She's left most of her stuff. She's left her records.'

'That was kind of her.'

Vincent realized that he wasn't particularly enjoying this conversation. He didn't want to analyse his feelings, preferring instead to feel urges and to act upon them.

'You *like* Ruby?' Steven asked, trying not to sound too sarcastic.

'What?' Vincent almost laughed. 'What kind of a question is that?'

At the same time, however, he thought, Caring and liking. Are they the same things? Can I like a person without really caring about them? He supposed so.

Steven walked back over to the bedroom and peered in

through the door. The whole flat looked like a tip. He turned towards Vincent. 'Before you go, can you tidy the place up? It's a mess.'

Vincent shrugged. 'She likes it like this. She made this mess.'

He pulled his legs up on to the sofa and lay down on it again, closing his eyes. He didn't want to talk about Ruby any more. He found discussing her with Steven depressing. He didn't like the idea, which any type of conversation between them implied, of some kind of common ground, something shared, any sort of similarity between them.

There's nothing to discuss. I won't commit myself to any one thing, to one place, one idea, one person. I have to commit myself to everything. If it'd only been sex – at first I thought it'd only be sex – then it would've been fine. Now everything's too confused. People shouldn't need to demand things from each other.

He liked this idea. He said, 'People shouldn't expect too much from each other.'

Steven was staring over towards the door, thinking about leaving, but at the same time peculiarly dissatisfied by this interlude with Vincent. When Vincent spoke, Steven couldn't understand what he meant. He paused and waited for Vincent to clarify his words. Vincent kept his eyes closed. He was smiling to himself.

'What a wanker,' Steven muttered, letting himself out and going down the stairs.

After Steven had gone, Vincent continued to smile. He was remembering the colour of Ruby's nipples.

The day stretched ahead of him. He knew that he was at liberty to fill it in any way he chose.

Ruby put her head down on the table, using her folded arms as a cushion. She closed her eyes.

'You're not ill or anything, are you?'

'No.' She didn't bother opening her eyes or lifting her head. It's only Steven, she thought, and he doesn't count.

Steven pulled out a chair and sat down. Ruby listened to the

dog as she shifted nervously under the table, concerned at his proximity.

'I just went to your flat.'

'Why?'

'I was going to give you a lift. Your friend was still there.'

'Vincent.'

'He said that Don phoned and that I should tell you. Does that make any sense?'

Ruby opened her eyes. 'Don? Why?'

'Didn't say.' He registered her expression. 'You can ring back now if it's important.'

'No. I'll ring him later.'

She calculated in her mind the number of days that had expired since she'd acquired the dog. Six. Her mind turned to Vincent and the money. When she'd said no, had she really meant no? Maybe then, but now?

Steven said quietly, 'You'll be all right here, won't you?'

'Yeah. I should think so.'

He looked at his watch. 'Are you working? It's nearly half-nine.'

'I'd like to go soon, but it won't look too good if I leave before they do.'

He pushed back his chair and stood up. 'I'll try and hurry them up a bit. They shouldn't be much longer.'

She popped her head under the table and addressed the dog: 'I'm going out soon. Can you hold your bladder for eight hours? I hope so.'

She hoped so.

Several pieces of paper were on the telephone table, some in a neat pile, others crammed into the directory. Eventually Sylvia found what she was looking for: a small piece of lemon-yellow notepaper. On it, in Sam's hand, Connor's name in capital letters and the ten digits of his phone number. She dialled.

It rang three times and was then answered: 'Hi. This is Connor.'

'Sylvia.' Her voice was clear and loud.

'You sound completely different from the last time we spoke.'

'So?'

'I was just saying. Why did you ring?'

Sylvia felt silly. She hated taking the initiative.

'I want you to come and pick me up.'

'What?'

She repeated what she had said, shaping the consonants and vowels slowly and carefully as though speaking to a child: 'I said, I want you to come around here and pick me up.'

'Why?'

'I want to visit your flat. Sam told me all about it. She told me how nice it was.'

'She did?' Connor was incredulous.

Sylvia grimaced to herself. She thought men must be very stupid.

'Will you come?'

He hesitated and then acquiesced: 'Maybe I could just visit you. How would that be?'

She scowled. 'Come now,' and cut him off.

She stood up. Her head felt too light. The walls slipped slightly and the carpet wavered. She closed her eyes for a moment and tried to focus herself.

Forty minutes later Sylvia stood damp and naked in Brera's room, staring into the dressing-table mirror. She'd had a bath and had washed her hair, which was wrapped up in a towelling turban.

Her naked body looked awful. Her hip and rib bones jutted out under her yellowy skin, the bones far too clear, too evident. Her breasts were small but droopy, like tiny bread rolls in two translucent plastic bags.

She inspected the stretch marks on her breasts, belly and buttocks, the small clusters of eczema on her arms and chest, on her hands and neck and on the arches of her feet. She wasn't particularly self-conscious, didn't care what people thought. She rarely tried to see herself as others saw her. She continued to stare at herself, her expression blank and uncritical. The air was warm.

She left the room for a while, then reappeared, minutes later, fully dressed. She wore one of Sam's dresses: a slightly old-fashioned, loose-fitting brown pinafore dress, which reached to well below her calves. Underneath it she wore a pea-green T-shirt. Her legs were bare, and on her feet were her old brown sandals.

She threw her head forward – an action which occasioned a wave of dizzy nausea – pulled off the towel, using it to rub dry the ends of her hair, then opened the top drawer of Brera's dressing-table. The sweet aroma of perfume and make-up which rose from the drawer forced her to step back for a moment. These smells shot straight up her nose and made it run. She sniffed and stepped determinedly closer again, holding her nose between finger and thumb this time and breathing through her mouth. She looked for make-up and creams which were unperfumed, and applied these products to her face with caution.

When she'd finished, she stepped back, pushed her hands through her hair, pulling down her wiry curls into some semblance of order, and inspected herself in the mirror. Her face still looked gaunt, thin, strangely moonish. She smiled. Her teeth were yellow. Over the past few days she'd been unable to put toothpaste – that sweet, awful, pungent stuff – into her mouth.

She closed the drawer, dusted down her pinafore and then walked into the hallway, pausing for a moment to listen to the scuffling, snorting sounds that the dog was making in the kitchen. She walked to her bedroom door, waited, held her breath, but could hear nothing. No sounds at all.

'I bet that bitch closed my window.'

The *smell*, though! It was still there. It made her head feel like her brain was stewing in vinegar. Of course she was able to smell it everywhere in the house, but here it was concentrated, heady and undiluted.

She returned to the living-room. She was nervous. She walked over to the television, switched it on and turned the volume down. Instead of sitting on the sofa, she primly tucked in her dress and sat down in a small armchair.

As she watched the screen she hummed to herself: snatches of a tune she'd been composing over the past few days. She listened to her own voice, pushed it out and pulled it in. She listened in amazement as the cords in her throat held a note, didn't waver, simply held on to it and expelled it with an alarming purity.

What did this mean? What had changed? She curtailed her thoughts, refusing to contemplate options, choices, possibilities. She didn't need choice. She stopped humming. She listened.

Someone was climbing the stairs outside. Connor. She recognized the sounds he made. He knocked at the door. She stood up and steadied herself by holding on to the arm of the chair.

How many days now since I ate? she wondered, and then, Will I answer or will I just let him knock and knock?

When she felt steady enough, she walked to the door and opened it.

An ambulance was parked on Wardour Street, blocking the one-way system. Its two attendants were uptight. They had struggled along the market with a stretcher, negotiating the stalls, the fruit, the rubbish. Ruby followed them into the shop.

Jason was pointing towards the men's toilets: 'There's a needle about a foot long blocking the cistern in there and blood sprayed all over the wall.'

To Ruby he said, 'Toro found him.'

'Who? Is he dead?'

'Looks like he swallowed his tongue. Toro's in the staff kitchen out back. I said he could make himself some coffee.'

Dawn was holding the toilet door open. Ruby walked over. She had to look. She glanced in. The white urinals. The blue tiles. Her gut turned. He was right. Blood. A bad smell. They were lifting the body. It wasn't even stiff yet. His head rolled back, his face, set, grey, his neck like a slack rope.

'Christ!'

She was sick on to her hand. Out it came, *swish*, on to her hand. Nothing substantial. Only water, saliva.

What had she done? And Vincent. What had he done? She was sick again. Bile and water. Someone would be punished. But who would it be? And how?

When the police came, later on, Dawn spoke to them. She said, 'Yeah, I'd seen him before. Last Saturday, a week ago, I chucked him out of here. He always had a bad habit.'

Connor was dumbfounded when Sylvia opened the door and he saw her for the first time. Like Sam, she was tiny. Bird-like, he thought, smiling. But she was white, not black like Sam, not beautiful. Nevertheless, he enjoyed her expressions. Her face, he decided, was like a security camera, projecting everything internal externally, for immediate perusal.

When she opened the door she peered at him suspiciously. He said, 'I'm Connor.'

'I know.'

Instead of welcoming him inside, she stepped out into the corridor and closed the door behind her. He was irritated by this. 'Couldn't we go in for a while?'

'Sure.' She smiled at him. Her teeth were small and yellow.

He waited for a few seconds but she didn't budge. 'Do you have a key?'

'No.'

She stared at him, as though expecting him to have one, then turned and started off down the stairs.

He followed her. He asked, 'Is someone staying with you? Someone who *does* have a key?'

Sylvia stopped for a moment. 'I've got to go slowly. I can't breathe and talk at the same time. Outside I have to breathe through my mouth.'

As she started to walk again he said, 'Will the birds be a problem out in the open?'

She stopped again. 'Not if someone else is with me. Smaller birds are naturally cautious. Pigeons . . .' She frowned. 'Well, just don't take me to Trafalgar Square.'

They caught a bus. Sylvia breathed through her mouth for the duration. If she could have pinched her nose for the whole trip

she would have. The smells – the stink of exhaust fumes, dirt, grime, other people – were appalling.

Physically, Connor found her charming. She was chapped and scuffed, scruffy and mauled, but there was something pure and tiny and strong about her. Obviously he found her terrifying. Obviously, he thought, she's completely mad.

On the tube, something odd happened. As they waited for a train, she put out her hand – a minute hand, dry to the touch, rough, scabby – and took hold of his. His body stiffened. He thought, Why is she doing this? He tried to catch her expression out of the corner of his eye, not turning his head, keen not to confront or embarrass her. He saw that she had her eyes closed. She swayed slightly.

'Are you all right?'

She nodded, still breathing through her mouth.

When the tube arrived, she moved very slowly and heavily. He prayed, God, I know it's selfish, but don't let her die on me. That'd finish me off completely.

At last they were home. By the time they'd arrived, she was panting. He opened the door and followed her in. She walked straight into the living-room and stood in the centre of the carpet, staring around her.

He said, 'I'll get you a drink. I bet your throat's dry after all that . . . breathing.'

'I only want water. Do you have bottled? Not Evian, it's too chalky.'

'My flatmate drinks bottled stuff.'

He went into the kitchen and opened the fridge.

Sylvia remained where she was. She didn't move, just closed her mouth and sniffed tentatively. This room, she decided, stinks of hippie oil. She didn't like it.

Connor returned with a glass of water. He offered her the glass and she took it. He said, 'Why are you pulling that face?'

'This room.' She was breathing through her mouth again. 'It smells like perfume. I don't like it.'

She looked around. 'Where's your room?'

He pointed. The door was half-open. She took several steps in

that direction and then her legs began to wobble. He noticed and moved to assist her, taking the glass from her and putting an arm about her waist.

Slowly he helped her into his bedroom and on to his bed. Once comfortably seated, she put her hand out for the glass, took it from him and drained it in several gulps. Some of the water splashed down her chin and on to her pinafore.

He squatted next to her. 'You don't seem very well.'

His head was only a foot or so away from hers. His face, however, was partially covered by hair. His hair looked soft. She liked the way that she could see only a fraction of his features, but also it maddened her. She put out her hand and roughly drew his hair to one side, tucking it behind his ear. His face expressed a mixture of surprise and concern.

She said, 'Let me be honest with you.'

She continued to stare at him and thought, What shall I say? Shall I tell him the truth? Shall I ask him to just leave me alone?

Her face projected her thoughts. He could see that she felt trapped, and was about to offer to leave her for a while, to say this to her, when her stomach interrupted them both with a loud, snarling, watery gurgle.

'How long since you ate?'

She glared at him, as though affronted. 'I won't eat anything.'

He rocked back on to his haunches, surveying her. Am I doing this for Sam? he wondered.

He tried to understand Sylvia, what it was that she thought she was doing. Eventually he said, 'Why have you been breathing through your mouth all this time? Are you still upset by the smell of things? Like you were the other day, on the phone, remember?'

She avoided his gaze, focused on his drums and said, 'Do you play those?'

'How long since you ate anything?'

'Recently.' She answered too quickly.

He said, 'I guess that's why you seem so weak. You've not been eating. Punishing Sam and Brera for going away.'

She laughed. 'I don't care what they do. I have my own life.'

He stood up. 'I'm going to make you something to eat, and if you don't eat it, I'm going to throw you out.'

He'd decided that firmness was best. She seemed far too manipulative to tolerate subtlety.

She stared at him coolly. 'I don't mind. I'll go.' She tried to push herself up, but couldn't stand.

'How long since you ate?'

She turned her mind back. 'Thursday morning . . .' then thought some more. Thursday morning she hadn't eaten either. She found it hard to remember her last meal: maybe a sandwich on Wednesday night.

Connor stood up. 'I'll get you something.'

She wanted to stop him. 'Wait a second.'

He paused on the threshold of the room. 'Now what?'

She said, 'I'm the sort of person who likes . . . discomfort. If I feel ill, I feel stronger. Do you understand what I mean?'

She knew this was a ludicrous question, so before he answered she said, 'I could go home.'

'Well, don't expect me to help you. You don't even have any money. How far do you think you'll get in your condition? Be sensible.'

She considered this. She thought, What if I collapse outside and someone calls the police? Maybe they'll have my picture, my description, on their files. Maybe they'll know all about the girl in the park and the geese. Or else . . . Now her mind was speeding. Or else I might collapse and get taken to hospital. They'll call Brera and she'll come back. They'd never forgive me. She and Sam. It'll justify everything they've both said.

She looked up at Connor. 'All right. Get me something.'

She flopped back on to the bed. Connor remained in the doorway long enough to notice that she didn't put her knees together when she lay down, but luckily the fabric of her dress fell between her legs.

She is like a man, he thought, remembering Sarah's comment.

Sylvia stared up at the ceiling. This bed, she decided, smells strange. She could smell Sam on the sheets – a scent of vanilla –

but it was mixed with something else. Sex, she decided. His smell.

She found him physically interesting. He was slight and thin, but also tall and in no way gawky. He had sensitive hands. His skin was healthy and smooth. His face wasn't actually handsome, but it was the sort of face a small mammal might have – not a rodent's face – a natural face. Clear and uncomplicated.

Her reverie was spoiled by the smell of real coffee. She felt physical alarm. She sensed her pulse rate quickening. She sniffed the air, inhaled it, digested it. Moments later she differentiated the aroma of bacon – a sweet, spicy smell – and the bland but startling fragrance of an egg frying.

She was cold. She touched her arms, which, she discovered, were rough with goose-pimples. She rubbed these vigorously until they melted away and then pushed herself up into a sitting position. Every sense, every pore, every orifice felt aroused.

Connor piled the coffee, juice and fried breakfast on to a tray and picked it up. He hoped that this combination of food wouldn't be too fatty and rich for someone who hadn't eaten in a while. Porridge would probably have been better for her, he thought, and weak tea. He carried the tray into his bedroom.

Sylvia was no longer on the bed. She was standing behind his drum-kit, staring out of the window.

He put the tray down. 'Come on. Eat it while it's still hot.'

She turned and faced him. Her eyes were wild and round. 'Don't make me.'

He didn't want her mood to infect him. He couldn't help thinking what an affecting person she was. He picked up a knife and sliced into some bacon, into the egg, and scooped these and a couple of slices of mushroom on to a fork. He stepped around his drum-kit and carried this small offering over to her. She pushed herself up against the window, her mouth tightly shut.

'Open up.'

She shook her head, but he noticed her nostrils twitching. The food was inches from her face. Her eyes began to turn back in her skull, rolling, white, like the eyes of a frightened pony. For a second she looked as though she might topple into the window.

He put out an arm to support her, curling it around her back. Her mouth opened, and a small moan, a tiny groan, escaped from her lips. He took this opportunity to slip the forkful of food into her mouth, afterwards closing her lips with his fingers.

She tried to swallow and to spit at the same time, staggering sideways, away from him. She put her hands over her ears, as though taste were sound and sound was too, too full of flavour. Something exploded within her, like an engine firing in her mouth, starting up, revving itself, gathering energy, a sensation so violent, so total, so acute, that she could only close her eyes and shake her head and think about screaming, but not scream because her mouth was too full, her head was too full. Again she tried to spit and swallow. Fragments of food choked her, while other pieces flew from her mouth and into the air. She threw out a hand to push them away, further away, then, at the same time, pulled in her hands as if to catch them. Everything was moving so slowly now, so brightly, that she almost felt able to do so.

Connor watched her, alarmed. What the hell is she doing?

She ran forward, straight into his drum-kit, kicking into his bass drum, clutching his cymbals, embracing them, pulling them towards her and then tossing them sideways, like a discus thrower: up, over and against the wall. She fell forward, scrambled forwards, collapsed on to her knees, crawled to the bed, put out both hands to the tray, on to the plate of food and grabbed hold of a fistful of beans.

Tomatoes! she thought. So red, so bloody red and soft and smooth and full of pips and tart.

She rubbed the beans across her cheeks and down on to her neck.

Connor stumbled over the drums, across the room, towards her. She picked up the egg he'd fried, still warm, still soft, pushed part of it into her mouth and the other part she pushed from her ankle to her thigh, feeling it kiss her skin, like a slippery vulva, like the keen, wet lips of a lover.

Connor was standing beside her now, stunned, desperate to say something, anything, but not knowing what.

Sylvia picked up the juice, fresh orange juice with bits of

orange in it, tiny fragments of fleshy, tadpole orange in it swamping the liquid. She inhaled it and squealed, throwing out a hand ecstatically, and finding, blindly, Connor's leg, the coarse fabric of his trousers. She held firmly on to the glass and then yanked herself up, pulling at his trousers, almost toppling him over. Once up straight, she tipped the orange over him, but his clothes swallowed the juice, so she put her hand to the throat of his shirt, grasped it and ripped at it, seeing the buttons pop away like so many tiny white frogs, bouncing from the edge of a pond into thin air.

Under his shirt was his chest – hairless. She rubbed the juice on to it, into it, up his neck, on to his mouth, then pushed her mouth against his to suck it off.

'Oranges,' she said. 'Oh God! Like sherbet, like toothache, like a terrible, terrible aching, like a mouse nibbling at your lips.'

Connor stood still, his arms at his side, terrified. She's eating me, he thought. She's ferocious.

She turned away from him, dropped the empty juice glass and picked up the cup of coffee. He put out a warning hand. 'Don't throw it. It's burning hot.'

She ignored him, inhaled the aroma, smiling widely, and then poured the coffee down her neck, chest and the front of her dress. It was scalding hot but she didn't scream. The coffee was like a cat's tongue, rasping at her flesh, tickling her. *The smell of it! The taste!* She licked her fingers and said, 'I want to swallow it through my skin.'

Connor saw her clothes steaming and her skin redden. He grabbed hold of her, pulled her pinafore clumsily over her head, then her pea-green T-shirt. Underneath she was naked. She didn't seem to care. She bent over, picked up a piece of bacon and pushed it into her mouth. He touched her chest, which was staining a bright red. She swallowed the bacon. Her tongue felt alive. Before, she thought, it was only a piece of damp muscle in my mouth. But now I must use it. I must taste everything.

She picked up the coffee cup again and drained the bitter dregs from the bottom of it, then tossed the cup on to the bed. Connor watched her breasts as she threw the cup.

This is terrible, he thought.

She turned to him. 'Where's the kitchen?' but she didn't wait for an answer. Instead she followed the trail of cooking smells, sniffing them out like a bloodhound, letting her senses lead her there.

She pulled open the fridge. Milk, cheese, butter. In the freezer compartment: vanilla ice-cream. She took out these things and went back to Connor, who was still in his bedroom, bare-chested, immobile. She opened the carton of milk, pulled at the waist-band of his trousers and poured the milk down inside. The milk was cold.

'Stop!' He tried to move away. 'Stop that!'

She laughed at him. 'I can't!'

She threw down the empty carton and picked up the tub of ice-cream, ripped off its lid and pushed a handful of it into her mouth.

Connor's trousers were wet and heavy. He began to unbutton them, but couldn't help noticing as he did so how the skin on her chest and neck seemed even redder and angrier. He stopped what he was doing and instead took the carton of ice-cream from her, put in his hand and scooped some out. He applied it to her throat and her chest.

She enjoyed this sensation: the coldness of the ice and the warmth of his skin underneath it. She pulled him to her. He still smelled of oranges. She pushed her face on to his neck, into his hair and smelled him properly. What did he really smell of?

She felt his hands on her breasts, her back, but they held no ice now, were simply touching her. She whispered, close to his ear, 'What do you taste like?' and took a tentative nibble.

'Christ!'

He jerked his head away, slapping a hand on to the spot she'd bitten. He checked his fingers to see if she had drawn blood. The expression on her face implied that she had. He frowned at her. 'That's dangerous.'

'You taste like tomatoes.'

He couldn't help smiling. 'You've still got bean-juice all over your face, it's probably that you can taste.'

He put out his hand and gently wiped some of the mess from her cheek. She grabbed his fingers and pushed them into her mouth, sucking them, tasting salt and garlic and resin. The feel of her mouth excited him. His trousers felt strange, though, as if prematurely full of creamy semen. He wanted to take them off but was embarrassed by his sudden state of arousal.

She sucked his fingers and then his hand, covering it in speculative licks and nibbles. He was being savaged by an irrepressible toy dog. She ran her nose from his wrist to his armpit, savouring him, chewing at his underarm hair and tasting the nasty bitter taste of his deodorant. She spat and screwed up her face. To quell the taste she grabbed hold of the pat of butter and bit into it. He said, 'Don't eat that! It's butter! Don't eat butter like that,' while he tried, at the same time, to pull off his trousers. She watched this and laughed when she saw the head of his penis jutting out from the opening in his boxer shorts. Roughly she shoved him backwards, on to the bed. Her mind was crammed full of buttery things, yellow things, oil and excess.

He lay on the bed, at once hopeful and hopeless. She knocked the remnants of the tray on to the floor, picking up some mushrooms in the process, one of which she pushed into his navel, then straddled him, low down, squatting either side of his knees and staring at his manhood.

She had never seen a penis before and was both fascinated and amused by what she saw. He looked like a pink leek, a radish, a red asparagus. He smelled milky.

His eyes widened as she leaned forward and took the tip of him into her mouth. She said, her mouth now full, 'You taste like an oyster, like a prawn.'

She was not overly impressed by the taste, but it seemed a natural enough flavour so she pressed down her teeth, ever so slightly. He sat bolt upright – 'Don't bite it! Please God!' – and jerked her head away.

He saw her face, so stupid, so child-like, so full of impulse, and wondered what they were doing, what they could do. At the back of his mind he knew that he would make love with her, if he could, but he didn't know, couldn't be sure, that she wouldn't

change her mind half-way through, get bored or get angry. She wasn't emotionally consistent.

He pulled her closer to him and touched the redness on her chest and neck, then took her nipple into his mouth as she sat astride him. She pulled it away. 'That's my job.'

Is she joking? he wondered.

Her face was serious. 'If we have sex now . . .' she frowned, 'will it be interesting? Will it taste of anything? I mean, what would we do?'

Even as she spoke, he felt himself diminishing. He said, 'I suppose the point is that you do it because you want to be close to another person.'

She pulled back slightly and stared at him. His face was covered by his hair, his body was lean. Like the bacon, she thought, not too much fat on it.

She pushed his hair away from his face. Underneath it, his eyes were uncertain. She liked that. She felt herself warming inside, bubbling a little, like milk before it boils. She pushed him gently down again and pulled off his shorts.

This is a real, live, proper man, she thought, delighted.

She pulled the covers over him, as though tucking him up for the night, scooped another mittful of ice-cream from the tub, and then slipped in beside him. She pushed down her creamy hands and took hold of his now somewhat flabby member. He gasped at the coldness of her touch.

'Where does this go?' she asked quietly. Then added, 'Don't tell me, I'll guess.'

Where was Sylvia? Out. Already?

Ruby collapsed on the sofa. The dog had been locked inside all day. She'd have to take her out soon. She didn't move, though.

In the kitchen, Buttercup sat under the table, her nose peeking out between two chairs. Close to the sink was a large puddle of urine. The kitchen smelled strongly of dog.

Ruby surveyed this scene, then squatted down and spoke directly to her: 'How can I be angry with you?'

The dog stared back at her, blankly.

She pulled out a chair and sat down on it. Her mind was clean and empty.

Steven had booked them into a small hotel within walking distance of the bridge.

At four they'd completed their sound-check in the club. At five they had a light meal in a tiny café, close to the hotel. At six Brera got up to order another pot of tea.

Sam and Steven watched her as she strolled over to the counter.

'Excited?'

Sam had been staring after Brera, not really concentrating. 'Pardon?'

'I asked whether you were excited.'

She shrugged.

'You've been quiet.'

'Yeah.' She looked down at her hands.

Sometimes she hated being away from home because things could so easily spin out of proportion. At home everything was balanced by a kind of regularity: possessions, routine, family. But when you were away, stupid, small, tiny impulses, thoughts, notions, could take over and dominate everything. She couldn't stop thinking about Sarah. About herself and how separate she felt.

Steven was staring at her, as though expecting her to say something.

She said, 'Did you get to meet my friend Sarah the other day?'

He considered this question for a moment and then shook his head. 'I don't think so. Why?'

'No reason.' Sam focused on his tie – a bright, wide, ugly thing. 'I just wondered.'

Ruby gazed at the dog.

'Dog,' she said eventually, 'You are not enough.'

She stood up and strolled around the flat. Eventually she arrived outside Sylvia's door. Inside, when she listened carefully, she could hear a combination of low clucking and cooing, a

deep, meditative humming and a whirring noise. She leaned her body against the door, submerging herself in these sounds. After several minutes she reached inside her jacket pocket and took out a bunch of keys. The metallic jangling that they made and the noise of steel against steel as the key turned in the lock jarred on her nerves. She pushed the door open and stepped inside.

The smell was terrible, but she didn't mind it. She accepted it. Inside the room were birds, birds, birds. Everywhere, like feathery wallpaper, glued to their perches, silent, watching. In the dusk their faces glowed. It isn't dusk yet, she told herself; just seems that way.

She walked over to Sylvia's bed and sat down on it. So many eyes watched her. Why don't they fly away? she wondered. They should do. But they didn't.

Something was tickling her. For a moment she thought it was a feather in her nose, in her throat, but then she realized that it was love. *Love.* An infinitely soft fur-ball of enchantment, an amiable, intimate contentment.

She lay down on the bed and closed her eyes. When she'd closed them, she remembered a dream: a bird at her window and the red sky. A thought floated into her head. *All these things go on, and you don't even notice, but they go on anyway.*

She felt something soft and scratchy on her hand, heard the buzz of tiny wings, the fan of feathers. One by one the birds surrounded her. Some of the smaller ones landed on her arms and chest, balancing on the landscape of her body.

Eventually a small sparrow alighted on her nose. She wanted to laugh and to twitch, but did nothing.

I am so flat, so empty, she thought, and felt suffused with joy.

Connor stroked her cheek, leaning over the bed. She opened her eyes and saw that he was fully dressed. He said, 'I'm going out now. We've got a gig in West London. You're welcome to come along and listen.'

What is this? she thought. I don't want anything else from him, apart from what I've already had.

She rolled over, sniffing the pillows, appreciating the smell of his hair on the cotton covers. 'Go. I've got things to try.'

He didn't really want to leave her. Tonight, he decided, I'll do something by Big Star as an encore, something from *Sister Lovers*.

He said, 'I'll dedicate a song to you.'

'Will you?' She didn't sound particularly interested. 'That's good.'

She closed her eyes. 'See you, then.'

What would Sam think of all this? he wondered, and then realized that he didn't actually care. Sylvia's indifference amused him. Her passion amazed him. These two things balanced each other.

She heard him leaving the flat. 'Come and listen' she thought contemptuously. The fool!

She wanted more than that, and she would have it.

Vincent was icing a cake. Ruby's tiny kitchen was covered in flour and sugar.

He had decided around lunch-time, in a moment of boredom, that baking Ruby a cake would be almost as good as apologizing. Easier, certainly. He couldn't really understand what it was that he should apologize for, so the cake served a dual purpose, was an evasion, of sorts.

He told himself, as he baked, that any sort of relationship between himself and Ruby was impossible. The main problem was that he liked her too much. She deserves worse, he decided, someone who cares more about stupid things. Someone who isn't independent, and who doesn't respect her.

The stage was small and cramped. As they plugged in their guitars and adjusted their microphones, Sam thought wryly, The problem with being a middle-of-the-road band is that your audiences are middle-of-the-road. She considered this for a second and then decided that a short while ago it wouldn't have bothered her, but now it did.

They started their first song after a perfunctory introduction from Brera and an even more perfunctory round of applause from the audience.

Sam squinted out, beyond the lights, at the crowd. How many people altogether? she wondered. Sixty? Seventy? Some sat at tables, but the majority milled around over by the bar. Mainly men.

Sam was glad that they had dressed down. She looked over at Brera, who seemed cheerful enough, her cheeks slightly pink, her mouth singing and smiling. The light that shone on them – two spotlights from above – was filled by swirls of cigarette smoke, as though all the cigarette smoke in the entire place was funnelled into these two bright tunnels. Sam tried to make this halo of light, this nimbus, the edge of her consciousness. She didn't want to see beyond it. She felt as though her mind was programmed to transfer everything before her into nastiness, obscenity and ugliness. She tried to tell herself, But it's my mind that does that. It isn't actually the case, it's only me.

She strummed vigorously on her guitar and harmonized.

The next song started. What we're doing . . . she thought, it *is* right.

She glanced over at Brera again and Brera caught her eye and grinned. But in glancing, she caught several other eyes. Some people, close to the front, were watching her intently, their eyes cutting into her.

She peered down at her guitar, focusing on her fingers, imagining for an instant that her hands were strumming not the instrument but her own body: calming her, relaxing her.

I've never been afraid of performing before, she thought, and then, seconds later: At least, not of being watched. I don't mind people staring. People always stare.

She looked up and out at these people, stared back, but it didn't feel right. It felt as if she were offering an invitation. It felt promiscuous, like responding cheaply to a cheap proposition. She focused on the stage, at a space just in front of her feet.

The point of a performance, she told herself, is that you have to be secure in your own world. You have to show the audience your world, your confidence, your self-containment, and they should appreciate it. They should respect it.

But what was her world? Who was she? She was different. No wonder they stared. The only black woman here.

The song ended and several people clapped. Brera leaned over and said, 'Let's do something light, something funny. This lot could do with cheering up.'

'No.' Sam pointed with her foot at their song list, which was stuck to the bottom of an amp. 'Let's stick with it.'

After a short pause they started to play again.

She's really trying, Sam thought desperately; I can't let her down.

She looked up, focused her eyes and tried to smile. She caught the gaze of one man, standing close to the bar, and realized that he was staring at her breasts. Only at her breasts.

He knows that I'm here with my mother, she thought primly, and it doesn't make a blind bit of difference.

In that instant she doubted everything that she had previously established, in her mind, about the two of them: the show, the act – two women, a mother and a child, taking a stand. Ideas don't translate into life, she thought. Marxism, monetarism, conservatism, communism, feminism. Things can't translate because people are stupid. They won't believe.

She stared at the man by the bar and tried to communicate her anger, her sudden hatred. But he didn't notice *her*, only her body. She sang automatically, she played automatically, but all the while, inside her, a private mantra repeated itself. *I have to carry on. I have to carry on.*

This was Sarah's fault. She knew it. Why am I so bloody suggestible all of a sudden? How can I let her get the better of me?

I have to carry on.

It felt to Sam as though her mind had opened up, like a flower. It was a strange and terrifying sensation. Usually her mind was closed, had one small door and a door-keeper who carefully selected the things that would be let in and the things that would be left out. But suddenly the door was wide open, and the supporting frames were cracking, crumbling, letting in more and more light, more and more air. And *people*.

She closed her eyes, continuing to strum and play. Now she could only imagine everyone watching her, but imagining was bad enough. She knew that simply not caring was a solution, but she did care. She did care and she couldn't stop caring.

Life is a terrible violation.

One song.

Life.

Another song.

Terrible.

The last song.

Violation.

She opened her eyes and turned to Brera. 'That's it. Let's go.'

Brera scowled. 'Not even an encore?'

'Let's go.'

She jumped down from the stage, into the crowd, using her guitar to keep people distanced, stumbled through the club, beyond the bar, out of the exit and on to the street.

She breathed in the night air, looking up at the sky but seeing only clouds.

Brera was behind her.

'Stage fright,' she said, sagely.

Sam wanted to disappear, but couldn't.

When Ruby came to it was dark. The room was empty. The birds had flown. She stared up at the ceiling, trying to establish her whereabouts. Something was bothering her, upsetting her, but she didn't know what. The doorbell rang. She sat bolt upright. 'That's it. The doorbell.'

She jumped up and ran to answer it, hoping it would be Sylvia. Instead it was Vincent, holding a cake.

She pulled the door wide open. 'I was asleep.'

He offered her the cake. She took it and used her free hand to switch on the light. Everything sprang into clear relief. The cake was ineffectively covered in a scrappy piece of clingfilm. She pulled it off, careful not to damage the icing. It smelled of fruit and spice.

'Weird cake,' she said, sniffing it. He pushed past her and

went into the living-room, turning on the light and sitting down on the sofa.

She followed him. 'What's this for?'

He shrugged, smiling. She watched his smile. Could she forgive him? This was his way of saying sorry. What for, though? Which particular thing was he apologizing for? For not fancying her? For nearly losing her her job? For not giving a shit about anybody else?

'I fucked Sarah.'

'Sarah?' she said. 'Isn't she Sam's friend?'

He nodded. 'I fucked her.'

'Thursday night,' she said, feeling sick.

Why had he told her? She stood up, holding on to the cake with both hands. She felt like throwing it at him but thought, No, that'd be too easy.

She walked over to him. 'Take the cake.'

'What?'

'Take the bloody cake!'

He took the cake. He was still smiling at her. He was setting her free.

She walked from the room, down the hallway and into the kitchen. The dog was still there. She looked at her and said, 'I'd forgotten about you.'

She picked up her lead from the table and attached it to her collar.

'Guess what?' she said. 'You're going home.'

She pulled her along the corridor and towards the front door. Vincent emerged from the living-room.

'What're you doing?'

She stopped and turned. 'What does it look like? I'm taking the dog out.'

'Where?'

'Back.'

'Back where?'

Before she could reply he said, 'Don't do that. Don't take her back.'

'Why not?'

'Well . . .'

He thought for a moment and then said, 'She's interesting. She makes you interesting.'

'You're a dishonest bastard. A dirty lying bastard.'

She meant it. She yanked open the door and pulled the dog behind her.

He stared after her, smiling. She was free. He had set her free.

He listened to the noise of her shoes on the tiles in the hall, on the stairs. The tapping of the dog's toe-nails.

When she had gone, Vincent rang for a cab. He was still holding the cake. He considered what she'd said.

There are two worlds, he decided, one in which being honest means something mundane, another in which it means being true to yourself, to real things.

He stared at the cake and debated which world it was that Ruby inhabited until a car horn sounded outside.

I'll take the fucking cake, he thought, getting to his feet; I'll take it.

Sam borrowed Steven's mobile phone in the car on their way back to the hotel. Initially she rang Jubilee Road, but no one answered. Next she tried Sarah.

As she dialled Brera turned and asked, 'Who're you phoning?'

Sam put up a hand to silence her, evading any explanations.

What did she want from Sarah? She couldn't decide. Affirmation? Confirmation? Justification? Sex?

Sarah answered, 'Hello?' Her voice seemed troubled.

'It's Sam.'

'Sam!' She sounded delighted. Sam's heart lifted, but before she could say anything Sarah said, 'She's still in the bathroom. She's driving me insane.'

'Who is?' Sam asked this automatically, not even thinking.

'Your sister. Your mad bloody sister. She's made such a mess. I don't know what Connor was playing at, bringing her here.'

'Connor?'

'Hang on.'

Sam listened. In the background she could hear squawking and

splashing: sounds like a gang of children might make in a public pool. She also heard Sarah shouting, saying, 'Do you know how much that costs? A whole bottleful? Do you have any idea?'

After a further pause and more splashing, Sarah returned to the phone. She said, 'I slapped her earlier and she asked me to do it again. She *enjoyed* it.'

'You slapped Sylvia?'

Brera turned in her seat. 'What about Sylvia?'

Sam ignored her. 'You slapped Sylvia?'

Sarah sounded unrepentant: 'Yes. I slapped her and she *enjoyed* it. She asked me to do it again.'

Sam laughed. Like me, she thought. If she slapped me, I'd probably enjoy it too. What a fool. A complete fool.

'You said Connor invited her?'

'He must've. He's out now, though. At a gig or something.'

'Is she OK?'

'Orgasmic.'

Sam smiled. That'd be right, she thought. We are sisters, after all. Something else popped into her head, inexplicably: *It wasn't fear I felt before, only ecstasy*. She knew instantly that this wasn't coherent, but feelings, she decided, like ideas, didn't have to be, weren't *obliged* to be. She said briskly, 'And where's Ruby?'

'Ruby?'

'The blonde woman who's looking after her.'

'Oh.' Sarah paused for a second. 'I don't know where she is.'

Sam endeavoured to take stock of the situation, ignoring Brera's desperate gestures from the front seat.

'OK. Well, thanks for putting up with her. I'll see you.'

'What do you mean? Is that it?'

'I think so.'

She used the cut-off mechanism on the phone and handed it to Brera. 'It's all yours.'

Brera was in a state of intense agitation. 'Who was that? Who slapped Sylvia?'

Sam laughed. 'Someone who should know better,' she said.

*

Shortly after Sarah had hung up, Vincent arrived, demanding money for a cab, clutching, somewhat incongruously, a large iced cake which smelled of apples and cinnamon.

Sarah said, 'Hi,' and made as if to give him a hug, but he put out a restraining hand.

'Hold on. This is precious.'

'Who's it for?'

'Nobody.' He glanced over his shoulder. 'Would you pay the cab? He's waiting outside.'

Sarah went to get her purse. Vincent walked into the living-room and was about to switch on the television when an assortment of peculiar noises captured his attention. They were radiating from the bathroom. He walked in and found Sylvia.

She was in the bath, up to her neck in water. The bathroom smelled like a perfume counter. Sylvia was naked but seemed unembarrassed.

'Hello,' she said, recognizing him from their previous encounter. She sloshed around lazily in the water, grinning, watching as waves of liquid spilled over the rim of the bath and on to the floor.

Vincent tried not to fall over on the tiles; which were now wet and slippery. He held his cake aloft. Sylvia spotted it as she peered over the edge of the bath. She sat up. 'What's that? Is it for me?'

He shrugged. 'I suppose it could be.'

She stretched out an arm towards him. He saw that her hand was covered in eczema.

'You shouldn't stay in there for too long.'

'Sod it. Give me the cake.'

Her face shone out wetly at him: a round, yellow, exuberant moon.

There was something in her that he found suddenly irresistible. What was it? A carelessness? He said, 'No cake until you get out of that bath.'

She scowled. 'Yeah? Is it really worth it?'

He showed it to her. 'Smell it. It's delicious. It's all natural.'

He saw her nostrils twitch and her eyes ignite. She tried to

snatch at it and water spilled from the bath in even greater quantities.

'Out,' he said authoritatively, 'out or no cake.'

She turned her back on him. 'I'm not a bloody kid, or a dog.'

He enjoyed this little display. He liked her unreasonableness. He put down the lid on the toilet and sat on it. 'Fine.'

He then said, 'Ruby must be worried about you.'

'Ruby?'

Sylvia considered this for a moment. He smiled at her expression, which was so expressive, suddenly so serious. Eventually she said, 'From now on I'm living only for pleasure.'

He put a finger into the icing on his cake, scooped some off and ate it. Sylvia watched jealously, her mouth watering. She stood up, stepped out of the bath and grabbed a large fistful of it, shoving it into her mouth. It was delectable.

Vincent watched her, offered her the plate to hold. 'Hedonism,' he said. 'You've become a hedonist.'

She ignored this. She didn't understand what he meant. She said, 'Where's this from? I want more of it. Different kinds, different types. I want to build a world out of tastes like this. A life. Something so beautiful, so delicious, completely full of touching and tasting and smelling and seeing.'

Vincent passed her a towel.

'I made it,' he said calmly. 'And I can make more. I can show you how.'

'Right.'

Sylvia was pleased by this notion. 'I'll get my clothes. Let's go.'

Vincent watched her as she padded from the room. His gut tightened. Ruby was cheap, he thought.

He was cheap too. He had to spread himself very thinly.

So much happens here on a Saturday night, Ruby thought, as she walked from street to street through Hackney – from Pembury Road to Amhurst Road to Mare Street, then along this main thoroughfare for a long, long time.

Eventually, outside the Bethnal Green Museum of Childhood, she ground to a halt. The dog had been behaving perfectly

pulling on her lead only where appropriate, for the most part trotting amiably at Ruby's side, obliging and obedient.

'Good girl,' she said, squatting down next to her. She stared up at the bright lettering on the front of the museum and thought, Hackney Wick and Bethnal Green. How far between the two?

She decided to take a bus.

After several false starts she established herself comfortably upstairs on a number 6. The dog clambered on to the seat next to her. It was empty up here, apart from the two of them. She stared out of the front window. The scene before her, lit by orange lights, dark but not yet properly dark – The city, she thought, is never really dark – seemed inexplicably grand. The dog sat beside her, also watching, but her eyes saw things differently, saw everything in monochrome, like fragments of an old film, every detail rendered stark and formal.

The dog sat next to Ruby like another person, upright on the seat, her legs tucked under her, her back ramrod straight. But with every unexpected jerk she fell forward, sometimes only a couple of inches, but other times almost crashing into the window, on to the floor. On these occasions Ruby tightened a possessive arm around the dog to save her from falling, from injury. The dog was too big, too bulky and unsuitable. Like so bloody many of the things in my life, she thought, and then instantly dismissed this idea. Instead she decided, My life is too *small*, that's the problem. Maybe I'm too small.

She tried to map out in her mind the basic constituents of her immediate future. I'll take the dog back, I'll leave her there. I'll return to Soho. I won't see Vincent again.

These were all things she could imagine happening. Also, though – and this was the wonderful part, the amazing part – she could imagine, just as easily, these same things not happening.

Sometimes, she thought, you can get on to a bus and the bus driver forgets to stop, or he loses his way, or he has to change his route because something unexpected happens – roadworks, or a traffic jam, or a flood – and then everything is changed; because of that, everything is different.

She relaxed and smiled to herself. In life, she decided, there's

an outside and an inside. Things happen outside and things happen inside your body, inside your mind . . . ideas, decisions, feelings. Happiness is just a question of balancing the two.

The bus stopped abruptly and the dog fell forward. She caught hold of the dog, falling forward too.

In that split second – as she moved through the air, hearing the bus's horn and the squeal of brakes, feeling the dog's ribs, her fur, her breath – in that tiny dart of time her mind became a microscope. It took in everything, and every detail was significant.

This could be the beginning of something immaculate, she thought.